THE
SISTERS

THE
SISTERS

Cynthia Victor

AN ONYX BOOK

ONYX
Published by the Penguin Group
Penguin Putnam Inc., 375 Hudson Street,
New York, New York 10014, U.S.A.
Penguin Books Ltd, 27 Wrights Lane,
London W8 5TZ, England
Penguin Books Australia Ltd, Ringwood,
Victoria, Australia
Penguin Books Canada Ltd, 10 Alcorn Avenue,
Toronto, Ontario, Canada M4V 3B2
Penguin Books (N.Z.) Ltd, 182–190 Wairau Road,
Auckland 10, New Zealand

Penguin Books Ltd, Registered Offices:
Harmondsworth, Middlesex, England

First published by Onyx, an imprint of Dutton NAL,
a member of Penguin Putnam Inc.

 REGISTERED TRADEMARK—MARCA REGISTRADA

ISBN : 0-7394-0288-9

Printed in the United States of America

For Marnie Hagmann Pavelich, whose sensitivity, beauty and intelligence left their mark on all of us lucky enough to have known her. . . .

And for Carly Sarah Steckel, who dazzles us every day and fills the future with such bright promise.

ACKNOWLEDGMENTS

Special thanks to the following people for their expertise, support and affection: Harriet Astor, Carole Baron, Richard Baron, Michael Barrett, Karen Bergreen, Leona Blum, Reva Blum, Carolyn Clarke, Denise Evans, Susan Ginsburg, Lawrence Goldstone, Jean Katz, Mary Macy, Susanna Margolis, Susan Moldow, Matt Pavelich, Nick Pavelich, Riley Pavelich, Harriet Rattner, Diana Revson, Ellen Seely, Jennifer Skurnick, Mark Stark, Jenna Steckel, and Mark Steckel.

For their insight and dedication, warmest gratitude to Amy Berkower, Audrey LaFehr, Genny Ostertag, and Jody Reamer.

THE
SISTERS

Prologue

Molly Ross was busy sorting through the summer clothing in her large walk-in closet and hadn't heard anyone enter the bedroom. She pushed open the closet door and emerged, her attention on the short-sleeved navy sweater she was holding up before her. The sweater momentarily blocked her view, but as she lowered her arms, she was startled to discover she was no longer alone.

"You scared me," she exclaimed, with a nervous laugh.

The laugh quickly died in her throat. The expression she saw on the face of the person before her was so intense in its fury, she actually took a step back.

No one said anything. Disconcerted, Molly cleared her throat. "What are you doing here?"

The answer came as an angry retort. "What do you think I'm doing here?"

Molly slowly came around to the foot of the bed, raising her hand in a placating gesture. She tried to keep her voice calm.

"Look, why don't we sit down and talk."

There was a sharp, bitter laugh. "I don't see any point. Do you?"

"Of course," she said, hoping her tone was soothing. "There's no reason we—"

Even as the words were coming out of her mouth, her eyes widened with shock at the sight of the gun being raised and aimed directly at her.

There was a loud blast as the gun was fired and Molly was struck squarely in the chest. Her arms went flying out to either side as the force knocked her onto the bed. The navy sweater dropped from her hand and slid off the side of the bed onto the floor.

Blood spurted from her wound, then gushed out, soaking her clothes and the beige damask bedcover beneath her. Her eyes were open, staring unseeing at the ceiling. An acrid smell filled the air, mingling with wisps of smoke.

The silence was unbroken for several long moments. Then there were only the sounds of the bedroom door being opened and closed, and footsteps going down the hall.

Chapter One

1992

"Will I ever forgive my friend for moving to Charlottesville? Definitely not."

Standing, with wineglass held aloft, Elizabeth Ross smiled warmly at her former college roommate Diane Figueroa, seated beside her at the table. "I'll be bereft without her advice, her jokes, her lunatic way of viewing the world, as I'm sure you all will. But do we want her to be happy? We do. So we must graciously step aside and permit the sensational Charlie Arlen to drag our friend away from us. May they be forever deliriously in love."

Elizabeth sat down to the applause and amused chatter of the eight other women at the table. Diane gave her a quick hug of thanks, then rose to say a few words of her own.

Elizabeth listened with mixed emotions as she pushed her long, curly hair back from her face. It would be difficult to say good-bye to Diane, who had been one of her closest friends since they had met during their first week at Columbia nine years before. But Diane had fallen in love with a man who wanted to move back to his southern hometown, and she had chosen to accept his marriage proposal and go along with him.

"First, I want to thank you all for coming, for the gifts, for everything," Diane began. "If I really thought about how hard it's going to be to leave New York, I'm not sure I could actually do it. And to my dear friend, Elizabeth, who so graciously made this beautiful party, I can only say thank you yet again. She's been making me birthday parties and celebrations since we met. Aside from being a perfect person—gorgeous, brilliant, *and* nice, if you can even stand it—she's a perfect friend."

Elizabeth groaned at the lavish praise. "Embarrass me to death, why don't you?" she said to her friend laughingly.

Diane raised her glass. "To friendships that remain the same despite the swirl of change around them."

There were murmurs of "Hear, hear" as everyone drank.

Diane continued. "Wish me luck finding a house. I'll be back next month to see you all at the wedding."

The guests started saying their good-byes and gathering their things. Elizabeth caught the eye of the maître d', who nodded. He disappeared for a moment, then returned to give her the credit card she had handed to him before they all sat down to dinner.

"Thank you, Ms. Ross. It was a pleasure."

She smiled. "Everything was wonderful. Thank you so much."

It was another ten minutes until all the guests had left and only Diane and Elizabeth remained. Reluctant to see their time together end, they slowly made their way outside

"Want to share a cab?" Diane asked.

Elizabeth shook her head. "I'm meeting my parents at the opera, so I just have to run over to Lincoln Center."

"Now?" Diane asked in surprise. It was after nine o'clock.

"I'll catch the last half." Elizabeth leaned forward to hug her friend. "God, I'm going to miss you. Call."

Diane pulled away, her eyes damp. "I'm getting out of here before I wail like a baby."

At last, with a wave, they separated. Elizabeth headed downtown on Columbus Avenue in the direction of the Metropolitan Opera House. She was glad to have a chance to get some fresh air and stretch her legs. It had been a long day at the office, and she had barely made it to the party on time. Typically, she didn't leave her desk until eight o'clock at the earliest; getting out by six was no easy trick.

She inhaled deeply as she walked. She was genuinely glad for Diane, who had been through a bad breakup the year before but was now absolutely certain she had found the man to marry. It must be great to be that sure, Elizabeth thought. She couldn't imagine ever having that kind of feeling herself. Marriage to her meant lies and betrayals. Dating was one thing. Marriage was definitely another.

The spectacle of Lincoln Center lit up at night struck her anew each time she saw it. She hurried across the outdoor plaza to the Metropolitan Opera, enjoying the gentle whooshing sound of the spouting water in the circular fountain and the sight of the blazing lights around her. Inside the building, she was pleased to see that intermission was just ending. She paused outside the door to her father's box, smiling at the usher who approached to unlock it for her.

She thanked him as she hung up her coat in the small anteroom.

"The second act starts any second," he said, turning to go. "It will last ninety-three minutes."

Elizabeth opened the inner door to find her parents seated with another couple. She remembered her father mentioning that he had invited the Marlers, both of whom worked in the mayor's office. All four people turned to see who had joined them.

"Darling." Jack Ross smiled fondly at the sight of his older daughter. "I'm so glad you were able to get here."

"Hi, Dad. Me, too." She bent down to give him an

affectionate kiss, although she had seen him several hours earlier at the office. Her father was the Ross of Ross, Jennings, and Trent, the nationally known law firm where Elizabeth had worked ever since graduating from Yale Law School two years before. As usual, he looked supremely elegant in his expertly tailored suit, his thick silvery hair perfectly combed.

"Hello, Elizabeth." Molly Ross leaned forward to see around her husband.

"Hi," Elizabeth answered briefly. She took the empty seat behind her father.

"Have you met Neil and Virginia Marler?" Jack asked as the lights went down.

Both members of the couple smiled at her and she reached over to shake their hands. Then they all settled into their seats to enjoy the rest of *Madama Butterfly*.

Elizabeth had seen it several times before. Her father had been taking her to the opera with him since she was a young girl. Back then, her younger sister, Joey, would come as well, but she had stopped as soon as she was old enough to get away with it, and Jack had long ago given up trying to persuade her to join them. Sometimes her mother went as well, but in years past, it had frequently been just Elizabeth and her father.

This box at the opera had special meaning for Elizabeth. When she was a child, those nights with her father had been a special treat, wonderfully exciting. She had been dazzled by the glamour of the women in their furs and jewels, the magnificence of the opera house, the thrill of sitting next to her father on the red velvet chairs, feeling so grown-up. The opera itself had been a big bore to her, though she hadn't minded because of everything that went with it. Still, over the years, she had learned to appreciate it. She now found it relaxing, as she sat back and just let the music take over.

Caught up in the story, she watched sadly as Butterfly brought out her son, revealing him to be the child of B. F. Pinkerton, the husband who she refused to believe had abandoned her. Elizabeth sighed, knowing what tragedy was still to come. She glanced in her mother's direction and saw her leaning over, scribbling notes onto her program in the darkness. Jack started to whisper something to his wife, but she raised an index finger to indicate he should wait a moment until she was done.

Elizabeth watched with mild irritation. No doubt Molly was writing something about the costumes, her own area of professional expertise. Whenever she was at a performance of any sort, she would make notes about what she might have done for the costumes if she had had the opportunity to paint them, the rarefied type of work in which she had come to specialize. Elizabeth could never see the point of that exercise. But she was more annoyed at the way Molly held Jack at bay, holding up that finger so dismissively.

God, Mother, she told Molly silently, would it kill you to give him a little respect? To give him *anything?*

But of course she already knew the answer. Her mother would never change. Jack Ross loved Molly with all his heart, but he was unable to see the truth behind his wife's eyes. Only Elizabeth knew the way Molly Ross actually felt about her husband. And she could never forgive her mother for it. Her father was so wonderful to all of them. But it had brought him only deceit and disloyalty.

For the thousandth time, Elizabeth wished that her sister understood the truth so she could talk to her about it. Maybe then Joey would stop sniping at their father, always looking for an argument with him, ready to criticize him at every turn.

Elizabeth gave an inward shrug. The truth was, it wouldn't help either her or Joey to talk about it because they couldn't talk about anything. And they never had been able to. From the time they were small, most of their interactions quickly degenerated into fights, and little had changed as they approached their late twenties. Joey was just so damned prickly.

She seemed to have contempt for Elizabeth in every area—her friends, her dates, her awards, whatever she accomplished. Joey didn't know and didn't care how incredibly hard Elizabeth worked for everything. She always acted as if things just came to Elizabeth by accident or luck.

Well, Joey would doubtless continue to be a pain in the neck, and to be so damned inconsiderate of their father, Elizabeth thought unhappily. And why not? She hadn't been the one to overhear her mother on the telephone when she was ten years old. She had no idea that their family's foundation was nothing more than a house of cards.

Elizabeth had an excellent memory, but she had wished a thousand times that she could forget the day she learned the truth about her mother. It was during those strange years, the time when Molly never went out of the house and always seemed too tired to play with them. Back then, Elizabeth didn't have a name for what she knew now was agoraphobia. Elizabeth had been downstairs in the kitchen with the babysitter, having a snack of oatmeal cookies and milk. Coming out, she had noticed that the small red bag containing her jacks and rubber ball was on the floor near the front door, and she darted over to retrieve it. As she passed by the living room, she heard her mother's voice on the telephone.

"How can you ask if I love my husband? That wasn't even a consideration when we got married. I did it in some kind of fog, and I still feel that that fog may swallow me up and kill me."

Elizabeth had continued what she was doing, grabbing the bag. But when she got upstairs, she went into her room and shut the door. Then she had sat on the floor, her legs crossed, her hands folded, for a very long time. She thought of her father, so good to all of them, so helpful to their mother. It would be terrible if he ever knew what Elizabeth had just learned.

Besides, she thought, if that was how her mother really felt about her father, who knew how she might feel about Elizabeth and Joey? No one had to tell Elizabeth that other mothers weren't like hers, staying at home, in bed half the day. Elizabeth always told herself that her mother would do all the regular mother stuff if only she were well enough. But now it seemed that wasn't the case. Maybe she didn't even care about her children. Maybe she even *hates* us, Elizabeth had thought, tears stinging her eyes.

Still, she felt worse for her father than for herself. She couldn't bear to think of what it would feel like for him if he ever found out what her mother had just said. Something inside Elizabeth knew right then and there that it was her job to protect him from that pain.

Suddenly she felt angry. They were a family. The mother was supposed to love everybody. What kind of a mother didn't? Elizabeth wanted to run back downstairs and punch her mother. She wanted to pound on her, scratch her eyes out.

"I wish you were *dead*," she had whispered fiercely.

She imagined her mother lying in a coffin, the horrible truth about to be buried along with her. But what would her father do then? He would be lonely and miserable, she realized. He was a good father, and he loved everybody, the way a parent was supposed to. It would only make him sad if his wife were gone.

But she might leave them alone anyway. The realization hit Elizabeth with horror. Maybe her mother had had enough of living with people she hated. Maybe she was getting ready to go.

No, that simply couldn't happen. It would be too awful.

But, Elizabeth reasoned, if she behaved and kept everybody as happy as she possibly could, maybe it wouldn't have to happen. Maybe her mother wouldn't tell her father that she didn't love him, but would just go on with life the way it was, believing no one knew the rotten truth about her. She might not decide to leave all of them.

As that afternoon had turned into early evening, Elizabeth remained in the same spot, thinking. Two knots of feeling hardened within her, taking permanent hold of her heart. One was her resolution to protect her father. The other was her bitter fury toward her mother. Underscoring both of them was her determination to keep the family together.

And that's never changed, she reflected, shifting in her seat. God knows, she was doing her best.

She tried to push her thoughts away and concentrate again on the opera. Pinkerton had returned, bringing his new American wife. He was too cowardly to face Butterfly in person. Tears came to Elizabeth's eyes as she watched Butterfly pick up the knife and prepare to kill herself. Love didn't get *you* anywhere either, did it? she asked Butterfly silently.

As the story drew to its tragic close, Elizabeth joined the rest of the audience in enthusiastic applause. Eventually, she, the Marlers, and her parents filed out of the box and downstairs, then out onto Broadway.

"Joey's coming in for the weekend," Molly said to Elizabeth as they exchanged a quick kiss good night. "Will you come for dinner?"

Elizabeth nodded. Joey was at Harvard Law School, a fact that astonished Elizabeth, considering her sister's historic disgust with their father's profession. "If she wants me there."

"Good night, sweetheart." Jack wrapped her in a bear hug. "See you tomorrow."

"Thanks, Dad. Love you." Elizabeth gave him a loud smack on the cheek.

She stepped off the curb to hail a taxi. "West End and Seventy-eighth Street, please," she said over the sound of screeching wheels as the driver veered away from the corner. She sank back in the seat gratefully, realizing how tired she was. It had been a long day, but certainly a good one.

She stopped to exchange pleasantries with the building's doorman for a few minutes before heading up in the elevator. She had a two-bedroom apartment on the fifth floor of the elegant prewar building, and she never failed to appreciate how fortunate she was to have such a comfortable place in such a good location in the city. It had been a surprise, finding the co-op already purchased for her when she returned from graduation at Yale Law, a present from her parents. Apparently, as soon as she had mentioned that she wanted to live on the Upper West Side instead of around Gramercy Park where she had grown up, her father had gone to work to find her the perfect apartment. Elizabeth felt somewhat guilty at her good fortune in living there. But, as Joey so acidly put it, not guilty enough to refuse it. How could you let someone else pick your *home,* Joey had asked in horror. But it happened to be everything Elizabeth wanted; she couldn't come up with any reason not to be thrilled.

It was midnight by the time she crawled into bed and pulled the comforter up around her shoulders, happy to feel the cool white sheets envelope her. She sank into the soft mattress and was asleep within minutes.

The next morning, she woke up and rolled over to see that the clock radio on the night table said seven o'clock. If she hurried, she could be at her desk by eight. She jumped up to shower.

By the time the elevator reached the ground floor, her mind was already on the day before her. She had to prepare for a deposition she would be taking tomorrow. At ten, she had a meeting with her father about the DeMeering matter. That case was going to eat up a lot of time; she knew it already. It would be a real challenge, but it was an important one for her father to win. She quickened her pace. There was nothing as satisfying as unsnarling a difficult legal problem.

At ten to eight, she emerged from the subway onto Fiftieth Street, rapidly making her way through the morning crowds of people to the tall building five blocks away on Park Avenue that housed the law offices of Ross, Jennings, and Trent. She could never see the office building rising up before her without getting a thrill. The towering gray edifice was so emblematic of New York City itself.

She loved the sound of her heels clicking on the cool marble floor of the cavernous lobby as she crossed to the elevator bank. Everything had been built with such care, even the floor numbers in the elevator decorated with ornate carvings and fine brasswork. Happily, she stepped out on the fourteenth floor and waved to the receptionist.

"Good morning, Lucy," she said. "How does your day look to you?"

The middle-aged woman standing behind the large curved desk nodded politely, busy arranging flowers in a tall glass vase. Lucy Forrest had been the receptionist at Ross, Jennings since Elizabeth was a little girl. Humorless and efficient, she was a stern fixture in the elegant surroundings of the reception area. Only once had Elizabeth seen her laugh, after the birth of her grandson the year before.

Elizabeth gave herself over to the sense of excitement that filled her every morning when she walked down the long corridor, busy by this time with the lawyers and secretaries getting a jump on their day. Her father had started the firm with two other men, but he and Richard Jennings hadn't been able to get along, and her father had bought him out twenty years earlier. Sheldon Trent had died of a heart attack in 1982.

Elizabeth approached her secretary's desk. The young woman had been working there for seven months, but she was still making so many mistakes that Elizabeth wondered if she could justify keeping her on. Elizabeth genuinely liked her. She only hoped the girl would straighten things out in the next few months.

"Hi, Linda," Elizabeth said pleasantly as she came near. "What a nice dress."

Linda glanced down at what she was wearing, then smiled. "Thank you, Ms. Ross." She picked up two interoffice envelopes. "These came for you. I was just going to put them on your desk."

"Thanks, I'll take them."

Elizabeth reached out to get the envelopes as she went past to enter her own office. It was a large room, situated right next to the enormous corner office belonging to her father. She liked the fact that it resembled a library more than an office, with rich beige and green tones, and bookshelves filled with legal tomes covering an entire wall.

She set her briefcase down, taking in the view of the city as she came around to stand behind her desk. The *New York Times* and the *Wall Street Journal* were waiting there.

She dropped down on the leather chair and swiveled around to her computer to check her E-mail. Eight messages, all of them demanding her immediate attention.

Elizabeth swiveled back to face her desk. The large appointment book she kept was already open to today's date; she slid it closer, simultaneously leaning down to retrieve a gold pen from her briefcase, a gift from her father for passing the bar. After thinking for a few moments, she began to make notes in the book. There was a lot to be done that day.

Damn, I love this job, she thought.

Forty-five minutes later, she had returned all the important phone calls and was nearly done reading through the notes for a case she was working on, a medical intern who was being sued after stopping to help at the scene of a car accident. Although Matt Golan had clearly saved the drunken driver's life, the man's family blamed the young intern for the fact that he was paralyzed from the waist down. Already in debt for medical school loans, Golan had virtually no money to pay for an attorney, so Elizabeth had decided to waive most of her fee. The lawsuit's unfairness infuriated her. She was glad that she worked at a firm where she could right such an injustice. Matt's entire future was on the line, Elizabeth reflected, closing the folder, reaching to put it to one side of her desk. She wanted to win this thing for him.

Her secretary buzzed. "Ms. Ross, there's a Peter Grier on line two. Says it's personal."

Elizabeth froze, the hand holding the folder still in midair.

Peter.

Elizabeth didn't know what she felt, but before she could decide, she reached for the telephone receiver.

"Hello?" Her voice sounded oddly high in her own ears.

"Lizzie, is that you?"

Peter was the only person who ever called her by that nickname. The sound of his voice was so instantly familiar, it was as if she had heard it the day before.

"Peter, my God, how are you?" A sudden pang shot through her. Images were rushing through her mind, memories of their time together. It seemed a million miles away.

"I'm well, I'm very well. So you're at your dad's firm, just as you intended."

"Yes. And you, where are you?"

"I'm in New York." He paused. "And I wonder if I could see you. Actually, I was hoping to ask your advice about some locations I'm considering for a restaurant. I've been gone a few years and I know precious few people here anymore."

She smiled. "Just want to pick my brain?"

"Cut right to the chase. That always was you," he said with a laugh. "Of course I'd like to see you, sit down and talk. It would be great."

"Weren't you living in Vermont?" Elizabeth asked, remembering what she had heard about him at her last college reunion. Apparently he had opened his own restaurant and wound up marrying the woman who was his chef.

"I've moved back. I missed the city. I had a restaurant, which I sold for a good piece of change, I'm happy to report. That means I can open up something here."

"Your wife would be the chef, I guess." Elizabeth groaned inwardly at her own lack of subtlety.

"No." He seemed to hesitate. "Actually, we got divorced about a year ago."

"Oh," she said in a small voice.

There was a long silence.

Peter spoke first. "Well, that was awkward," he said cheerfully. "Now, what do you say we plan a meeting? I don't suppose a busy person like yourself would be free tomorrow night for a drink."

Elizabeth glanced at her appointment book. She had drinks scheduled with a client, after which she had set aside a few hours to come back to the office to do some research.

"Seven-thirty?" She felt an odd fluttering in her stomach.

"Done. I'll pick you up at your office."

"Do you know how to find it?" she asked.

"Hey," he laughed, "I may have been gone, but I haven't been transformed into a foreign tourist. The address is right in the phone book here. I'll see you tomorrow."

He hung up. Abashed, she put the receiver down in its cradle. I don't know how to talk to him, she thought, getting up, then immediately sitting back down again. I can't believe how nervous I am. What am I worried about? He's probably fat and bald and old and repulsive by now. I'll wonder what the hell I ever saw in him. There's no reason to be nervous. This is just Peter.

How long had it been since they had talked? Senior year at Columbia, she realized, which made it a good five years. Exhaling loudly, she picked up the telephone to cancel the next day's appointment for drinks. Peter Grier had been her boyfriend for the last two years of college, and there hadn't been anyone else like him, before or after. But he had started talking about getting married, and Elizabeth knew that was an impossibility. She wasn't ready, and what was more important, she didn't expect that she would ever be ready. Just the idea made her feel as if the walls were closing in on her. She had made it clear to him how she felt about marriage. Still, he argued, it was crazy to throw away something as good as what they had.

But as much as she loved him, she couldn't bring herself to say yes, at which point he had broken things off with her altogether.

After graduation, he had disappeared. But now here he was, right here in New York.

And she was nervous. She stayed that way throughout that day and the next. The feeling didn't ease until the following evening, when she finally lost herself in drafting a brief. She became so engrossed that she was completely unprepared to look up and see Peter Grier standing in her office.

He was leaning against the far wall, his arms folded. Beneath his tan overcoat, he was wearing a navy blue suit, with a sky-blue shirt open at the neck. Apparently he had been there for a while, watching her. As their eyes met, he smiled. It was the same blindingly white smile she remembered. His large, deep-set hazel eyes, his thick brown hair—everything about him was exactly as she remembered, except that she couldn't recall ever seeing him in a suit. He had always been in blue jeans and flannel shirts when they were together. In fact, she realized, that was the one thing that was different: he looked like a man, rather than a boy.

"Hello, Lizzie," he said quietly.

She rose, dropping her yellow legal pad and pen onto the desk. "Peter."

She came around from behind her desk to greet him, and he took a few steps forward. She recognized his movements, the easy way he held himself, as if they had been forever imprinted in her brain. She felt a funny clutching sensation in the pit of her stomach.

As if it had been planned, they moved together to embrace. Feeling him encircle her waist, she closed her eyes with pleasure, moving her hands up his arms and around his broad shoulders.

It was as if they'd never been apart. She found herself melting into his embrace, exactly as she'd yielded to him years before. And, in response, his arms tightened around her, his mouth moving from her lips to her neck.

This is crazy, she said to herself sternly. I don't even know this man anymore. She tried to say as much to Peter, but his lips had come back to cover hers once again. It was so much easier to kiss him back, to explore his mouth with her tongue. In fact, when words finally came, she heard herself sighing.

"Oh, Peter," she murmured as he drew her even closer, his hands going lower on her back, gliding over the curve of her hip, lightly stroking her thighs.

Don't, she wanted to say, as she saw him kick the door shut behind him. We can't, she tried to insist as he sank down to the floor, taking her with him as they imprinted themselves on the beige carpet.

"This is crazy," she uttered, finally managing to get actual words out of her mouth. But the words didn't keep her from running her hands under his shirt, taking in muscles that hadn't been there years before.

"My God, you're so beautiful," Peter said, groaning with pleasure as her hands made contact with his skin.

This is exactly what wasn't supposed to happen, she thought ruefully, unable to stop herself from responding to the touch of his fingers as they lingered on her secret places, kneading her, caressing her through the thin silk of her skirt. She thought she was pushing his hand away, but instead realized she had lifted the skirt herself, had guided his hand to the black satin tap pants she was wearing underneath, that she was lifting her body to meet his hand, urging him forward.

I can't give you what you want. Go away and don't come back for another ten years. Leave me in the safety of my life. She longed to say all of that and more. And this time she found a sentence actually forming in her mouth.

"You'd better lock the door," was what came out.

She moaned in the rhythm of the hand that moved inside her.

"There's no one here," Peter responded in a husky voice. "The cleaning crew was turning the lights off when I walked in." He withdrew his hand, leaving her longing for more. "In fact," he added, now sliding her underpants down her legs, "They told me you were the only one here, and you were not to be disturbed."

Once again, his hand moved toward her center, but this time he slid it underneath her body, raising her up. Tantalizingly slowly, he lowered his mouth to meet her essence. She shuddered as he penetrated her with his tongue, clearly reveling in the taste of her. She heard herself cry out in ecstasy.

"So, is it all right if I disturb you?" Peter asked as he withdrew his mouth from her, coming up to kiss her lips once again.

Oh, hell, a voice in the back of her mind said as their lips came together. Here we go again.

Chapter Two

"Well, I'm off. How do I look?"

Elizabeth spun around in the narrow doorway to Joanna's room, the full skirt of her off-the-shoulder blue taffeta dress rustling.

Lying casually across her unmade bed, Joanna Ross lowered the constitutional law text she was reading and regarded her sister through narrowed eyes.

"Well," she said, lifting the book once more and staring at its pages, "if what you're going for is Barbie, you've succeeded admirably." She pretended to go on reading, although she wasn't really taking in a word. As usual, all she could focus on was the complex mix of emotions that always seemed at war with each other whenever she and her sister found themselves in the same place at the same time.

She knew how wounding her remarks were to Elizabeth, but she couldn't help her annoyance. There her sister was, indeed looking like a vision from heaven, but what she chose to do with all her gifts tonight was to accompany their father to yet another *de rigueur* fancyass lawyer festival. Was it the New York State Trial Lawyers' annual ball or County Lawyers? Or, for all she knew, another fund-raiser for the latest trendy radical movement. Papa always loved to play it both ways—the perfect hero for every occasion. Robin

Hood to the poor, Sir Galahad to the rich and famous. It had always sickened Joey, but Elizabeth was a sucker for it every time.

"You are, of course," Elizabeth snapped back, "a world-renowned sartorial expert. It's no wonder my wardrobe is beneath your notice."

"At least I get to pick my own clothing," Joey retorted, remembering the countless times she'd watched her father sit in an upholstered chair outside the dressing room at Bonwit Teller, beaming at his other daughter as she modeled some treacly full-skirted outfit for his approval. She knew that he had bought this particular dress for Elizabeth just the month before. She was also certain that the garment more accurately reflected her father's wish for his daughter to look like Cinderella at the ball than it did her sister's taste, which tended more to the expensively tailored.

"Excuse me, Your Highness," Elizabeth answered. "I apologize for being grateful to someone who's laid out a few hundred dollars to buy something just because I happened to like it. And I'm so terribly sorry for loving my father. What a *stupid, horrible* human being I must be."

Elizabeth turned around and began to walk down the hall. "By the way, in case I forget," she called back over her shoulder, "the next time I have my apartment painted, remind me not to do it while you're home on spring break. Assuming we could both stay here at the same time was just plain crazy."

Joey listened to her sister's retreating footsteps. She felt slightly ashamed of herself, something she never would have allowed Elizabeth to see. After all, both women had been out of their parents' house for years now. Joey had spent four years away at Brown, followed by the last two and a half at Harvard Law School, while Elizabeth had her own apartment uptown. They'd hardly been under the same roof in a decade, yet, at twenty-five and twenty-seven respectively, they inevitably fell into the same sniping they'd done throughout their childhoods.

You'd think one of us would be smart enough or brave enough to change the rules, Joey thought, knowing even as the notion crossed her mind that that person was very unlikely to be Joey herself.

She put the book facedown on the bed and turned to look in the mirror that hung over the dresser across the room, studying her reflection. Her curly, brown, medium-length hair was wildly disarrayed, as always, and her navy blue corduroy jeans and white sweater weren't exactly clinging to her body. As wiry and thin as she was, Joanna Ross always wore her clothes baggy and loose, as if at any moment she was prepared to gain a hundred pounds or hide thirty bananas inside her shirt.

Not that either scenario was very likely. In fact, Joey found most food uninteresting, and, for that matter, most people too. Be honest, she'd say to herself when the latter thought would come into her mind—most people don't seem to find *you* very interesting. As opposed to the golden girl temporarily residing in the next bedroom, she mused.

Elizabeth was fascinated by—and fascinating to—virtually everyone who crossed her path. In a secret place in Joanna's heart even *she* loved her sister, a fact that she'd be hard-pressed to admit. As beautiful as Elizabeth was on the outside, she was just as well-meaning and kind on the inside. But being the golden girl's sister, two years younger, three inches shorter, and about a million times less attractive wasn't exactly a plum assignment.

Joey tried to shake off her thoughts and go back to studying *Barenblatt v. United States.* The 1959 case in front of the Supreme Court involved Communist infiltration in education, and ordinarily Joey was fascinated by matters involving free speech. But the erudite prose of Justice Harlan didn't capture her attention tonight. She couldn't rid herself of the vision of her sister, aglow with anticipation. So foolish on the one hand, yet so hopeful and lovely on the other. Neither hopefulness nor loveliness had ever marked Joey herself. She put the book down yet again. Well, she thought with minor satisfaction, at least I'm smart.

Of course, she acknowledged to herself, Elizabeth was probably even smarter. With about one-tenth the effort. She lay back against the pillow and shut her eyes. What am I that Elizabeth isn't? Mysterious, maybe. Aloof, maybe. Downright cold, maybe.

The thoughts made her chuckle. Those were the adjectives various teachers had ascribed to her all through grade school. Later, at Merryman, the public high school for gifted kids that she'd attended from the seventh grade on, she'd made a place for herself. Okay, so she was never one of those popular, outgoing, cheerleader types. But she had one friend she ate lunch with every day in the school cafeteria. They even went to the occasional movie. Yeah, she said to herself, frowning at her reflection. Marianne Wolfson lived in the apartment right underneath the Rosses and had been in the same class as Joey every year of their lives, from preschool through Merryman. What choice did she really have?

That wasn't completely fair, Joey realized. Marianne was actually fond of Joey. You have to show people how great you are, Marianne would urge Joey at the beginning of each school year. Is it an actual law? Joey would answer disingenuously. Suddenly, she missed Marianne, wishing she still lived downstairs, that she could call her and meet her for a drink or a movie. But Marianne had entered the Foreign Service right after college and was now a junior something-or-other in the United States Embassy in Turkey.

Joey had had a friend or two in college. Junior and senior years, she'd even had a boyfriend. Ted Vargas hadn't exactly set her on fire, but his rare intelligence and passion for American history had awakened a kind of intellectual curiosity she'd never really felt so clearly before.

It was because of him that she'd gone to law school.

Up until junior year at Brown she'd avoided any thoughts of becoming a lawyer. Her father's insistence that she join him and her sister at his firm only cemented her resistance. But, along with Ted, she'd spent a couple of summers interning at a small Boston newspaper, and she'd found herself fascinated by the legal issues that arose between a paper's right to publish and an ordinary person's right to privacy.

So, after fighting it all her life, she found herself in law school. But she'd be damned if she would capitulate to dear old dad, as Elizabeth had done so joyfully. She was never—*never*—going to join Ross, Jennings, and Trent. She was never going to join any big, prestigious firm. She had never even interned in the big firms during the summers, as most of her classmates had. Instead, after her first year of law school, she'd offered her services to the *Hartford Courant,* a newspaper midway between Boston and New York City. She spent most of her time there as a researcher for Kevin Thomases, the paper's international affairs reporter. The work was hard, hour after hour in libraries, staring at microfiches or searching through legislative journals, but the genial middle-aged journalist had been a real mentor, someone who made her feel essential while in actuality he taught her everything she needed to know.

She would have returned to the paper the summer after her second year, but Thomases had been stolen away by *The New York Times,* where he had already made a name for himself with a column that ran on the op-ed page twice a week. There was no room for her there, but she stayed in New York, devoting her hours to doing free legal work for Columbia's School of Journalism. It wasn't quite as fascinating as her time at the *Courant* had been, but when she graduated this coming June, she was already assured of a job in the school's legal department, vetting articles, handling any matters of jurisprudence that came up. Okay, maybe it wouldn't make the fullest use of her talent for legal matters, which, despite her best efforts, she seemed to have inherited from her father. But at least it put her into the world of journalism. Well, she amended silently, not quite into the middle of it, but it secured her a place right around the edges.

"Anybody home?"

Joey heard her mother's voice coming from the entrance hall downstairs. She put the book aside and rose, stretching her arms overhead as she left the room.

Her mother smiled up at Joey as she walked down the staircase.

"You look comfortable," Molly said, glancing at her daughter's mass of uncombed hair and bare feet.

"And you look tired," Joey replied, greeting her mother with a warm hug.

She took the heavy bag Molly had been carrying and deposited it on the small oak table across from the doorway. "Have you eaten?"

Molly looked chagrined. "Isn't that the question I'm supposed to be asking you? After all, I'm the mother here." She walked toward the kitchen. "Such as I am . . ."

Joey caught up with her. "You're the stuff mother-dreams are made of," she said reassuringly, knowing how sensitive Molly was on this issue.

Together they entered the kitchen and opened the refrigerator door, standing there wordlessly as they surveyed the contents.

After removing a bunch of carrots and carrying them over to the sink to wash, Joey broke the silence. "Has Hansel started showing yet?"

Molly laughed. She'd been painting costumes for *Hansel and Gretel* at the New York City Opera, and it was an open secret that the mezzo-soprano singing the role of the older brother was expecting a baby. Hansel was played by a woman in every opera house in the world, but rarely if ever by a woman who was in her fifth month of pregnancy.

"I think she'll last until it shuts down five weeks from now," she said. "Otherwise," she added, taking a plastic container of salad out of the refrigerator and bringing it to the table, "suspension of disbelief will be required at the door, along with the very expensive ticket."

"Why would they hire someone who's pregnant when there are so many singers out there who could do the role?" Joey asked, taking a bite of her carrot.

"Because she brings in the crowds, dear," Molly answered. "Besides, Monique Valeria would probably bomb Lincoln Center if they dared to replace her."

Joey smiled thoughtfully. "It must make your job harder."

"On the contrary, honey. If she weren't pregnant, there'd be no need for vertical stripes to be painted on her pants, hence no need for me." Molly took a forkful of the salad.

"I'm really proud of you, Mom," Joey said.

She saw that her words brought sudden tears to her mother's eyes. "Hey, that's not exactly something to cry about."

"No," Molly said, dabbing her eyes with her hand. "I'm glad to hear you say it. I only wish . . ."

"I know," Joey supplied, "you only wish your older daughter hadn't been struck both dumb and blind at birth."

Molly shook her head. "Oh, Joey, stop blaming your sister for my very real flaws. I didn't give either one of you enough time or attention, and I'm not much better now. And you know what? If I were a better person, I'd be with your father at the Plaza tonight, instead of hanging out backstage at the Met. Your poor sister always gets roped in."

"Oh, please. Elizabeth loves being 'roped in.' She gets to play her Little Princess fantasy, and Daddy doesn't even have to get wounded in a war."

"Don't be mean, darling. There's nothing wrong with a daughter making a father happy." She beamed at her. "After all," she said, reaching across the table to ruffle Joey's hair, "look how happy you make me."

* * *

"You both should have been there," Jack Ross enthused as he waved his glass of orange juice toward his wife and his younger daughter. "We raised over a million dollars last night."

His wife smiled at him, although her fullest attention seemed to be on the swatches of fabric lying on the table in front of her.

Joey knew she should keep her mouth shut, but she couldn't help herself. "Does the mil go directly into Elizabeth's account or do I get a hundred thou or so?"

Jack looked at her sharply. "Don't be ridiculous, Joey. You of all people shouldn't be sarcastic about a fund-raiser for the American Civil Liberties Union."

"Sorry," Joey said, sounding utterly unapologetic. She finished the bagel she'd been eating and pushed her chair away from the table. "See you later."

"Where are you going?" her father asked querulously.

"To rob a bank," she answered brightly.

Her mother looked at her with a reproving glance. "Don't be rude, dear."

Joey knew her father couldn't help himself. He'd experienced terrible things in his own childhood, and his worries about his wife and his children were understandable. But as a woman in her mid-twenties, it was unbearable to be treated like an irresponsible four-year-old. In fact, it had been just as unbearable when she actually *was* four.

"I'm going up to Columbia to talk to some of the people I'll be working with come June." She kept her voice as patient as she could as she started to walk out of the sunny white-tiled kitchen.

"I ran into someone interesting last night, Joey," her father said, succeeding in stopping her before she got out the door.

Joey turned around, leaning against the side of the broom closet. "And who might that be?"

"Your personal hero—Kevin Thomases." He smiled at the attentive expression that immediately appeared on Joey's face.

"In fact," he grinned even more broadly, "I've taken him on as a client."

Surprised, Joey went back to the table and sat down.

"Why does he need a lawyer all of a sudden?"

Her father lifted a coffee cup to his lips, took a long sip, then patted his mouth with a paper napkin. Joey knew he was just building suspense, but she wasn't about to give him the satisfaction of acknowledging her eagerness.

"Mr. Thomases is being sued for ten million dollars, a fact that neither he nor his new employer is very happy about."

Joey was taken aback. "Sued by whom?"

"Do you recognize the name Burton Herlihy?"

"No," Joey replied. "Should I?"

Jack sat back in his chair. "Actually, yes, since he was the subject of one of Mr. Thomases' columns a month or so ago." He looked at his daughter. "Of course, you were in Boston last month. I'll recapitulate for you. Dr. Burton Herlihy is—or I should say *was*—a professor at SUNY Purchase. Four of his students were arrested for smuggling guns to Northern Ireland. In his column, your friend Kevin suggested that the real blame lies not with the kids, who were hotheaded and impressionable, but with their English-history professor, the aforementioned Burton Herlihy. It seems his version of English history stems more from the Belfast perspective than from the London perspective."

"What does that have to do with a multimillion-dollar lawsuit?" Joey asked.

"Well, according to Dr. Herlihy—who, I might add, was fired two days after the column ran in the *Times*—the column constitutes both libel and defamation of character, in response to which he's suing both New York State and *The New York Times*. And, of course, Kevin Thomases."

"But that's ridiculous," Joey exclaimed. "According

to *Times versus Sullivan,* to prove libel he'd have to show malicious intent. Which is next to impossible."

Her father raised an eyebrow. "Maybe not so impossible in a sympathetic state court."

"But the core part of the case, the civil rights aspect, is federal," Joey objected, pondering what her father had said. She stared thoughtfully at the wall, picking up her father's coffee cup and taking a sip without realizing she'd done it. "Of course, the defamation is a state cause of action, but there's no reason not to combine it all into federal court."

"You're absolutely right," Jack responded warmly. "But even in federal court, this case will be hard fought."

"Why?" demanded Joey. "Freedom of the press is not exactly a new concept in these United States."

"Nor is freedom of speech," her father answered, "which right Dr. Herlihy claims our client abused."

Joey looked over at her father abruptly. "*Your* client, Dad."

Her father looked mildly abashed. "You know, Joey, I'm not sure I can do right by Kevin Thomases, at least not without some help."

Joey felt a chill creep slowly up her spine. "You're the managing partner of one of New York City's most eminent law firms, Dad. You've got all the help you need."

Jack smiled sadly. "Eminent, yes. Large, no. We have only five senior people, plus a handful of associates, clerks, and paralegals. Not exactly a population explosion."

"You've kept it elite, Dad, not underfed. There's a difference."

"Listen, sweetheart, I know this doesn't fit in with your current plans. But I need someone on this case who actually cares. Who loves the journalistic side as much as the legal side, who's close enough to campus life to evaluate the adversary's position as well as our own. And no matter how capable my people are, none of them is as well equipped as you are to fight this."

Joey was speechless. Thomases was her mentor, a man to whom she owed so much. Now he was in legal trouble, already relying on her father's firm. And here she was, almost a lawyer and in a position to help him. If she didn't help and something went wrong with his case, she would never be able to forgive herself. But that meant doing the unthinkable. She found herself holding her breath. Without a hint of traffic, she'd been in a two-car collision and hadn't even heard the crash.

"I'm completely taken over by Stern and the Stevens thing." Jack tossed off the names of two of his most demanding cases, which had been going on for months.

"How about Elizabeth?" Joey finally reclaimed her powers of speech.

"Your sister is sitting second-chair on all my stuff, plus twenty-odd cases of her own are waiting in the wings."

Now the rear tires of the car were traveling over Joey's body, back and forth, flattening her into the concrete.

Jack's voice became a soothing murmur. "It doesn't have to be forever. . . . Just until we settle this for your friend Kevin. Think how fascinating the case will be. How grateful your client will be when it is all over."

"I . . ." Joey tried to think of something to say. Anything. But it was as if she had taken her last breath. The car that had run her over had left the scene. It was over. She was already dead.

Chapter Three

"So what do you think, Mrs. Ross?" Adele Fellenbach's mouth was tight with anxiety as she handed Molly the sketch of a floor-length dress, its softly falling full skirt awash in soft blues and greens. "Can you get the effect we're after?"

Molly examined the piece of paper carefully. "I think this calls for a heavyish silk," she said, closing her eyes for a moment as she envisioned how she would approach the job of painting all those yards of fabric. The dress fell in wide panels, each of them featuring a pastoral scene, which would be invisible to most of the audience but give the overall impression of the regal but down-to-earth character that the lead actress was supposed to project.

"It reminds me of Pissarro," Molly said finally, opening her eyes and looking at the sketch again. "I'll work it up and have a bid for you by Tuesday."

"That will be fine," Adele answered, leaving the sketch with Molly as she swept out of the studio.

Molly walked across to the bookshelves that completely covered one wall of the room. She surveyed the assortment of oversized illustrated books, then pulled down an art history text and turned to the index. There it is, she thought, as her finger came to rest on *A Cowherd on the Route du Chou, Pontoise.*

On the page listed she found the painting of the small French village, its short brushstrokes and soft colors evoking exactly the feeling that Adele Fellenbach had been describing. What a perfect model for Molly to be drawing on for her very first European work assignment. Her first assignment outside of New York City, she thought with a thrill of anticipation.

Using the painting as a reference, she began to sketch out a sample with an array of colored pencils. As she worked, she thought about how much she should charge for the job. She wouldn't be the only costume painter bidding on it, that was for sure. Despite the fact that so few people did this kind of work, competition for every single job was fierce.

"Hey, um, Molly, how about a cup of coffee?" Michael Weaver stuttered nervously as he entered Molly's studio.

Molly looked up, surprised by his sudden appearance. A sculptor whose studio was one floor beneath hers, Michael stopped in a little too often as far as Molly was concerned, but she didn't have the heart to tell him so. The fear and vulnerability in his large brown eyes always seemed to be pleading *Pay attention to me, don't hurt me, love me.* And despite the discomfort she always felt in his presence, she couldn't just ignore him. Today, his dark hair looked as if it hadn't been washed in months. Equally filthy were the overalls he wore, not just plaster-splattered but covered in what looked like food stains. Molly felt pity and distaste in equal measure, as she often did with Michael, but right now she had no time to give in to his demands.

"Sorry, Michael," she said more brightly than she felt, "but I have a job I have to finish by tonight."

His face grew apologetic instantly. "Oh, of course you do, I mean, absolutely you're busy, and I'd never disturb you, never . . ." As he spoke, he was backing up toward the door. When he got just outside, he stopped and looked at her once again. "Maybe tomorrow . . ."

"Actually, Michael," she explained, "If I get the job I'm working on, I'll be going out of town within a few days, and there's so much I'll have to take care of before that . . ."

She let the sentence hang in the air, hoping that he would understand. Knowing how sensitive he was, she expected disappointment from Michael, but not the expression of pure anger that crossed his face. He caught himself immediately, replacing the look with a too-wide smile.

"Whenever, Molly," he said, finally turning around and shutting the door behind him.

Molly stared after him. She was surprised to realize that she'd been almost frightened of him, and relief coursed through her body now that he was gone.

But there was no time to dwell on Michael, she realized, once again concentrating on the task in front of her. Her eyes darted between the picture of the Pissarro painting and the sketch pad. This would take a few layers of paint, and she'd have to go over it more than once, she knew. She would paint the skirt panels with thickened analine dye, then steam the fabric and wash it out. For the next layer, she'd have to perform the process all over again.

When she finished the sketch, it looked beautiful. Just right for a play based in nineteenth-century France, she thought, pleased with what she'd done. She put the pad down and walked over to the sink, which stood alone on the wall opposite the bookshelves. A toilet and a shower were hidden behind a door nearby, but in this old downtown studio building no one had ever bothered to combine the elements of a bathroom into one space.

Which was just fine with Molly. In fact, she loved her studio on Nineteenth Street. Up here, on the sixth floor of the old warehouse building, she felt more herself than anywhere else. She washed the paint off her hands and filled the kettle that rested on a hot plate near the sink. As the water started to heat, she began to feel the excitement that always arrived with the start of a new job.

She looked around the studio with satisfaction. Fifteen years ago she hadn't even known there *was* such a job as painting costumes. Nor that she would be a card-carrying member of Local 829 of the Scenic Artists Union. What a long road she'd taken to get here!

For that matter, she realized, it was pretty much a miracle that she could even leave the house, let alone contemplate a trip to Paris. How many years had she spent in the confines of her apartment, unable even to go to the drugstore on the corner or a school conference with one of the girls' teachers?

In the first year of her marriage to Jack, she'd realized that she felt comfortable only inside the one-bedroom apartment they had rented on Amsterdam Avenue. By the time she became pregnant with Elizabeth the following year, she had to force herself to let Jack take her to the obstetrician's office for the scheduled checkups. It was only because Jack stayed at her side for forty-eight hours straight that she was able to endure being at the hospital when the baby was born.

After that, she stopped going out altogether. She was just so frightened, panicked at the thought of the people, the noise, the idea that she might get lost.

Gradually, everything had become overwhelming to her. She spent long hours sleeping or just lying in bed, constantly exhausted. She couldn't do anything. She couldn't even feel anything. A succession of nannies took care of Elizabeth and then Joanna, when she was born two years later. By that time, Jack had found a physician willing to come to the house for Molly's prenatal checkups, and she was sedated for the trip to the hospital for the birth. The move to their current apartment overlooking Gramercy Park was the last time Molly went out for years. Her world was the apartment, almost the only people she spoke to were Jack, her daughters, and their baby-sitters.

Molly was ashamed of herself every minute of those years. She felt as if her children were growing up at arm's length from her. She could hug them and sit with them for a while, but she was too tired for much else.

And she had been powerless to do anything about it. It was as if she were buried alive, the force of the earth pressing down upon her. When thoughts of suicide began to overwhelm her, she finally decided to get some help. For several months, she consulted with a psychiatrist—by telephone. For two years after that, the psychiatrist came to the apartment to work with her. It was only then that she was ready to venture outside for the first time. And slowly but steadily, she made progress.

Oh, the cost of those lost years, she thought, sinking into a chair and covering her eyes with her hands. She was still, even after all this time, swallowed whole by the guilt. She hadn't been there for her children, nor for her husband. God knows she *wanted* to be there, longed to be a regular person living a normal life. But during those years, really feeling a part of things came so hard for her. Always in the background was the shadow of her own childhood, her own parents.

The memories made her sink even lower in the chair. Whatever happy times she'd had in the big house in Riverdale, playing with her neighborhood friends, going to school, daydreaming as she tried on her mother's dresses and high heels when she was a little girl—all that was lost. Displaced by that terrible Monday afternoon, the day she virtually never allowed herself to think about.

What was the use of thinking about those years, she asked herself wearily. That was then. This was more than thirty years later, thirty years in which she'd become Jack's wife, been protected by him, maybe even overprotected. He continued to take care of everything. It was as if none of the terrible things had ever really happened.

She had gone along with him for so many years. Avoiding the pain, burying the memories. It meant that she had buried most of her other feelings as well.

But, she told herself yet again, this was her life. No better and no worse than anyone else's.

Oh, stop it, she chided herself as she listened to her thoughts.

The kettle began to whistle and she got up, rummaging around a small cupboard and removing a white ceramic tumbler and a peppermint tea bag. Pouring the boiling water into the cup and swirling the tea bag around until the liquid turned a pale yellow color, she picked up the cup and discarded the used bag. Then she walked back to her work area. The tea was too hot to drink, she knew, so she just inhaled the aroma. She blew on the liquid for a moment, then took a long sip.

She hadn't really felt so isolated and useless since she'd been plucked out from behind the scenes at Joey's school by Corinne Fontaine. She smiled at the memory. It was the year before Joey graduated from Merryman. Just on instinct, she'd chosen to paint the lead's costume for a performance of the musical *Brigadoon*. The dress that Leslie Fontaine wore as Fiona for her first romantic scene was a lovely purple color, but under the lights it looked pale and lifeless. Molly had imagined how vivid it would be with actual paint added, purples and light blues mingled to make the skirt shiny and alive. The fabric would look so much richer, she'd told the drama teacher. And it had come out perfectly, the heather colors evoking mist and timelessness in a way regular fabric never could have.

Leslie Fontaine's mother had asked to be introduced to Molly after the performance. It turned out she was directing an off-off-Broadway show down at a tiny theater on Second Street, a play that involved Harlem nightclubs of the forties. "I'm trying for exotic and tragic all at the same time," Corinne had explained to Molly, "and I think you could paint the ambiance I want right into the wardrobe. In all honesty," she'd added, "professional costume painters would cost a fortune."

That was the first time Molly had heard that cos-

tume painting *was* a profession. And she wasn't put
out by the notion that she was not being paid. After
all, Jack made plenty of money and with the girls
growing up, what else did she have to do with her
time?

She'd agreed readily, although she hadn't really
known what to expect. But she'd been surprised at
how much fun it was. Then, a month or two after
Corinne's play closed, Molly got a call from one of
the people she'd met backstage. "My costume painter
is stuck in Milan!" Gregory Borenstein had cried.
"Please, please, you must help me out!"

Gregory's play had been off-Broadway. An Equity
production. Suddenly Molly found herself working in
professional theater. Not just plays, but operas and
ballets too. As if she were taking a crash course, she
called a couple of other painters and got their permission to watch them as they worked, learning from
them. So few people were versed in the art of costume
painting that she found herself with plenty of projects.
She'd rented the Nineteenth Street studio when Joey
was a junior in college. By then, Molly was working
full-time, meeting her own circle of friends, finally
having her own frame of reference.

And it had changed her. She knew it. Little by little,
she was letting herself feel things. Sad when she lost
a job she wanted. Elated when a dress came out just
right. She still felt guilty about Elizabeth and Joey. If
she had been emotionally unavailable when they were
little, now she was so busy painting that she was often
physically unavailable. "I'm finishing a job for Frank
Miceli," she'd explain to Elizabeth when her daughter
would ask her to come to dinner. "I have to finish
steaming the ball gown," she'd told Joey just last night
when she had called her mother from her office at
Ross, Jennings. She couldn't blame the girls if they
were irritated, but she was doing her best. Someday
there would be time to catch up.

Taking a final sip of tea, she forced the thoughts
out of her head. It was depressing to dwell on regrets

this way. She just had to stay cheerful. This was no time to give in to whatever lingering darkness she might still have inside. She put the cup in the sink and went back to the sketch she'd made. Already more had occurred to her—a hint of pink in the bodice, another layer of aqua in the skirt.

Her full attention now back to the work in front of her, she was startled by the ringing of the telephone.

"Hello," she answered distractedly.

"Hi, there, love."

The sound of her husband's endearment sent a prickle of discomfort up her spine. She knew she should appreciate his solicitude, but whenever he called her "love" it made her feel constricted. The way she used to feel when she was bound in her apartment. Caught. Like a bird in a gilded cage.

Cage, indeed, she chided herself. This man had not only saved her life, he had fed her and dressed her and loved her for thirty years.

"Hello, darling." She forced extra warmth into her voice. "I'm glad you're calling. Something very thrilling might be happening."

"What is that?"

She knew she had her husband's full attention, something she shouldn't ever take for granted. After all, how many women married to men as busy as Jack Ross could make the same claim?

"Well," she said, her excitement bubbling up, "Adele Fellenbach might be sending me to Paris for three weeks. I can't believe it!"

Jack didn't answer right away, and she wondered if his attention had been drawn away by something in his office.

"Did you hear my news?" she repeated. "I might be working in Paris."

"I'm not deaf, Molly," Jack answered, his tone sharper than usual. "I'm just not certain that France is feasible."

Molly caught her breath. "What do you mean, 'not

feasible'? France is six hours away by plane. People go there every day.''

"I know that, darling," he responded more softly, "but my schedule is overcrowded right now. I can't possibly get away until summer at least. And I assume she'd need you right away?"

"Well, yes," Molly answered, wondering why he wasn't understanding what she was trying to tell him. "But you don't have to be available. This trip is work for me. I wouldn't even have time to spend with you if you *could* come. I'll be working all day and most of the evening in the theater, then getting on a plane and coming home. I doubt I'll have the time for dinner out, let alone sight-seeing or going to a museum with you."

"Since when don't you want me with you?" he answered, his voice suddenly boyish.

"It's not a question of *wanting* you with me. It means that a whole new world is opening up for me. It's the opportunity of a lifetime. Surely you understand that." She realized that her words were unlikely to soothe him. Carefully, she modulated her tone, keeping her enthusiasm to a minimum. "I always like to be with you, Jack, you know that. If you were there with me, it would be absolutely perfect."

For a moment, she hated herself. What she was saying was a lie. It was exciting to think about being in Paris alone, working on such a splendid production. Amazing, in fact, to think with pleasure instead of fear about being so far away on her own. Years ago, this would have been impossible, beyond her wildest dreams. But Jack got so frightened whenever she seemed to pull away. She had to understand that.

She wasn't sure her reassurance had had any effect. There was total silence on her husband's end of the telephone. Finally, when he spoke again, the longing in his voice was palpable.

"But the girls and I simply can't do without you for that long a time, especially that far away."

"The girls are in their twenties and living under

their own roofs," she replied, exasperated. "And Paris is the same phone call away that all your business trips have been for the past three decades."

She realized she was sounding snappish, but her patience was about to give way completely. Somehow, her husband was taking one of the happiest moments of her life and transforming it into an Ibsen play.

But, she realized, sighing inwardly, now clearly wasn't the moment for a debate. "Why don't we talk about this later tonight? I'm sure you have a hundred things to do."

"That will be fine, darling," he responded, his voice actually frail. "We'll work all this out. You wait and see."

Molly felt deflated as she replaced the receiver. Jack didn't mind substituting one of the girls when he needed a companion for a business event. Well, substituting Elizabeth, she amended, since Joey wouldn't dream of accompanying her father. But he liked the family together, all four of them within shouting distance of each other, each of his three girls in her proper square. The notion reminded her suddenly of pieces on a chessboard, but she pushed it out of her mind. In fact, within moments, she was completely consumed once again by the sketches that lay in front of her.

Jack put the phone down slowly. He couldn't bear the apprehension that was spreading through his chest, the sudden weakness that left his legs feeling like rubber. He saw the light flashing on his other line, knew he should pick it up and answer it, that his secretary wouldn't be bothering him if it weren't important. But he could barely move.

How could Molly be contemplating such a step? How could she think of going thousands of miles away from him, leaving him stranded a continent away?

There was a discreet knock on his door, and after a few seconds, Jane peered in.

"Sylvia Michaelson is on line two, Mr. Ross," the young woman said apologetically. "It sounds urgent."

Jack forced himself to speak. "Keep her on hold. I'll be with her in a minute or two."

As soon as Jane closed the door, Jack reached into the lower drawer of his desk, removed a bottle of Scotch, and poured two fingers into his empty coffee cup. He drained the cup in one long gulp, then put it down, waiting for the liquor to take effect. The warmth of it was bound to soothe him, bound to keep him going.

The Scotch tasted good, but his uneasiness remained. He hated this feeling, had hated it since he was a little boy, alone, trying to find his way in a world that wanted him dead.

To Molly, Europe was Paris. A wonderland. A world where culture and beauty lay in abundance. To Jack, Europe was Hungary. The land of his birth.

As a child in war-torn Hungary, Jack had gone through more before the age of ten than most other people would go through in their entire lives. While his parents had fallen victim to the concentration camps, Jack and his brother had hidden out in plain sight, their blond hair and winning grins making people smile at them, offer them food and shelter. Theo, two years younger, was shy and withdrawn; left by himself, he probably couldn't have done it. No, it was Jack who would clasp the people's hands, kiss their cheeks, show them that he recognized what wonderful people they were inside, heroes, going unappreciated by everyone but him. Poor little angels, he'd hear them say as they settled the boys into a corner of a room or a pile of straw in a barn.

The people who helped them never guessed they were Jewish, enemies of the state, never saw anything but their big blue eyes and golden hair. And Jack had made sure that neither he nor his brother had ever gone hungry, not even for a day. He wouldn't have let anything happen to his brother.

He found that he was shaking. Taking a handkerchief from the breast pocket of his suit jacket, he wiped perspiration from his face, realizing as he did so that the wetness came only from his eyes.

Of course, he couldn't really protect Theo at all. He had thought that when the war was over, everything would be all right. He would never forget that October night in 1956, almost a decade after having survived the horrors of the war, when he and Theo joined the massive student demonstrations against Soviet domination. What had started as support for the Polish revolutionaries not so many miles away became a clarion call for the freedom of Hungary. And at first the peaceful rally was tolerated. But later that night, the security police began to shoot at the demonstrators. One minute he and his brother were shouting along with thousands of others against the evils of collectivism and proclaiming the need for a democratic Hungary, and the next, Theo was lying on the ground, a single bullet to the heart ending all of their dreams.

Jack felt his tears start to flow once again. Angry at his weakness, he poured another finger of Scotch into his cup and drank it down. He had put all that behind him. Had gotten to America, had married the beautiful girl with the white tennis shorts and the alligator on her shirt. She'd been the daughter of the surly man in the big, beautiful house in Riverdale while Jack himself had been making his way through law school by mowing lawns and taking out rich people's garbage. He knew he would amount to something. He'd always known. But he hadn't known why. Not until he saw Molly, holding her books in front of her as she'd walk to school, so pretty, so clean, so *American.* She'd been the beginning of everything good, the culmination of all his dreams.

Out of the corner of his eye he saw the flashing telephone, knew he had to pick it up, deal with whatever was going on right now. There was nothing he could do about what happened decades before.

But there's plenty I can do to protect my family now, he vowed. And that included keeping his wife and his daughters safe. Safe and close, that was the only way. Maybe he hadn't really told Molly the complete truth on that terrible day years before, but it had kept her safe.

Perhaps they didn't always understand or agree. Certainly his daughter Joanna fought him every way she knew how. But he had nothing to apologize for. He was the only one who understood how dangerous the world really was.

He finally felt the alcohol take hold, felt the tension begin to ease out of his muscles. Taking a deep breath, he pushed the button for the waiting call and heard the voice of Sylvia Michaelson, the wife of a man he had represented in a tax case three years before.

"Jack, thank goodness you're there!" she said, her voice almost hysterical.

"What's the matter, Sylvia?"

"Oh, God, everything."

He heard a sob, which she obviously was attempting to stifle.

"Easton is trying to can me," she answered after successfully collecting herself. "First, they hold out the executive vice presidency. Now they're making my life a living horror."

Sylvia Michaelson had been an executive at Easton Technologies as long as Jack had known her. An attractive woman, she'd always seemed extraordinarily self-assured and competent. In fact, her husband had bragged to Jack about how his wife's salary was slightly higher than his own, which had been a source of comfort during his own litigation. Whatever else Sylvia might be—and truth to tell, Jack had always found her slightly intimidating and cold—for her to be on the edge of losing it this way, things must really be terrible.

"Sylvia, you should come in and see me. Can you do that this afternoon?"

"Damn," she answered, "I'm in our Maryland office. I won't be home until late tomorrow night."

"Well," Jack said, thumbing through his Rolodex

and finding the card with all the Michaelsons' numbers on it. "I have your office number here. Why don't we talk when you get back?"

"What you have is my old number," Sylvia answered bitterly. "They've given my office to the young guy who just came in. I've been relegated to a space as small as a fingernail."

"I don't quite understand, Sylvia. Have they actually said anything about firing you?"

"Oh, no. They've just made my life such a misery that I've finally decided to leave."

"Ah," Jack said, immediately getting the picture. "Constructive termination. The tool of the nineties." He thought for a few seconds then spoke once again. "How old are you?"

"Forty-nine. A little too young for age discrimination."

"Anything special coming up in the next couple of years, in the way of stock options or the bonus plan?" he asked.

"Well, yes," she answered thoughtfully. "There's a whole package that kicks in at twenty years, which would be, well, about eighteen months from now."

Bingo, Jack said to himself. Cases like these were becoming more and more common. And it almost always happened to people exactly Sylvia's age. Right around the time they were eligible for their greatest financial prize, they would either be fired outright or simply made so uncomfortable that they would choose to leave. When he spoke again, his voice communicated the optimism he was beginning to feel. He loved finding the angle that would rescue a client.

"You know, Sylvia, that's the nastiest part of age discrimination. The bastards do it in such a way that even the very people being discriminated against don't have the satisfaction of knowing what's really going on." He began to sound angry now. "These sons of bitches are playing with fire. It's good that you called me now, before anything is cast in stone."

"What should I do?" she asked, her voice a bit more hopeful than it had been.

Jack pulled a pad of paper in front of him and wrote down his advice as he gave it, making sure that he didn't forget anything. "First of all, amass every piece of your work history you can put your finger on—your annual reviews, what may have been done to you that hasn't been done to anyone else around you. Try to remember any comment ever made about your age—and about your being a woman, for that matter. And look around you. Who else might they be grooming for your job? Is it someone younger? I bet it is."

He heard her intake of breath and knew he had struck a nerve.

"I can't believe they'd be that obvious, that stupid," Sylvia said.

"Well," he answered, "if they have a feel for subtlety, it may not be that direct. Ask around. See if there's a job that's just been filled or that's going to be filled that sounds like yours but has a different title. Generally that's one of corporate management's favorite tricks. Trust me, dear, it won't go over well in court. I promise you that."

"Jack," she said warmly, "you're a lifesaver."

"Just a worker bee among all the other bees," he laughed, "but one with a powerful sting."

He smiled as he hung up the phone. He still had it, no matter how upsetting the day had been. He would solve Sylvia Michaelson's problem and he would solve his own, one step at a time, just as he always had. His eye caught the bottle of Scotch, still sitting on top of his desk. For a second, he thought of pouring some more into the cup, celebrating his competence. But he stopped himself this time. He had work to do. He was a successful lawyer, the managing partner of a fine legal firm, and head of a wonderful family. The Scotch could wait until later.

Chapter Four

1995

Peter Grier tapped his fork on the table, looking around the restaurant appraisingly. Elizabeth knew that his frown was one of professional assessment, not irritation, despite their having been seated for a full five minutes without anyone coming over to take their drink orders.

"The hot place. It's crowded," she said, reaching for a roll. "Mmm, this is nice and warm."

Peter squeezed one of the other rolls in the basket but didn't pick it up. "No excuse. They're not billing it as noisy, wait-forever, hip. This is supposed to be a serious place."

"Well, you run a tighter ship." Elizabeth smiled. "Your waiters wouldn't let customers languish like this without a martini."

"Damn straight." Peter gave her a smile in return. "I'd shoot them dead."

"Torture them first," Elizabeth said facetiously, biting into her roll.

"You really should run a restaurant—you've got that Management Attitude," he teased.

Elizabeth laughed. She admired Peter's skill in running his two restaurants, Hey There on Broadway and

Seventy-fifth Street and Grier's on East Sixty-third Street, just off Lexington Avenue. It had been quite an education for her, watching him over the past few years as he developed the concepts, had the spaces built, and presided over the endless details of preparing them for opening night. By now, both restaurants were bustling, successful places, and he worked long days and nights to keep them going smoothly.

A harried waiter appeared beside them. "What can I get for you?"

Peter looked up. "Two menus, one vodka martini straight up, two olives, and a glass of red wine, please. Wine—right, Lizzie?" he asked.

She nodded. "Thanks."

The waiter left, and Peter leaned forward to take her hand. "Now, tell me what's new in the world of my powerful lawyer friend. It's been what, four or five weeks?"

"Has it been that long since we went to that movie?" Elizabeth was genuinely surprised. "God, I've been so caught up in this case I'm on, I guess the world is passing me by. Or at least this month has."

"It's not exactly a new story," Peter said as their drinks were set down before them. "You've been known to get caught up before. But why state the obvious."

Elizabeth looked rueful. "Thank you for keeping track of me and making sure I get out at night."

"It's for my own selfish pleasure." Peter brought her hand to his lips, turning it over and kissing her palm lightly before releasing it.

"You flatter me."

Peter raised an eyebrow. "Do I? Well, I hope you get some selfish pleasure out of it too. You can have all you want, you know. Selfish pleasure on sale, forty percent off this month. Lifetime guarantee."

She laughed, not answering but pleased nonetheless. They had resumed seeing one another, just as she had known they would the instant she saw him in her office that day, right after he had moved back to New

York. They still made love with the same passion as when they were first together. Elizabeth was thrilled to find that he was still just as much fun, just as nice. She cared deeply for him. Yet she knew that nothing inside her had changed; the thought of making anything permanent with Peter stopped her in her tracks. She had to admit she also had a convenient safety net in the fact that she was always busy with her job at the law firm. She was simply too preoccupied with work to give any relationship the attention it required. For his part, Peter knew better than to question her. There were no conversations about marriage or even about increasing the amount of time they spent together. Still, every so often he made a comment indicating that he was hoping for something more. Elizabeth usually ignored it, and he would let the matter drop.

As he did now.

"By the way," he said, suddenly recalling, "my friend Alex's girlfriend has a golden retriever that just had puppies. Do you want one?"

"Me?" Elizabeth looked surprised. "You've got to be kidding. The poor thing would be alone in my apartment all day. I don't have any time for a dog."

Peter nodded. "I figured, but I thought I'd ask. You never know. What about your sister?"

Elizabeth frowned. "I don't know, but I'd rather not ask her. She's always so testy with me. She'll probably have some nasty interpretation of why I'm offering it to her." She sighed. "Joey will forever think of me as some kind of glossy, superficial princess. She's always so difficult. I don't know why she has to be."

Peter smiled. "Is it because you're beautiful and talented and smart? Anyone who has that kind of older sister is bound to be pissed off by it."

The waiter handed them menus. Elizabeth opened hers, shaking her head. "You know she's always been that way. As if my life is so easy, and hers is . . . she wouldn't say harder, but somehow more *real*."

"It's too bad you two don't get along better. I'd love to have a sister or a brother."

Elizabeth made a face. "Don't be so sure. When I was little, I thought a baby sister would be the greatest thing in the world. Who ever thought I'd get the crankiest, most sharp-tongued sister of all time? If we weren't related, she would step over me if she saw me lying in the gutter. Hell, she might step over me anyway."

"I'm sure she has her lovable side," Peter said, signaling to the waiter that they were ready to order.

"Well, if she has, she keeps it hidden from everyone except my mother." She looked back to her menu. "What do you hear about the swordfish?"

Peter shook his head. "Go with the red snapper. I'm having the hangar steak. Want to share? I'd like to check them both out."

"You're on."

After dinner they took a walk, window-shopping, talking, enjoying the cool May night. Even though it was nearly eleven o'clock on a Thursday, Columbus Avenue was brimming with life. Peter lived only twelve blocks uptown from Elizabeth, but they invariably spent their rare nights together in his apartment. They strolled aimlessly for a while before heading toward his building on Broadway.

Upstairs in his apartment, they quickly retreated to his bedroom.

"I have a seven o'clock meeting tomorrow," he said teasingly, as he pulled Elizabeth down onto the bed with him. "I don't know if I can afford to stay awake even a minute longer."

She laughed. "Hey, I'm the one with the seven o'clock meetings. You can't steal my lines."

He started unbuttoning her shirt. "But it's true." His tone grew exaggerated. "And, frankly, I'm *exhausted.*"

She kicked off her shoes, reaching for his belt buckle. "Poor baby."

He brought his face close to hers. "You're going to have to find some way to keep me awake."

She nodded, her expression serious. "I think I can do it. I'm going to try my damnedest."

"My money's on you," he whispered, as his hands traveled up her arms, and he slipped the shirt off both her shoulders in one fluid motion.

"The forensics expert should arrive that Monday. That should give us enough time, don't you think, Dad?"

Elizabeth glanced up from the pile of papers in her lap at her father, who was standing across the room from her, looking out his office window. He seemed absorbed in something he saw on the street below, but she was afraid he might really be thinking about the bottle of Scotch she knew was hidden away in the bottom drawer of his desk.

"Dad?" she repeated. "Is that plan okay with you?"

"What?" He turned to her.

"The forensics expert," she repeated patiently. "He'll be here that Monday."

Jack nodded, apparently making an effort to concentrate. "Fine, fine."

Elizabeth bit her lip. This next part was a little more difficult to say tactfully.

"You know," she started slowly, "if I think of myself doing Barcell's opening argument, I get this urge to put the implausibility of his alibi right up front. Deal with it from the outset with the jury. If we admit it seems ridiculous on the face of it, we can show why it must be the truth." She shrugged. "Just my thoughts."

Her father gazed at her, apparently turning her words over in his mind. Then he straightened up slightly and brushed off an imaginary piece of lint from his navy suit jacket. "Hmmm," he said mildly, still examining his jacket. "Interesting."

"Thanks." She smiled. Okay, she said to herself, he got it. He'd reorganize his opening statement.

Elizabeth returned from her father's office to her own more than an hour later. They had spent most of that time going over the Sayres case in more detail, along with a few others, all in different stages, all of them needing careful research and thought. She wasn't sure how much her father even remembered the cases when she referred to them. But that was all right; she would handle things.

She had to be careful in assigning the backup work she needed; it was usual for associates and paralegals to do research work, but she didn't want anyone to suspect that she was actually piecing all the cases together. Certain requests should appear to come from her father, and the facts should be delivered to him. She could then retrieve the files and integrate all the information in a way he could digest.

She furrowed her brow, thinking about the smell of Scotch when she had kissed him on entering his office, knowing it was an almost daily late-morning occurrence now. She wished he didn't drink so much. But, hey, she thought, if Jack Ross wants to knock back a few, he's earned the right. Her father was one of the all-time-great attorneys, practically a New York institution. Even if he weren't her father, it would be a privilege to work for him.

She picked up the telephone receiver as she flipped through her Rolodex, stopping when she reached the card she wanted. Her friend Diane was home with the flu. Diane had come to love Charlottesville, where she now resided in an enormous colonial house in the countryside with her husband, two children, and two dogs. She had given up working to be a full-time mother. Elizabeth couldn't have been more delighted by her friend's happiness, although she found the picture of her old New York buddy in blissful southern domesticity difficult to conjure up. Every so often, Elizabeth tried to imagine herself in the same situation. Can't be done, she would say to herself, shaking her head. Just can't be done.

It was only because Diane was so happy where she

was that Elizabeth could continue to tease her about coming back north. Now, she dialed a mail-order company whose gift baskets she particularly liked, and ordered oranges and grapefruits to be sent to her friend, who had been miserable in bed for over a week.

"Could you please have the card read, 'If you were here to get the right kind of chicken soup, you'd have been better long ago. It's all too sad. Love you, E.'"

As she began gathering papers for the meeting she was going into next, she felt a pang of longing to see her friend. She had plenty of friends, but there weren't many with whom she shared as long a past. And it was so difficult to make time to keep up with the friends she did have. Even her time with Peter had to be shoehorned into her schedule. Well, she thought, it was a good thing they had the kind of understanding they did.

Chapter Five

"Only one more mile," Tom gasped as he and Joey made their way across the Brooklyn Bridge.

Joey felt as if her heart were about to burst out of her chest, but there was no way she would give in to her fatigue. "Tell me more about Henry."

Tom Abrahams looked at her, his expression bemused. "You just want some entertainment to get you all the way home."

"You betcha." Joey pulled a tissue from the pocket of her gray sweatpants and wiped the perspiration from her face. "Please, tell me about your parents' new patio furniture. Tell me about the weather. Tell me anything."

Tom laughed. His own, much larger frame was bathed in sweat, but his preparation for the New York City Marathon just a couple of months before meant he was now less exhausted than Joanna. For him, running ten miles or so through Brooklyn Heights and Carroll Gardens, then returning to Joey's loft in Tri-BeCa was ordinary weekend exercise.

"Okay, my dear," he said, pulling ahead of her, "I'll be the entertainment committee, but you'll have to go a little faster as payment."

Joey winced. "Not fair. You do this all the time—"

"—while big bad Daddy keeps you chained up in

the office, threatening to beat you with a stick if you don't earn your five million dollars a year," Tom interrupted.

"Closer to five thousand than five million, believe me," Joey said, but she didn't put much heart into her demurral.

Tom slowed down slightly and told Joey about his date with the man he'd met while he'd been roller-blading along the West Side Highway the weekend before. Joey was interested in her friend's social life—after all, one of them had to have one—but his jokes about her job left her uncomfortable. She found herself lost in her own thoughts as Tom's voice helped keep her feet moving.

In fact, she earned more money working for Ross, Jennings, and Trent than she deserved. No, she amended as she tried to keep up with Tom, more than *anyone* deserved—certainly anyone who helped rich codgers hold on to their money instead of turning it over to the IRS and protected cheating husbands from having to pay their soon-to-be-ex-wives what they surely were entitled to.

Not that her father's firm didn't handle other, more interesting cases. Jack Ross loved nothing better than seeing his name in the paper associated with someone perceived to be an underdog. Glowing editorials would describe how brave he was, how committed to morality. All she saw was a frightened, narcissistic guy with one hand on a bottle of Johnnie Walker.

To be fair, her father had continued to feed her some compelling cases after she'd successfully defended Kevin Thomases. In a way, that was the problem. The good cases came just often enough to keep her there, but not quite often enough to cover up how uninspiring at best and immoral at worst most of her cases were. The fact was, she just hated it. Every working minute of every working day. Hated the loopholes, hated the partisanship every lawyer had to embrace, hated the confrontations and the negotiations.

She'd tried to talk to her mother about it once,

when they'd gotten together for dinner. Molly Ross had attempted to listen, but Joey might as well have been speaking in a foreign language. When trouble was about to start, Joey's mother could go very far away very fast. Not physically, Joey reminded herself. Despite her mother's troubles in the early years of Joey's childhood, she had been there through chicken pox and a broken arm and even a couple of really bad dates that had left Joey more vulnerable than usual. But anything *real,* and her mother went to that place in her head where no one else was welcome. Joey had often imagined it, cartoon-like, a lush green pasture amid the axons and neurons.

"Hey, Joey, are you with me?"

Surprised by the sound of Tom's voice, Joey looked up and realized they had arrived at her building on lower Broadway.

"See, Tom," she said, stopping in front, "your stories make me forget time and place."

He looked at her skeptically. "Repeat one word I've said in the past ten minutes. Just one."

"The," Joey answered, straight-faced as she unlocked the front door and walked toward the industrial-sized elevator in the lobby. "You used the word 'the' at least twice, if not three or four times."

"Not even once," he answered, pulling open the heavy metal gate and holding it as Joey walked inside. "What were you thinking about, anyway?"

"Your friend Henry," she said, looking him in the eye. "I was dreaming of his handsome face, his fabulous pecs."

"If you'd been listening, you'd know that he's a librarian who looks more like Dudley Moore than Arnold Schwarzenegger." He opened the gates once again as the elevator stopped at the seventh floor. "By the way, why haven't you found some fabulous pecs to daydream about? Not that my life isn't fascinating, but aren't you ever going to start one of your own?"

The question almost made Joey shudder. She thought about the married people she knew. As far as she could see, they were imprisoned. Her mother was so stifled by her father that she had to go inside her head to escape. And the two couples from her law school class who'd married at graduation had both separated. Marriage, men, all of it seemed like some fantasy meant for somebody somewhere, but certainly not here, and definitely not for her. Besides, few men had been interested. Okay, she sometimes admitted, maybe her sister was right, maybe there weren't many men who were brave enough to confront a woman as tough as she appeared. But if there were anyone smart enough to notice that she was mush inside, anyone who would even care, she hadn't found him.

It was easier to hang out with Tom. He was smart and funny and completely nice. So what if his romantic attentions would always be reserved for Bob or Bill or John? At least Tom was there for her, a friend, someone who actually thought about her occasionally, even when she wasn't standing right in front of him.

"One thing about those millions," Tom said lightly as Joey opened the door to her loft. "They buy some very happy furniture."

Joey smiled. Her apartment really *was* beautiful. Even she wasn't so jaded as to be unaware of that. A huge space, it had a perfect kitchen and dining area, with sparkling new all-white cupboards and appliances, two bedroom areas, each furnished eclectically but expensively, handsome maple furniture from an artist on Wooster Street in one, an Art Deco bed and chest of drawers in the other. The living room area was delineated by a glorious blue and maroon rug her grandparents had had in their house in Riverdale. For some reason, her mother refused to have it in her apartment, keeping it stored in the building's basement until giving it to Joanna when she moved out. The beautiful shades of the carpet were echoed by two matching couches bathed in rich velvet, another gift from Joey's parents. The view of the World Trade Center and the Hudson River just beyond made the room even more dramatic.

"Back after the shower," Joey said, knowing Tom would understand. Whenever they ran together, Tom would stop at Joey's, have a snack while she got dressed, then he'd run the rest of the way to his apartment in Chelsea.

Her bathroom, with its gunmetal fixtures, its steam shower and hot tub, had been another parental gesture. Her father had known someone who knew someone who knew someone, and before she could stop them, she had the bathroom of a pasha instead of a working woman of twenty-eight. She opened the glass door to the shower and stepped inside. Pulling open the plastic bottle of shampoo and foaming some of the amber liquid into her hair, she thought about how ungrateful she was. Even her soap was meant for an empress, she thought with disgust as she reached for her washcloth. She looked at the perfectly formed white swan that would bubble up and smell like perfume. That had been a birthday gift from her sister. The soap. The luxurious apartment. The spectacular view. The truth was she despised it. All of it.

"It was a joke," Joey heard Dan Sachar saying as she washed her hands in the bathroom off the conference room. "I mean, if I told him to jump off the Brooklyn Bridge and he did it, would that make it my fault?"

"For the sake of the deposition, tell us the actual words you used, Dan. We know you meant no harm, but we need all the information we can garner."

She noted that her father was using the smooth lawyer tone he must have worked hard to develop when he'd first arrived in the United States. She wondered unkindly if his words would sound any more genuine with the Hungarian accent he'd so assiduously removed even a trace of. She soaped her hands slowly as she listened, evaluating just how long she could linger in the bathroom. Not that what she was doing was exactly fascinating, but anything was better than going out there again.

Joey looked in the mirror above the sink, disgusted by what she saw. Her black wool Armani jacket lay perfectly against the silk of her white blouse. The simple gold ring on her right hand, given to her the year before by her parents, had small but perfect ruby chips molded around the sides.

Just about everything in Joanna's life sparkled on the outside—even those four boys seated in the conference room at this very moment. Four pieces of expertly tailored human slime whom she was busily defending, she thought as she ran the water, splashing it over her face again and again as if it could erase what her reflection had shown her.

She and Elizabeth had both been helping their father out on the Taylor University case, which had attracted national attention. These four young men, all from wealthy families with endless money to support their offspring, had egged on a fellow fraternity brother to rape a freshman girl who wandered into the wrong room of their fraternity house at the wrong time. A party was going on downstairs and Mary Leahy, fresh from a small town only sixty miles away from campus, happened into an upstairs bedroom where the five boys were playing poker. She'd been looking for a bathroom, and she tried to back out as soon as she'd realized she was in someone's room.

Almost immediately, the boys started in on her, their whistles and catcalls making her uncomfortable. She wanted to leave, but one of the boys, Dennis Ahearn, stood up and blocked the door. Shy to begin with, Mary felt stupid and unsophisticated; she couldn't seem to extricate herself from the situation. Then the scene turned rougher, and the four preppily dressed seniors started urging their slightly younger fraternity brother to take advantage of the confused and not completely sober young woman. Too dazed to resist successfully, she wandered downstairs after the rape, crying her eyes out and asking for help.

That night, little help was available. A girl that Mary recognized from her English class took her back to her dormitory room, not entirely sympathetic but at least willing to get her out of there. And, for the first day or so, Mary had said nothing. She felt too guilty about her own helplessness, too stupid about having had so much beer. But when she told the story sobbingly to her mother the next evening, Patricia Leahy was incensed. Not at her daughter, who had acted like every college girl who'd ever gone away to school. And not only at the rapist, whom she excoriated. It was the coldhearted bystanders for whom she reserved her greatest anger.

As her parents rushed to her support, Mary found herself growing more confident. Together with her mother and father, she presented her story to the campus police. Unfortunately for the girl, they were indifferent. And several days later, when the family took the case to the local police, they were told they were too late. No evidence had been collected, no rape kit done, and of course no sample sperm remained. And none of the boys involved in the incident was about to step forward and testify on her behalf.

But now, months later, the girl and her family were bringing civil charges against all five of the young men, for violation of Mary's civil rights. Jack Ross had been hired by the parents of the four onlookers. "I never would defend a rapist," he'd assured his daughters when they wondered if this was a case he should take on, "but the case against the four boys is a free-speech matter. This girl and her parents are just in it for the money," he kept saying in explanation, trying to excuse his position.

To Elizabeth, their father's claim of "free speech" seemed to be a powerful justification. But it made Joey feel sick to be representing people like this. And she'd made her feelings clear to her father when he'd first taken the case.

"Joey," he'd said condescendingly, "to preserve free speech, you have to protect even the most evil people. After all, when they lose their rights, we all lose ours."

When she hadn't looked convinced, he went on and

on about the sanctity of flag burners, the inalienable rights of pornographers, the right of every man to state his case no matter how repulsive or idiotic. "That's what makes America America," he'd said with a flourish when his lecture had come to an end.

No, she'd thought, that's what makes you rich. Her father was annoying enough when he fought for real causes, his self-satisfaction making even a good cause slightly questionable. But when he used the law to rationalize personal gain, it revolted her.

Of course, after the thrill of successfully defending her old mentor, Kevin Thomases, she'd been influenced to stay at Ross, Jennings by her father's continuing declarations of upholding the Bill of Rights. And there had been a number of cases that had captured her attention, involving issues of substance, people of moral courage who really needed her support. She had been counsel to people unjustly accused of crimes, and to several small-business owners about to be mowed under by huge corporations bent on monopolizing their industry. But cases like the one she was working on today left her feeling not just useless but downright dirty.

"We didn't make anyone do anything," she heard Matthew Dalish say, whatever fear he may have had well hidden beneath a tone of absolute certainty. "Ben did what *he* wanted to do and Mary was free to leave. The four of us never even got up from the card table," he added self-righteously.

Joey felt sick to her stomach. Once more she looked at her reflection, but then, abruptly, she turned off the tap and reached for the thick navy blue towel, with the monogrammed *R J and T* embroidered in gold. She examined the monogram in disgust. If I stay here, I'm just as bad as he is, she told herself. I don't have to do it. Indeed, this *is* America, and I have a choice.

Without wasting another moment, she turned the doorknob and walked back into the conference room.

All three people seated at the oval table looked up as she entered.

"Glad you're back," her father offered, his grin making him look to his daughter like a used-car dealer. "We miss your valuable input when you're gone."

"Well," she said, looking back at him, "you're just gonna have to miss me, I guess." With that, she walked out of the conference room and back toward her office three doors down.

"Maggie," she called out to her secretary as she passed her, "do you think you could find me a couple of boxes?"

In her office, she started rummaging through her desk, pulling out items at random. She stuffed some papers on an upcoming trial into her leather briefcase, then took them out again. *Wherever it is I'm going, I won't need these*, she thought, rifling through the drawers more thoughtfully now, wondering if there was anything at all she really needed.

She was stopped by a photograph, tucked under a box of staples and some index cards. There they were, the whole Ross family—Elizabeth looking beautiful, of course, her mother staring off somewhere other than at the camera, her father seated, as always, in the middle, looking ready to leap into action, even in a still photo. Joey herself was slightly behind Elizabeth, her expression unreadable, her eyes watchful.

She started to put the photo back inside the desk, then hesitated. Finally, with a sigh, she stuck it inside her purse.

"What in the world do you think you're doing?" Elizabeth had burst through the door without Joey's even hearing her.

"I'm leaving." Joey kept going through her things.

"Leaving?" Elizabeth's face was red with anger. "Leaving for the day? The week? The year?"

"For good," Joey answered, keeping her tone as calm as she could.

"You can't just walk out on us this way. It's indecent. Why, it's right in the middle of a case!"

Joey looked at her sister. "If it weren't in the middle of this case, it would be in the middle of some other case." She snapped her briefcase shut with a definitive click. "And besides, Daddy has you. You're much better at this stuff than I could ever be. You actually believe in it."

Elizabeth seemed to be trying to quiet her voice. "If you're leaving because of the Taylor case, Daddy and I can do that alone. You don't have to work on it anymore."

Joey's eyes implored Elizabeth as she came around the desk, her purse and briefcase in hand, stopping directly in front of her sister.

"You don't get it. I don't want this, any of this. I never even wanted to be a lawyer. And I certainly never intended to end up as one of Jack Ross's puppet daughters."

"How dare you say that!" Elizabeth shot back, the hurt obvious even through the anger. "Daddy has given us the opportunity of a lifetime. We've been given a chance to do what anyone in his right mind would kill for. Daddy—no, this whole firm—stands for everything that counts, everything that's important."

Joey spoke so quietly that her sister had to strain to hear her. "This firm stands for our father's ego, pure and simple, and I no longer want to be a part of it."

"Ego!" Elizabeth was almost screaming now. "What is more egotistical than always being so sure you're right? No—not just being sure you're right, but that you're the *only* one who's right. Always looking down your nose at the rest of us. How dare Daddy try to make a good living? How dare I wear a nice dress or put a brush to my hair? How morally inferior the two of us are compared to Joanna Ross, the paragon of all earthly virtues!"

Without answering her sister's charge, Joey walked away from the desk and started toward the door.

"How can you abandon your own father?" Elizabeth cried, her voice breaking.

Joey continued walking. "Daddy has all the support he could ever want. You. Every one of the New York papers. All his wealthy, hypocritical clients. Everybody in town knows what a fabulous citizen our father is."

The door opened from the outside. "Evidently not fabulous enough for my younger daughter." Jack Ross's smooth lawyer's voice resounded with rage, but his face had gone white and his efforts to control his shaking hands were all too obvious.

Joey looked at him. Her father had used pathetic neediness to keep his family in line all her life. No, she realized. Probably all *his* life. His manipulations had helped to cripple her mother, had made Elizabeth so much less than she could be. Yet, as contemptible as his need was, Joey felt the strength of it. How would he survive without his anchor, the three women who made him feel whole?

But she wouldn't give in to it, couldn't let herself be pulled back. If she didn't get out now, she never would. "I'm sorry, Dad. I can't do this anymore."

Her father's face crumpled. "What can I do to make you stay?" he asked, sounding as if he were almost at the point of tears.

Joey looked at him pityingly. But this was right. She felt it in her heart. "There's nothing, honestly, nothing at all. I just wasn't cut out for this."

"Honey," his voice suddenly held the folksy sweetness he often used in his jury summations, "you're absolutely made for this. Why, along with your sister, you're the best attorney in the city. How would Jorge Rodriguez have been shown to be innocent without your skills?"

His reference to a trial Joey had conducted the year before in which a Brooklyn janitor had been cleared of theft caught her off guard. That *had* been a very worthy, satisfying case. She knew her father was sharp enough to sense her hesitation, so she began walking once more toward the doorway, her purposeful foot-steps meant to hide her weakness.

"And where would I have been on the Hunter case without you?" Her father allowed her to pass by him but followed her as she moved toward the glass doors that led to the building's elevators.

Joey remembered the Hunter case all too well—invoking it was not a clever move on her father's part.

"Perry Hunter is a pornographer and a criminal." She opened the door and turned toward her father. "The fact that I helped keep him out of jail is part of the reason I'm leaving."

Her father put his arm across the door, keeping Joey from moving forward. A reddish flush was apparent on his handsome face, robbing it of the sweetness it had shown moments before. "I'm damned proud of our defense of Perry Hunter."

"Good," she said, ducking underneath his arm and making her way to the elevator. "It's your firm. You should be proud of it."

"As opposed to the morality queen," he answered roughly. "You always were above the rest of us poor mortals. Joanna Ross, keeper of her own flame."

"Good-bye, Dad." She pushed the Down button. "I'll let you know when I've landed."

"You can't leave!" her father shouted, tears streaming down his face. "We're a *family.*" He spoke the word as a more conventionally religious man might utter the word "God."

Joey didn't let herself look at him. It took all her concentration to stare straight ahead. "I'll call you, Elizabeth," she said, not at all certain whether her sister was even there to hear her.

As the elevator descended toward the lobby, Joey waited to feel guilty, to feel as if she should press the button for fourteen and go right back up again. But all she felt was relief so strong it left her almost weightless.

Chapter Six

1998

As Joey entered the diner, she saw her friends sitting opposite each other in a booth near the back. Lisa Martin held up a package and smiled broadly. The wrapped box was swathed in gold foil, with heavy gold and white ribbons intertwined to form a perfect bow. How like Lisa, Joey thought, the gift displaying the same intricate preparation and concern for detail that Lisa herself embodied.

"Happy birthday, stranger," Lisa said, her blunt-cut dark blond hair falling in a smooth pageboy, emphasizing her carefully applied makeup—nothing obvious, nothing exaggerated—and the tailored lines of her gray wool pants suit and sparkling-clean white silk blouse.

Lisa's birthday greeting was echoed by the other woman at the table. Younger than Lisa by at least twenty years, Cornelia Wrightson was more careless in her appearance, her worn purple sweater bearing a stain on the left shoulder that marked her as the mother of an infant.

Joey sat down next to Cornelia, grinning at both women as she reached out for the gift. Pulling open the wrapping, she was shocked to see a dark green silk scarf that was almost identical to one she had often worn when she'd lived in New York.

"You look as if you'd seen a ghost," Lisa commented, picking up one of the menus that had been placed on the edge of the table and running her eyes down the list of breakfast offerings.

Joey raised an eyebrow. "Actually, in a way I have." She lifted the scarf appreciatively, pulling it around her neck and tying it in a casual knot. "I used to wear something very much like this in my old life in New York. It's kind of nice to have it back."

"It's returnable," Cornelia said apologetically, "that is, if you're willing to drive the two and a half hours to Missoula."

Joey reached out and took Cornelia's hand. "I wouldn't dream of returning it. The scarf I'm thinking of was one of the only things I was sorry to leave behind, believe me."

"How could you have left that wonderful job and that fabulous family to come here?" Cornelia asked, a glint of envy reflected in her large green eyes. This was not the first or even the twentieth time she had voiced her frustration at rarely having left the small town she was born in. The birth of her baby three months before, which made her feel even more attached to Torrance Falls, had unleashed stronger feelings of entrapment. She took a piece of toast from the bread basket in the middle of the table. "I saw the article about your father in *Time* magazine a few weeks ago. According to that, he's practically saving the world single-handedly."

And amplifying his glorious reputation, Joey thought, but as she turned to face Cornelia, she kept her annoyance to herself.

"You'd be amazed at how easy it was to leave. Moving to Montana is the best thing I ever did for myself."

Cornelia shook her head. "Gosh, do you have that backward! Now, getting out of here—that would be the charm."

"You understand," Joey said, turning to Lisa. "You

know what it's like to settle in here from someplace else."

"Hey," Lisa answered, "I know what it's like to settle in here after living *everyplace* else." She took a sip of coffee. "When you've moved around to fifteen or twenty different army bases, Torrance Falls is like heaven."

Lisa's peripatetic youth as the daughter of an army major was a constant source of conversation among the three friends. She always claimed that as a result, she wouldn't travel more than twenty miles in any direction ever again. In fact, Joey couldn't even remember Lisa going as far as Missoula. Not to a concert, not to shop, not for any reason at all. Joey was virtually certain that Cornelia was the one who had traveled to the department store to buy the beautiful birthday scarf, while Lisa would have taken charge of the fancy wrapping. It constantly amazed Joey that given the tiny parameters of Lisa's existence, she nonetheless managed to look picture-perfect at all times, displaying none of the casual ease that most of the women in town wore almost as a badge of honor on all but the most formal occasions.

"So, happy thirty-two, Joey," Lisa said, signaling the waitress over to take their order. "I think the occasion requires something more exotic than your usual poached eggs on wheat toast."

"Oh, caviar at least," Joey said, glancing quickly at the menu before ordering scrambled eggs and hash browns. "Does that meet with your approval, Madame?" she asked.

Lisa wrinkled her nose. "I'll have apple pancakes," she said, closing up her menu and looking expectantly at Cornelia, who quickly ordered fried eggs, hash browns, a muffin, and a rasher of bacon.

"I haven't had time for a real meal since Adam was born," she explained, slightly abashed at how much food she had ordered.

"I don't know how you have time to breathe," Joey said, having seen firsthand how difficult Cornelia's days were since the birth of her son. When Joey had visited the Wrightsons' small frame house, she had watched her friend prepare dinner for her family while carrying Adam, who didn't stop crying once during the hour that Joey had been there.

"The real issue isn't how little time Cornelia has," Lisa said archly, "it's how little time for their friends certain people *without* new babies have."

Joey sighed. "Whatever could you mean?" she asked disingenuously.

"Dear Constance Truggle," Lisa Martin said, holding a napkin in front of her face as if it were a newspaper, "my two best friends are mad at me for not spending enough time with them. I don't want to hurt their feelings but, frankly, they bore me to death. How can I break it to them without causing too much pain?"

Joey looked at her and shook her head. "Your subtlety leaves me speechless. Not to mention heartless and friendless."

Joey's tendency to stay alone most of the time, working on her advice columns for the *Torrance Star,* or just listening to music or reading a book, had made her the butt of her friends' jokes many times before.

"If I had as little to do as you," Lisa said airily, "I'd be spending all my time in the town square begging people to talk to me, picking up tourists and inviting myself along on hikes."

The mother of twelve-year-old Josh and fourteen-year-old Karen, Lisa was also compulsively busy with her hobbies, working on her church newsletter, running various charity drives, singing in a local choir, not to mention driving her children to basketball, baseball, football, hockey, and cheerleading, and doing scores of errands for her husband, who was the only accountant in Torrance Falls.

Unlike Lisa, Cornelia had a job forty miles from Torrance Falls, doing clerical work for the state housing authority. But since Adam's birth, her entire existence revolved around the baby. There weren't

enough hours in the day even to comb her hair, let
alone shower or wash her face. With one month remaining of maternity leave, Cornelia was aching to get
back to work, a fact that Lisa was often critical of.
"These are the most important months you'll ever
have!" she would say over and over again when Cornelia would talk about escaping from her house. "For
a woman who spends twenty-three hours a day in her
car racing around town, you have a lot to say," Cornelia would answer cheerfully.

Both women were constantly on the go, yet, of the
three friends, it was Joey who was hardest to get hold
of. Meeting for breakfast one day a week was about
the only thing she would commit to, and she always
looked forward to it. In the four years since she'd
moved to Torrance Falls, she'd come to count on Lisa
and Cornelia for support and cheer and good company. They were like siblings, but without the rivalry,
she would often think to herself after she or Elizabeth
made one of their rare phone calls. These were always
the same: a couple of minutes of affectionate conversation followed by ten minutes of yelling at each other.
Sometimes, it would be set off by a sarcastic remark
from Joey; other times it was Elizabeth who started
it, still angry after all this time at what she perceived
as her sister's betrayal of their father.

So Joey's uncomplicated friendship with Lisa and
Cornelia was not just pleasurable but important to her.
Yet, when they wanted to go out to dinner once in a
while or if Cornelia tried to commandeer her into a
trip to buy a dress or go for a hike in Spokane, just
a couple of hours to the west, Joey was loathe to
agree. How can I ever explain it to them, Joey often
wondered, frustrated at the gap between her and her
friends and at the same time touched by their fondness
for her.

For Joey, the move to Montana had been an opportunity for solitude. And for finding work that would
provide her with all the satisfaction the legal profession never had. For a few weeks she spent most of

her time finding a house to rent, fixing it up with a minimum of furniture—most of it used—and trying to figure out where the supermarket was and how to get to the bank. But pretty soon she realized that the thing she looked forward to most each day was going through the local newspaper, her interest in journalism once again piqued as it had been when she was in college. She had subscribed to the *New York Times,* and she read it with interest each day, but it was the local Torrance Falls paper that gave her a direction, one that she would never have expected.

She was reading an article about a local woman who'd written a letter to the editor, complaining about how she'd been treated in the movie theater on Main Street. Several small children sitting in front of her had been rude and noisy, and the theater staff didn't take her displeasure seriously enough for her liking. Joey found herself wishing she had the woman in front of her to tell her what she should have done, how she could have gotten what she wanted from the theater manager if only she'd said the right things. That was the one part of being a lawyer that Joey had liked: getting to make someone's life better by giving a piece of advice that the person was too close to the situation to see.

Just for the fun of it, she composed a letter answering the woman. Given how trivial the woman's problem was, her response came out funny and more than a little ironic, but she worked hard to avoid actual meanness. Too embarrassed to send it in under her own name, she signed it *Constance Truggle,* the pun amusing her for the moment, and sent it to the editor of the paper.

The following week, she was shocked to see how deeply she had underestimated the impact of a single letter. Any number of people wrote to the paper, praising her advice, asking for more suggestions for their own problems. And pretty soon, under the protection of her pseudonym, she had a humorous advice column that ran Monday through Friday. After a couple of months in the tiny paper in Torrance Falls, she'd had calls from several other Montana papers. By now, her advice column was published in several of the leading newspapers in the state.

It didn't pay much, but she'd managed to save some money from her days in New York, and the sale of her apartment, which Elizabeth had been kind enough to handle, had given her a nest egg that wouldn't run out for quite a while. Joey had relished every minute of building a career that had nothing to do with the law, with no prominent people on the horizon, no fancy suits to wear, few trips to the dry cleaner, endless hours of silent contemplation, and almost no complaints.

She'd met Lisa and Cornelia during her first week in Torrance Falls. Both of them had been in the local doctor's office when she'd come in with a gash in her thumb from accidentally cutting herself while slicing a loaf of bread. Cornelia had been recuperating from bronchitis—a common problem during the harsh Montana winter—while Lisa had been there with her son, who'd broken his leg in a football game. The local doctor took care of people within a hundred-mile radius, not unusual in a state as big and relatively unpopulated as Montana, and he'd been called out on an emergency, so the three women were left with hours to fill until his return. Cornelia, always the one who was interested in other people, started asking Joey questions, which Joey responded to as monosyllabically as possible. But soon enough, Lisa started teasing Joey about her reticence, a wicked wit belying Lisa's well-groomed exterior, and by the time the doctor had returned to his office, the three had become fast friends.

The waitress approached their table, her arms filled with plates. Joey tasted her eggs, then sat back and watched Cornelia take a huge bite of the hash browns. Lisa's eating style was more refined, her table etiquette as respectful as her appearance. How lucky she was, Joey thought, as she listened to the pair begin to discuss their children, Cornelia enthusiastic about Adam's ability to smile on demand, and Lisa describing her daughter's heroic soccer goal the week before. Sometimes, when Joey listened to these conversations, she felt a yearning for a family—even an impulse to get on a plane and visit her parents and her sister. Then she would remember what her family was really like—not the Brady Bunch fantasy in her head but people who, when they stood right beside her, made her feel more alone than when she was living thousands of miles away.

Even the phone calls she got from her sister or her mother reminded her of how uncomfortable families could be. She was glad her mother's work was going so well. At least Molly sounded happy when they spoke. But lately, she'd been so busy she'd hardly had time for a real conversation with her younger daughter. It didn't bother Joey really—she and her mother had always had a bond, even when there wasn't time for words—but she detected a slight distance that had to do with more than miles. And, of course, she didn't have to worry about her father's communication skills because he hadn't said a word to her since she'd left the firm. Jack Ross had crossed Joey off his list completely.

And then there was the matter of her love life. Sometimes, alone at night, she would feel the urge to have a man next to her, to be held by someone, loved by someone, but she never let herself think about it for very long. Under the pen name "Constance Truggle," she was happy to solve other people's problems. Her own would just have to wait.

Joey turned to Cornelia. "How about you? Anything you feel the need to discuss with Constance Truggle?"

"Well," Cornelia said, narrowing her clear green eyes and tilting her head to one side, "my eggs are a little runny. Anything the great journalist can do about that?"

"If I were the dragon you two make me out to be,"

Joey answered with a smile, "I could just breathe on them and they would dry right up."

Ordinarily the trio didn't attract much attention in the small diner where they ate every Thursday morning. Most of the customers would be truckers driving through Montana on their way to Washington or all the way up to Canada. The rest would be a few people from the town of Torrance Falls who might nod pleasantly over a roll and coffee and quickly go back to their newspaper or their own conversations. But today there was a change in the atmosphere. One of the people seated at the counter, a man dressed in a sport jacket and impeccably pressed white shirt, seemed to be monitoring everything the three women were saying to each other.

Joey had become aware of it ten or fifteen minutes earlier, but she had decided to ignore him. Lisa, however, seemed riveted by his attention. Joey had observed her looking at him in the mirror that hung over the end of their booth. When he winked at Lisa's reflection, she almost turned her glass of orange juice over.

"Sorry, ladies," the man said politely, standing up and walking the couple of small steps to their booth. "I didn't mean to interrupt your fine time. I heard you talking about Constance Truggle. Does she live around here?"

Joey had no intention of answering, but Cornelia burst right out. "Why, this is Constance Truggle, right here," she said enthusiastically, pointing to Joey.

Joey forced a small smile. She didn't advertise her real identity, but she didn't want to make Cornelia feel bad. "Nice to meet you."

"Are you a fan?" Cornelia continued.

The man answered her question but kept his eyes fixed on Joey. "I certainly am. In fact, she's—that is, *you're*—the reason I'm in town."

"And why is that?" Lisa asked, her eyes running over the stranger as if she were memorizing his appearance.

He sat down in the booth without asking permission, forcing Lisa to move toward the window. Before any of them had a chance to say anything, he pulled a card out of his pocket. "I'm Philip Gallent, from New World Syndicate." He pushed the card across to Joey. "We're interested in picking you up nationally."

"Wow!" Cornelia was the first to speak, although Lisa followed quickly with congratulations.

Joey was transfixed. It was like an answer to a prayer. New World Syndicate was famous. She had even done some contract work for one of their subsidiaries when she'd been working for her father. Suddenly she wondered if that was why this man had come looking for her.

"What made you come here to Torrance Falls?" she asked, taking another cautious bite of her eggs.

"Well," he answered, obviously pleased with himself, "the column first appeared in the *Torrance Star.* I figured if I hung around long enough, I'd get someone to tell me who Constance Truggle was." His eye wandered over to Cornelia's plate. It seemed as if he were about to reach out for a taste of her hash browns, but he caught himself just in time. "I never thought I'd be this lucky. I mean, finding you right off."

Joey felt uncertain. Would her father have arranged this? Given that he didn't even speak to her, it seemed unlikely.

"Hey," Philip Gallent leaned forward and addressed himself to Cornelia, "how would you feel about my taking a piece of your bacon?"

Joey was comforted by his rudeness. No one associated with Jack Ross could have gotten away with being gauche. To her father, the self-made American icon, this guy would be anathema.

Her uncertainty melted away completely with his next question.

"So," he said, finishing off the bacon and looking back at Joey, "what's your real name anyway?"

"You can make the checks out to Joanna Ross," Joey answered. Raising the glass of water in front of her, she smiled at her two friends. "Happy birthday to me," she said, finally breaking out into a happy grin.

Chapter Seven

"Clarence Winter's mother is on the line, sir."

Jack Ross pushed the telephone's intercom button. "Tell her I'm in conference, Jane. I don't want to talk to her until the day after tomorrow."

"Yes, sir," Jane Ebner said impassively.

Jack reached for his glass of Scotch. Christ, that Winter woman wouldn't leave him alone. She kept calling, trying to find out "in what direction," as she put it, he was going to take her son's defense. If I get your son off, he thought, it'll be because of a god-damned miracle, not because of any stupid *direction.*

He finished his drink and refilled the glass from the bottle of Johnnie Walker on his desk. There was no point in getting worked up over Winter's mother; he had dealt with plenty of family members before, who were everything from irate to sobbing to plain crazy. He just wished he hadn't taken on this case. The kid had mugged a seventy-five-year-old woman who had a stroke two days later.

Well, he would leave it up to Elizabeth to dream up some way out of this mess. She had come through for him in tight spots before. He was so proud of her quick intelligence, her analytical abilities. Her instinct for what would work with a jury was nothing short of incredible. Of course, he supposed they had a sort of understanding. He never asked for her advice, and she would never dare to presume to give him instructions. But in the course of their preparations, she always talked about what she would do if she were the one arguing the case, and he had long ago stopped questioning her thinking. He had turned a brief but frightening losing streak around as soon as he began letting her orchestrate things behind the scenes.

The two of us make a great team, he thought with pleasure. It never failed to warm his heart that he had produced such a truly fine attorney, someone who could take over the firm when the time came. Right now, it wouldn't be to anyone's benefit to know how much work she was putting into Jack's cases, but her day would come. Hell, I can't live forever, he told himself, finishing the second drink.

He refilled his glass yet again, ignoring the guilty thoughts that tried to crowd his mind. Elizabeth could have been a star at a big firm by now if she weren't occupied with his cases. No one knew it was really she who planned his strategies, wrote his openings and closings, organized his every move at trials.

Jack stood up, moving idly to the bookcase. He stared at the titles, seeing nothing. He was tired, that was all, that was why he was letting things get him down today. So what if he needed a little help at this stage of the game. He'd been a fantastic lawyer in his day, and just being able to say that Jack Ross represented you was still a defendant's dream come true.

He certainly had the same hunger to win as always. But the terrifying truth was that he no longer had it in him to do the work. Maybe it was the Scotch or maybe it was just age—he really didn't know. Even the simplest efforts at concentration were becoming overwhelming. Without Elizabeth, he would have to throw in the towel.

I'd lose it all, he thought, the familiar feeling of panic setting in, the feeling that had been with him during his entire life. There was no one who knew that the great Jack Ross vomited before every appear-

ance in court, did it even in the days when he had
been at the top of his game. He had always been
petrified of blowing a case, certain that somehow he
would do something that would lead to his losing his
practice and everything he'd achieved.

Nobody had to tell him that he was taking a big
risk, leaning on his daughter to do his work. Being
found out would be the most humiliating thing imaginable. Still, he couldn't face giving up his job. He would
be just an old out-of-work lawyer with a bunch of war
stories. Jack Ross could never be a has-been. I'd
rather die, he thought, turning back to sit at his desk
once again, knowing he meant it.

His intercom buzzed. "It's time for your meeting on
the Sayres case," Jane announced. "The others are
waiting for you in the conference room."

"Thank you."

Jack drained his glass before putting it away in a
cabinet, along with the bottle. He moved over to his
private bathroom, grabbing the mouthwash he kept in
the cabinet. He filled his mouth with the green liquid,
drinking straight from the bottle, and gargled as quietly as he could before spitting into the sink. He had
no interest in hearing that any gossip was traveling
around the office about his drinking. That's all I need,
he thought as he buttoned his suit jacket on his way
into the hall.

When he opened the door to the conference room,
two women and a man were already seated at the far
end of the enormous, gleaming oval table. One of the
women was Elizabeth, who smiled at him before looking back down at the papers on the table before her.
The sight of his daughter gave him a small lift, as it
always did, her expression so guileless, her blue eyes
bright and ready to meet the world head-on.

The other two lawyers fixed their gazes on him expectantly. Jack gave himself an inward mental pinch,
trying to work up some energy. Bring on the Jack
Ross we know and love, he said to himself.

"Good morning, good morning." His tone was jovial as he strode along the thick beige carpeting to his chair, left vacant for him at the head of the table. "Let's see what brilliant work we're all going to do today."

Reda Mathias was seated to his left. "How are you, Jack?" She spoke with concern, leaning slightly forward in her chair, her silk blouse straining against her large breasts. She put a hand over his.

"I'm fine, Reda." Jack pulled his hand away gently to pick up the folder resting in front of him.

He had no interest in reading the file, but it served as a convenient excuse to free his hand. The forty-six-year-old blond attorney had been with the firm for a year and was fierce in her devotion to Jack. At least, that was how he described her to other people. The truth was that she was relentless in her romantic pursuit of him. He chose to make use of her legal talents, but he had no intention of taking her up on her unsubtle sexual hints and innuendos.

Reda leaned in still closer, giving Jack a better view of her cleavage, and lowered her voice conspiratorially. "This is a spicy one."

"Oh?" Jack put on his reading glasses and made a show of flipping through the documents before him, not bothering to take in any of the many pages of notes and deposition transcripts. He looked up. "Who wants to fill me in?"

"I will." Elizabeth raised her hand slightly. "Our client, Alexander Sayres, was employed as a handyman in the Fifth Avenue building where Mrs. Lucinda Leeds lived. The two were having an affair, and had been for approximately eight months, when her husband, Roger Leeds, discovered them together in bed. A fight ensued, during which Alex Sayres shot Roger Leeds with Leeds's own gun. Fatally, that is."

"But here's the adorable part," Reda broke in animatedly. "Mrs. Leeds says she deeply loves her poor-but-noble handyman and that this was no tawdry affair. Mind you, he was working his way through college with this job and is an impressive young man. I myself would have to describe him as gorgeous. The husband, on the other hand, was a mean, rich bastard who she says made her life miserable."

Jack nodded, looking thoughtful. He desperately wanted a drink. Reda was obviously titillated by the soap-opera quality of the case, but he had no interest whatsoever in the lurid details of his client's idiotic behavior.

"So, Bruce, what's your take?" Jack asked as if he had himself already considered it but was willing to hear another viewpoint.

Bruce Dermott cleared his throat. He was in his early thirties, a slight, balding man who was perpetually damp with nervous perspiration. Jack found it irritating to listen to his halting presentations, but he knew the man was a good lawyer, excellent at synthesizing information once he could force himself to verbalize it.

"Uh, the scuffle gives us a good self-defense claim. He's a very sympathetic defendant, uh, what with, uh, his being young and attractive to, um, women jurors. Student, holding down a night job, all that. The husband's cruelty can be played up. The wife loves our client and is . . . uh, still willing to say so."

Reda smiled mischievously. "So he gets to walk away with the woman and all the dead husband's money. I love it."

Jack ignored her. "Elizabeth?"

She nodded. "Clearly self-defense is the way to go."

"I take it the wife is paying our bill." Jack looked at Bruce.

"Right, uh, yes."

"Ah, who knows where true love will strike." Jack grinned as he got up. "Thanks for bringing me up to speed. Who's going to be my second chair on this?"

"I am," Reda answered.

"Great. We're going to knock it out of the park." Jack gave them all a small wave as he headed for the door, forcing himself to walk slowly. He could barely wait until he got back to his office and the Scotch waiting there for him.

Elizabeth, Bruce, and Reda all stood as well. Just before Jack reached the double doors leading out of the conference room, Reda caught up with him, putting a hand on his arm to stop him. She brought her face close to his.

"I'm really looking forward to working on this with you. It's going to be a juicy trial."

Jack happened to catch sight of Elizabeth watching the two of them. He saw the disgust on her face as she took in how close to him Reda was standing, the intimate way she was stroking his arm.

Reda smiled invitingly. "Would you like to discuss it over dinner? I have some good ideas."

She never gives up, Jack thought. Aloud, he answered, "I'm not available tonight, but I'd love to hear your ideas. They're always good ones. Can you put them in a memo?"

Her face fell, but she recovered quickly. "Of course."

He broke away. "Good. I'll look for it."

He exited before she could answer, hastening down the hall toward his office. As he reached his door, it struck him that he had already forgotten the names of everyone in the case, including their client, as well as everything about it other than that it involved a murder and a woman.

Hurrying inside, he retrieved the bottle of Scotch from the cabinet with an audible sigh of relief. He downed a drink and put the bottle away, knowing Elizabeth would be in at any moment. It wasn't that he felt he had to hide things from his daughter, but he didn't see any need to draw attention to his drinking.

He was startled by the sharp buzz of the intercom.

"Elizabeth is here." This time it was his other secretary.

"Fine, Miriam."

He shoved the glass into the cabinet and moved to sit behind his desk. It had become customary for

Elizabeth to come to his office right after a meeting to go over things in a little more depth. What she does is hold my hand and tell me what the hell to do, he thought wryly.

Elizabeth entered, her long legs carrying her swiftly across the room to him. She kissed him on the cheek, something she did in the office only if they were alone.

"How's your day going?"

"Fine, sweetheart."

If she could smell the Scotch on his breath, she gave no indication of it. He motioned to the seat across from him.

"So, what's your take on our client?" Jack asked, leaning back in his chair and stretching his legs out under the desk.

"I think it'll be okay. Sayres says that the husband drew the gun and took aim. He leapt across the bed toward the husband and wound up with the gun in his hand. It went off by accident while they were fighting. The wife does seem a little uncertain as to the order of events, which I don't like at all. But I think she'll hold up. Frankly, I think she'll back him even if she doesn't really remember, because she clearly does love him. Assuming the jury believes that it happened the way Sayres says it did, it looks pretty good. We just want to make sure nobody gets the impression the lovers were in on it together so they could get the husband's money."

"Sounds like you've got it nailed down." Jack crossed his arms behind his head, hoping he looked relaxed and in control. "By the way, Clarence Winter's mother is calling again. She's still demanding to know how we're going to get Clarence off."

Elizabeth nodded. "I've been thinking about that."

"Can you put some notes together on it for tomorrow?" Jack asked.

"Sure, tonight. After dinner."

Jack beamed at her. "That's the way, kiddo."

Her mind on the Clarence Winter case, Elizabeth walked down the hall toward her office lost in her thoughts. But as she passed the half-open door to Reda Martin's office, the sound of the lawyer's voice caused her to stop suddenly.

"Mr. Ross has decided he wants to cancel that order," Reda was saying sweetly. "No, no roses or anything else to Mrs. Ross. That's right. Thank you."

There was a click as the telephone was hung up. Elizabeth stood very still for a moment, considering what she had just overheard. Reda's coy little come-ons to Jack were one thing; this was something else. Slowly, she turned around and went back down the hall. She walked over to Jack's secretary and paused in front of her desk.

"Miriam," she began quietly, "by any chance did my father order flowers sent to my mother today?"

The woman looked at her with mild surprise. "Well, yes. He said she had lost out on some job, and he wanted to cheer her up. He asked about it as soon as he walked in this morning. Of course, I had to wait until the florist opened up to place the order, though."

"He asked you to order them from his florist in this neighborhood?"

"That's right."

Elizabeth thought. "Did anybody hear you order them?"

Miriam regarded her quizzically. "Well, no, I don't think— Wait—yes, Reda Martin was standing by my desk when I called the florist. She was waiting to ask me something about Mr. Ross's schedule. So I guess she would have heard me on the phone, if that's what you mean."

"Did my father tell you he wanted to cancel the order?"

"No." The woman furrowed her brow. "Is something wrong?"

"Oh, no," Elizabeth said hastily. "Nothing at all."

Miriam looked relieved. "Good."

"I just need another minute with my father," Elizabeth said, walking to the door. "I'll be right out."

She knocked and waited for his muffled reply telling

her to enter. He was seated at his desk, making notes on a pad, but he put his pen down when he saw who it was.

"What's up?" he asked.

Elizabeth wasn't sure how to proceed. "Dad," she said hesitantly, "there's something a little odd I have to tell you."

He waited, but she was quiet.

"Yes?" he prodded.

Elizabeth shook her head in bewilderment. "I just overheard Reda cancel the flowers you ordered for Mom. She told the florist you had changed your mind. Did you?"

"You heard what?" One of Jack's eyebrows shot up questioningly.

"I'm not kidding. Reda apparently took it upon herself to tell the florist to forget about it."

Jack's expression turned to one of bemusement. "That is a bit peculiar." He laughed. "But it's not as if I don't know the woman has a slight crush on me." He gave a modest bow of the head. "And who could blame her?"

"Dad," Elizabeth retorted in annoyance, "it's not funny. That's not a normal thing to do. It's nuts. It's downright scary. You should do something about it."

Jack waved his hand dismissively. "Honey, Reda is a great worker and really produces. If she wants to play games, I don't really care. It's not as if I'm going to get involved with them. You're making too much of this."

Elizabeth felt a sudden surge of irritation at her father's patronizing tone. Hey, she thought, if he didn't want to take her warning seriously, he could deal with the consequences.

Quickly, guiltily, she stifled the thought. "Okay, Dad, I told you, and you can do what you want with the information. I won't mention it again."

"Really, sweetheart, don't worry." Jack picked up his pen and resumed writing. "Though you know I appreciate your concern. But Reda's harmless."

Elizabeth resisted the urge to reply as she left the room. The truth was, she reflected, Reda could develop a truly obsessive attachment to Jack Ross without anyone noticing. Because no one would want to. When it came to the firm's strong lawyers, everyone shut their eyes to any personal trouble that might be brewing. If it was a poorly performing employee, that was a different matter. But no one would go looking for problems with an attorney whose track record was as good as Reda's. Elizabeth was shamed by the realization.

As she approached her own office, her secretary put a call on hold.

"It's your mother," she said to Elizabeth.

"Thanks, Linda."

She went into the office and punched the flashing button as she picked up. There was no point in mentioning anything about the flowers to Molly, she decided. It would just cause a big mess. Besides, her father didn't seem to care.

"Hello?"

"Hello, darling. It's me." Molly Ross's voice was cheerful.

"Hi, Mom." Elizabeth cradled the receiver on one shoulder while she looked at her appointment book to see where she was due next. "What's up?"

"I want to remind you that it's your sister's birthday," Molly replied. "I just got off the phone with her, and I know you'll want to call her and wish her a happy birthday too."

"I knew there was something in the back of my mind bugging me," Elizabeth said.

"She's home now, so you can call her and have a nice talk. It's so wonderful for sisters to have each other."

Elizabeth rolled her eyes. "Will do, Mom. Thanks. What else is new?"

"I have to run, darling," Molly said, her mind already on some other subject. "I have a dress here waiting to have an enormous sun painted on it by five o'clock. Bye, hon." With a click, she was gone.

For a moment, Elizabeth stared at the ceiling, fighting her mounting irritation. Cutting off conversations with that bright little "Bye, hon" had become her mother's pattern. She was always so busy with her work, she rarely had time to talk on the telephone about anything she didn't perceive as important. It was ironic. When Elizabeth was little, Molly Ross never ever left the house; now she was virtually consumed by her career.

With a loud exhalation of breath, Elizabeth put her mother out of her mind and pulled her address book out of a desk drawer to look up Joey's number in Montana. She had never memorized it, and considering how rarely they spoke, it wasn't likely she ever would.

She dialed the number and heard it ring four times before her sister picked up.

"Hello, yes?" Joey said distractedly.

"Hi, it's me, Elizabeth. I wanted to wish you a happy thirty-second."

"Oh, yes, thanks. Sorry—I was in the middle of something. What, did Mom call you?"

Elizabeth tried not to get annoyed. "Yes, but I would have called you anyway."

There was silence for a few seconds. "Well, thank you. How are you?"

"Good, good. How's life out there in the great wide-open West?"

Joey's voice turned goofy. "Oh, we hicks shur do make ourselves laugh, spittin' tabacca and pickin' the fleas off each other."

Elizabeth bristled. "Knock it off, Joey. I was just asking."

"I know what you think of 'the great wide-open West,' Elizabeth," her sister said. "It's not New York, so it's nowhere."

"That's ridiculous. I can't say I understand why you want to live there, but I'm not quite that small-minded. I'm well aware that there are plenty of other great places in the world."

"You just wouldn't want to be caught dead in any of them," Joey finished up for her.

"Oh, brother," Elizabeth muttered, mostly to herself.

"How's everybody? Mom says she and Dad are wonderful, but of course, what else would Mom say?"

"They're fine. She's telling the truth."

"You and Peter still together in that *not*-together way of yours?"

"Yes, thank you," Elizabeth said sharply. "Are *you* seeing anyone?"

"Can't say as I am," Joey replied airily. "And Dad—are you still covering up for him?"

"I'm not sure what you mean," Elizabeth said stonily. It was time to end this call.

"Oh, come on, Elizabeth, I'm not some stupid flunky you can fool. Jesus, he's had a great career, but now it should be your turn. What the hell are you doing skulking around in the shadows? You should be on your own, not propping him up."

Elizabeth exploded. "What the hell do you know about anything, running away the way you did? You're a real model to follow, holed up in the middle of nowhere, avoiding everything. Is it easier for you there, big Harvard-educated lawyer getting down with the common folk?"

Joey spoke with disgust. "God, you are the worst snob in the world."

"No, *you're* the one who thinks she's superior," Elizabeth spat back. "Don't tell me what I should be doing with my life. You haven't done crap with yours."

"No, but I should listen to you and come back to the fabulous Ross, Jennings, right? So I can be like you with your little high heels and Prada briefcase? Give the uneducated and the oppressed their moment in the sun so I can get rich and famous."

"Joey," Elizabeth shouted, "HAPPY BIRTHDAY! *And go to hell!"*

She slammed down the receiver. Joey would never be anything but an irresponsible wiseass who always knew better than everyone else.

"I only called to say happy birthday, for crying out loud." Elizabeth shook her head as she reached for the folder she was planning to work on next.

Chapter Eight

"For Christ's sake, the man just killed her brother! He's not about to stand facing the audience with a Shirley Temple grin on his face. It makes him look like a fucking moron."

Molly watched Jimmy Tate's broad face redden to a festive beach ball as he screamed at the actor playing Tony. She'd had no idea going into this particular revival of *West Side Story* that it would turn out to be so unpleasant. The notion of Leonard Bernstein's beautiful music being performed by trained singers from the Repertory Light Opera Players had sounded like a great idea. The lyricism of "Maria" and "Somewhere" rendered by classically trained singers should have made the production a coup. Instead, every rehearsal was marked by the open scorn and belligerence of the young director, whose temper was checked only when the more mature producer was around. It was interesting, Molly thought, how correct the director's barbs were at their core, yet how unusable they were for the actors. Barking at people, especially at creative, sensitive people, wasn't exactly the best way of getting a great performance out of anyone.

It was unusual for Molly to be so near the stage for days at a time. Generally, most of her work was done in her studio. But the production was opening in two days, and various patches had to be painted right in the middle of dress rehearsals. She tried to concentrate on her work, but Tate's grating voice was hard to block out. She looked carefully at the skirt she held as she methodically trailed gray threads of acrylic paint down the front. Who would have imagined that costume painting would be used to make a garment look grimier, she thought as she heard the more soothing tones of Dennis Foley, followed by an immediate softening on the part of Jimmy Tate.

She'd been on the set for three days now, and she found the impact of one man on the other remarkable. Tate would be screaming his head off and then Dennis would come along and keep the essence of his criticism but couch it in terms that the actor could hear. And instead of resenting Dennis for what might have been construed as interference, the hotheaded director would sound more like a human being for the next hour or so. It never lasted much longer than that, but when he erupted all over again, Dennis would once more make his way to the stage and bring the boil down to a healthy simmer.

Even now, the twentyish actor playing Tony sounded more arresting, more complex than he had a few minutes before. And his voice, as he broke into song, sounded as if it had come straight from heaven.

Molly stopped painting while the actor sang. The music was truly beautiful. In fact, she realized, almost surprised, when all this tempestuous rehearsal was finished, Jimmy Tate was going to deliver an absolutely fabulous musical to Broadway. The thought should have elated her, but, strangely, she felt almost hollow. Why is that, she wondered, as she went back to her painting. Well, of course, she thought, dipping her brush into a muddy brown mixture to accompany the gray, she should have been in Barcelona now. Yet another overseas opportunity her husband had forced her to decline.

Damn you, Jack, she thought, surprised by her own vehemence. She felt guilty about her sudden anger.

Her husband had done everything for her, given her anything a woman could want, loved her passionately, wanted only the best for her.

Done everything to keep her dependent on him, a voice inside her head answered insidiously, given her everything but the freedom to grow, to flourish, wanted only the best for her just so long as it kept her within the borough of Manhattan.

You're being unfair, she chided herself, too unsettled to go on painting. Jack had saved her from a terrible situation when she was seventeen, had protected her from a prison sentence, for God's sake. How ungrateful could she be?

Unnerved, she put down her tools, and walked offstage. There was a small room with a stove and some comfortable chairs in the back of the theater. She would take a break for a cup of tea and eat the sandwich she'd brought that morning from home. She made her way to the room and set a kettle of water to boil.

"So, how's the artist?"

Dennis Foley's voice caught her by surprise. She was surprised he even knew who she was.

"Fine, Mr. Foley," she answered shyly. Taking in the friendly glint of his brown eyes, she smiled.

"Dennis," he said, smiling back at her. "You have enough in that pot for two cups?" he asked, seeing the empty cup with the tea bag hanging out of it and reaching up to a cupboard to lift another cup off the shelf.

"Sure," she said. She pulled out another tea bag from the box and lowered it into his cup, then looked at the kettle, waiting for it to boil.

"Kind of like watching Mr. Tate, isn't it?" he asked, the twinkle in his voice making the remark funny rather than malicious.

Molly raised an eyebrow. "He does have a temper."

"Yoga, that would be the answer," the producer answered, "or perhaps a lobotomy."

"Gosh!" As soon as it was out of her mouth, Molly

felt embarrassed at her response. She wasn't a five-year-old child, and Dennis Foley had obviously meant his remarks to be taken with a grain of salt. In fact, the producer had shown extreme kindness any number of times since she'd begun to watch him in action. And Jimmy Tate blew up at least twenty times each day.

"I've shocked you," Dennis said, obviously surprised himself at her response. "Jimmy's a great director, and I don't mean to be making fun of him."

Steam began to pour out of the kettle, and Dennis lifted it from the stove before Molly had a chance, pouring water into first her cup, then his, and walking over to the round table in the corner. His wave toward Molly indicated that she should join him, so she sat across from him, seeing him up close for the first time.

He must be nearly my age, she realized, his extraordinary good humor and smiling countenance making him seem younger than the fine lines around his forehead indicated. Not much taller than Molly herself, he was solidly built, and quite attractive, with a long, straight nose and a generous mouth. He also had the thick gray hair that Irish men so often sported, a feature she had always found particularly appealing. And, his yoga joke aside, he seemed to radiate the sense of grounded calm that kept this troubled production going forward. She could actually see his talent for leadership in the fix of his jaw, the comfort with himself that his relaxed posture indicated.

He raised an eyebrow as he noticed her appraising him. "So, do I pass?"

Molly flushed with embarrassment. "I'm sorry. I guess I was trying to figure out where your ability to calm the waters comes from."

He cocked his head to one side. "Calm the waters, huh? Well, that was not exactly my strong suit for quite a few years, but I guess I've gotten pretty good at it."

"How do you do it?" she asked, then was aware of how intrusive the question might seem. "I'm sorry," she added quickly. "I don't mean to pry."

He looked at her, then took a sip of tea. "Actually, I don't mind answering. Producers are paid to keep things going, and that means striking a fine balance between letting creative minds go their own way and keeping things moored so everything can move forward."

"Well," she said, "you're very good at it."

"Thank you," he answered.

He seemed lost in thought, and Molly began to feel uncomfortable. She ought to leave him alone. Clearly he'd needed some time to himself or he wouldn't have wandered into the kitchen to begin with.

"I learned the hard way, to tell you the truth." Dennis took another sip of tea. "I've had to deal with some difficult people in my life, and I suppose I've discovered when to stick around and try to control someone and when the only thing to do is walk away and let them make their own mistakes."

She kept silent, although her curiosity was overwhelming. Within moments, her reticence was rewarded as he went on without her having to prompt him.

"Both my brother and my wife had severe drinking problems. For a long time, I kept trying to stop them, get them on the wagon, tell them over and over again how dangerous their actions were. Then, one day, I realized it wasn't up to me. That the best thing I could do was leave them alone to carry their own weight."

"That must have been hard," she murmured in response.

His answering grin was ironic. "Yes, I suppose it would have been easier either to kill them outright by carrying in bottles of liquor or to just nag them to death, trying to be their conscience. But, in the end, you have to let people live their lives."

She couldn't help asking the next question. "So, are they all right, both of them?"

He nodded. "Well, my brother's been in AA for the past seven years and is doing fine. And my wife finally started going two years ago." He smiled ruefully. "She's not my wife anymore, but that's all right too. It turned out that without the Chardonnay we didn't have much to talk about."

"Wow," Molly said, once more sounding to herself like a child.

He looked at her seriously, but not, she noted, sadly. "You can't make people be what they're not. You can't force them into your corner and keep them there. It ends up creating a cage that kills both of you."

She was stunned not just by what he had revealed to her, but by how resigned to all of it he seemed. What if Jack had not made it so easy for her when she'd been unable to go outside all those years. Had his "help" really kept her imprisoned? The thought was unsettling.

The sound of Jimmy Tate screaming at one of the players interrupted the silence.

"I'd better go back to the lions," Dennis said, drinking the last of his tea and placing the cup in the sink. "Thanks for listening," he added as he walked out of the room.

She couldn't believe *he* was thanking *her*. That such an eminent and fascinating man had taken her into his confidence was the highest compliment she could imagine. But she was still discomfited by the thoughts his remarks had set loose in her mind. What if her husband were the kind of man who could let her live her life? Make her own mistakes even. She would be in Barcelona now, standing on her own, learning things about herself she might otherwise never get to discover.

But that wasn't the only thing that was bothering her. She suddenly saw the whole pattern of their marriage differently from the way she'd always thought of it. Had Jack saved her or had he isolated her so she had nowhere else to turn? And all those years of agoraphobia. Had Jack made it all so easy for her because he wanted her to get better, or was it his way of keeping her right where she was?

Jack was always telling her how he loved her. But was it really love? She had always half suspected that it was what she represented that he loved, not really the woman she was. His years as a child had been so tortured. She must have seemed like an American princess. And that was how she felt with him sometimes, even early in their marriage. Like the clean, scrubbed trophy of his attaining the American dream.

What would it have been like, she wondered, staring into her cup, to have been married to a man who saw her as a whole person, an equal?

Her discomfort at this line of thought was so acute that she stood up, pouring the almost full cup of liquid into the sink and returning to her work. But, as she stirred the brown pigment for the skirt, she found the image of Dennis Foley in her mind, his strong face smiling at her as she walked alongside him through the boulevards of some magnificent European city.

Molly's going to love this, Michael Weaver thought proudly as he beheld the tiny giraffe in the palm of his hand. He covered it carefully with his other hand as he walked up the flight of stairs that led from his floor to hers. It was so fragile, after all. He'd sculpted the original version of the animal in bronze six months before, and Molly had raved about it. So he'd decided to make her one of her own. But this time, he'd crafted it in porcelain, a perfect miniature just for her. It had taken weeks of precision craftsmanship, but it had been worth it.

His excitement grew as he knocked on her door. She'd done so much for him over the years of their friendship. Sometimes he wondered what he'd do without her. But Molly would never desert him, not even when he had one of his bad times. She wasn't like the other people he knew. His parents even. No, he thought sourly as he knocked one more time, his parents *especially*. Molly Ross didn't let a friend down. And Michael wasn't just a friend. He was practically family. Okay, he admitted to himself, maybe he didn't mean quite as much to her as her precious daughters, but Molly loved him. He knew it from the way she spoke to him, how she always made time for him, was always interested in what he had to say.

Impatient now, he knocked for the third time. When once more she didn't answer, he held his ear against the door, listening for some sound from inside. Damn, he thought, looking at his watch. She's always here in the afternoon. Where was she? He heard the elevator and felt embarrassed suddenly. What if someone got off and found him standing here alone in a corridor with the stupid giraffe in his hands? He'd look like an idiot. Like a little kid nobody wanted to play with. Luckily, the elevator didn't stop.

He was relieved, although he felt agitated anyway. It was starting in the pit of his stomach, just as it always did. He knew that if she didn't show up soon, it would spread to his chest. In the end, he'd have a pounding headache and it would all be Molly's fault.

"Molly," he called out, knowing there would be no answer yet unable to stop himself.

Incensed now, he kicked at her door. "If you're in there, let me know! I need to see you! It'll only take a minute, I swear it!"

There was no response. Angry tears were forming in his eyes, and he couldn't keep them from spilling down his face.

"How can you do this to me, Molly?" he screamed, kicking the door even harder.

Suddenly he heard a door open behind him. Monique Vergasse, the dressmaker whose studio was opposite Molly's, stepped out and stared at him scornfully. His heart beat wildly as she held her fingers to her lips, quieting him the way a librarian would an obstreperous seven-year-old. Enraged and humiliated, he held his breath and stood completely still until she went back into her studio.

When he heard her lock her door, he gasped for air. He felt powerless. No, he thought, not powerless—

furious. Goddamn you, Molly Ross, he screamed inside his head. This is your fault!

He spread out his fingers and regarded the giraffe in his hand. Suddenly, with all the strength he could muster, he flung it at Molly's door, weeping as it broke into tiny shards at his feet.

Chapter Nine

Joey followed Philip Gallent across the crowded hotel lobby. For three days, she'd been on display, trailing behind him at the Chicago Convention Center, talking to editors and publishers from around the country. Already her column was syndicated in all fifty states, but Philip wasn't going to be satisfied until Constance Truggle was an international phenomenon. His energy never seemed to flag, and that, by now, seemed a miracle to Joey. He remembered just about everyone by name, evinced sincere enthusiasm for their wives, their husbands, their children, the local concerns they'd discussed the last time they'd met. Philip seemed a miraculous dervish, filled with adrenalin, and, more amazingly, with genuine kindness. And Joey would dutifully try to smile each time he stopped to present her to yet another old friend.

"Mack, this is Joanna Ross, the real Constance Truggle," he announced with absolute ebullience, just after they passed through the revolving door of the small but elegant hotel where they were staying, not far from Michigan Avenue.

The man Philip was introducing her to was from the *Detroit Free Press,* and he actually seemed interested—fascinated in fact—to meet the face behind the recently syndicated advice column. But, although Joey tried to look alert, she knew her eyes were glazing over. She was exhausted. For the past few years, she'd spent the bulk of her time working alone in her small home, barely speaking to anyone at all outside of Lisa and Cornelia. To find herself a celebrity of sorts was shocking.

As Mack Fowler went on at some length about the flight of Whites to the Detroit suburbs, a subject he and Philip had clearly discussed before, Joey slowly pulled one stockinged foot out of her shoe, hoping the men would not notice. She longed to lean down and rub her toes, which were almost completely numb, but, for the sake of her dignity, she merely flexed her foot. Fowler went right on talking, but Philip chose that moment to look down. Suppressing a grin, he put a supportive arm around Joey's shoulders.

"Let's talk more over dinner next week," Philip said warmly, shaking Fowler's hand before moving away.

"Sorry," he said apologetically as he took Joey's arm and led her toward the elevator bank. "I'm used to this. It must be a little overwhelming for you."

Joey looked at him skeptically. "Overwhelming?" she answered, widening her eyes. "How about mind-blowing?"

"Come on," he responded, pulling her along with him into one of the elevator cars and pushing the Door Close button before anyone else could join them. "It's time for a drink. Just us. No more meetings. Not even a dinner, I promise."

Joey slumped against the metal railing, yawning loudly.

"Oh, come on," Philip said, watching her with amusement. "It hasn't been that bad."

"No," she said, looking him straight in the eye, "who wouldn't love wearing high heels for twelve or fourteen hours, meeting several hundred strangers and having to be funny on cue?"

Philip looked genuinely abashed. "I'm sorry," he said. "You know, except for the part about the high heels, I actually *do* love all this."

Joey looked at him in amazement. "You couldn't. No one could."

"Shoot me," he said brightly, "I'm gregarious." He looked at her more intently. "I'm sorry, kid," he said seriously. "These meetings with the papers that carry you are important, but if I'd realized how difficult they'd be for you I wouldn't have kept you at it for so long."

Joey shook her head and grinned. "God, I'm a bitch," she said ruefully. "I should be thanking you, not making you feel guilty. You've gotten me into every important paper in the country and all you've asked in return is one lousy weekend in Chicago."

She stepped out as the doors opened onto the eleventh floor. Together, they walked down the hall toward their rooms, which were just across from each other.

"You are certainly good at the schmoozing thing," she said, stopping at his door as he searched through his pocket for a key. "You actually seem delighted to meet every one of those five million people."

Philip opened the door and stood back to let her through. "Five hundred, but who's counting," he said as he followed her inside. "And, yeah, the truth is, I love it. The more the merrier." He shut the door behind them and walked over to the minibar. "They say there's a gene for gregariousness."

Joey looked at him skeptically.

"Seriously. Just as there seems to be a gene for risk-taking and certain kinds of cancer. I swear it. Well, my brother Will says that what I need is a gene for shyness."

Joey laughed. Imagining Philip shy was like imagining Placido Domingo unable to carry a tune or Matisse color-blind.

"Listen," Philip said earnestly, "I would love to be able to be quiet and just listen once in a while. Not to feel connected to every person who crosses my path. I long to be so mysterious that I make someone nervous."

"Oh, Philip," Joey said, sitting down on the gold-threaded couch and putting her feet up on the shiny black coffee table, "the whole world would die for a personality like yours. You make everyone feel like a million bucks. It's a gift not many people have."

Joey herself felt comfortable with Philip in a way she'd rarely felt with any man. He was unfailingly courteous—no, courtly, making her feel valued not just as a client but as a friend. She'd seen him every couple of months since he'd first sought her out, and she'd found herself trusting him absolutely, telling him things she'd never told anyone. No matter how easily he conversed with all the people he knew, nothing confidential would ever come out of his mouth.

It was like having a brother, she'd decided after she'd known him for a while. And, actually, she realized, easing her back into the soft cushion, Philip wasn't so different from her sister. Universally loving and universally lovable. So why did Elizabeth make her want to scream and Philip seem so delightful? It was a question she hadn't been able to answer, and, tired as she was, she knew she wasn't going to figure it out tonight.

She watched as Philip poured sherry into two glasses and brought them over to the couch. Lifting Joey's feet up, he installed himself on the seat beside her and replaced her feet in his lap.

"Maybe you're right," he said thoughtfully. Maybe ultra other-directedness has its uses." He rubbed her toes slowly, not even seeming to realize he was doing it. "It certainly comes in handy in business," he continued, laying his head back against the cushion. "But that's not everything."

Joey was surprised to see the bitter set of his mouth.

He turned toward her and saw the curiosity on her face. "My wife didn't find it that amusing, that's for sure," he said, looking off into the distance.

Joey pulled her feet away and sat up straight. "I didn't know you had a wife."

"And two kids," he said glumly. "They left for California about a year and a half ago."

"Oh," was all Joey could think to say.

"It seems that an outgoing nature is not much when you compare it to a few million dollars and ownership of a nationally advertised business." Philip tried to employ a joking tone, but the muscle twitching beneath his right eye belied his attempt at humor.

Joey took his hand, holding it gently. In the time since they'd met, Philip had been efficient, caring, smart, gregarious, and endearing. But this was the first time she'd ever seen him sad.

"Do you feel like talking about it?" she asked.

"Not much to say really," he answered. "Barbara fell in love with a guy she met in a coffee shop." He shook his head. "A coffee shop, for Christ's sake. What do you say to someone you love—drive carefully, use a seatbelt, get to bed early and whatever else you do, don't go into any coffee shops?"

Joey watched his face contort with pain. She could have sworn his eyes were about to tear. Moving toward him, she put her arms around his neck, her legs now lying higher up in his lap. They stayed that way, clutching each other, almost swaying as they sat together. Through the half-opened window they heard the buses continue to make their noisy way down the wide Chicago streets. Outside in the corridor, someone slammed a door loudly, then ran toward the elevator. But Joey and Philip remained as they were.

Philip's face was touching Joey's, the cool softness of his skin a surprising contrast to the slight stubble of the late afternoon. Slowly, he seemed to come to life, his cheek moving until it almost caressed hers, his lips moving like a shadow across her neck.

And in the dimming light, Joey felt everything change. Philip put his arms around her back, and suddenly he was holding her more tightly. She felt an odd tremor as his fingers trailed softly through her hair before traveling down her spine. She pulled away, surprised, looking at him as if to ask what was happening.

But instead of saying anything, he touched her cheek and brought her face close to his. He kissed her, softly at first, then with a passion that was as thrilling as it was shocking.

Joey found herself responding, her tongue meeting his, almost gasping with the pleasure of his mouth, offering herself as his lips left hers and claimed her throat, then her breast.

This is my friend Philip, she thought, trying to make sense of what was happening, but logic was not working. Instead, she found her hand on the back of his head, bringing him to her more urgently. Together they lay back, entwined around each other on the soft cushions of the couch. Philip tore Joey's blouse from the confines of her skirt, then raised it up, his hands coming under her bra. As his fingers traced her breast, she felt her nipples harden, urgent desire filling her everywhere, taking her over completely.

Impatiently, she pulled the blouse over her head and threw it on the rug. Within seconds, Philip had removed his own shirt, adding it to what was becoming a pile of garments. She shuddered as he took off her bra and his lips encircled her nipple. She could feel him hardening against her. Drawing even closer now, she explored the muscularity of his naked back, the surprising softness just between his shoulder blades.

Philip raised his head once again, taking her lower lip in his mouth, and Joey couldn't believe what she was feeling. Not frightened, as she had felt so often before, with boys in college or with the few people she'd dated since. This was her friend, her confidant, someone who would never hurt her. And that feeling of safety gave her the freedom to explore stirrings of ecstasy that she'd never even imagined were there.

"So, why isn't William Randolph Hearst here with you?" Cornelia asked, her eyes sparkling mischievously.

"Leave her alone," Lisa answered, having observed the embarrassed flush creeping up Joey's face. "Just the three of us for breakfast has always been enough.

Why should that change just because Philip is in town?"

Joey rolled her eyes. "Philip would have been here, but he had a lot of calls to make. He has to go to Los Angeles tomorrow, and there were all kinds of meetings to be set up."

Cornelia picked up a piece of toast Joey had left uneaten on her plate. "He could have at least shown his face and said hello."

"I promise, next time he's here. We'll have an inspection party. He'll wash his hands and face, and do all his times tables for you." Joey pushed her plate away, the eggs she'd ordered almost completely uneaten.

Cornelia eyed the plate, then dug her fork into a clump of hash browns. "He may not have time for us, but he seems to have had quite an effect on you."

She watched as Joey removed a lipstick from her purse and applied it carefully. "This Philip seems to have taken you right from tough to tender, with very little time in the oven."

Joey swatted her with a napkin. "Stop it, both of you. Just because I have a hint of a social life doesn't mean I've become an idiot. Wouldn't you like to hear how my work is going? Wouldn't you like to tell me about the baby's latest sentence?"

Lisa and Cornelia looked at each other, their eyes meeting.

"No," they answered simultaneously before dissolving into laughter.

Joey took her wallet out of her purse and extracted a twenty-dollar bill. "Since there seems to be nothing left to discuss," she said, laying the money on the table and sliding out of the booth, "I might as well get back home and see about doing some work."

"Oh, yes," Lisa said sarcastically, "I think you're going to get a lot done this morning. Not to mention this afternoon. And especially tonight."

Joey looked at both her friends in disgust. "Why do I feel as if I'm back in my high school cafeteria?" she asked, walking to the door of the diner. "Maybe next weekend we can pretend to be adults once again."

"Okay, Buffy. But don't forget to study for trig." Cornelia's accent had turned pure Valley Girl. "And make sure he gets you home by ten or Dad's gonna shoot you!"

Joey shook her head and walked out to the parking lot. Getting in her car and turning on the engine, she had to laugh at the reaction of her friends to Philip. It's not exactly life-altering, she said to herself, knowing full well she was lying. In fact, she'd been happier in the past couple of months than she'd ever imagined being. She and Philip had spent the rest of that week in Chicago rarely leaving his room. And they'd spent several weekends together since. He'd come to Montana on Friday, making an unnecessary stop between his home in St. Louis and his next destination, Los Angeles.

And from the start, she'd felt exactly the way her friends had suspected: like a teenager with her first crush. Who the hell am I? she thought with wonderment, turning onto her street.

As she pulled the car into her driveway, she heard Philip through the screen door. He seemed to be winding up a call to one of the people he'd be meeting with.

"Two o'clock is fine, Mel," he said, catching sight of her and smiling.

She walked straight into his arms as he hung up the phone. He held her close, then kissed her hungrily.

"Just one more call, honey," he said, releasing her and picking up the receiver again. "I want to arrange to see the kids on Monday when I get in."

Joey nodded and walked out of the room. He didn't need her breathing down his neck when he was talking to his ex-wife, that was for sure. She went into her bedroom, straightening up for a few minutes. When she stopped hearing the hum of his voice, she decided to go back inside.

But, as she neared the doorway to the living room,

she realized he was still talking. His voice was low and intent.

"Can anyone stay that wonderful forever?" she heard him asking. "Now he grabs the moon out of the sky and presents it on a breakfast tray every morning. What happens a year from now, or five years from now, when he starts scratching his ass in front of you and gets grumpy once in a while, or forgets to shave on Saturdays?"

Joey stayed where she was, frozen, as Philip's voice turned bitter.

"God knows, I tried every way I knew how to be the man you wanted. If I could have been taller or smarter or richer, I would have done that, too. There wasn't anything you asked me for that I didn't want to give. That I wouldn't try to give you even now . . ."

The pain and yearning were obvious. She didn't know what Barbara was saying on the other end of the line, but she could see his shoulders slump in sadness.

"There won't be a next time, you know," he was saying. "I'm not something you can throw away and get back anytime you choose."

Joey didn't want to hear any more. She walked outside, shutting the door behind her, a pain deep inside her chest. Without much thought, she walked around to the back of the house, where the former owners had erected a swing set, now drooping and rusted. Sitting down on the hard metal, she felt a curtain descend over her happiness.

So this is what I was escaping all these years, she thought, considering the self-imposed isolation she'd created for most of her life. Maybe she was right the first time, she decided, as misery burned through her.

She heard Philip slam the back door, but she didn't dare look at him.

"Hey, Joey," he said a little too cheerily, coming up behind her and rubbing her shoulders with his hands. "You didn't have to leave the house. It was just another fight in the long war."

Joey didn't answer right away. She swung slowly, pulling away from his hands, inching forward until her feet hardly touched the ground. Then she stood up, releasing the swing behind her. She turned around.

"The problem isn't the war," she said sadly, finally meeting his eyes. "The problem is you're still in love with the enemy."

She walked back into the house. Philip followed, entering the kitchen and sitting down on a chair. "When I told you my marriage was over, I meant it," he said pleadingly.

She sat opposite him, too far for him to reach out and touch her.

"I know you meant it. But I didn't realize how much feeling there still was between you."

When he started to demur, she stopped him.

"I know you want to be free," she said, standing up and walking over to him for what she knew would be the last time. She stroked his dark hair, her hand coming to rest on the side of his face. "The problem is, you aren't. And there's nothing you can do about that. Not yet."

She moved away abruptly. "And I can't wait around to start hating you. I like you too much. You're too important to me."

"Joey," he said, standing up and coming toward her. "I wouldn't have hurt you for anything in the world."

She held out her hand to stop him from coming any closer. "I know that. And that's the saddest thing of all."

Chapter Ten

The tension Molly had been feeling all morning only intensified as she approached the theater's stage door. The amount of time she had spent thinking about Dennis Foley since their last meeting had made her extremely uncomfortable. No, she amended, make that humiliated. It was disturbing to have her thoughts constantly interrupted by the image of his face before her, recollections of their conversations. Nothing like that had ever happened to her before.

Still, she had assumed it would all fade away with time. There was no reason to see him again, as her work for the production was done. But yesterday she had been called back to repair a costume she had painted for Anita's rooftop dance during the song "America." Apparently, the director explained sarcastically, some curious friend of one of the cast members had felt it necessary to inspect the hand-painted dress more closely. But he didn't feel it necessary to put down the cup of coffee he was holding while he did it. The dress now featured a large brown stain down the front. It appeared to be ruined.

Molly had said that of course she would be there first thing in the morning. But it hadn't been the damage to the costume that had kept her stomach in knots. The prospect of coming face-to-face with Dennis again was downright nerve-racking. She prayed she wouldn't make a fool of herself. Maybe she would get lucky and he wouldn't be around that day.

But Dennis was the first person she saw as she came inside. She was disconcerted at how very happy it made her when his eyes lit up at the sight of her.

"Molly," he said, coming over and taking her hand, "what a treat. I wasn't glad to see the costume destroyed, but I'm pleased it brought you back."

She loved the feeling of his hand over hers. "I don't think the audience will buy Anita as *that* big a coffee drinker. I'll see what I can do." She smiled, hoping he couldn't see her nervousness.

"And later," he said quietly, "is there any chance we could get some dinner together? There's a new place on Forty-seventh I was hoping to try."

Molly looked away, utterly disconcerted. *He's asking me out,* she thought. Dear God, what do I do now?

Every fiber in her being wanted to say yes. She could envision the two of them seated at a table, sharing a bottle of wine, talking. It sounded like heaven to her. But of course she wasn't free to have dinner with him or any other man. She was married to Jack. I'm not really *in* the world anymore, she wanted to burst out.

She made no effort to hide the regret she was feeling. "I can't." The words were almost a whisper. "I'm sorry, I can't."

He took in her expression, then nodded and smiled gently. "I understand. Even though I'm sorry. There was some actual business I wanted to talk to you about. I'm doing a play next year that takes place in post–World War II Ireland. It's a rich family, two grown daughters. It's Kevin O'Hara's latest. There are a lot of outdoor scenes, and I need to evoke that feeling on a small stage."

She caught her breath at the prospect of working with him again. "Why don't I start with a few sketches, and then we can talk in detail?"

He leaned in and kissed her lightly on the cheek.

Molly's heart seemed to jump at the sensation of his lips against her skin. "Maybe we can have dinner another time," he said quietly.

"Maybe," she said in return.

She watched him walk away. God, she wanted so desperately to call out to him. To tell him that she had changed her mind, they could go to dinner and anywhere else on earth he wanted to go after that. But she stood there, rooted to the spot, her feelings a riot of confusion. The sensation of desire was so unfamiliar to her, she simply didn't know what to do with it. All she could think was that it was terrible and wonderful at the same time.

Molly awoke suddenly, wet with perspiration, her eyes springing open in the darkened bedroom. She put one hand over her heart, feeling it race. It took a few seconds for her to realize where she was.

She turned her head to see Jack asleep, his back to her, his breathing quiet and regular. Throwing off the covers, she sat up and reached for her robe, which was lying at the foot of the bed. She slipped into it and tied the sash as she left the bedroom quietly and, still barefoot, went downstairs to the kitchen.

She flicked on the overhead light switch. The shining white room gleamed brightly, hurting her eyes. The kitchen was large only by New York City standards, but it had professional-grade appliances. Virtually every item in it was white or chrome. Molly liked its starkness. She privately regarded this room as her domestic equivalent of the Museum of Modern Art, compared to the more traditional Metropolitan Museum that was the rest of the apartment.

She sat down at the kitchen table. Ever since her encounter with Dennis the day before, she had been unable to stop thinking about all those lonely years she had stayed inside. She kept coming back to the frightening thought that Jack was perfectly content to let his wife, his *prize,* as she knew he regarded her, remain under glass, as it were, on display for only him at home. Having a wife with agoraphobia assured him that she would never leave him—in the most literal sense imaginable. Back then she had never thought to question how he had the groceries delivered, the dry cleaning picked up, every little household need attended to. Wouldn't someone else have tried to get his wife out of the house or get professional help earlier on? She knew the answer, but it was beside the point.

She had never pretended she loved Jack Ross. But she had tacitly agreed to live as if she did. She had forced herself to look away from her husband's overbearing personality, his bottomless need for more of everything, be it money, people, or approval. She had known it was all there, but she had simply refused to see it.

Suddenly Molly was filled with a longing for her mother so painful that it nearly took her breath away. But her mother had died nearly twenty years before. I should have told her the truth, she thought in anguish. *She* was the one who should have handled things, not Jack. I handed over my entire future to this man. Her sense of loss was almost unbearable.

She wandered out into the living room. I should have stuck with my family. Whatever happened, even if it meant prison, I would have had my own life the way I was supposed to. Instead, I completely gave up being who I was. Living in my own gilded cage, forever waiting for . . . She didn't even know how to finish the thought.

She *was* grateful to Jack. He had protected her when she was too weak to stand on her own. And they'd had Elizabeth and Joey, the best things in her life. Yet she had never wanted the marriage to begin with. And the truth was, she realized, he'd done it for himself.

She was overcome with a sense of grief as she thought about how much she had lost. She had been only seventeen. There had been no college, no staying up late talking through the night with a girlfriend, or necking with a boy after curfew. She'd never held a job, never had the excitement of learning to do things for herself, shaping her own destiny.

Maybe, if she hurried, she could still have some years for herself, years in which she could be *alive* again in some way. The girls were grown up—they didn't need her anymore. And she had certainly repaid Jack for whatever he had done for her.

It was time to look at that day back in Riverdale. Time to face up to it once and for all.

Molly went to a cabinet and got out some paper and a pen. She sat on the couch, pulling a large book onto her lap to rest the paper on. For a few minutes she sat quietly, just thinking. Then she began to write.

She had to stop several times to breathe deeply before forcing herself to go on. But she finished. Every detail was there. She almost expected lightning to strike her for daring to put the actual words on paper after keeping them hidden away for so long. For a while, she just stared at the pages, knowing she was holding in her hands the moment in which her life, her independence, had been lost to her.

The sun was coming up as she rose, clutching the papers tightly. They would go into a hiding place; in time she would probably show them to her daughters.

An overwhelming sense of relief washed over her as she went toward the staircase to go back up to the bedroom. She felt lighter and actually younger than she had in years. It was time to go to the studio. She had work waiting for her there.

I'm free, she thought in amazement. I'm finally free.

Molly and Jack both waved as the Normans got into a taxi. They were standing outside of Claudio's on Lexington Avenue, where they had all just had dinner together. Jack was in an expansive mood after the meal. Not to mention after his four or five Scotches, Molly thought, frowning. She would have preferred that he be sober for the conversation she was about to broach. Unfortunately, there were few times when she could expect to find him that way.

She had known that he was drinking more and more heavily over the past several years, but she had paid little attention to it. Now, however, things were different. Everything was different.

"Let's walk a little, Jack," she suggested, taking his arm.

He looked at her, his face flushed from too much alcohol. "Why? There are plenty of cabs."

She gave a gentle tug of persuasion to his sleeve. "It's a lovely night, and I want to talk to you. The air will be good for us. Please."

He shrugged slightly. "All right."

They turned onto a side street and walked in silence for several yards, feeling the warm night air, Molly with her arm still in his. She searched for the best words to start with, but her mind was a blank. Somehow, she just had to come out with it.

"I've been thinking," she said hesitantly.

"Never a good idea," he joked.

She stifled her irritation at his remark and began again, this time getting right to the point.

"I know this will upset you, but there's no avoiding it. I appreciate what you've done for me, I truly do. And we've been together a long time. But it's time to bring it to an end. I need to leave this marriage."

There, it was out. She took a deep breath, waiting for his reaction.

But Jack merely chuckled and kept walking. "Molly, what are you going on about?"

"No, no, I mean it." She looked at him. "I want a divorce."

He stopped and stared at her. "You aren't serious, are you? This has got to be a joke."

She shook her head. "No, it isn't."

Anger appeared on his face. "You can't do this. You're my wife. We've been married, what, thirty-four years?"

"Thirty-six, actually," Molly corrected him.

"Thirty-six. You're my wife. That can't change."

"Jack," Molly said gently, "of course it can change." She paused, collecting her thoughts. "We got married when I was still a teenager, for God's sake. And for all the wrong reasons."

"I resent that," Jack said. "I loved you and you loved me."

"Do you really believe that?" Molly asked quietly.

He didn't respond. She knew he couldn't argue the point.

"I took care of you, Molly." His voice was growing louder. "Who else would have done what I did?"

She bit her lip. "Maybe it would have been better if you hadn't. Maybe I just should have stood up and told the truth."

"You would have gone to jail," Jack said furiously. "I saved you."

"Well, perhaps I deserved to go to jail. At least I could have paid my dues and been released. As it was, I've never been free of it. It's had complete control of my life all these years."

"I don't believe this." Jack looked around as if he were going to find answers somewhere in the air. "This can't be happening."

"I gave you my life," Molly said, struggling not to buckle under the force of his words. "I'm not ungrateful. But now I want my life back."

Jack shook his head. "This is insane."

In exasperation, Molly blurted out her words. "You knew I didn't love you, Jack, and you didn't care. You just wanted me to marry you. God, I don't even *know* what I wanted. But this can't be the way my life ends up. It *can't* be."

Jack looked stricken. He turned and walked away. "I'm not going to entertain this discussion any further," he said desperately. "We'll talk again when you've come to your senses."

Molly was about to let him go. Then, without thinking, she ran up behind him, grabbing for his arm once more.

"Listen to me, Jack," she implored. "I'm leaving you. I'm not going to change my mind. You can hear me, or not. But I'm leaving you just the same."

He whirled around to her. *"You can't. I won't allow it."*

Stunned, she didn't reply for a moment. Then she said, "You won't 'allow' it?"

His face was growing more flushed as he pointed a finger at her. "You can't do this to me, Molly," he yelled. She could see him casting frantically about in his mind for a way to stop her. His next words came out in a fevered rush.

"I'll tell it all, the whole sordid story. I'll tell everyone how you killed your father. And how you lied about it, even to your own mother."

Molly gasped. They stood there in silence, his words hanging in the air between them. She felt a coldness spreading through her. She didn't know for whom she felt more contempt, her husband, or herself, for having stayed with him all these years. Finally she spoke, her voice low with an icy fury.

"You would *blackmail* me?"

Jack grabbed both her hands. "You will *not* destroy me this way. *You can't leave!*"

Molly snatched her hands away. "You can tell anyone anything you want. I don't care what you do." She paused, anger hardening her face. "But while you're spilling secrets, be sure you tell them yours. How you're drunk every day at the office and barely sober when you show up in court. How you take credit for everyone else's work because you're too drunk or lazy or addled to do your own. How you even use your own daughter to disguise the fact that you're no longer competent to practice law."

Jack looked as if he had been struck. His voice dropped to a hoarse whisper. "How long have you known?"

"I've always known," she said in disgust. "I just didn't want to admit it, even to myself."

She moved past him. This time it was her turn to

walk away. But Jack didn't follow her. As she rounded the corner, she looked back to see him still standing there, staring after her, shock evident on his face. Tears stung her eyes, but she wasn't sure if she was crying for herself or for him.

"Mom?"

Elizabeth's voice rang out through the apartment. She had used her own key to let herself in the front door.

"I'm in here, sweetheart," Molly called to her. "In my sewing room."

Elizabeth appeared in the tiny room. It was the place where Molly kept her papers and books, and whatever else she needed to store. Jack had dubbed it the sewing room, and the name had stuck, despite the fact that Molly didn't sew.

"Hi, Mom." She entered and gave her mother a kiss on the cheek. "What's so important that you had to see me? I don't have much time." She looked at her watch. "I have a meeting at ten."

Glancing around, she took in the cartons, half packed, and the fact that the room was being taken apart.

"What on earth is going on here? Are you re-decorating?"

Molly had put down the pile of books she was holding when Elizabeth came in. She was watching her daughter, hoping as she had during the long night she had just passed that Elizabeth would understand.

Jack had never returned the night before. It was obvious to Molly that she would have to be the one to leave the house. There was no other way. She had lain awake all night, thinking about how to tell her daughters, worrying about how she would work things out. What kept her resolute, though, was the sense of how right it felt when she imagined living on her own, being in a small apartment somewhere and setting up her own life. It was almost breathtakingly exciting to her. At five A.M., when she had given up on sleep altogether, she arose and started to pack. At seven, she had called Elizabeth and asked her to stop by on her way to work.

As she went through old papers and items she had collected over the years, she was upset to see how little she could remember in connection with the various events they represented: birthdays, wedding anniversaries, vacations. I never let myself feel anything if I could help it, she reflected sadly. By the time she started sorting out what was in her sewing room, she was more certain than ever that she had no other choice but to leave this house for good. Because of the time difference she was planning to call Joey later in the day to tell her. First, she would break the news to Elizabeth.

"Darling, sit down," she said soothingly.

Elizabeth crossed her arms over her chest. "Why?"

"I need to talk to you about something important."

"Mom, what's happening? Out with it."

Molly sighed. She should have known Elizabeth wasn't going to let her get this out in her own way. Her daughter was far too direct.

"Honey," she began, "you may know that your father and I haven't had the ideal marriage. I know you don't see us argue, but that's because I never allowed myself to argue with him. There are other ways in which a marriage can be unhappy."

Elizabeth's eyes opened wide. She uncrossed her arms and dropped down onto the wing chair behind her.

"Go on," she said slowly.

Molly picked up a piece of white linen that lay on the desk next to her. It was a swatch of fabric from a costume she had painted two months earlier, a production of *Sweeney Todd* at the Roundabout. She rubbed it between her hands.

Then, abruptly, she looked up, into her daughter's eyes. "Sweetheart, I've decided to leave your father. I *need* to leave him."

"*What?*" Elizabeth burst out in disbelief.

Molly nodded unhappily. This wasn't going to be easy.

"I told him last night that I want a divorce. You and Joey don't need me here with him anymore. And I want to have some time for myself, however many years I have left."

Elizabeth gripped the arms of the chair. "Mother, you can't be serious," she said urgently. "This would be a terrible, terrible mistake."

Molly was surprised by her daughter's choice of words. "Honey, why would you say that? I can understand you might not be happy about it, but you can't say it's a mistake."

Elizabeth jumped up. "But it *is* a mistake. You and Daddy belong together."

Molly shook her head. "I'm sorry to say that's not true." She decided not to add that she had never been in love with him; it wasn't necessary for Elizabeth to know that. But she was surprised that her elder daughter, typically so keenly perceptive, had never seen beyond Molly's facade. I guess I'm not the only one who's seen only what she wanted to, she thought.

"Mom, you can't do this to Daddy," Elizabeth said, anger in her voice now. "It's not fair to leave him alone at this stage of life."

Molly, unsettled, put down the fabric she was holding. "Now, just a minute. He's not frail or ill. He can manage just fine. And he can afford any kind of household help that he might ever want."

Elizabeth began to pace. "I don't believe this, I just don't. How could you do this to him?" The question came as a shout.

Molly drew herself up. "Don't yell at me, Elizabeth."

"Of course I'm going to yell," she screamed back furiously. "This is crazy. You *can't* do it."

"I notice you don't ask anything about me. What I'm going to do, or why this might be better for me," Molly said sharply.

"That's a good question." Elizabeth was shouting, out of control. "You've never lived alone. Can you even balance a checkbook? You have to go off on some journey of self-discovery and leave Daddy, after all he's done for you? *How could you do this to him?"*

Molly was so taken aback by the fury in Elizabeth's outburst, she could only stare at her. Her daughter was glaring back, waiting for an answer. The silence was broken by voices in the building hallway, people talking as they passed by the Ross apartment.

"I'm amazed at your reaction," Molly said. "You have hurt me deeply. I know how attached you are to your father. You always were. But you're taking his side blindly when there shouldn't even *be* sides."

Elizabeth's anger hadn't abated. "This is just flat out wrong of you. You haven't tried to fix it."

Molly laughed bitterly. "You don't know what you're talking about. And don't spout platitudes to me. I'm the queen of platitudes."

"Mother, don't do this," Elizabeth urged passionately. "It'll kill him."

Molly regarded her for a few moments. "Sweetheart, I have to tell you that I'm surprised—unhappily surprised—at your reaction. You're a grown woman, and you're taking this as if you were still a little girl. I know it's upsetting, but you're not even interested in why I would do such a thing at this stage of *my* life. You only care what will happen to your father. And you're acting as if it's the end of the world for him. It's not. I'm not the villain here. No one is."

"Oh, no," Elizabeth shook her head, "this is all your fault. Daddy's not leaving *you*. You started this and you can stop it."

"Elizabeth, that's enough," Molly said. "You work all day with your father, and you're totally wrapped up in his life. You've focused on him all *your* life and this is the result. I wish I'd seen this coming." She waved her hand, trying to convince herself to dismiss the thought. "Just another thing I can blame myself for," she said mostly to herself.

"Mother, what you're doing is wrong," Elizabeth shouted.

"Darling," her mother answered, "you need to get out from behind your father. Attend to your own life. He took the best years of mine, and now it looks like he's taking the best of yours."

"That's a vicious lie," Elizabeth yelled contemptuously.

"Is it?" Molly asked.

Elizabeth snatched up her jacket and briefcase. "I'm leaving. I'm too angry to discuss this now."

She slammed the door behind her.

Dear God, Molly thought, lowering her head and rubbing her eyes, exhausted.

Chapter Eleven

"Do you want to fax the contract over now?" Elizabeth sat in her desk chair with her legs crossed, dangling one high heel from her toe. "I'll be happy to look at it right away."

She didn't hear the answer from the attorney on the other end, because her intercom button starting buzzing frantically. She frowned.

"Hold on, could you?"

She punched the button rapidly. "Yes, Linda, what is it?"

Her secretary sounded almost frightened. "It's your father. He was yelling for you, like, I don't know, crying or something."

Disconcerted, Elizabeth immediately returned to the call she had been on. "I'll have to get back to you later, Lauren, okay?" she asked briskly, then picked up the other line.

"Dad? Are you all right?"

There was a choking sob on the other end.

"Dad?" Elizabeth sat up straighter, frightened. "What is it?"

"It's—it's—"

She had never heard her father sound this way before, his words muffled by crying. Just the idea of her father in tears was difficult to take.

"Talk to me, Dad," she said soothingly. "Let me help."

"Your mother," he managed to get out at last, "Elizabeth, it's your mother."

"Is something wrong with Mom?" Elizabeth was on her feet.

"*She's dead.* She's been shot."

Elizabeth froze. "What do you mean? What are you saying?"

"She's been killed."

"Oh, my God." Elizabeth caught her breath. "Oh, dear Lord." She was too stunned to say anything else.

"Elizabeth," her father whispered, "I need you."

She nodded, too shocked to realize he couldn't see her. Then she seemed to snap back to the conversation at hand. "Where are you?" she asked her father urgently.

"At home. With her," he replied.

"She's at home?" Elizabeth asked in disbelief. "Dead at home?"

"I found her." Jack had started to cry again in earnest. "I came home and found her on the bed. Shot. She's covered in blood—" His sobs overwhelmed him.

Elizabeth was afraid she would be sick. She struggled to compose herself. "Okay, Dad," she said as soothingly as she could. "I'm on my way. Did you call the police?"

"No," he whispered hoarsely.

"I'll do that. Should I call an ambulance? Is there any chance she's still alive?"

Jack's voice rose to a scream. "She's *dead,* I told you. Do you understand?"

"Okay, calm down, Daddy," Elizabeth urged, taken aback by the outburst. "I'll be there as fast as I can."

"*Hurry!*"

The desperation in his voice was frightening. She put down the phone, grabbed her bag, and ran out of the office.

Chapter Twelve

Elizabeth felt increasing anger at the police detective leaning against the doorjamb of her parents' bedroom. Even though his posture seemed to imply casualness, it was obvious to her that he was purposefully keeping her from entering.

"What time did you leave the apartment this morning, Ms. Ross?" he asked for at least the second or third time since she'd arrived.

"I was with my mother until, I don't know, maybe nine-thirty or so, as I've already told you," she answered, trying to keep her tone from getting too sharp. It would do no good to alienate the guy, she kept telling herself, although Detective Sergeant Gary McCullough was certainly doing nothing to be the least bit ingratiating.

She'd been home for almost half an hour now, and she felt the urgent need to see her mother for herself. My mother's *body,* she amended with horror, not really believing it even as she thought it.

"Please, Detective, I need to go into the bedroom for a few minutes." Tears stung at her eyes. "That is my *mother* in there."

"All in good time," he answered, his blue eyes flashing with some emotion Elizabeth couldn't quite name. "You know, until the forensics team finishes, we can't allow anyone to contaminate the crime scene. Can we get back to this morning?"

Elizabeth looked at him furiously. "What is the matter with you?" she asked, her voice anguished. "My mother has been brutally murdered, my father is half out of his mind with pain, and all you can do is ask me pointless questions!"

The detective's gaze didn't falter. But he did move away from the wall, taking her arm and leading her toward the den. Directing her to a chair, he sat down in one opposite her. "I'm very sorry about your mother. Clearly your father isn't up to handling this right now, leaving everything pretty much up to you, and I'm sorry about that, too. But you're a lawyer— a good one, I hear—and you of all people should understand that my job is to find out who killed your mother." He shifted uncomfortably in his chair. "Now, can you please tell me your mother's state of mind when you left her this morning?"

Elizabeth could hardly bear to think about her last conversation with her mother, let alone tell this man about it. "My mother was in a perfectly fine frame of mind when I left her."

Which, Elizabeth thought somewhat bitterly, was actually true. It was Elizabeth herself who was frightened and furious. Her mother was like a convict being let out of prison, for God's sake, like some New Age convert on her way to adventureland.

The policeman took his notebook out of his pocket and unscrewed the top of a dark-green fountain pen. "Can you think of anyone who would have wished your mother harm?" he asked.

Elizabeth's mind was a blank. "My mother was a very nice woman," she sighed. "Everyone who met her liked her."

"Someone didn't," he snapped, shutting his pen and getting up. "Where are you and your father planning to stay tonight?"

"I don't know," Elizabeth replied, realizing that she hadn't given any thought to where everyone would stay.

Her mind hadn't gotten past thinking about what time Joey would arrive. But, of course, she realized, they couldn't sleep in this apartment. Not tonight. Maybe never again. They would all have to stay at her place, she thought, her mind wandering to whether she had enough linen for all of them. My God, she suddenly realized, Dad and Joey under one roof. It was . . .

"Where is your sister?"

The detective's question interrupted Elizabeth's musings. She had practically forgotten that he was in the room. "Joanna lives in Montana. Her plane should be arriving at eleven-thirty."

"Are you sure that's where she is?" he asked icily.

Elizabeth was momentarily confused, then realized what he was implying. "My sister has been in Montana for about five years," she said, shaking her head in disgust. "Besides," she added cryptically, "my mother would be the last person Joey would ever kill."

"And who would be the first?" McCullough asked pointedly.

This time, she didn't attempt to leaven her hostility. "Given your intuitive powers, my mother's murderer should be caught sometime late in the next century." She strode to the door, looking back at him abruptly. "I *am* a lawyer, as you so kindly noted, and I am now exercising my civil rights and going to see how my father is."

With that, she swept out of the room and hurried to the guest bedroom, where her father sat, slumped in a chair. She walked over and put her hand on his shoulder. Despite her bravado, since his phone call she had felt completely numb. Nothing was able to penetrate the invisible wall that had sprung up around her. From the moment she had learned about her mother, she had simply shut off. Doing what needed to be done was fine; feeling anything at all was not.

Is this what they mean by being in shock, she wondered idly. No, probably you wouldn't know you were in shock if you really were. I'm not that lucky.

She gazed down at her father. Eyes closed, sipping from a glass of Scotch. His face was etched with pain.

"It'll be all right, Daddy, you'll see," she mur- mured soothingly.

She knew her words were meaningless, knew that it was impossible for her to imagine what he must be going through. It was tragic enough for him to lose the woman he had loved so much for so many years. But to lose her like this, in such a violent, senseless way, had to be unendurable.

Jack didn't respond to her words of comfort, but he had said practically nothing since she had arrived back at the apartment. It was as if getting through the phone call to her was all he could manage. It broke her heart to see him so shattered. He'll never be the same without her, Elizabeth thought. With a jolt, she remembered that her mother had been in the process of leaving him. Abruptly, she dropped her hands to her sides.

"It'll be okay," she said softly as she came around to kneel next to her father on the floor. She leaned in close to him. They hadn't talked about Molly's plans to move out, not before or in the hours since she'd died. It was, of course, the moment Elizabeth had been dreading since she was a child. Molly had finally decided to go.

Jack opened his eyes. They were bloodshot.

"I need a refill." His voice was dull as he extended his glass to her.

Elizabeth took it and stood up, refraining from pointing out that this would make five—and that was only what she had seen since she got there.

Well, who wouldn't drink in his situation, she thought sympathetically. She went to the dresser, pick- ing up the bottle he had put there, only to see that it was empty.

"I'll be right back," she told him.

At least he *could* feel something, she reflected as she went into the living room to get another bottle of Scotch. At least he had a pure love. He feels clean grief, without guilt, without regret. With time, he should be able to come to some kind of terms with his loss.

I, on the other hand, she thought cynically, am sentenced to torture myself forever. I can berate myself into eternity for not being a better daughter to her. For not loving her enough. For having our last conversation be one in which I screamed at her and walked out.

Elizabeth tried to ignore the black pain she suddenly felt welling up inside her. It was as if a nightmare was waiting for her around the corner and she was compelled to walk toward it even though it should be avoided at all costs.

She simply hadn't been able to think about it, not any of it. Not when her father called, not when she rushed here to sit with him as he drank and wept. Not when she made the call to Joey to give her the news. But she had taken charge as best she could. She had called the office to cancel her father's and her appointments for the next few days and delegate what couldn't wait. Next, she had made a list of what would have to be attended to in the aftermath of death. She would take care of the funeral arrangements so her father wouldn't have to bother with them. She'd even tried to straighten up the apartment, knowing it might be a while until she came back, but the police had stopped her. "Don't touch anything," one of the officers had said sharply. Still, she felt nothing.

She spotted two bottles of Glenfiddich and reached for one. "It'll just be a second, Dad," she called out reassuringly.

As she walked back to her father, she could see that he was trembling uncontrollably, his face ashen, his eyes red from hours of tears. As she poured some of the liquid into his outstretched glass, she felt almost jealous of his grief. After all, when you know what you feel, there is at least the smallest hope of feeling better. How do you help yourself when you don't feel anything at all?

"Hello, Dad."

Jack awoke with a start. He had dozed off in the chair. He looked over to see Joey standing in front of him, dressed in jeans and a white shirt. Her eyes were puffy from crying. She had a black bag slung over her shoulder. She dropped it on the floor before coming over to kiss him on the cheek. Elizabeth followed her into the room.

Joey's eyes searched her father's face, taking in his hollow complexion and red-rimmed eyes. "My God, Dad, are you okay?" she blurted out.

"Of course I'm not okay," he snapped. "Your mother's dead. What the hell's wrong with you?"

Joey was momentarily startled by the harsh words, but she nodded understandingly. "I'm sorry, I didn't mean anything."

Elizabeth came to stand behind the chair, putting a protective arm on her father's shoulder. "Leave him alone, Joey."

Joey glanced at her in irritation. "What are you, the gatekeeper? You're in charge of all his conversations, too?"

Elizabeth bristled. "Not now, Joey, for crying out loud. Jesus, you haven't been here three minutes, and you're causing trouble."

Joey stopped and took a deep breath. "Okay, you're right. Let's start over again."

She took her father's arm. "Dad, I'm here to help."

His words were barely audible. "You can help by bringing your mother back."

"Oh, God, how I wish I could." Joey's voice was a strangled sob. "I can't believe it." She looked back at her sister. "What *happened*? What on earth happened to Mom?"

Jack stood up abruptly. He threw his glass against the wall with all his might, the noise of its shattering making Joey and Elizabeth both jump.

"What difference does it make what happened?" he yelled. "She's dead. That's all that matters. It's over and it can't be changed."

Elizabeth came around, both she and Joey reaching out in comfort. Jack shook them off roughly.

"Get away from me. You don't understand," he

screamed, his face reddening. "Nobody will ever understand."

He rushed out of the room, unsteady on his feet, smacking into the doorjamb as he went. He grabbed at his shoulder in pain, crying out something in Hungarian, a language neither of his daughters had ever heard him use.

The two women started after him.

Elizabeth stopped and shook her head. "Let's give him a few minutes alone."

Joey turned to face her sister. "Christ, why didn't you tell me how bad he was?"

"What do you expect from a man whose wife was just murdered? He's drinking to ease his suffering."

"Elizabeth," Joey said in exasperation, "that's not the face of a man who's been drinking for a few hours. That's a man who's been drinking for years. Heavily. And he's not 'easing his suffering.' He's falling-down drunk."

"Look, you've never had a whole lot of compassion for him. I don't even know why you came," Elizabeth retorted.

"I came for my mother's funeral," Joey snapped. "I happened to love my mother. And I'll thank you not to make me out as some kind of monster. I'm here for him too, even though he was a bad husband and a terrible father. Mom's being dead isn't going to change that, you know."

Elizabeth waved a hand in annoyance. "You never give up on that."

Joey sat on the edge of the bed with a loud sigh. "Listen, I don't have the energy to argue with you. I've had a long flight, and I'm sad, dammit."

Elizabeth bit her lip. "I'm sorry. I'm upset, too."

She hoped Joey couldn't see that she was lying. She hoped she was doing a good job of hiding the fact that she was like some kind of zombie, unthinking, unfeeling, just trying to get through this day.

Joey's eyes were wet with tears. "I don't get how

this happened. Why would anyone shoot Mom? It wasn't a burglary?"

"They can't identify anything as missing so far," Elizabeth said. "I certainly haven't seen anything missing. I mean, I haven't gone through Mom's things . . ." She trailed off, disconcerted by the idea.

Joey began to cry. "Poor Mom. It must have been so terrifying." She wiped her nose with her hand.

With a slight smile, Elizabeth reached into her jacket pocket and extracted a small package of tissues. She moved closer to the bed and held it out. "Here," she said in an amused tone. "You always were a total slob. At least that much hasn't changed."

Joey wiped at her eyes with her hands. "Keep it," she said curtly. "I'll just go on being a slob, although I appreciate your patronizing contempt. Besides, you might actually shed a tear before all this is over, you never know. You and Mom may not have been bosom buddies, but still, you might need a tissue or two." She cast a critical eye at Elizabeth's suit. "What is that? Your old boyfriend Armani?"

Elizabeth gave her a hard stare. "I almost wish you hadn't come back."

"I'm not here for you. I'm here for Mom. The poor woman had a lousy life and now she's had a lousy death."

"You always felt so sorry for her," Elizabeth said disgustedly. "You always took her side against Dad."

"Somebody had to. Besides, there isn't room for *two* Daddy's girls in this family. You're it, Elizabeth. Always have been and always will be. You never wanted to see anything that didn't make him look good. Even if it was the truth."

Elizabeth couldn't bear it any longer. Without another word, she walked out, heading for her parents' bedroom. The police had to have left by now. And, as numb as she felt, she knew she needed to see the place her mother had died.

They had taken away her mother's body. The duvet lay crumpled in a heap, the bloodstains covering it having left a pattern of red that looked obscenely like batik. Elizabeth lifted the cover, beginning to fold it in half, then realized that she had no idea what to do with it. She surveyed the room. Powder used for fingerprinting was sprinkled on every surface, and the pillows, too, were covered in blood, as was the pale blue carpet that the housekeeper had always kept pristine.

She sat down on a small clean patch at the foot of the bed. It was the first time she'd been alone all day, she realized, almost one in the morning and all she wanted to do was go home. And that's exactly what I'm going to do, she decided, getting up just as the door opened. She looked up to see her sister coming toward her, a cup of tea in her hands.

"I'm going to get going," Joey said, offering the cup to her sister.

"Thanks," Elizabeth said, gratefully taking a sip of the hot liquid. "I'm ready myself. Let's collect Daddy and get a cab. I can put him in my second bedroom and I'll sleep on the couch. You're welcome to my bed—you must be exhausted with the flying and all."

Joey looked her questioningly. "I appreciate the offer, but I have a room at the Mayflower."

"You're staying at a hotel? You can't do that. I figured out the whole thing. We can all be together." Elizabeth knew she sounded almost hysterical, but she was too damn tired to sound any other way. "We *need* to be."

"Elizabeth," Joey said gently, "don't take it as an insult, but the news syndicate keeps an apartment at the Mayflower, and they offered it to me. I think it would be better if I were on my own."

"Better for whom?" Elizabeth snapped.

Joey gave her a determined look. "Better for me, and probably better for you."

"Why don't you trust me to know what's good for me?" Elizabeth asked belligerently.

"Listen," Joey answered angrily, "I need to grieve for my mother, an act you probably won't require, so leave me the hell alone."

Elizabeth's eyes blazed with fury. "And just what does that mean?"

Joey walked away from her, disgust written plainly on her face. "You didn't like Mom when she was alive, and I don't expect you to miss her now that she's gone. That's what that means." She turned to go, throwing one last look back to her sister. "Is that plain enough for you?"

Both girls were shocked as a voice came from the hallway.

"It seems quite plain to me," Detective McCullough said, looking from one sister to the other.

Elizabeth stood up, laying the cup of tea down on the night table. "I thought you'd left hours ago."

"I did," McCullough responded. "Your father let me back in about fifteen minutes ago." He made himself comfortable on a tall wooden chair across the room from the women. "I gather this is the famous Joey."

"Joanna Ross. Ms. Ross to strangers." The look she gave him could have iced over a forest fire. "Despite the fact that you were listening in on a private conversation, I don't know you and will happily assume that that state can continue."

"Absolutely," he answered, bowing slightly with mock courtesy. "I do want to ask your sister a few things, though." He turned to stare at Elizabeth. "If you can spare a couple of minutes."

Being interviewed again was the very last thing Elizabeth had the energy for, but it wasn't worth arguing. "What is it you want to talk about now?" she asked in an exhausted voice.

"If you would excuse us," he said, nodding to Joey.

Joey hesitated, then addressed her sister. "I'll come to your apartment at eleven tomorrow morning, if that's okay."

Elizabeth sensed that her sister was being exquisitely polite in the presence of the police. Why can't you show me the same courtesy when we're alone? she wanted to ask, but she only nodded her assent.

The detective waited to speak until Joey had left

the room. "No more games. What was it you and your mother talked about earlier today?"

Elizabeth flushed. "We had a disagreement," she acknowledged.

"About what?"

Elizabeth looked down. It was wrong, she knew, but wild horses couldn't drag the truth out of her. There was no way she would be the one to announce to the world that her mother was planning to leave her father.

The detective repeated his question, more sharply this time.

"My mother wanted to know when I would be getting married." Elizabeth spoke as convincingly as she could. "I was annoyed. We had a slight argument."

"From what I hear, it was more of a knock-down-drag-out fight," McCullough threw back at her.

"Who told you that?" The lawyer in Elizabeth was slowly taking over. "My mother and I were alone in the apartment."

"Several of your neighbors overheard the yelling," he answered.

Elizabeth stayed silent, following the advice she had given clients hundreds of times.

"Your father claims he was with a client, and we're checking that out. According to your secretary, you came in late this morning. Were you with your mother until you went in?"

Elizabeth thought. "Well, no. In fact, I was here a relatively short time."

"So where were you the rest of the time?"

"I took a cab to a meeting on Thirty-ninth Street. Then I stopped for a bite to eat and walked back to the office."

He pulled his pen from his pocket. "So you sat in a restaurant for some time. I presume people there will remember you."

"Actually, I picked up a sandwich from a deli. I ate it sitting outside an office building."

"And what deli would that have been?"

She threw up her hands. "How in the world would I

know? It was on Forty-first Street," she said, then caught herself. "Maybe it was Forty-third, I'm not really sure."

"And the building you ate in front of?"

She raised her shoulders as if to say, who knows? "There were about a hundred construction workers eating there at the same time. Maybe one of them could tell you."

"It's hard to find the workers to interview if you can't tell me what building it was," he said. His voice hardened. "You know, your fingerprints were on the barrel of the murder weapon. Everything else was wiped clean."

"It was my gun," she answered simply.

"You carried it with you to visit your mother?"

Elizabeth shook her head. "On the contrary, I never used it at all. In fact, I'd given it to my mother to hold. Neither of us thought I needed a gun."

"And where did your mother keep it?" he asked.

As irritated with herself as she was with him, Elizabeth closed her eyes. She hadn't even wondered about that. I shouldn't be talking to this man, she told herself.

"Detective McCullough, I have no idea where the gun was kept. I let go of it well over a year ago." She moved toward the door. "I really have to go home. My father and I need to get out of here, please."

He sighed, whether with empathy or annoyance she couldn't tell.

"In a minute. Just one more question." He stood opposite her, his eyes searching her own. "Just how much did you dislike your mother?"

"What?" Elizabeth could barely keep herself from screaming. "My mother was murdered today, and you're asking if I'm glad. Is that the implication?"

"Well, are you?" he said, evidently unfazed by her clear contempt.

"My mother and I had our difficulties like every other mother and daughter throughout history," she finally answered. "I loved her. She was the only mother I am ever going to have."

The detective looked at her quietly, then walked to the door. "You're sure there's nothing else you wish me to know?" he asked softly.

Elizabeth felt a shiver go through her. His gentle tone might have been meant as comfort, but it scared her more than his bullying ever could have.

"My father and I will be leaving now," she answered. "I assume you have the number if you want to get in touch with us."

"I've got it," he replied, following her out the door. "By the way, I wouldn't go anywhere far away if I were you—but I assume you already knew that."

She turned back to glare at him. "I wouldn't assume too much if I were you, Mr. McCullough."

"Rest assured, Ms. Ross," he responded coolly. "All we do is gather facts and let them speak for themselves. It should be interesting to hear what they have to say when this is all over."

Elizabeth walked out to the living room. She saw her father sleeping soundly in the large brown-velvet wing chair, heard the sounds of snoring that always accompanied his heaviest drinking.

"Come on, Dad," she said, shaking him awake.

He woke up, staring at her through bloodshot eyes. "Where's your mother?" he asked drowsily.

Elizabeth couldn't answer. She had spent the day in a nightmare, and suddenly she realized that it was not going to end tomorrow or the day after that.

As she helped her father up from the chair and led him out of the apartment, she pondered the questions the policeman had asked her. No, she thought, ringing for the elevator, this was a nightmare that might very well last for the rest of her life.

Chapter Thirteen

Elizabeth turned on the water, reaching for a sponge and the bottle of dishwashing detergent. She heard her father turn on the television in the living room. Picking up one of the plates from their just-finished lunch, she sighed. She could barely recall ever seeing her father sit in front of a television, unless it was for some special cultural event or political debate. But in the past eight days, both when he had been staying with her and since he had returned to his own apartment, he kept it on constantly, not really watching but allowing it to calm him. Or really, she thought, frowning, to numb him.

She finished washing the plate and put it into the dish drainer. Since Molly's death, he had eaten less than half of any meal, slept fitfully, and spoken very little. He was in a state of shock, that was obvious to Elizabeth. His doctor had prescribed sedatives, but she often found them untouched with the glass of water by his bedside. He preferred his Scotch to do the medicating for him.

I could use some Scotch right about now myself, she reflected, washing out the large salad bowl. Nobody had to tell her that the police weren't satisfied with her lame explanation of what she and her mother were arguing about the day Molly was killed. She knew she should just come out with the truth. But the words were locked away, far out of reach. She couldn't bring herself to utter them, and there was no point pretending she could. All she knew was that she damn well wouldn't be the one to humiliate her father publicly. Let him keep what dignity he had left.

But the incredible thing was, she was the primary suspect in Molly's murder. The police saw it very simply: she had been there, she owned a gun, she had never gotten along with her mother, and she had fought bitterly with her that morning. Nobody else was around, and Molly turned up dead. So, they figured, Elizabeth killed her. Neat and clean.

"It's insane," she muttered angrily, shutting off the water with a sharp twist of her hand.

The telephone rang as she was drying her hands on a dishtowel.

"I'll get it," she called to her father, knowing full well he would have no intention of answering it even if he were alone.

She reached for the white telephone on the wall. "Hello."

"Elizabeth? The office said I'd find you here. It's Malcolm."

Malcolm Brothers was an old friend of Elizabeth's from law school who now practiced criminal law. He was well connected with the New York Police Department, both because of his work and because several of his family members were on the force. Elizabeth kept in touch with him only sporadically, but he had called a few days before when he heard about her mother. Glad to talk to him, she was especially appreciative when he promised to find out where the police were going with the investigation.

"Hi, how are you? Have you found something out?" she asked.

"Yes, but it's not good news." He paused. "They think you did it, they really do. They'll be picking you up. Tomorrow morning, from what my sources tell me."

"Oh, my God," Elizabeth breathed. "They're arresting me? Are you sure?"

"I'm sorry, but, yeah, you can trust this information."

"Malcolm, what do I do?" she asked, panicked.

"Gee, Elizabeth, I can only tell you what you yourself would tell anyone in the same position. Get the best lawyer you can find."

Elizabeth closed her eyes. "Well, thanks, Malcolm. I appreciate—"

"Listen, don't thank me. Just use the rest of the day to get all your ducks in a row."

She nodded but couldn't answer.

"You okay?" he asked, concern in his voice.

"Sure," she managed to get out. "Thanks again."

She hung up. Slowly she walked into the living room, where her father sat in an armchair, gazing out the window. She turned off the television and came to stand in front of him. He brought his eyes to her face.

"Dad," she said, "I have a problem. They're going to arrest me for Mom's murder."

Jack's eyes opened wide with what looked to Elizabeth like fear, but he didn't speak.

"Dad, did you hear me? I need your help. What do I do?"

"Oh, dear God," Jack whispered. "When will it end?"

Elizabeth nodded, trying not to let him see her own fear. "I know. But tell me—legally, what's the best thing to do here?"

Jack dropped his eyes down to his lap, twisting his hands together. "This can't be happening," he said, so quietly she could barely hear him.

"Who should I get to represent me? Someone from a different firm?"

Her father didn't answer, but she saw his shoulders begin to shake. He was crying.

Elizabeth took a long, deep breath. Her father wasn't going to help her. He couldn't.

"That's okay, Dad," she said softly, putting a hand

on his arm and patting him gently. "Everything will be all right."

She turned away from him. All her life, she had known with a pure certainty that Jack Ross would take care of her, would always be there for her if she were ever in trouble. The moment had come. But it was he who needed taking care of.

She went back into the kitchen, wishing desperately there were someone there to talk to, someone who could tell her what to do, or at least tell her that everything would be all right, the way she had just told her father. They didn't even have to mean it.

Diane. That's who she wanted now. Diane knew all about Molly's death, and they had talked frequently over the past week. Elizabeth grabbed the telephone and dialed the number in Charlottesville. She almost sagged with relief when she heard her friend answer on the other end.

"You're home. It's me, Elizabeth."

"Oh, hon, how are you?" Diane's voice immediately warmed with sympathy.

"Diane, you're not going to believe this. They're arresting me. Tomorrow morning."

"*What?*" Diane gasped. "You're joking, I hope."

"No. I wish I were."

"Elizabeth, this is nuts. Don't they have any other suspects?"

"No one as convincing as me, I guess," she said grimly. "I don't know what the hell to do."

"Oh, Christ," Diane moaned. "I'd just want to pull the covers up over my head and pretend I was invisible. Just disappear until it was all over. What *can* you do?"

"Get a lawyer. Tell the post office to hold my mail." Elizabeth's stomach was beginning to hurt.

"This is terrible. You can't go to jail."

"Apparently, I can."

"What does your dad say?"

Elizabeth pursed her lips. "Diane, he's not saying

much of anything these days. He's not in such great shape."

"Damn," her friend said unhappily. "Listen, should I get on a plane and come up there?"

"No, no, that's not necessary," Elizabeth said quickly but gratefully. "Your family needs you, and I'll be fine."

"You're sure? I'm glad to do it."

Elizabeth smiled. "Thanks. But no." She sighed once more. "I'd better get off. Get myself organized, figure out what the hell to do in my last hours of freedom."

"Will you call me later if you have a chance? I want to hear what's going on."

"Of course."

"Take care of yourself."

"You, too."

Elizabeth hung up, but remained where she was, staring at the floor. Then, suddenly, she felt an urgency to get home, back to her own apartment. She didn't know what brainstorm she would come up with once she got there, but she had to figure *something* out, that was all there was to it. Surely, she would.

Staring at the ground, lost in thought, Elizabeth didn't notice that the light had turned green until a man jostled her as he passed. She crossed Seventy-seventh Street and continued down Broadway. Although the street was far from deserted even at eleven P.M., she was grateful for the darkness and relative quiet of the night.

After an entire day, she was no closer to knowing what to do than she had been when Malcolm first told her she would be arrested the next morning. She had just been going around and around in mental circles. All the circumstantial evidence pointed to her. She would be locked up, which meant she would be trapped in the system, unable to take any active role in proving her innocence. A few legal mistakes, a few turns of bad luck, and she could end up in jail forever, convicted of murdering her own mother. She needed to figure out how to keep that from happening. She needed to find the killer.

But the only thing that kept coming back to her was Diane's reaction on the phone earlier. *I'd just want to pull the covers up over my head and pretend I was invisible. Just disappear until it was all over.*

One word had been in her head ever since.

Run. *Run.*

But she kept pushing the idea away. It was impossible, out of the question. She was a lawyer, for God's sake. Still, here it was again, sounding in her brain, fierce and insistent.

Run. Run now, before it's too late.

If she got away now, she could try to find out the truth on her own. But it was a terrifying risk. If she got caught while she was in hiding, there would be no bail, no nothing. They would lock her up and throw away the key.

Of course, she thought, I don't have any idea exactly *how* you hide from the police. Could someone like her actually get away with it?

She was amazed at her audacity in even contemplating such a notion. An image appeared before her—there she would be, alone, roaming the streets, unable to communicate with anyone she knew, nowhere to turn for help. She hugged herself as she walked, not from cold but from fear. The whole idea was almost incomprehensible. But she was trapped, and time was running out.

A middle-aged woman walked by, peering inside her pocketbook. Elizabeth gave a slight gasp, her hand flying to her chest in surprise. The woman was the same height and build, with the same shoulder-length, thick brown hair, as her mother. To Elizabeth, it was as if she were about to look up and smile in greeting at her daughter.

She paused, recovering from the odd sensation. I'm never going to see my mother again, she reminded herself. Her brain should have registered it, should have taken in the funeral service, the long drive to the cemetery, the sun beating down on the hundred-odd people clustered around the open grave as somber words were spoken. There was nothing more final than that to make the living understand that they would never see the person again. Yet it hadn't seemed to work. She simply didn't believe her mother was really dead.

She resumed walking, wondering if the burial service had helped her father. He had sat through the funeral in a daze, oblivious to what was going on. At the cemetery, he had bowed his head, refusing to look up the entire time. He had brushed off all attempts to comfort him.

Her sister had handled things in her typical isolated manner, Elizabeth recalled with a frown. Joey kept to herself throughout the service, weeping quietly into a handkerchief. She hadn't sought solace—or offered it—to Elizabeth or their father. She had been quiet in the hours afterward as people gathered at the Gramercy Park apartment, polite but distant to all those murmuring condolences. Elizabeth noted that she took a flight home at the first opportunity, not a second too early to be considered rude, but not a second later than that either.

Still, in the same way Elizabeth had envied her father's ability to feel grief, she envied Joey her tears. Joey wasn't racked with guilt over her coldness toward Molly. Joey's last words to their mother hadn't been ugly ones. Elizabeth herself had sat through it all dry-eyed, chilled by her own lack of sensation.

She went another few blocks, forcing herself to look in the store windows. She tried to keep herself from thinking about anything at all. Suddenly she stopped short. Without meaning to, she had walked to one of Peter's restaurants. The bright red canopy had the words "Hey, There" scrawled across it in a jaunty yellow script.

She looked in through the glass front. Many of the tables were still busy with people having late dinners.

Peter had already told her he would be out that night with some potential backers for a third restaurant, so she knew there wasn't any chance of seeing him as she peered in. She stood there for several minutes, observing the waiters maneuvering platters of steaks, the house specialty.

Peter was another subject she had been trying to avoid. If she went away, it would have to be completely in secret. He would become a casualty of the whole damned mess that was her life right now. There was nothing she could do about it. But standing there, gazing in at the place that represented his hard work and all his dreams, she was seized by an almost painful longing to see him. The image of lying warm and safe in his arms made her shut her eyes for a moment.

Enough, she told herself sternly. She turned quickly and headed back uptown.

When she entered the lobby of her building twenty minutes later, she was startled to see Peter sitting on one of the leather armchairs, wearing a suit and tie, reading a newspaper. She was even more surprised at how incredibly happy the sight of him made her.

"Hi, there," she said softly, approaching.

He looked up and grinned. "I know it's against the rules for me to make surprise appearances, but I hope the panel of judges will allow it this once."

She made a face of disapproval. "I don't know," she said teasingly, "it is most irregular."

He folded the newspaper under one arm as he stood, leaning over to kiss her. "My meeting went late, and then I was too wired to go home. I dropped by hoping to spend a few minutes with you, although I was afraid you might already be in bed. Little did I know you were out living it up."

They walked to the elevator. "How long have you been here?"

He shrugged. "Twenty minutes. It gave me a chance to catch up on the news."

Elizabeth dug around in her jacket pocket for her

keys as they rode up. "I took a long walk. A very long walk."

"Yeah, sure." His eyes crinkled as he smiled.

"No, really." She got out ahead of him and unlocked her apartment door. "I had a lot on my mind."

His expression grew more serious. "I'm sorry, I shouldn't be flippant. It's been a terrible time for you. Would you rather I left?"

"No, no," Elizabeth said quickly, slipping off her jacket and coming to stand in front of him. She was wearing jeans and a red T-shirt, and her hair was loose, untamed curls cascading around her shoulders. "You can't imagine how glad I am to see you."

His eyebrows shot up in surprise. "Well, I have to admit that sounds good. And the feeling is mutual, in case you were wondering."

He brought his arms around her and she nestled against him. She held him tightly as he stroked her back.

"Mmmm," she said, the sound muffled by his chest. "That's nice."

He kissed the top of her head. "How's your dad holding up?"

She sighed. "Not too well, actually." Pulling her head back to look up at him, she smiled. "But could we not talk about any of that? I have something else on my mind now that we're here alone, and it's pretty much all I want to think about."

"And that would be what?" he brought one hand up to stroke her cheek.

She kissed him in reply, her need for him evident in the urgency of her mouth. Their bodies pressed against each other. She slid her hands beneath his suit jacket, stroking his chest, moving around to feel his muscular back through his shirt, then slipping his jacket off. She loosened his tie, her breath coming quickly as his hands traveled up and down her body, as the kiss deepened. They mutually yanked off his shirt, then her T-shirt and bra.

Peter stopped and gazed at her. He hooked his fingers through the belt loops of her jeans and pulled her to him.

"God, Elizabeth, you're so beautiful," he whispered, lost in his passion as he buried his mouth on hers once more.

They sank down to the floor, struggling to get the rest of their clothing off. When they were naked at last, his hands were everywhere, caressing her breasts, sliding up and down her slender waist, gently probing between her legs. She groaned with pleasure as he found what he was seeking and stroked her, more and more intensely until she thought she would explode. When he entered her, she climaxed almost at once, her legs wrapped around his back, her face buried in his neck. He waited until her shuddering had subsided, then ever so slowly he began to move again inside her, his kisses and the motion of his hips building until a fresh wave of desire washed over her.

They rolled over together, Elizabeth on top of him, the grief and fear and anger of the past week all spending itself in her frantic lovemaking. Peter responded in kind to her need, holding her tightly to him until he felt her begin to tremble again in orgasm above him and finally let go to climax with her.

When it was over, she collapsed down onto him. They lay on the floor, bathed in perspiration, their chests moving up and down together as their breath slowed. Finally, she pulled away and rolled over onto the carpet, stretching her body out alongside his, her hand lightly stroking his shoulder. He put an arm around her and drew her more closely to him.

She stared at his profile. It occurred to her that her decision was already made. She knew what she had to do. And it was time to tell him.

"Peter." She raised herself up on one elbow.

He turned his head to her, his eyes half closed. "Hmmm?" he murmured.

"Can you look at me? I need to talk to you about something."

He gave his head a little shake to wake himself up more fully. "Okay, go ahead."

"They're going to arrest me for the murder of my mother." She exhaled loudly. "So I'm going to go away."

"What do you mean?" he asked in alarm, raising himself up on his arms.

"I'm leaving. Disappearing." She sat up fully. "I have to."

"Now, hold on here." Peter sat up to face her. "What on earth are you talking about?"

"Peter," she said, "I can't trust my life to hoping the police or anybody else will believe me when I tell them I didn't do this. Once they arrest me, they'll stop looking. And what if it goes to trial? Anything can happen at a trial. There's nothing to say I'll be cleared."

He stared at her in disbelief. "So you're going to take off?"

She put her hands out, palms up. "What else can I do? I *can't* let them take me in. And in the past year or so, I've seen too many affluent suspects denied bail—a bit of political correctness I've supported. Until now. At least if I'm free, I can try to find out who killed my mother."

He shook his head. "You're losing your mind. You can't do something like that."

"Why not?" she asked, more defiantly than she felt.

"Come on, now." He reached for her hand. "What'll happen when they catch you? If they really are going to arrest you, you're talking about becoming a fugitive. This is *you* we're talking about here. Besides, what the hell are you going to do? Where would you go? Have you given any thought to what it is you're actually contemplating?"

She held up her hand to stop him. "I know, I know. But innocent people aren't always cleared. I can't take the chance. I'll do what I have to do to keep out of sight. It's as simple as that."

"And exactly who will know where you are?"

"Nobody can know. Nobody at all."

He was silent for several seconds. "That includes me, I suppose."

She paused before answering. "Yes. You can't be in the position of lying if the police ask you where I am. I wouldn't let that happen. As it is, I'm asking you to pretend that this conversation never happened."

"I don't believe what I'm hearing." Peter stood up and began pulling on his pants, his back to her. "This is insane."

Elizabeth gathered up her own clothes and started to put them on. "It's not as if I want to do this. I don't see any other way out."

Grabbing his shirt, Peter spun around to face her. He was visibly upset. "You can't!" he shouted. "I won't let you disappear on me."

Elizabeth tucked her T-shirt into her jeans, her expression grim. "If I go to prison, I'll disappear for a lot longer."

"Jesus." Peter ran one hand through his dark hair, searching for the right words to stop her. "This isn't a game, Elizabeth. You don't just take off, like it's a weekend in the Hamptons."

"I don't regard it as a game. This is about saving my life."

He stared at her. "But I love you," he said. "I can't lose you again."

She stopped and looked at him.

"Yeah, yeah," he went on bitterly, the words spilling out, "we're not supposed to get tangled up, it's all just a lark. A few meals, a few movies, great sex. I'm the guy to call when you feel like getting out of the office and having a few laughs. But that's all been a big lie for me, and you know it. I love you. I want to marry you." He dropped his gaze. "Shit. I'm sorry. I can't help it."

"Peter," she said pleadingly, "don't do this. I have to get away before they lock me up."

He didn't answer as he finished getting dressed.

Elizabeth stood in silence watching him. When he was done, he finally brought his eyes to meet hers.

"When will you be coming back?" he asked.

"I don't know," she said softly.

"You're expecting me to wait for you?"

She rubbed her cheek with one hand. "I can't ask you to do that."

His face revealed a sadness greater than she had ever seen there before.

"Nothing can induce you to tell me where you're going, or to let me help you? Nothing at all?"

She shook her head. Her eyes filled with tears.

When he spoke, his tone was resolute. "Then goodbye. If you need anything, call me. You know where to find me."

"Thank you." She barely got the words out as a whisper.

He stared at her as if committing her to memory. "I've always loved you, Lizzie," he said softly. "Every day since I met you. I've never stopped. I played this stupid game with you these past couple of years, pretending I didn't care that much. But that wasn't ever the truth."

He turned around and left without looking back. Elizabeth stood there, tears streaming down her cheeks.

I can't think about this, I just can't, she said to herself. Summoning up all her will, she pushed the image of Peter out of her mind. I'll deal with it another time, she reassured herself. As soon as things get straightened out.

She took a deep, ragged breath and forced herself to turn her attention to what she was about to do. How do I prepare for this? she wondered. Pack a bag, for starters.

She headed for her bedroom, then stopped. There was something else she needed to do first. She picked up the telephone in the kitchen, pressing the memory button and the number twelve, the spot where she had stored Joey's phone number in Montana. Her stomach tightening, she listened to the beeping sounds as the telephone automatically dialed.

Her sister picked up on the third ring. "Hello."

"Hi. It's Elizabeth."

Joey's response was polite. "Oh. How are you doing?"

"I'm okay, thanks." Elizabeth hesitated, unsure how to continue. "Everything okay with you?"

"I'm upset about Mom, but you must know that." Joey didn't offer anything more.

"Okay, listen," Elizabeth pressed on. "I need to ask you something."

"What is it?"

"I need a promise from you. That you'll look out for Dad."

"What?" Joey exclaimed. "What do you mean, look out for Dad? You're there, looking out for him. Hell, you've been looking out for him since the day you were born. I couldn't begin to do half the job you've done at it even if I wanted to. Which I don't."

Elizabeth fought back her urge to snap at her sister. "Joey, really, if something should happen, if for any reason he were without my help, I'd be grateful if I knew you'd be there for him."

Joey sounded exasperated. " 'Without your help'? What on earth are you getting at?"

"Please," Elizabeth said more forcefully, "this isn't a joke. Please give me your word you'll take care of him, regardless of how things have been between you two in the past."

"Look," Joey said in annoyance, "I'm not some kind of devil woman. If my father were in trouble, obviously I'd be there to help him, despite his many faults, flaws, selfish acts—"

"I get the point," Elizabeth broke in. "So you promise?"

"What are we, Girl Scouts?" Joey retorted. "Okay, I'm holding up three fingers." She recited in a dutiful tone: "I promise to look after my pathetic Daddy should the need arise, regardless of how rotten he's always been. Amen."

"Thank you," Elizabeth said, as if Joey had been perfectly serious. "I appreciate it. Just remember you made the promise."

"Something tells me you're not going to let me forget."

Elizabeth sighed. "Okay, well, thanks." She spoke almost tenderly. "And good-bye, Joey."

Her sister's tone became insistent. "What's going on? Why do you sound like that?"

"No reason, really. But I have to go now. Thanks."

Joey wasn't satisfied. "You're up to something."

Elizabeth spoke gently. "I'm saying good-bye now."

She hung up the phone. Would the words she had just uttered so sarcastically mean anything to Joey when push came to shove? Well, at least after this peculiar conversation, Joey was certain to remember she had made the promise. What she would do about it was another question altogether.

And what I'm going to do about—well, just about everything—is also another question, Elizabeth thought grimly as she opened the hall closet to get out a suitcase.

Chapter Fourteen

"Was Daddy's grandmother from Torrance Falls?" Josh Martin grasped his pen tightly, waiting for his mother to reply.

Lisa looked up from the hem she was sewing, smiling at her son's openmouthed stare. Ever since he'd been a baby, he'd had that same expression when he was utterly focused on something. This week's homework assignment was filling out a family tree, and she was surprised at how it seemed to capture her son's attention.

I really shouldn't be so surprised, she thought proudly. After all, there was very little that didn't interest her son. Or, for that matter, her daughter. Her children had grown up to be extremely bright and shockingly well mannered. And overflowing with interest in everything around them.

If only I could drive with them across the United States and show them the Grand Canyon or the Statue of Liberty. There are so many interesting places to see, she thought sadly. Quickly, she covered her unhappiness with a smile and offered up the answer Josh was seeking.

"Your great-grandmother was from Maine. She came out to Montana during the Depression to teach school, and then she met your great-grandfather."

"What did she teach?" he asked as he noted her answer on the pad he was holding.

"Hmmm," Lisa said, pondering the question, "I'm not exactly sure." She went back to the hem. "Actually, she probably taught everything. I think in those days, in towns as small as Torrance Falls, a teacher covered just about every subject."

"And how about *your* grandparents?"

Lisa frowned slightly. "They lived in the Seattle area, honey."

"And your mother and father too?"

"Yes, honey, we were all in Seattle."

His mother's response had been so soft he almost hadn't been able to hear it. He regarded her curiously. "So why don't we go there and see if we have any relatives?"

Lisa kept her eyes on her sewing. "Because both my parents were only children and when they died, there was no one left."

"There must be someone," he said stubbornly.

Lisa finished the hem, making a tiny knot with the black thread and cutting away the excess strands. She folded the skirt neatly and stood up. "I'm it," she said, abruptly walking out of the den.

As she picked up the remains of a chess game that had been left in the middle of the carpet, she was nonplussed to see that her son had followed her.

"I don't get it," he said. "You must have *somebody* else in your family. A cousin. An aunt." He shook his head stubbornly. "I mean, jeez, everybody has someone. It's *weird* to have no one."

Feeling her face flush, Lisa faced away from him. "Honey, some people have big families and some people have small families. It's perfectly normal."

Josh walked around to stand straight in front of her. "There's nothing normal about our family. It's like we have half a family. Like a house with people living in only half the rooms." He stuck his hands into his pockets, as if embarrassed about what he was about to say. "I mean, Mom, you don't ever leave Torrance

Falls. How would you even know that you had relatives? For all you know, you've got some second cousin living right in Missoula."

Lisa sighed deeply. "Josh, baby, my family is my family. I can't manufacture people for you. Sometimes things just are what they are."

Josh walked away, his disgust plain. "I'm telling you, Mom, it's *bizarre*." He rolled the word around his mouth, as if savoring its unfamiliarity. He stopped walking suddenly, once more turning toward his mother. "What if we took a trip to Seattle after school is over? All of us. We could drive there when Dad is on vacation."

"We'll see," Lisa answered, eager to end the discussion.

"Which means no," Josh responded, annoyed. "We never go anywhere. Every kid in my class has been all over the country. The McKenzies went all the way to Italy last year! But no, not the Martins. They just walk around Torrance Falls every day. My God, Mom, I've just about never met anyone I haven't known since the day I was born. It's pathetic!"

"I'm sorry I'm such a pathetic mother," Lisa retorted angrily. "Maybe you'll do better in your next life."

Looking at Josh's face, she realized that her fury had left him bewildered. Not knowing what else to say, she walked out.

Going into her daughter's room, she unfolded the skirt she'd been hemming and hung it in the closet, frowning as she began to wade through the masses of clothing Karen had piled up in the relatively small space. If her son had inherited her own neatness, her daughter had her father's complete unwillingness to organize. "It keeps me creative," Karen would say, echoing her father's sentiments when Lisa would try to get her to do even the most rudimentary sorting or cleaning.

And Karen *was* creative, thank goodness. It made Lisa happy to watch her daughter bubble over with enthusiasm for whatever her latest project was. Like Lisa herself, Karen was a good singer, who'd performed with the school chorus every year since third grade. Now she was starring in the play the eighth graders would put on at the end of the year. How thrilling to have normal, cheerful kids, Lisa thought, coming to face herself in the mirror over her daughter's dresser. Eyeing her reflection critically, she pondered her conversation with Josh and wondered if they'd manage to stay that way.

In the mirror she saw a perfectly sensible middle-aged woman, attractive even, she thought without vanity. After all, she said to herself, carefully shutting Karen's door so Josh wouldn't catch her unawares, why shouldn't she find the reflection attractive? It had nothing to do with her. The well-tended woman in front of her was a manufactured product. It was no more real than the family stories she'd just told her son.

Josh and Karen had no idea who Lisa was. Nor did her husband, Hal. In fact, she thought, staring at her reflection, she wasn't so sure that even she knew who she was anymore.

Oh, you know who you are, she scolded herself silently. You're the woman who lies to everyone you love.

She thought back to the night her friend Joey had returned from her mother's funeral in New York. Her grief had been so plain, so open. Obviously she'd adored her mother. Oh, God, she thought, almost clutching her chest as the sadness rose inside her, how wonderful it would be to have a mother to love, sisters and brothers to talk to, to share your problems and your joys. She couldn't bear the pain she was feeling.

"How long can you keep this up?" she whispered to the empty room.

Dear Constance Truggle,
Sometimes, I think my husband just doesn't under-
stand me. The other night, I asked him to go out and

get some milk, and two hours later, he came home with two cases of Heineken, a box of Pringles, and his mother. I told him I was living with an overgrown five-year-old, and instead of answering me he turned on the television set and started watching the basketball game. As of now, the beer is gone, the chips are gone, and his mother seems to have made a permanent home in our den. What should I do?

Joey stared at the letter, then tossed it back into the pile in front of her. There were so many problems out there, so many people who were sick, who were unhappy or unloved, who just wanted some kind of connection. Even the silliest letters contained a kernel of real pain. She picked up another envelope, it's thin blue paper indicating a foreign mailer, and began to slit it open. She noticed spots of darker blue as she ran her nail under the flap, then realized they were her own tears.

Since her mother's death, almost anything could make her cry. Seeing Cornelia's baby take his first steps two weeks before, watching the sunset, even a Hallmark card commercial—she'd be fine one minute and the next she'd find herself weeping. Just the night before, she'd had a call from Marianne Wolfson, her oldest friend. It had been so long since they'd last spoken, and she found out so many things about mutual neighbors of theirs from New York that she'd never known about before. As she was hanging up the phone, she found herself looking forward to dialing her mother's number. *Guess what Marianne told me,* she could almost hear herself saying. Then she remembered that her mother could no longer listen.

Listlessly, she pushed the pile of letters around. It used to be so easy to answer these people. Do this, don't do that. It was a lark. Now it seemed like a chore. In fact, everything seemed like a chore.

"I want my mommy." She said the words out loud, in a tiny voice that parodied childhood. But what she felt wasn't funny. It was real, and it was as infantile and deep as if she truly were a little girl.

The sound of the telephone startled her. For a hint of a second, she thought it could be her mother, magically responding to how much she needed her. She got a grip on herself and reached for the phone.

"Joanna—"

She recognized her father's voice before the sound broke off into sobs. Be nice, she urged herself, certain that it was the alcohol that was doing most of the weeping.

"Dad," she said quietly, "how are you?"

"Never mind me," he answered. "It's your sister."

"What's the matter with Elizabeth?"

She heard her father blowing his nose, waited for him to get control of himself.

"She's gone. She's run away, gone somewhere the police can't get to her. You have to come back here and help me with this."

Joey felt a pounding in her head. "Dad, I don't know what I can do. I mean, I'm sure Elizabeth knows what she's doing . . ." She tried to sound confident, although she felt a leaden dread take hold of her. What in hell was her sister thinking?

"Joey, you can't just leave me here with nothing!"

Her father's vehemence should have made her sympathetic, she knew, but instead it made her angry. *Work for me. Take care of me. Me, me, me.* It was all so familiar.

"Daddy," she said, "I can't just leave here all of a sudden. I have responsibilities. I have a life."

"Your sister would want you here. I know she would."

Her father sounded like a stubborn child, and once again it made her furious. Yes, if Elizabeth had had her way, Joey would never have left. She would have been under her father's thumb for the rest of her life. Jack's little pawn, keeping the old man afloat while her own life drained away. That's what Elizabeth had chosen and that's what she would have had Joey choose. But that was just what she had run away from, and no matter what her sister had suddenly done, she wasn't about to volunteer now.

"Dad," she said, choosing her words carefully, "I'm sure Elizabeth will be back. She's a sensible woman— she's a lawyer, for God's sake. Everything will be fine if you give it a day or two."

Would it really? she asked herself as she heard her own voice. This was so unlike Elizabeth. The good one. The golden girl. Was she underestimating how terrible things really were?

She stopped herself. To think that way was to give in to the stranglehold she'd always fought. She couldn't go back. She couldn't accede to her father. She'd done it before and the consequences had been deadly. Elizabeth would be all right. She had to be.

Suddenly Elizabeth's words on the phone resounded loudly in Joey's head. *Promise you'll look after Daddy if I'm not around. Promise me.* Joey groaned. Damn her.

"Please, Joey, I need you here."

The words tore at her, but she willed herself to harden her heart. "I'll call you tomorrow, Dad, and make sure everything is okay. Honestly, it will be fine. I promise."

She put down the phone before he could say anything more. Oh, Elizabeth, she thought, what have you gone and done?

It took hours for her to get to sleep, then she startled herself awake a little after three-thirty. She was still shaking as she thought about the dream that had awakened her. She'd seen her sister running down a dark highway, right into the path of an oncoming car. *Stop,* she was screaming, but the words weren't coming out. She couldn't make herself heard, couldn't keep Elizabeth from going headlong into the lights.

"Oh, God," she said into the silence of her bedroom.

By the time she got back to sleep, it was close to six, and only an hour later she heard her doorbell ringing. She looked at her alarm clock, bleary-eyed. Now,

who would just show up so early in the morning, she
wondered, getting out of bed and wrapping a terry-
cloth robe around herself. She walked to the front of
the house and looked out the living room window.

"It's me." Lisa Martin's voice was instantly
recognizable.

Joey opened the door and ushered her inside.

"I'm sorry to wake you," Lisa said, entering and
giving Joey a quick kiss on the cheek.

"Hey, it's nice to see you whatever time it is," Joey
answered. She looked at her friend curiously as she
made her way to the kitchen, taking a seat at the
table. As always, Lisa was neat as a pin, her dark-
blond hair pulled back in a tortoiseshell barette, her
makeup carefully applied down to the perfectly drawn
lipliner. But beneath the grooming, Lisa had an uncharacteristically serious expression on her face. She
kept looking down at her hands, as if her fingers could
reveal something she badly needed to know. Her extraordinary energy seemed depleted, her movements
more ponderous than usual, her eyes dull beneath
the mascara.

"What's going on?" Joey asked as she took the seat
next to her friend.

She watched Lisa carefully, waiting for her to say
something. Lisa and Cornelia had both come over the
night after Joey had returned from New York, helping
her through what they knew would be a tough time.
And it had made her feel better to know that her
friends were there for her.

She caught Lisa's eye and smiled at her encouragingly, but her friend seemed to be having trouble saying anything at all. Once again, Joey found herself
looking at the time, but now the significance of it was
turning her sympathy to alarm.

"Lisa, what's going on? What's wrong?"

"I'm not Lisa."

Joey stared at her friend openmouthed. "What do
you mean?"

"Joey—" Lisa started to speak, then fell silent.

It took another minute for her to start up again, but Joey waited patiently.

"Joey, I want to give myself up to the police."

"For what terrible crime?" Joey asked. Her friend's utterance sounded so ludicrous that Joey almost started to laugh.

Lisa bit her lip, clearly struggling to keep the tears at bay. "I'm wanted for murder."

Joey knew her friend could see the shock on her face. Quickly, it turned to concern.

"Whom exactly are you accused of murdering?" Joey drew her chair closer to the table, unconsciously rubbing her hand across her forehead as if she had a headache.

"Does the name Alice Lynn Carter ring a bell?" Lisa was watching Joey closely now.

Joey pondered the question. There might have been something familiar about it, but she couldn't put her finger on it. Finally, she shook her head no.

"How about the Peekskill Six?" Lisa asked.

Joey leaned back in her chair. She had studied a variety of radical groups in a political science class at Brown, and she immediately recognized the group Lisa had referred to. "Are you telling me that you were one of the people involved in the bank robbery all those years ago? The one where they shot the bank guard?"

Lisa expelled a long breath. "That's exactly what I'm telling you. And I can't live with it anymore. I need to set my life in order."

"Why, it must be almost thirty years since that happened," Joey exclaimed.

Lisa took a tissue out of her purse and dabbed at her eyes. "Twenty-nine years, five months and three days," she said bitterly.

"But who's counting," Joey finished for her.

Lisa smiled sadly in response. "I'm sorry to be presuming on our friendship, but I need your help. Your father's help, really."

Lisa's words brought back the phone call from the

night before. Yes, the bank robbery was in New York, and a New York lawyer was exactly what Lisa needed. But Jack Ross? Right now, her father couldn't deal with a traffic ticket. Oh, no, she realized, as she thought about what he had told her. The person she needed was Elizabeth, but God knew where Elizabeth was. Or, a small voice within her murmured, whether her sister would ever be home again.

She'll be fine, she told herself, averting her eyes from Lisa's face so her friend would be shielded from the pain she might see there. She's smart and resourceful and—the anguish that threatened to rip through her body kept her mind from going forward.

It's Lisa I have to think about now, she thought, forcing herself to consider the story her friend had laid before her. It took only a few seconds for her to come to the only conclusion she could.

"I'm afraid what you need right now isn't my father, but me. We're going to go to New York together and deal with this."

She covered Lisa's hand with her own, smiling encouragement. But, inside, she was screaming. Damn you, Elizabeth, and damn you, Dad. One more time, it's you win and I lose. As usual, they were going to get exactly what they wanted.

Chapter Fifteen

Jack looked at his watch as he entered the building. For a moment, he couldn't tell if the hands indicated that it was eight-thirty or six-forty. Don't be ridiculous, he told himself, straightening his shoulders and walking purposefully to the right. Expecting to see the bank of elevators he had used for decades, he was shocked to come to a blank wall. He turned slowly, looking back, noticing finally that the elevator bank was located all the way at the other end of the lobby. Flushed with embarrassment, he walked back to where he was supposed to be.

The uniformed man behind the desk next to the elevators tipped his cap as Jack walked by.

"A terrible thing, Mr. Ross," the familiar-looking dark-haired fellow said sympathetically.

Jack felt the rush of tears running uncontrollably down his face. He wanted to hug the man, this near stranger who seemed to understand the depth of his loss. Get hold of yourself, he thought. The man was simply offering condolences, as so many had in the past week.

For days now, he had sat alone in his apartment, comforted only by the bottle of liquor in front of him. He would try to sleep, then drink some more, his days and nights a haunted blur of emptiness. There was no

Molly, coming home breathless with excitement from a job at some theater downtown. No Elizabeth walking into his office, organizing his cases, his day . . . his life. Everyone who had meant anything to him was gone. His mother. His father. His brother. Elizabeth. Joey. Molly . . .

The sound of his weeping shouldn't have surprised him, yet it did. And it obviously alarmed the uniformed man standing awkwardly in front of him. The man reached out toward his shoulder, but Jack pulled away abruptly and walked to an open elevator door. He had to get upstairs before he made any more of a fool of himself.

He had to get used to being in public once more. After today, he thought as he entered the elevator and rang for his floor, everything will start to go back to normal. Today was the first day back. That's why his nerves were shot. Soon, everything would become as it had always been.

He got out on the fourteenth floor and strode quickly down the hall, shaking his head briefly at the receptionist, who was trying to speak to him. What was the use of stopping? So he could acknowledge how terrible it was? How some monster killed his wife? Well, as he knew all too well, that was true. But what the hell was he supposed to say about it?

He walked down the hallway, looking neither to the left nor the right, then entered his office, closed the door, and sat down behind his desk. Slowly his eyes perused the objects he'd lived with for so long. The large walnut desk, the conference table in one corner, the soft leather couch in the other. The lawbooks and framed pictures that defined his entire career. It was as if he'd stepped into someone else's life.

"Shall I come in now, Mr. Ross?"

The voice from the intercom rattled him. Instinctively, he reached into his pocket and withdrew a silver flask. The Scotch he'd poured in that morning felt warm going down his throat.

"Sure, Jane," Jack said as he pressed his own intercom button. "That would be fine."

Quickly, he placed the flask back into his pocket. When his secretary entered the office, all she would see was her boss, seated with sad dignity behind his desk waiting for his day to start. As he heard the door open, he had a moment of panic. What if it all showed? What if he couldn't hide the fear he felt?

But he managed to sit still as Jane seated herself in front of the desk. He even managed a gruff "thank you" as she indicated how sorry she was about Mrs. Ross.

"Shall we start?" Jane asked, placing several files on Jack's desk.

He nodded.

"Well, as you probably remember, you have the pretrial conference coming up for the Kendrick case. The clerk from Judge Parker's chambers called to confirm it for Friday. Is that all right?"

Jack nodded once again, although he barely remembered what the Kendrick case was. It was probably something Elizabeth had handled. She handled so much, he thought, his eyes misting at the memory of his daughter, seated right next to Jane at so many of these morning reviews. Elizabeth would always look so beautiful, dressed in some flattering shade of gray or navy blue, her eyes sparkling, the shape of her lovely face so like Molly's.

He suddenly realized that Jane was peering at him oddly.

"Yes, go on," he muttered as the mist threatened to turn into another deluge of tears.

Jane looked back down to the papers in front of her. "Harry Landes called about his appeal. I told him you'd get back to him next week. And Tamara Harland wanted to know how soon she could expect to see some money."

Jack frowned. That case he remembered all too well. The famous but aging Broadway dancer had slipped in her local supermarket. Maybe there was some liquid on the floor. Maybe she had fallen on purpose and was lying through her reconstructed teeth. With Elizabeth's help, he had sued the store and the entire supermarket chain. Tamara Harland would probably never have to work again a day in her life.

What a way to make a living, he thought miserably. Personal injury cases featuring spoiled divas as clients. A living, surely, but not a life. A life was a wife, children, a home filled with people who loved you. His mind became crowded with images of Molly. As a teenager, carrying her books on the way home from school. As a young wife, pregnant with Elizabeth, her face aglow, her belly not showing at all until well into her sixth month of pregnancy.

And Elizabeth. When she was two or three, she'd leap into his arms when he'd get home each night.

God, how he missed his wife. And his daughters, both of them. He'd lost everyone, just as he'd always known he would. Maybe Joanna had never loved him the way Elizabeth had, but when she was a baby, she was content to lie in his arms, pulling his reading glasses off his nose, chewing on them until he took them back.

But that was then. Joey hadn't been close to him for years. Why should she, after all? He hadn't even spoken to her since she'd moved to Montana. God, what he'd give to have her in this room right now. He knew how hostile she'd be, how much resentment she'd built up by now, but it would be such a comfort to have her with him, a daughter, linked to him by blood.

". . . and Rob Casamiglia called again from CBS, asking about your response to *Whitmore v. Coe*."

Jack noticed Jane looking at him expectantly. He had no idea what she'd been saying, how long he had been lost in his own hellish thoughts. He longed to pull the flask out of his pocket, to take a gulp, to escape back to a place where he had no thoughts at all.

Jane was quietly watching him, but Jack couldn't offer any response. Finally the secretary forged ahead. "And your daughter is waiting in the outer office with a friend of hers."

Jack felt a thrill of pleasure shoot through him as he stood up and strode toward the door. He couldn't believe he hadn't seen her when he walked in. "Oh, thank God, Elizabeth's come home," he said, reaching for the doorknob.

Jane caught up to him, her confusion evident. "No, sir, it's actually your younger daughter. Joey's been waiting for a couple of hours."

Jack threw the door open. He saw his daughter sitting on one of the black leather chairs, engrossed in conversation with a neatly dressed woman well into her forties.

Jack walked over to Joey and pulled her up into his arms. She remained stiff as he held her, but for once she allowed it. Seeing her, he felt a burst of his old energy suddenly filling his veins. After releasing Joey, he turned to the woman beside her.

"How do you do, Ms. . . ."

"Martin," the woman said. "Lisa Martin."

He ushered both women into his office and took a seat behind his desk. "Joey, darling," he said, "I'm so glad you're back. It means everything to me."

Joey looked at him evenly. "I'm not exactly back, Dad. At least, not for the reason you think." She looked to her friend reassuringly, then plunged ahead. "Lisa has a legal problem, and since Elizabeth is still gone, I'm going to stay long enough to handle it." She looked at her father. "That is, if it's okay with you."

Jack smiled broadly. "It would be okay with me if you sat in that chair for the rest of your life."

"This isn't a joking matter, Dad," Joey answered impatiently. "Lisa's in terrible trouble, and there's a lot I'm going to have to do."

"What's the matter?" he asked, looking at Joey's friend. He couldn't imagine what kind of trouble this woman would be in, with her attractively made-up face, her tailored pale-blue dress neatly outlining her carefully maintained figure. She looked like a person to whom moderation was second nature. A model of self-control, that much was certain. In fact, he realized, she was almost too well maintained to be a friend of Joey's. Most of the young people she'd been friendly with over the years had been anything but well put together. The few people she'd brought home had been almost slovenly. Then there was her best friend, that gay man she liked so much. Well, Jack thought with reluctant approval, at least he was tidy.

He looked at the woman seated across from him and realized his mind had wandered. She seemed to be on the verge of saying something, and he scrambled to remember what it was he had asked her.

Joey's answer reminded him sharply.

"She's wanted for murder."

Jack felt uneasiness running through his veins. I'm not up to this anymore, he thought, as perspiration snaked down the back of his neck. "What happened?" he asked, frightened that whatever the answer, he would have no idea how to proceed.

"I was part of the Peekskill Six, one of the people the police never found after the bank guard got killed. I want to turn myself in."

Jack was genuinely surprised. Who would ever have associated this woman with antiwar politics of the sixties?

He knew he ought to say something to her in response, but he couldn't think what it was he should say. Was this a matter for the federal courts? For the state? Were there special procedures after so many years? All the alcohol he'd consumed that morning suddenly seemed to overwhelm his ability to think at all.

"Well . . ." he said slowly, reaching over to a pitcher of water on the side of his desk and pouring himself a glass. When he finished taking a sip, he just sat there. He saw his daughter eyeing him oddly.

"Dad," he heard her say through his blur of fear,

"I'm going to see to everything. Lisa's going to give herself up to the police. But I want her to be able to say that Ross, Jennings represents her."

Lisa leaned forward in her chair and looked at him gratefully. "I want to thank you for letting me come here, for helping me."

Jack found he couldn't sit any longer, couldn't contain his relief and sudden excitement. Getting up, he paced around his office. "On the contrary, Lisa," he said, standing behind their chairs and touching Joey lightly on the back, "I want to thank you for bringing my baby back to me."

He didn't look down at Joey's face, didn't see the resignation etched in her eyes. In fact, he found himself smiling, barely remembering his panic of a few minutes before.

After all, he was still a good enough lawyer to know when he had won.

Chapter Sixteen

Elizabeth poured the egg mixture into the pan and swirled it around with a fork, watching it make the transformation from yellow liquid to fluffy solid. When the eggs were fully scrambled she scraped them neatly onto a plate and sprinkled pepper on them. Sunlight streamed in through the windows that surrounded the kitchen. It's going to be another beautiful day, she thought as she took the plate and a glass of orange juice over to the kitchen table. That's three in a row.

What would I normally be doing on a perfect Saturday in June? she mused as she ate. Playing a game of tennis, doing errands, having lunch with a friend, putting in some extra hours at the office. What does a fugitive do on a gorgeous, sunny afternoon? She grimaced. I guess I'll find out when I do it.

She carried her empty dish and glass to the sink to wash them. As it had been since she had arrived six days before, the silence in the cottage was everywhere, as strong a presence as another person would have been. Elizabeth had never realized how accustomed she was to the noise of New York. The stillness of the country—and the fact that she was so totally alone every day and night—made her more aware of the quiet than anything else around her.

Well, almost anything, she amended. It was the

pitch-blackness of the night that brought out a fear she hadn't know she was capable of feeling. Once night fell, she kept every light in the house blazing to ward off the darkness that surrounded it. In retrospect, it seemed to her that New York barely registered nighttime as dark, with the millions of lights radiating cheery warmth from the streets and apartment windows. Everything functioned at all times. The city was still alive. Nature had been beaten back.

But here in Maine, nature was still in control. Each night Elizabeth forced herself to step outside, trying to overcome the irrational terror she felt. But when she peered into the vast, inky night, there was no sense of depth or ending. She felt she was about to be drawn into the void. A chill would grip her that frightened her to her core, and she would flee inside, defeated. Then there was the loneliness that enveloped her as she sat on the couch, a woolen throw tucked around her, a book in her lap. When she finally went to bed, trying to put her tortured thoughts aside for a while, she slept badly.

Still, she knew it was a miracle to have this place. The cottage belonged to Diane's parents. Elizabeth had visited the cabin with Diane at least half a dozen times over the years. But it wasn't until she was zipping her suitcase shut, ready to leave New York but still uncertain where to go, that she stumbled upon the idea of hiding here. She knew that Diane's parents were in Europe for the summer, and Diane was at home in Charlottesville. No one would be around. Elizabeth was slightly horrified at herself for coming up with a plan to use someone else's house without their knowing it, particularly people who cared for her and trusted her. Still, it was a perfect place in which to disappear. And she was desperate.

Breaking and entering turned out to be simpler than she had thought. She had left her apartment at six in the morning, with only her purse and the suitcase in hand. She drove to Boston, then left her car in a garage and took a bus the rest of the way to Maine. The key to the house was in a flowerpot by the back door just as she remembered it. Flushed with guilt, she had let herself in. And there she was. Gone from New York, away from the police, in hiding. She continued to feel bad about using the house without asking anyone's permission. But she had to smile at the idea of actually asking for it and explaining the reason why. She would just have to find some way to make amends.

She had started the coffeemaker earlier. Now she went to pour herself a cup. With the steaming mug in hand, she walked to the front door and opened it. The question, she thought, as she gazed out at the peaceful vista of meadows and mountains, is what on earth happens now? Just finding a place to hide out for a bit had seemed the logical move when she first left the city. But she needed to get moving, both to avoid the police and to start her search for whoever shot her mother.

She pushed her hair back from her face. It was still difficult to get used to how weightless it felt now that it was six inches shorter. The day after arriving at the cottage, she'd cut it off to chin-length to make herself less recognizable. But it hadn't been a radical enough change, so she had taken the next step and bleached it blond. At the kitchen sink that day, she was struck with the reality of her situation. Up until then, she realized, she had just been going through the motions. As she watched the curly brown strands of hair turn to blond, she actually understood for the first time that she was running away from the law. It had taken her breath away.

By now it would be obvious that she was gone. Everybody would know—her father, the police, Joey, everyone at the law firm. The police would no doubt have discovered that her car was gone, and that she had withdrawn thirty thousand dollars in cash from her bank account. They would have gone into her apartment and searched through her things to see what they could learn. They had no doubt questioned her friends, people she worked with, acquaintances, shopkeepers in her neighborhood. And, of course, Peter.

She turned and went back inside, into the small extra bedroom. It was the room she had used when she had come here as a guest. She wouldn't have felt right sleeping in any of the other beds. Like Goldilocks, she thought, imagining Diane's parents standing there wondering, Who's been eating *my* porridge?

She set her coffee down and started to get dressed. It was time to go back to New York. She hoped she had covered her tracks well enough that the police wouldn't be waiting for her with open arms. But she had to get cracking if she was going to accomplish her purpose.

She had another reason for wanting to get back. Somehow, without letting him know it, she wanted to make sure her father was all right. She could only imagine how awful this week had been for him, his daughter disappearing into thin air right after he'd had to bury his wife. He was tough, but he had seemed so fragile in those last days. She only prayed he could take it, at least for a while longer.

What surprised her was how much she wanted to see one other person. But she didn't dare try to get a look at Peter without his knowing; for some reason, she was certain she wouldn't get away with it. Besides, she didn't want to see him from a distance. It had taken her aback to realize how much she wanted to talk to him, to touch him. Before all this had happened—was it a million years ago she wondered—she would go days without thinking much about him. He was always there when she wanted him. Now she couldn't be with him, and it hurt. She'd had no idea how much she would miss him.

Grabbing her purse, she left the cottage and walked down the main road toward the one street that constituted town. Fortunately, the house was less than a mile away, so she had been able to purchase food at the small general store and bring it back on foot.

Otherwise she might have had to rent a car, and she wasn't quite sure how to do that without giving away her identity.

At the moment, she had no particular purpose in going to town. She wanted some exercise and the opportunity to see a few other people. God, I could never have lived in the country, she mused as she walked. Too much healthy fresh air and quiet. She smiled, but it faded quickly. Might this be her last real taste of freedom? Her heart clutched with fear.

She squinted up at the sun. You can do this, she reassured herself. An image suddenly came back to her of her mother sitting on her bed, reading aloud from *The Little Engine That Could,* as a young Elizabeth listened, freshly bathed and snug in her flannel pajamas.

Sadness washed over her. Softly, she chanted aloud in rhythm with her steps. "I think I can, I think I can, I think I can."

She saw the general store up ahead. There was a public telephone inside, and Elizabeth realized that was where she had been heading all along. Nobody would be trying to trace her call, but it seemed smarter not to call from the telephone at the house, even if only to protect Diane's family from somehow becoming involved later. The bell above the door jingled as she went into the crowded, dimly lit store.

The girl behind the counter was about sixteen, with long, stringy hair and lots of dark-blue eye shadow. She was flipping through a magazine, chewing gum and popping bubbles noisily. Elizabeth handed her a five-dollar bill.

"Hi. Could you give me change for the telephone?" she asked pleasantly. "The whole five in coins, if that's possible, please."

Dully, the girl glanced at her before taking the money and opening the cash register drawer. Elizabeth wondered if the girl would remember seeing her should the police discover she had been here. It struck her that it might actually be exciting for this teenager to be able to say she had waited on a suspected killer. Quite the icebreaker at a party. She almost laughed at the thought.

"Here." The girl looked at her suspiciously.

"Thank you."

Elizabeth took the silver and made her way through one of the narrow aisles to the telephone in back. She dialed Peter's number, following the operator's instructions to deposit two dollars and eighty cents.

"Hello?"

A pang shot through Elizabeth at the sound of his voice. What's come over me, she wondered.

"Hi. It's me." She lowered her voice, although she realized the girl couldn't hear her from so far away.

"Elizabeth? My God, where are you?"

She felt a flood of relief at the urgency in his voice. After the way they parted, she wasn't sure what he was thinking anymore. In her lonely, late-night worrying, she had almost convinced herself he despised her by now.

She ignored his question. "I just wanted to say hello."

"Hello?" he echoed in disbelief. "You want to chat? Jesus, Lizzie, I've been going crazy here. I can't believe you actually did it. Are you okay?"

"I'm fine. I just wanted to hear your voice."

He paused. "You're not coming back? This is serious. It's already been in the paper, how you took off."

"No, I'm not coming back." She had no intention of letting him know she would be in New York by that night. It was too risky for both of them.

"Your father called me, you know. He was asking if I knew where you were. Presumably he called everyone you hang around with."

She tensed. "Is he all right?"

"I can't really say. I told him you talked about going, but you wouldn't say where. He turned very quiet and got off the phone pretty fast. I told him I'd get in touch if I heard from you."

"Please don't tell him I called," she said beseechingly. "It won't help for everyone to be lying to the police. Lies have a way of making themselves visible sooner or later."

Peter spoke forcefully. "I want *you* to make yourself visible. This is too dangerous."

Elizabeth pictured him holding the receiver, his hair falling across his forehead. "I miss you," she whispered.

"Then come home to me," he burst out.

"I can't. Listen, I'll call you again sometime if I can. Now I have to go."

"Wait—"

"Take care of yourself, Peter." She hung up.

Outside in the bright sunshine, she shielded her eyes and looked around. That was selfish of me, she thought. I upset him just because I needed to hear his voice. I can't do that again.

She went back up the road toward the cabin. It was time to pack and attempt to make the place look as if no one had ever been there. She would call a taxi to pick her up in town and take her to the bus station. Tonight she would check into a hotel in the city. What a mess, she thought. Peter, her father, her entire life.

Just then, she had an eerie sensation, a strange feeling that everything was supposed to happen the way it had. That there was a reason she was being wrongly suspected. That *she* would have to be the one to find out who killed her mother.

Is this something that's meant to be between you and me, Mom? she asked silently. Despite the heat of the day, she shivered.

Chapter Seventeen

Joey could hardly believe that the woman in front of her was Lisa Martin. Waiting for Lisa to appear in the visitors' room of the Metropolitan Correctional Center, Joey somehow expected her friend to look just as she had each time they had met for breakfast in Montana. More than anyone Joey had ever known, Lisa embodied consistency and perfection. Even in Jack's office, Lisa had managed to somehow be herself. But the woman Joey was facing now was at least ten pounds thinner, dressed in regulation blue cotton shirt and pants, with unkempt hair that fell haphazardly around her shoulders. Her face had a gaunt, almost haggard quality, her skin making her a pale replica of the woman she used to be. In fact, her entire posture breathed equal measures of negligence and depression.

"Not a pretty sight, huh?" Lisa said, noting the surprise in Joey's eyes.

Joey leaned across the table and took her friend's hand. "For someone who's going through all this, you look just fine."

"Well, at least it's finally gotten me out of Torrance Falls."

Joey couldn't help but laugh. "That's certainly true." The laughter didn't last long. "In the crush of the past couple of weeks, I never thought about that. I guess I never did understand your reluctance to leave town. Now, I get it."

Lisa sighed. "There have been pictures of me in post offices and police stations for almost thirty years. Even a trip to Missoula was potentially dangerous."

Joey found herself shivering. She realized suddenly that even after all these days in New York, she was still reeling from the fact that Lisa was one of the six people who'd left Henry Langdon dead that day in Peekskill. She'd have been less surprised by being carried off by a UFO in the middle of the night than by the notion that her most conventional, well-behaved friend hid such an enormous secret.

"Well," Joey said, opening the briefcase that lay in front of her and pulling out a yellow pad and a pen. "I guess we'd better get down to business."

"I'll go through it all one more time, though nothing's going to make what happened any less terrible." Lisa stopped suddenly and bit her lip. "I can't tell you how grateful I am that you're here with me to do this."

"You know it's what you would do for me if the shoe were on the other foot," Joey responded, hoping the unhappiness she actually felt was well hidden.

Entering her father's law offices after all this time had been profoundly upsetting. Even wearing her old suits made her feel stuck in a time warp, one in which she'd been miserable. The only thing that had really changed in the past few years was her father, who seemed almost like a ghost of his former self. Seeing him frail and despondent didn't exactly mitigate her anger at him; in fact, watching him sneak that flask out of his pocket every time he thought no one would see made her sick. And he was so pathetic, so old-looking all of a sudden. Still, he had lost his wife and his favorite daughter. She couldn't deny the pity she felt for him.

Nor could she hide from herself the fears she had for her sister's safety. She couldn't think of a thing she could do for Elizabeth, and half the time what she felt was absolute rage. How could she have been so stupid as to run away? It only made her seem guilty. And Joey couldn't believe that anyone could really believe that Elizabeth Ross could commit murder. For God's sake, she was incapable of stepping on a lady-bug, let alone lifting a gun against her mother. But, between bursts of anger, she would find herself, in the middle of some random conversation suddenly think-ing about Elizabeth, wishing her sister would come home. She would prove to Joey and her father that she was all right, that something terrible hadn't happened.

Something terrible, she thought bitterly. What could happen that was more terrible than what had hap-pened already?

The single good thing about being back in New York was that she was staying with her friend Tom Abrahams in his apartment in Chelsea. Coming home each night to the warmth of his friendship made her feel human. For an hour or two, he would regale her with stories of his disastrous dates and his misadven-tures as a math teacher at Evander Childs, an over-crowded high school in the Bronx. Only the next morning, when she'd pull on a silk blouse and a well-tailored suit and walk through the doors of Ross, Jen-nings, would she feel that horrible uneasiness that used to make up her life.

But she was back here for a reason, and it was time to go to work. After today, Lisa would be transferred up to the federal authorities in Westchester, the county where the original crime took place, and once she was placed in the Valhalla Correctional Facility, it would be much harder to see her.

They'd had so little time to talk about the actual case. First, there's been the hurried trip to New York. Lisa had been so emotionally drained that she slept through the whole flight. Then they'd gone together so Lisa could turn herself in. After that, there'd been reams of paperwork, meetings with prosecutors, prece-

dents to check before the case could begin. Joey
hadn't even had time to have a real conversation with
her client.

"So," she said, "why don't you start with the robbery in Peekskill. Assume I know nothing, because
that's pretty much the truth."

Lisa seemed to be searching for the right words.
"It's so hard to explain this in the context of the nineties. You have no idea what it was like back in the
late sixties. The four kids had just been killed at Kent
State. Johnson was secretly bombing Cambodia. I was
a sophomore at Barnard, and all of us were adamantly
against the war in Vietnam. But carrying signs and
participating in sit-ins began to seem almost silly.
There was so much carnage in Vietnam and Cambodia. We saw the dead bodies every night on the six
o'clock news. So some of us felt compelled to do
more, to raise money for the groups that were really
accomplishing something."

"Groups like the Black Panthers and SDS?"

Lisa nodded. "Exactly. The Panthers were pouring
their hearts into community work, feeding people, ed-
ucating children. And the people in SDS were the
ones really putting themselves on the line against the
war." She shook her head as if in wonder. "My God,
we were so young, all of us. There was so much we
wanted to do."

"And robbery became the means to raise the
money?"

Lisa laughed bitterly. "We were such idiots. Take
from the rich to give to the poor. Punish the evil pow-
ermongers. It seemed almost heroic when we talked
about it. Then that poor guy ended up dead."

"Were you actually at the bank in Peekskill when
Henry Langdon was killed?"

Tears were beginning to well up in Lisa's eyes. "I
was in the car, waiting for the three people who'd
gone in. Freddie Shore and Bobby Sarkalian were
standing outside, watching for the police. Janie Saltzman, Paul St. John, and Tony Raffia came back out-

side with the money, got in the car, and the four of us drove away. Freddie Shore fired off the gun at least five minutes after the four of us had already left." She looked straight at Joey. "I never understood exactly what happened. Everything was over with, and it seemed to have gone smoothly. But that doesn't make it any less my responsibility." She pulled a wad of tissues out of her pocket and dabbed at her eyes. "That I caused a man's death. It's the thought that has awakened me at three in the morning for the past twenty-nine years."

"Well, you didn't take an active part in shooting the man. But even without your actually carrying a gun or firing a shot, they can try you for felony murder," Joey said, thinking the matter through out loud. "The fact that you took no part in the act itself doesn't mean anything according to the letter of the law, just so long the act was committed in the course of the robbery."

Lisa nodded glumly.

Joey wrote a brief note on her pad and looked up again. She smiled softly this time. "So your father was never in the military, huh? You lived all those places when you were on the run."

Lisa spoke almost in a whisper. "I was raised in a tiny town in Michigan, and my parents were strict Catholics. There were five of us brothers and sisters, and we went to church every single Sunday of my childhood. When I was moving around, before I settled in Montana, I got to whatever church was near as many times as I could." She smiled. "Even when I was going around calling myself Shirley Greenberg, I used to take communion at Immaculate Conception in Buffalo, New York." She closed her eyes, obviously trying to hold back a flood of tears. "I never even lied as a kid, never took a candy bar, never spoke rudely to my mother or father, never got less than an A in school." Her tone turned ironic. "I was the goodest girl who ever was."

"Well, maybe you still are a good girl. You have

certainly been a good wife and a good mother and a good friend." Joey smiled at her encouragingly.

Lisa couldn't even meet her eyes. "How good a mother can you be when you're not even the person you claim to be, when your name is Alice Lynn Carter instead of Lisa Martin, and your parents are alive instead of dead, and you come from Alberta, Michigan, instead of Seattle, Washington? How good a wife can you be when everything you've ever told your husband is a lie?" The tears started flowing freely. "And how good a person can you be when you murdered an innocent man?"

Joey stood up. She didn't want to subject Lisa to any more today. "Enough for now. I want you to write down everything you remember about the day of the robbery and everything you know about the other five people involved in it with you. And try to list everyone who knew Freddie and Tony. After all, they're still out there, and they may have said something to friends over the years that could help you." She stopped, wondering if there was anything else to add to her instructions. "Don't leave out anything," she said, unable to think of anything specific, "even the stuff that might seem inconsequential."

She leaned over and kissed Lisa lightly on the cheek. "And please try and remember, if you weren't a person of good conscience, you never would have given a damn about the war, and you certainly never would have chosen to turn yourself in. You know, they never would have caught up with you. The official investigation was closed at least ten years ago."

"I know," Lisa answered in an exhausted voice. "I just couldn't live with it anymore."

Joey gave her friend a brief hug and began to collect her things. "We're going to work this out, I promise you. Please don't lose heart."

Lisa smiled weakly. "I'll try not to. Really, I feel relieved. Once I told Hal and the kids, I began to feel better. I certainly brightened up Josh's term paper on his family tree," she added ironically. The moment of levity didn't last long. "Whatever happens, at least I can be myself. You can't imagine what it felt like to sign my real name when I came in here. It was something I'd been terrified of doing by accident for so many years."

Joey turned and walked toward the door. "You were always yourself in the ways that counted," she said, turning back to Lisa one last time. "I'll see you up in Valhalla, tomorrow or the day after."

Joey was lost in thought as she left the correctional center. She strolled past the federal courthouse nearby, thinking how ironic it all seemed. How could it be that women like Lisa Martin and Elizabeth could be in so much trouble? They were the good ones.

The thought stayed with her block after block. Was that somehow why they found themselves in the predicaments they were in? Was it the very same goodness—that quest for perfection that had made Lisa such a devoted daughter and such a wonderful student—that had contributed mightily to her ultimate destruction? The goodwill, the heartfelt concerns about humanity? And how had Elizabeth managed to turn herself into a murder suspect? Oh, God, she thought, unbearable sadness filling her completely, how badly it had all turned out.

"I hear you're keeping some excellent company, Ms. Ross."

The voice startled Joey. She looked up to see a familiar-looking man, although she couldn't quite come up with his name.

"Detective Gary McCullough, at your service," he said, putting out his hand to shake hers, then pulling it back when she failed to respond.

"If you're talking about Lisa Martin, she is excellent company, thank you."

She strode on ahead, but the detective caught up with her easily.

"What is it about you that makes you so admiring of criminals?"

Joey felt a flash of anger but forced herself to stay

calm. She looked past him to the many groups of policemen smoking and laughing on the steps of the
building. "What is it about you policemen that makes
you want to hang out with criminals? Of the two of
us, I'd say you're the one who's chosen to make it a
way of life."

His voice grew steely. "I've chosen to put people
who hurt people behind bars, not to get them off with
light sentences or support them when they run away."

"If you're referring to my sister," she said, unable
now to keep the anger out of her voice, "she is not
a criminal."

"Generally speaking, people who run away and
evade arrest don't do so because they suddenly feel
the need for a vacation," he answered.

Joey found his sarcasm hard to bear. She stopped
moving and looked up at him, realizing, to her discomfort, that in other circumstances she might have found
him attractive. Much taller than she was and dressed
casually in a brown tweed jacket and corduroy jeans,
he had warm brown eyes.

"First of all," she said, catching her breath and
speaking slowly, "I have no idea where my sister is.
Second, the closest Elizabeth ever came to doing anything criminal was wearing a navy blue skirt a dye lot
away from her navy blue blazer one Monday in the
seventh grade. She would no more be able to shoot
my mother than I would be able . . ." She hesitated,
looking for the appropriate analogy.

". . . to come and have a beer with me," he finished
her sentence, smiling at her unexpectedly.

Joey felt stung by confusion. What was this guy
doing? She couldn't decide if he was flirting with her
or just warming her up to get something out of her.
Well, she thought, there's nothing to get out of me,
and I'll be damned if I let him get under my skin.

"You know, Detective, oddly enough I tend to
drink beer sometime *after* eleven-thirty in the morning. But your affection warms my heart. Maybe we'll
do it another time, possibly when the snowdrifts in

hell reach six hundred feet." She walked away from him, searching through her purse for a subway token.

"I have a proposition I'll leave with you," he called out to her. "Just in case you really don't know where your sister is—which, frankly, I doubt—you might want to work with me on finding her. Because, trust me, as long as she stays away, my friends and I have very little reason to look elsewhere for your mother's murderer. Your Phi Beta Kappa sister has done a great job of making herself look as guilty as guilty can be."

Joey had been intending to walk away without another word, but decided to ask a question instead. "And if Elizabeth hadn't run away, who else might you be looking at?"

He turned to go. "If you want to know the answer to that, you'll have to take me up on my offer. And I wouldn't wait for Satan's headquarters to be snowed in. I'd guess you won't have quite that long to decide."

"Do you know where my sister is?" she asked, struck by the implication of what he'd just said.

He didn't bother to turn around as he answered her. "You show me yours and I'll show you mine. Those are the ground rules. Any time you want to join forces, you can find me at the precinct."

His voice had grown fainter as he walked away, and she couldn't be certain she'd heard everything he said. But she didn't really have to. What he wanted was clear. Well, she thought, blushing in embarrassment, not exactly everything. The part about the beer felt something other than strictly professional. She felt unsettled by the memory of his grin, the intelligence that so clearly lay beneath his glib surface. Damn it, she thought, turning around and making her way toward the subway, why couldn't the detective in charge have body odor and weigh four hundred pounds?

Better yet, she thought, laughing at herself, maybe I should be the one who gains a few hundred pounds. It might not help either her friend Lisa or her sister, Elizabeth, but at least it would guarantee her the solitude to focus on everything she had to do.

Chapter Eighteen

"Know what you want?"

Pencil poised above her pad, the waitress glanced down at Elizabeth, who was seated in the small booth.

"I'd like the fresh fruit salad and a toasted English muffin, please," Elizabeth replied, closing the plastic menu. "And coffee. Thanks."

Nodding as she finished writing the order, the waitress moved away. Elizabeth turned her attention to the copy of *The New York Times* that she had bought just before entering the coffee shop. She separated the first section from the rest of the newspaper and began scanning the front page. The waitress returned, setting down a cup of coffee at her elbow.

"Thank you."

Elizabeth smiled up at her, reaching for the milk. When the woman returned the smile, looking her full in the face, Elizabeth realized her mistake and hastily dropped her gaze back down to the paper. *Stupid,* she reprimanded herself, as she picked up her sunglasses from the table and put them back on. You're not supposed to be going out of your way to imprint your face on the brain of everyone you meet.

She stirred her coffee dispiritedly. If hiding out in Maine had been something like a dream, these past twenty-four hours since she had arrived back in New

York City were more of a nightmare. It was disorient-
ing to be so entirely isolated from the crowds swirling
around her on the streets, to worry constantly about
keeping up her guard. She found herself hesitating
each time she spoke, fearful that she would somehow
blurt out her real name or give herself away. It's as if
I'm surrounded by cotton batting, wrapped in a co-
coon, she reflected.

In that same hazy way, she had checked into a small
bed-and-breakfast on Horatio Street in Greenwich
Village. She chose it over a hotel because she was
concerned about having to show identification. Her
bed-and-breakfast was a renovated town house with
three guest rooms on a small, quiet street. Under different circumstances she would have appreciated its
charms. Right now, she was just relieved that the el-
derly man who owned it asked few questions; he
merely nodded as he accepted her cash payment of
three hundred dollars in advance.

Still, her heart had been pounding as she told him
the name she had made up for herself, Stacy Hubert.
The name was one she had simply pulled out of the
air during the bus ride from Maine. In her work as a
lawyer it had always amazed her that criminals so
often chose aliases with their own initials. It must have
made it easier to keep track of their phony identities,
but it created such a damning trail of evidence, appearing somehow even more coldly calculated than a
random choice would have been.

So she was now Stacy Hubert, a woman without a
Social Security number, credit cards, or a driver's license. There was no way to open a bank account
under her phony name, so she put seven hundred dollars into her purse and sealed the rest of her money
in a Ziploc plastic bag, which she taped to the back
of a painting above the bed. Walking around the city
with a purse containing only a comb, lipstick, and
seven hundred-dollar bills made her feel almost naked,
a faceless being in a strange place without any protection. Equally disturbing, though, was the realization

that being cut off from her identity left her so utterly defenseless. She hated not being anyone.

I never realized what a straight citizen I really am, she thought as she turned the page of the newspaper. Or I guess I should say, I really *was*.

She stopped, staring at the page in front of her. "Dear God in heaven," she whispered.

There in the *Times* was a picture of her father, standing beside a woman Elizabeth didn't recognize, with a crowd of people behind them. And on the other side of the woman was her sister, Joey. The three appeared to be emerging from a building onto the street. Her father had his hand up as if to warn everyone to keep their distance.

Next to that picture was another one, much smaller. It was of Elizabeth herself, the formal publicity shot that had been taken back when she joined her father's law firm. She remembered the day she had posed for it, how carefully she had selected her dress, the way the photographer told her to turn down the intensity of her smile because she was supposed to look, as he put it, like a tough legal eagle.

She read the caption beneath her picture. *All in the family. Elizabeth Ross, the fugitive suspect.*

She recalled Peter telling her during their telephone conversation that she had been in the newspaper, but it hadn't meant much to her in the abstract. Seeing her own face staring out at her, her expression so earnest, made it painfully real.

Her gaze went to the caption beneath the photograph of her father and Joey. *Alice Lynn Carter, sixties radical, alias Lisa Martin, surrendering after three decades in hiding, accompanied by the father-and-daughter team of attorneys, Jack Ross and Joanna Ross.*

What the hell was going on? Joey was in New York and was working again as a *lawyer* with their father?

The waitress brought her fruit salad and English muffin. Elizabeth took a few quick bites of the food as she adjusted the paper so she could read the story from the beginning.

When she finished, she put the paper down and sat staring into space. Was this Lisa Martin one of the women Joey had become close friends with in Montana? Elizabeth could almost hear her mother going on about the wonderful friends Joey had made out west, really interesting women. Well, this woman was interesting, that was for sure.

For a moment Elizabeth wondered if her father had enlisted Joey's aid by telling her he needed the professional help now that Elizabeth wasn't on the scene. But she immediately rejected the notion. Despite Joey's promise to Elizabeth, she would never have returned to New York just because their father asked her to. Obviously, Joey had come because she wanted to help this Lisa.

She frowned. Lisa Martin wasn't the only one who needed Joey's help. Joey knew so much more about their mother than Elizabeth herself did. Joey and Molly had talked regularly on the telephone, which Elizabeth had never done. Her sister had a genuinely close relationship with her mother. She was in a much better position than Elizabeth to come up with the names of people who might have wanted to do Molly harm. Still, the thought of having to ask Joey for help made Elizabeth cringe inside.

She glanced up as the coffee shop door opened. Two police officers entered and took seats at the counter. They exchanged warm greetings with the waitress.

Elizabeth saw the picture of her face resting by her arm on the table. She snatched up the newspaper, folding it to hide the photograph, and signaled for her check. Trying to appear calm despite her mounting panic, she took the check from the woman's hand and hastened over to the register. The man behind the counter snorted in annoyance as he took her hundred-dollar bill but made change for her without further comment. She pretended to adjust her sunglasses so she could use her hand to shield the side of her face closest to the policemen. Even with her hair short and blond now, she had no idea whether she would fool anybody.

Am I that important a criminal that everyone will be on the lookout for me? she wondered. Unfortunately, she already knew the answer. Not only was her picture in the city's major newspaper, a paper read around the country no less, but the spotlight on her was going to be far more intense because of this case her dad and Joey were taking part in. They would be in the news constantly; that was the way her father always manipulated this kind of trial. That meant she would be in the papers constantly, too. Even she couldn't deny that it made for a great story, the father working with one daughter while the other was on the run, suspected of killing her own mother.

She left the coffee shop as quickly as she could without attracting attention to herself. What the hell did I think I was doing, running away, she asked herself. I can't pull this off.

She walked on through the unfamiliar streets. Except for forays to restaurants or galleries, she spent little time this far downtown. I shouldn't let my universe get so small, she thought, relaxing slightly as she took in the intricate carvings on the buildings and the eclectic store displays.

She glanced ahead and, with a small gasp, nearly stumbled. There, coming toward her, was Myra Connell. She and Myra had been friendly in law school, and though they had drifted apart since, they ran into one another at industry functions every so often. Elizabeth couldn't imagine that sunglasses and a dye job were going to keep Myra from recognizing her.

She turned hastily and stepped off the curb, narrowly avoiding being hit by a passing car. Her heart pounding, she raced across the street and stopped in front of a used-clothing store, staring in the window as if she saw something fascinating there. She waited to see if a hand was going to appear on her shoulder or a cheerful voice call out her name. After what seemed like an eternity, she dared to turn around.

Myra had continued on and was almost at the corner. She must not have seen Elizabeth. *Thank you, God,* she thought gratefully.

Elizabeth leaned against the store window, shaken. Running away from friends, terrified, was an unhappy new experience. The realization of just how isolated she really was pierced her yet again. There were countless strangers who might put her face together with the picture in the paper, but that still seemed kind of unlikely. It was dawning on her, however, that there were hundreds of people in this city she knew, friends and acquaintances who would all recognize her instantly. They would also know that she was being hunted by the police. It wasn't enough to stay in a different neighborhood and hope for the best. She had to take more radical steps.

She turned around to look back into the used-clothing store. Tie-dyed T-shirts and brightly colored bead necklaces were casually strewn over a chair in the window. Two mannequins off to the side, both looking as if they had been around for a good twenty years or so, were adorned with fedoras with big feathers sticking out of them and crushed-velvet jackets over bell-bottom pants. Ah, the sixties, she thought. She pulled open the shop's heavy door and went inside. It was dark and dingy. The smell of patchouli oil permeated the air.

Elizabeth gave a small nod to the man behind the counter, who was dressed all in black and sported two enormous hoop earrings in his left ear. He was writing something and didn't seem interested in her. Good, she thought. She began rummaging through the racks of clothing.

She slipped on a faded green army jacket and inspected herself in the narrow floor-length mirror at the back of the crowded shop. Good-bye, Calvin . . . Giorgio . . . Donna, she thought, wanting to laugh. The change was astonishing. Along with her blond hair cut in the uneven line that was the result of her unskilled barbering, the jacket made her look like someone else altogether, someone who actually belonged south of Fourteenth Street, rather than the displaced corporate lawyer she knew herself to be.

She looked at the handwritten price tag on the jacket sleeve. Twelve dollars. A vision of her closet flashed through her mind, the rack of expensive suits and silk blouses, pleated pants and narrow, sleeveless dresses. It's about time I broke out of my rut, she thought, inspecting a stain on one of the sleeves, amused at the realization that she meant it. Oddly, there was something wonderfully freeing about this jacket.

It's the new me, she said to herself, moving toward the shelves of blue jeans. Selecting three pairs, she went behind the curtain that barely covered a space for trying on clothes. The pair she settled on had a wide rip across the right knee, and several narrower rips high on the left thigh. She folded up the navy pants she had been wearing when she entered the store and held them under her arm as she emerged from the so-called dressing room. Next she chose a pair of black lace-up boots, then slipped on some long, dangling brass earrings.

Dressed in her new purchases, she paused long enough to pick out a striped knit shirt that zipped up the front and a long, gauzy skirt in a floral pattern. Waiting for her change at the register, she noticed a rack of granny sunglasses and tried on a few pairs hastily before choosing one. She was stunned at the change in her appearance created by the tiny frames and blue plastic lenses.

"I'll take these, too," she said.

She left the store and continued down the street. It was weirdly liberating, this feeling of being someone totally different. Catching her reflection in another window, she had to pause and stare. She wouldn't have recognized herself. Elizabeth Ross had vanished.

Two men in their early twenties approached, and one let out an appreciative whistle. "Hey, baby," he murmured suggestively to her as they passed by, not seeming to expect a reply.

She stood there. Who had he been talking to? It had to be Stacy.

It was only when she remembered that she might attract attention by standing in the middle of the sidewalk that she was able to force herself to move on. The boots felt very different from her usual high-heeled shoes, and she found herself walking more quickly, with a slight spring in her step.

Will Elizabeth ever come back, she wondered. Would she ever be able to?

Chapter Nineteen

The doorbell was ringing insistently.

"Coming!"

Jack hastened toward the door, pulling his wallet out of his pants pocket as he walked. It would be the deliveryman from the liquor store with his order. He pulled three twenties out as he yanked open the door.

"*Surprise!*" Reda Mathias had a bright smile on her face, and her voice was gay.

Jack could only stare at her.

"I saw the man from the store in the lobby, so I offered to bring up the package." She handed him a large brown-paper bag, the bottles inside clanking against one another. "I paid for it, not to worry."

"Reda," Jack said dully, peering inside the bag to make sure it contained the right bottles, "what on earth are you doing here?"

She stepped inside without waiting to be asked. "Tea and sympathy. To comfort you, of course. You've been through such a terrible time."

Jack couldn't be bothered to respond. He went back into the living room to pour himself a drink. Reda followed.

"Here, let me," she said soothingly, taking the bag from him.

He watched in annoyance as she opened the bottle

and got two clean glasses from the bar. Reda was wearing a short red skirt and a tight white silk blouse, with bright-red high heels. It was her idea of a sexy outfit, he realized foggily. What the hell was she up to? He wanted her to go away, and fast. Leave him to his drink, and to the stupor and perpetual headache that he had become accustomed to.

"One for you and one for me," she said cheerily, handing him one of the drinks she had poured. "Reda's here, so you don't have to worry about anything. I'll take care of you."

Jack knew he should hide his irritation, but he was past caring. "Reda, I didn't ask you here. I prefer to be alone."

She gave him a hurt look. "Jack, I only wanted to help." Her voice turned coy. "You're alone all the time now. Wouldn't it be nice to have a woman around again?"

He took a long gulp of his drink. "No."

"I know you're upset." Drawing near, she put one hand on his forearm. "But I can help you." Her tone grew suggestive. "Please let me. I've always wanted to."

Jack drew back in disgust. "I don't know what you're getting at. But let me be crystal-clear about this. I'm not interested in you. I never have been. I never will be."

The smile faded from Reda's face.

"That's right." Jack's head was pounding. He massaged his temples furiously. "Your little flirtations have been in vain. Go look elsewhere."

Turning away, he wondered if a hot washcloth would relieve the agony in his head. When Reda spoke, it was practically a shriek. Stunned, he turned back to her.

"How dare you! You have the chance to be with me, and you turn me down like I'm some little chippie? Do you know how many men would give anything to be in your position right now?"

Very few would give anything at all, he wanted to

snap back. Oh, hell, he thought in exasperation, he probably shouldn't have been so hard on her. Under normal circumstances, he would never have spoken to her that way. After all, he had always known it would only cause trouble to antagonize her on a personal level. But right now, he really couldn't care less what happened to Reda or her job at the firm.

"Reda, could you just go now?" he asked tiredly. "My wife died. I'm not interested in you or anybody else for the moment."

"Yes, your wife is gone," Reda said, nodding her head vigorously. "So there's no more impediment to us being together. It's what I want. It's what you want, I know it is." She walked toward him. "I'm a wonderful lover, Jack. I'll do things for you I know your wife wouldn't have dreamed of."

Jack stared at her. "Have you gone crazy?"

She stopped. "You're not saying no, are you?"

"Damn right I'm saying no," he spat out. "This is making me sick. Please leave my house."

Her eyes blazed. "You're making a big mistake. You can't throw me out like this. I won't tolerate it." She clenched her hands into fists. "No man says no to me. Never."

In some distant recess of his mind, Jack knew he should actually be a little frightened by this woman's reaction. But now he just wanted her to get out.

"My wife is dead. Can you please leave me?"

Reda's face twisted. "That bitch. She did nothing for you. If I were your wife, I would have been at the office every day, figuring out how I could help you, make your life better and easier. She didn't do a goddamn thing for you. Just went out for lunch and shopping, I'll bet."

Jack had had enough. He took Reda's arm and roughly escorted her to the door. Even drunk, he was far stronger than she was. She struggled with him, but he held on.

"We're going to pretend this never happened," Jack said as she shoved her into the hall.

Her voice turned placating. "No, no, you just think it over," she said, her expression softening again. "I shouldn't have rushed you. I'm sorry. But I'll be around when you're ready."

Jack didn't bother to reply. He shut the door. And he had always thought Reda was such a top-notch lawyer. What kind of a lunatic was she?

Chapter Twenty

There she was.

Elizabeth knew she should be moving, crossing the street to get to Joey, but she couldn't bring herself to take the first step.

Come on, she reprimanded herself. You need her help, irritating as that is. Besides, if you put it off now, you'll just have to wait around again tomorrow until she appears.

The prospect of spending another evening pacing up and down the alleyway across from the law firm was enough to propel Elizabeth forward. She hurried across the street, following several feet behind her sister, who she guessed was heading toward the subway station.

Joey was carrying a leather bag nearly overflowing with files and papers. She wore a simple navy blue dress and navy pumps. Glancing down at her white T-shirt and the gauzy skirt she had purchased at the used-clothing store, not to mention her newly acquired brown suede shoulder bag with its long fringe, Elizabeth couldn't resist a smile at the turnaround in their roles. She knew how much Joey despised dressing the part of corporate lawyer. This whole business had to be torture for her.

As they turned the corner, Elizabeth saw her

chance. There was a recessed doorway ahead. Coming up behind her sister, she grabbed her by the arm and yanked her into the dim recess.

"Hey—" Joey started to shout as she was pulled off balance, but when she saw who was holding her, the shout died in her throat. She stared at the woman before her for several seconds.

"*Elizabeth?*"

"Yes, yes, it's me," she said hurriedly. "We need to talk."

"Jesus, look at you with the funky blond hair!" Joey was taking in her clothes. She peered at the granny glasses, grinning. "Did you just leave a be-in or something?"

"Very funny." Elizabeth reminded herself not to tangle with Joey but to get on to the important subjects.

Joey suddenly seemed to remember why her sister would be dressed that way. "For God's sake, why did you take off? Are you out of your mind? And now you're running around like some crazy woman in a damned costume. They're going to crucify you if you get caught."

"Listen," Elizabeth said urgently, "I really need your help."

"You know how guilty this makes you look." It wasn't a question. "Running off is tantamount to a confession."

Elizabeth didn't respond.

"Elizabeth?" Joey seemed disconcerted. "You didn't actually . . . do it, did you? Could you have, I mean . . ."

Elizabeth stared at her coldly. "I ought to smack you for that."

Joey looked abashed. "I'm sorry. I mean, it's not like I ever really thought . . . But you know you can't just run away and have everyone say, 'Oh, yes, clearly the whole business was a mix-up,' It doesn't exactly make you look like the innocent party."

"Look, I can't stay here much longer." Elizabeth

glanced around to make sure no one was watching them. "Here's what I need."

Joey's face hardened at the way her sister had dismissed what she said without even responding.

Elizabeth continued. "You were a lot closer to Mom than I was."

"You think?" Joey answered sarcastically.

Elizabeth ignored the jab. "Give me a list of people who might have wanted to hurt her, get back at her, anything you can come up with. You know what I mean."

"The police have been over all this with me."

"I don't care what the police have or haven't been over," Elizabeth said in annoyance. "They think I did it, so they're not going to look into anybody else. I have to find the truth before they lock me up and forget about the whole business. Did you tell them about anybody worth pursuing?"

Joey shrugged. "I guess not. There was no one that came to mind."

"Well, think harder. I'll be waiting, let's say at this exact spot, tomorrow night at nine, and I'd like you to give me a list. Whatever you can come up with."

"This is ridiculous. You're a boring New York lawyer, not Magnum, P.I. You don't know how to find a killer."

Elizabeth wanted to shake her. "Okay, let me appeal to you on this level. The sooner I get cleared, the sooner I'll get back to Ross, Jennings. Then you get the hell out of New York, which I'm sure you can't wait to do."

"True. But first I have to finish something for a friend."

"Something for a *friend*? I read the papers, Joey. You mean the militant revolutionary accused of murder?"

Joey stiffened. "That's right."

"Well, hey," Elizabeth said with a shrug, "maybe she can give me a few tips on how to live as a fugitive. God knows I could use them."

Irritated, Joey started to speak, then stopped as she considered what her sister had just said. "What the hell *are* you doing?"

"It's better if you don't know. Suffice it to say I now pay cash. But I have no identification because I have to use a fake name. It's sort of like being in a Kafka novel."

Joey took this in. "What name do you go by?"

Elizabeth looked at her skeptically. "What difference does it make?"

"I'm curious."

"Okay, it's Stacy Hubert."

"Stacy Hubert." Joey exhaled loudly. "Jesus, this is really insane."

Elizabeth put a hand on her sister's arm. "Will you please help me? Don't tell anyone you saw me, and make up that list."

Joey shook her head disgustedly. "Make me an accessory—terrific."

"I'll take that as a yes." Elizabeth smiled. "Now, how is Dad?"

Joey's eyes narrowed. "As always, Dad is fine. Dad is drinking himself into the grave, but he's still playing the great defender. I don't know how even you could put up with him, much less do his scut work year in and year out."

The smile melted from Elizabeth's face. She turned to go.

"Tomorrow night, nine o'clock," she said tersely.

She could hear Joey muttering. "Yeah, yeah, yeah. Big rendezvous with the hippie sleuth."

Elizabeth gritted her teeth in anger as she sprinted back across the street. *Damn* her sister. She wondered if Joey could be so rotten that she might actually not show up. She was the last person on earth Elizabeth wanted to have to depend on. Yet Joey might be the only one who could save her from this nightmare.

Don't screw me up, Joey, she begged silently. You *can't* hate me enough to destroy my entire life. At least I sure hope you can't.

She headed downtown. Before getting her hands on Joey's list, she had at least one candidate of her own she wanted to check out. Her father may have thought Reda Mathias's clumsy overtures to him were flattering or, at worst, foolish, but Elizabeth saw things differently. She had observed the way Reda stared at her father when he passed, the way she tilted her head, studying him when they sat in meetings together. Everything about her behavior around him struck Elizabeth as peculiar. Most disturbing was that time Elizabeth had heard her cancel the flowers for Molly.

She hadn't thought of Reda as a possible suspect until she was lying in bed one night in Maine, unable to sleep. It was surprisingly easy to picture the woman deciding that Molly had to be removed from the picture so Jack could be freed up. She could even imagine Reda going to the apartment and shooting her mother during a confrontation. Maybe I'm reading too much into her behavior, Elizabeth mused, but, then again, I thought I was being overly suspicious about the flowers. And I was dead on about that.

She looked up, surprised to see that she was already on Twenty-third Street. She hurried along with the crowds. Up ahead she saw a mother and daughter, the young girl dressed in what was obviously her ballet class uniform. From the back, Elizabeth couldn't tell for certain, but she guessed the girl was probably six or seven. She had on a white leotard and a white chiffon skirt with pink tights and sneakers. A pink backpack with a picture of a cat on it was slung over one shoulder. No doubt her ballet slippers were inside, Elizabeth thought, watching as the mother put an arm around her daughter's shoulder and, smiling, leaned over to kiss the top of her head as they walked.

Elizabeth's mind flashed back to her ballet recital the year she was eleven. She had been given a solo, and when it was over, her father came to the edge of the stage to present her with flowers, long-stemmed roses wrapped in clear, crisp cellophane and tied with a wide pink-satin ribbon. It had been a glorious moment. Her mother, unable—or, as Elizabeth saw it, unwilling—to leave the house, had, of course, missed it. Later, when Elizabeth and Jack returned home, her mother was waiting to greet her. Elizabeth had dodged her open arms, but Molly had leaned over in exactly the same way as the woman in front of Elizabeth just had, managing to kiss the top of her daughter's head. Elizabeth could envision herself, still cradling her flowers in her arms, dressed in a pale-blue tutu, her mane of hair tortured into a bun wrapped in tiny white flowers. She had barely endured her mother's kiss, instantly slipping away to run upstairs to her room.

I sure didn't cut you any slack, did I, Mom, she thought heavily. And in all these days since you died, I still haven't even cried for you.

Her destination was up ahead. Keystroke was a computer bar, a place where people could get a bite while sitting at a computer. Elizabeth had heard about it from a woman she had met playing tennis a few months before. As she explained it, if you wanted to be sociable, you could talk to the people around you; if not, you could log on and amuse yourself in whatever way you chose. That was just the kind of anonymous setting Elizabeth needed right now.

She went inside. It was crowded and noisy, but, of course, she realized, it was the after-work crowd. This probably wasn't the best time to be here. She made her way to the back, past the bar to a row of computers set up on a long counter against the wall. Patrons perched on tall stools were engrossed in the words and images on the screens before them. She didn't want to risk standing in such a crowded place for what might be a long time until a computer became available. Maybe she would come back later that evening.

As she turned to go, she saw that a man was watching her. He was standing only a few feet away, beer in hand. Dressed in a denim shirt and jeans, he had brown hair pulled back in a short ponytail. He was startlingly handsome. His gray eyes bored into hers.

Elizabeth felt a sudden lurching in her stomach as he flashed her a lazy grin.

"I don't blame you for not wanting to wait," he said, just loudly enough to be heard over the crowd. "It's open all night."

Elizabeth turned away, not wanting to provide him with any more of a look at her than he had already gotten. Although it was too late, she thought, since he had clearly examined her at his leisure already. She hurried out and began walking downtown, anxious to get back to the isolation and safety of her rented room. She turned around to see if he was following her, but there was no one else on the block.

It felt better to walk than to be trapped in a taxi or bus, where someone might report her before she knew what was going on. In her everyday life she was usually so busy, rushing from one appointment to the next, she never had time to walk long distances. It was very pleasant, really, despite the circumstances. I'm going to walk more from now on, she resolved. Then she smiled grimly. Assuming there was a "from now on" that involved normal activities such as appointments and rushing to them, she amended. Already she felt as if her old way of life were receding into the distance.

Chapter Twenty-one

Joey clutched the piece of yellow lined paper in her hand as she walked down the dark street. The list Elizabeth had asked for had proved to be somewhat meager. It had taken only a few minutes to write down the couple of people who might possibly have wished her mother ill. Looking at how few names there actually were made Joey newly sad. It was the first time she had realized how few people her mother had been intimate with, especially in the years when she and Elizabeth had lived at home. She'd had to content herself with the knowledge that her mother's life had become fuller and happier in the past decade.

At six o'clock, Joey had had to go to the federal prosecutor's office to see about a procedural matter for Lisa Martin's case. That had taken longer than she'd thought it would, but it was just now nine o'clock; she would still be on time to meet Elizabeth. She hoped her sister would be there. God only knows, she thought, what it would mean if she didn't show up.

She found herself shivering with fear as she approached the building. How odd, she thought. Walking toward Ross, Jennings—something she'd done hundreds of times—suddenly filled her with tension. She peered at the people passing her on the street, as if they knew she was here to meet a fugitive. You're being ridiculous, she told herself, making certain that no one was watching her and then turning into the doorway her sister had dragged her into that morning. Where is she, she thought, annoyed.

She leaned against the brick wall along the alleyway. Jesus, she thought, I don't know if this is more weird than frightening or more frightening than weird. She tried to think of something to do that would ease the tension but came up with no ideas at all. For lack of anything better, she pulled back the sleeve of her blouse and checked her watch. It was exactly nine o'clock. In her anxiety she'd actually arrived a little early. As she raised her eyes, she saw her sister walking toward her from across the street.

"Expecting someone?"

Joey turned around, startled, and there in living color was her worst nightmare—detective Gary McCullough, staring at her from a few feet away. He was still on the sidewalk outside the alley, with a clear view across the street should he care to look in that direction. Thinking quickly, she walked to where he stood and stopped right in front of him. Then she took another step closer, locking her gaze onto his. She put her hand discreetly behind her back and waved it, praying that Elizabeth would understand her signal.

"Well, I certainly wasn't expecting you," she said, stalling for time while she thought up a plausible reason for her to be huddling in a dark alley at this time of night. It took only a couple of seconds for her to come up with something.

She opened her purse and dug around in it, finally finding a crumpled box of Marlboros. "Then again, I am expecting cigarettes not to cause cancer any day now. Alas, the forces that be in our building don't share my optimism and have stopped us from smoking anywhere inside." She dug back into her purse to extract a book of matches. "I know some see it as a filthy habit, but nowadays I see smoking as the gateway to the great outdoors. After all, working long hours inside as I do, the new nonsmoking regulations help me get outside more."

McCullough took the matchbook from her and struck one, holding it out for her. She inhaled as shallowly as she could without calling attention to it. In fact, she'd stopped smoking years before and the cigarettes had stayed in her bag all that time. She'd kept them with her on the theory that not feeling deprived would make her stick to her guns. And it had worked. Until now, she thought, realizing how much she enjoyed the feeling of the smoke going down into her lungs. Well, she thought, there's three years out the window.

"I wouldn't have taken you for a smoker," the detective said, watching her take another drag, deeper this time.

She looked at him cynically. "You should pay attention to such mistakes. Perhaps it means you've been wrong about a lot of other things as well."

She had purposely been standing straight in front of him, blocking his view as they spoke. Now, hoping for the best, she moved a few inches to the side. If Elizabeth were watching, she'd be able to see his face, and she would know to stay away. The trick was to enable her sister to see the cop without allowing him to notice her. Acting as natural as possible, she kept her eyes glued to his. Keeping him occupied was the best chance she had.

"Things like what, for example?" he asked, responding to her comment.

"Well," she answered, relieved that he seemed happy to keep their conversation going, "about me, about my sister, about lawyers in general." Slowly she began to walk east, away from the direction where Elizabeth might still be standing. "You don't seem to have much affection for the folks in my profession."

He stopped and for an instant she was certain he knew what she was trying to do. But after looking around at nothing in particular, he brought his gaze back to hers. Elizabeth must have caught her signal and disappeared, she thought, heaving a silent sigh of relief.

"What makes you so certain that what I think is so damn negative?" he asked, walking alongside her once again.

She found herself laughing. "Gee, officer, do you think it could have something to do with the fact that you're following me around at nine o'clock at night, looking for misconduct of some dire variety?" She kept her tone uncharacteristically coy. If flirting was necessary to keep him with her, then flirting it would be. The last thing she wanted was for him to walk away and catch up with Elizabeth, wherever she had gone.

"Why do you assume I'm following you? Maybe I happen to have business down here. Maybe I have a wife and six children living a block away."

"Do you?" She realized to her dismay that she actually wanted to know.

He lifted an eyebrow. "Do I have business here or do I have a wife?"

"It was the six children that interested me," she responded, her usual cynicism returning. "So much energy. The busy job. The countless soccer games and spelling bees."

"The weeks in Disneyland," he continued, obviously enjoying himself. "The new shoes every two or three months, the constant visits to the orthodontist."

"So, how old are they?" She eyed him curiously, completely uncertain about whether he was serious or not.

He held up his fingers, apparently intending to count them off, then shook his head as if he couldn't remember. "They range somewhere between eleven and thirteen."

She smiled. "Which means you either have twins and triplets or the most exhausted wife in America."

He shook his head. "No wife. Spontaneous combustion. First case in history."

Joey gave him the benefit of a grin. "I was a believer for a couple of minutes there, Detective. I especially loved the picture of all of you in a wood-paneled station wagon, heading to the drive-in window of McDonald's."

He laughed out loud. "No wife. No children. No station wagon." He looked around the dark street, which was marked by a few bars and restaurants, many of them rather elegant and sophisticated. "And most of all, no McDonald's." He touched her elbow lightly, leading her toward the entrance of a small, expensive-looking restaurant, marked only by a beautifully scripted handwritten sign. "Why, for God's sake, would anyone in New York eat fast food?"

She removed her elbow from his hand, but stopped alongside him. "You seem to be leading me somewhere. Should I call my lawyer?"

He went ahead smoothly, opening the door of the restaurant and escorting her through. "You *are* a lawyer. As a matter of fact, this establishment is known for its raw meat—as an attorney, you should enjoy it."

For years, she'd been the one making the bad lawyer jokes, but it wasn't that much fun being the butt of his. She longed to insult him in return, to walk away and leave him flat. But she didn't dare. If she stalked off, he might leave as well, and there was still a chance he could run into Elizabeth. Instead, she followed him through the narrow bar toward the surprisingly spacious restaurant area, taking the seat he indicated near the back wall.

"Hey, Gary," a blond, heavyset waiter called from across the room.

"Sam, meet Joanna," Gary replied.

Joey realized that it had been she who'd jumped to the wrong conclusion. "So, this was your destination all the time," she said, looking at him squarely. "You never were tailing me."

"True, true, true."

"Well," she said, starting to push her chair away from the table, "in that case, I'll be on my way."

He reached across and took her arm, urging her

back to the seat. "Don't. Eating alone, even in a familiar place, is pretty damn lonely."

Reluctantly, she sat down once again.

"What'll it be?" the waiter asked, coming toward them, a pad in his hand.

McCullough answered first. "A bourbon for me and—" he inclined his head toward Joey.

"A Diet Coke," she said, then changed her mind. "Some red wine, whatever you have by the glass would be fine."

The policeman overrode her. "That sounds great. Why don't you just bring a bottle of Cabernet Sauvignon for the two of us. Forget the bourbon."

Joey wasn't sure that drinking was such a good idea. She had barely touched liquor since she'd moved to Montana. Somehow, that life was all about health and sobriety. But being with Gary McCullough was making her nervous. She still wasn't absolutely certain that he hadn't been investigating her tonight. Besides, he was too attractive for his own good. And that was never her easiest category. Maybe wine wasn't such a bad idea, she decided.

Within minutes, Sam had brought them a bottle of wine plus assorted appetizers that they hadn't even asked for.

"I eat here a lot," McCullough offered in explanation, as he picked up a tiny square of parmesan cheese and popped it into his mouth.

Joey's mouth began to water. She realized that she hadn't eaten anything since breakfast. Hesitantly, she reached out and claimed a celery stalk.

McCullough smiled at her. "Try the clams. They're terrific."

She held up her hand. "Give me a minute. I haven't even made any headway with the celery yet."

He shook his head. "You'd better hurry. There'll be more very soon, and it will all be delicious."

Sure enough, within minutes, Sam was back, carrying an enormous platter. Joey looked in amazement at the assortment of meats and fish they were being offered. Baby lamb chops were surrounded by grilled shrimp plus slivers of what looked like rare filet mignon and strips of calfs liver.

"Did you order all this while I was in a momentary coma?" she asked, taking a long sip of the wine.

Sam responded before McCullough could say a word. "For Gary, the best." He walked away, starting to clear a table across from theirs.

"I helped out during a robbery attempt here a couple of years ago," McCullough said.

"And he was even off-duty," Sam called out with a laugh, obviously eavesdropping. His tone turned more serious. "He saved the life of everyone in this restaurant, including me."

"Oh, yes," McCullough answered lightly, "and most of the people in Tibet and Madagascar too."

The waiter came to stand over them, his hand briefly coming to rest on the policeman's shoulder. "He risked his life and got shot in two places." Sam strolled away once again, then turned back. "And, by the way, he always insists on paying for his dinner, which, believe me, he doesn't have to do."

Joey took another sip of wine, then watched as the detective refilled her glass. "You have a fan," she observed.

"It's nice to have at least one," he said in response, looking at her provocatively.

"I have nothing against you," she said, answering his implied charge. "You seem to be a singularly gifted policeman, and, by the way," she added airily as she waved the celery stalk in his direction, "a fine purveyor of meats and cheeses."

"I'm a regular Oscar Mayer," he answered, chuckling. "Now," he said, taking his fork and reaching over to the platter, "taste this and tell me it isn't the best thing you've ever had." He placed a slice of rare beef on her plate and waited expectantly.

She lifted it to her mouth, then sighed with pleasure as she chewed. "What do they do to this?" she asked.

"It's culinary magic," Sam answered from far across the room this time.

"And the privacy is wonderful as well," McCullough observed loudly.

"It certainly is," Sam bellowed in return.

Joey began to laugh. Everything about this night was crazy. She lifted her wineglass and drank. Here she was, keeping a fugitive at large by eating with the policeman who was chasing her, guarded zealously by a waiter who doubled as a Jewish mother. Well, Dorothy, she thought to herself, I guess you're not in Montana anymore.

"What are you doing about Constance Truggle?" he asked, taking her by surprise. She had no idea he knew anything about her column.

"I have a stash of pieces ready for the next month or so," she responded.

He brought a forkful of lamb to his mouth. "They're good, your columns," he said after swallowing.

"I wouldn't have expected you to be one of my readers," she answered.

His face turned more somber. "I wasn't until a few days ago."

She suddenly understood the implication. "Meaning I'm a suspect as well."

"Not anymore," he answered simply. "We checked with the airline."

Suddenly she felt depressed. No matter how surreal the night had seemed, reality now returned with a thud. "You know," she said earnestly, "my sister could never have done what you suspect her of."

He looked at her thoughtfully. "Unfortunately, I can't be as certain of that as you seem to be." he lifted his glass. "Here's to your sister's innocence and the real culprit turning himself in."

Joey smiled sadly, then lifted her glass and drank the wine down. McCullough finished his as well, then reached for the bottle, pouring a little into his own glass and the rest into hers. She looked at it, realizing that she was beginning to feel slightly displaced. Not quite drunk, but at a slight distance from what was going on. I should stop right now, she thought, watching him empty his glass one more time. But her musings about her mother and her sister had made her feel so unexpectedly emotional. Maybe the wine would calm her. She took another sip of the red liquid, relaxing in the warmth of it, savoring its flavor.

"You know, whatever happens, you're going to be fine," he said, rubbing his thumb under her mouth as her mother used to do to wipe away the milk remaining on her lower lip.

Shocked by how comforting it felt, she finally pushed his hand away a few seconds after she should have.

"You don't know anything about me," she answered harshly, mortified by the emotions he had raised.

"Maybe. Maybe not."

He was looking at her intently now, not touching her but seeming to take in everything about her. She felt naked, exposed, and longed to be somewhere, anywhere else. She stood abruptly, pushing her chair back, starting to walk away, disturbed to realize how unsteady she was on her feet.

"I'll put you in a cab," he said, standing quickly and pulling his wallet out. He extracted a few bills and left them on the table, then came up to her, holding her firmly by the waist.

" 'Night, Gary," Sam called out as the door slammed behind them.

They walked next to each other in silence as he looked for a cab. With the exception of a couple of cars, nothing was coming.

"We can find a taxi on Second," he said, guiding her steadily.

Joey shivered as his hand tightened around her waist. It should have felt like a noose; instead she longed for it to envelop her.

"What do you want?" she cried suddenly, stopping where she was and looking up at him.

Clearly surprised, he removed his hand and looked back at her. She felt unexpectedly empty, wishing he would put it back, then changing her mind and wishing he would leave her alone. She could see him taking in the confusion that showed on her face. He raised his hand, as if he were about to touch her cheek. Then, at the last possible moment, he pulled it back.

She had no idea what impelled her to do what she did, but without conscious thought she found herself reaching for him, pulling his face toward hers, tasting the warmth of his generous mouth. His arms went around her as he kissed her greedily in return. As if it had been choreographed, they moved together, toward the steps leading up to a brownstone building a few feet behind them. She found herself leaning against a short concrete wall as he continued drinking her in with his lips and his tongue.

Unable to hold herself back, she responded in kind, some part of her mind registering the expanse of his chest and his shoulders as he crushed her to him. She felt an almost physical thrill in her stomach as his fingers threaded through her hair, cupping her head to bring her even closer. Groaning, he sank down onto the steps, pulling her with him. Now his fingers were exploring her neck, trailing under the collar of her jacket to touch the warmth of her flesh.

Before she knew what was happening, both of them were stretched across the steps. She was shocked at how much she liked feeling his legs surrounding hers, how the weight of his body made her feel completely safe. She found herself helping him as he reached under the starched white blouse she'd put on that morning, impatiently tearing it free from the waistband of her skirt. His fingers lingered on her bare midriff, then came to rest just on the curve of her breast. She barely realized what he was doing; she only wanted more.

"We're going to be arrested," he said, his voice hoarse with desire as he finally pulled his mouth away from hers.

She couldn't let him stop, instead reaching for his hand and covering it with her own. She led him as he enveloped her breast, his supple fingers bringing her nipple to life. His mouth moved to her neck as he stroked her, his touch soft but sure. With his other hand he traveled beneath her skirt, caressing the insides of her thighs, slowly running up to her center. She could hardly keep from moaning as his kneading fingers caused her body to writhe in pleasure.

Only the sound of a car screaming around the corner made them stop. They lay there, transfixed and silent, until the noise of the car abated.

"Listen, I live around the corner," he said, finally, in a voice that was more of a whisper. He forced himself to stand, pulling her up as well. He paused after they walked the couple of steps to the sidewalk.

"You don't have to do this, you know." He let her hand go and stepped away to leave a few feet between them.

She stared at him for a long moment, absorbing the sight of his rumpled brown hair, the fire in his dark eyes. She felt awash in ambivalence. He was the enemy. He was everything she'd been afraid of all of her life. Worse than that, he was the one person who could eviscerate the remains of her already shattered family. She had no business being with him. No business having dinner with him, no business making out with him like a horny teenager in a Mustang convertible.

No business wishing the night would never end.

She walked toward him, her steps tentative. But as she spoke, she'd never felt so certain of anything before. "I do have to," she said, reaching once more for his hand.

Chapter Twenty-two

Elizabeth sat on a chair facing the window of her room and sipped from a cup of tea. Guests had free access to the kitchen of the bed-and-breakfast, so it hadn't been a problem for her to go downstairs at four-thirty in the morning to boil water.

When I'm serving eighty years behind bars, she thought wryly, I'll have to remember to recommend this place to the inmates who are getting out.

She set the cup down on the round wooden table next to her. From her vantage point, she looked down onto Horatio Street, which was nearly silent and lit only by a few streetlights. A man walked his dog, several cars drove by, a couple laughed and kissed as they passed below her window. Mostly there was quiet, the peacefulness a marked contrast to the agitation of her thoughts.

At five-thirty a taxi pulled up to the brownstone across the street, discharging a well-dressed woman who had obviously been out all night. Elizabeth saw her pay the driver and hasten up the stairs to her front door, key in hand. Did you have a good time, she asked the woman silently as she watched her insert the key in the lock. Are you going home to an empty apartment to be totally alone?

She sighed, taking another sip of tea. The loneliness

of hiding was almost more debilitating than the fear of being caught. She felt as if she were in one of those sensory-deprivation tanks she had read about, with no movement or sound. Being anonymous and alone, with no one to talk to, was wearing away at her. I'm like some kind of sociology experiment, she reflected, a woman stripped of identity. Too bad I can't write a paper about this for some college course. An easy A-minus at least.

She stood, her attempt to amuse herself serving only to make her feel worse. Idly she moved about the room, touching the candlesticks on the mantelpiece, straightening the pile of magazines in a basket near the door. The gnawing sensation she had been attempting to ignore for the past several hours wasn't going to go away. She had to admit it.

Molly. Visions of her mother were flying around in her brain, forcing her to recollect things she hadn't even known were buried in her memory. With growing dread, she realized she could no longer ignore the truth that was pushing forward through it all. Molly *had* loved her.

Clearly, her mother had had some serious problems of her own when Elizabeth and Joey were small. But somehow she must have gotten over whatever they were, because she had in fact started going out of the house, attending school functions and Elizabeth's tennis matches, and doing the rest of the PTA-type stuff. Looking back, Elizabeth realized that Molly had done much, if not most, of what loving mothers do for their daughters. She had praised them, comforted them when they were sick or afraid, made their Halloween costumes, and run their birthday parties. Maybe not all the time, but most of it.

It was Molly who had purchased forty boxes of Girl Scout cookies the year Elizabeth had gotten sick during the time she was supposed to be selling them. And when Elizabeth had wanted that red silk dress in eleventh grade, the one her father forbade her to buy because it was so grown-up—sexy was what he meant, though he hadn't used the word—it was Molly who had come through for her. Elizabeth recalled that she was at her desk, reading, when her mother brought the dress into the room, not saying anything, just hanging it in the closet with a wink and her index finger held to her lips to indicate that it would be their secret. Wincing, Elizabeth recalled how she hadn't even smiled at Molly but waited until her mother left the room before rushing over to the closet, thrilled, to admire the beautiful garment.

I can't believe myself, she thought angrily. I didn't want to give her the satisfaction of knowing how excited I was. I never did. Wild horses couldn't have made me grant her a genuine smile or a spontaneous kiss.

Elizabeth dropped down onto the edge of the bed. God, how I punished her, she said to herself. Relentlessly, year in and year out. Punished her for not loving Dad. I was the self-appointed judge, and I did my damnedest to make her pay for her crime.

With a wrenching sob, the tears that had refused to come since Molly's death were suddenly there. In anguish, Elizabeth fell across the bed, crying so hard she could barely catch her breath. The waste of so many years, years when they could have had some kind of relationship if it hadn't been for Elizabeth's stubbornness, was almost too terrible to contemplate. All her anger, grief, and confusion came out in a flood until she was too exhausted to cry anymore. Finally the weeping subsided, and she pulled the pillow to her, hugging it as her ragged breaths slowed.

"I'm sorry," she whispered to her mother. "I'm so sorry. But now you're not here to forgive me."

She lay there for a long while. At last, she was able to get up. She went into the bathroom, pausing to gaze at the unfamiliar reflection in the mirror, then splashing her face with water. All she could do now was find the person responsible for killing Molly. It wasn't much, but it was the only thing she had left.

By the time she had dressed and started the long

walk to Ross, Jennings, it was nearly eight. Elizabeth tried not to think about the narrow escape of the night before, when Joey had waved her away from their meeting in the alley. She'd seen McCullough approach her sister. Elizabeth could only pray that the detective was just fishing around, maybe following Joey, rather than knowing for certain that Elizabeth was on her way. She had to admire Joey's cool. She had obviously been distracting him and doing a good job of it. If he had turned his head even a little . . . well, there was no point going over it. She would just have to be more careful.

Unfortunately, she wasn't sure what move Joey would make next to get the list to her. The simplest solution seemed to be waiting outside the office this morning, and if Joey didn't turn up, returning later at nine P.M., the same time they were to have met the night before. With luck, Joey would be thinking the same way. Not that I ever had a clue how or what Joey thinks about anything, Elizabeth reflected as she strode along, making sure to avert her eyes from the gazes of those around her.

She stopped at a diner two blocks away from her destination to get a cup of coffee to go. Instead of standing directly across the street from the law firm's offices as she had before, she waited at the end of the block, assuming it couldn't hurt to vary her movements in case anyone was looking for her. The day was already turning hot. She drank the coffee slowly, trying to make herself as inconspicuous as possible.

By nine-thirty, there was still no sign of Joey. Maybe I missed her, Elizabeth thought. When Joey had worked there full time, she always arrived promptly at nine. But maybe now she actually cared about what she was doing and had taken to coming in earlier. Elizabeth was annoyed at herself for not having considered that possibility. But she remained where she was.

At a quarter to ten a taxi pulled up to the building entrance and her father got out. Elizabeth took several quick steps closer, still careful to stay out of sight. She had been so worried about him, and she certainly couldn't trust Joey to give her a reliable report on how he really was.

Seeing him now, her heart sank. She had been right to be worried. God, she thought, he looks about twenty years older.

She watched him button his suit jacket as he entered the building. He had always walked with a jaunty gait, as if he owned the world. There was no sign of it today. His complexion was pasty, his hair barely combed. There was an indefinable something about him that spoke of failure and a broken spirit. Her heart went out to him.

He's alive, he's at work, he's basically okay, Elizabeth reassured herself as she turned to go. Unfortunately, that was the best that could be said, but things could be a hell of a lot worse.

Dejected, she began walking downtown again. I need to wrap this up, and everything will be fine again, she told herself. But there was a small voice inside her that reminded her that nothing would ever be the same; no matter how it all turned out, everything was different now and forever. Still, she argued with herself, I've got to get some answers if there's any hope of resuming a normal life.

She walked on, thinking about her father, fighting the urge to just turn back and go up to the law firm to see him. She couldn't blow everything now.

There was a telephone booth up ahead. Hell, she thought, I'm going to do it.

Jack had a private line in his office, one that he always answered himself. Elizabeth dialed the number and waited, her heart pounding. She could imagine that her father was sick with worry about her. And he could certainly be persuasive when he wanted to be, a trait for which he was justly famous. She only hoped he wouldn't attempt to get her to drop what she was doing.

"Hello?"

His voice sounded almost weak. Elizabeth wanted to cry.

"Hi, Dad," she said softly. "It's Elizabeth."

"Oh, Elizabeth, my Elizabeth," he moaned into the phone. "Sweetheart, it's you."

"I'm taking care of things, Dad, but I wanted to be sure you're all right."

"You just disappeared . . ." he said sadly.

She searched for the right words. "You know I can't expect other people to prove I'm innocent. You always taught me that, if something's important enough, don't rely on somebody else to do it right."

"No, no, you have to come back," he said piteously. "I need you. I need you."

She thought she heard him sniffling on the other end.

"Dad, please," she said soothingly, "it's all right. I'm fine, really I am."

His voice rose almost to a shout. "I can't do this without you. You have to help me."

Disconcerted, Elizabeth closed her eyes and tried to concentrate. Her father hadn't even asked where she was or if she was okay.

"What do you need me for?" she asked slowly.

His voice dropped down to a dejected whisper. "I can't go on like this."

"I love you, Dad, and once I get this straightened out, everything will be fine again, you'll see." She paused. "I know you miss Mom. I'm sorry."

"Christ, you don't understand," Jack groaned.

Elizabeth waited, but he didn't offer any more. "I'm sorry," she said again, helplessly. "And I love you. Take care of yourself, please. I hope to be back with you soon."

Her father hung up.

Elizabeth replaced the receiver, then stood just staring at the telephone. Jack Ross was always the strong one, the one to offer her comfort and solace. Not today. Was her father going to pieces? She had to do something fast so she could get home, back to reality.

Unhappily, she continued on her way. It was helpful to walk, the motion serving to comfort her. She couldn't afford to worry about her father the way she normally would. This was not a normal situation. As she went on, she forced herself to clear her mind, attempting to think about nothing at all.

Turning the corner of Fifteenth Street, she glanced up and took a sharp breath. The man she had seen at the Keystroke bar was approaching, the one who had given her the blinding smile. He was carrying a large box, a pale-blue drawing of a computer keyboard on the front.

He saw her at almost the same second, and apparently recognized her as well, for he instantly grinned. I wasn't wrong, she thought. This guy could knock you flat out with that smile.

"Hey, did you ever get on a computer?" he asked.

She shook her head. "Want to lend me that one?" she replied jokingly.

He came closer to her and stopped. "Is it for a good cause?"

If you only knew, she thought.

"It's to pry into the lives of others, digging into their darkest secrets." It wasn't that she told him the truth that surprised her as much as that she couldn't believe she was flirting with this total stranger. I'm losing my mind, she said to herself.

He raised one eyebrow. "Interesting. And oddly enough, that happens to be a specialty of mine."

His eyes were warm and friendly. Elizabeth, she reprimanded herself, this man is probably a mass murderer. Don't be an idiot.

He was maneuvering the carton over to one side so he could extend a hand.

"Kent Patterson. And you are . . . ?"

"Kent," she echoed, ignoring the question as she shook his hand. "Interesting name."

"It's short for Kentucky. Stupid, but true. My father was a die-hard Southern gentleman. The less said about him, the better."

Elizabeth's first instinct was to assume he was playing some angle. But she had dealt with a lot of con artists and liars in the course of her legal career, and something told her this man wasn't one of them.

"Did your father teach you about computers?" she asked disingenuously, hoping to find out just how much he knew about the subject.

"Bourbon and horses were more his speed. He lived on a lost planet." His expression turned slightly more serious. "You were checking out the screens at the Keystroke, and now you're checking out what I can do with a computer. You really need help with something, don't you?"

He isn't stupid, she thought. At least we know that much. "I know a little about computers, but not enough."

He tilted his head, appraising her. "They're actually my business. I install them, train people, all of that good stuff. I work out the software glitches when people get lost or confused or accidentally blow them up. I know a lot about them." He paused. "Like what information you can get from them. About basically anything or anyone."

"Are you available for hire?"

He flashed that smiled again. "You offering me a job?"

"Maybe. Is there some place we could go to discuss it?" She looked around, searching for a restaurant or some place where they might sit down. Elizabeth didn't pick up strange men on the street, she thought, but apparently Stacy did.

"You're in a rush, aren't you?" he responded. "Look, I'm booked all day with jobs. How about we meet tonight, let's say eight o'clock, at the NoHo Star on Lafayette? We can discuss your project."

She had to look for Joey that evening. "Can we make it ten?"

"Okay, ten it is."

"Thanks. I'll be there." She nodded. "And by the

way, my name is—" She stopped, making sure she was about to say the right thing. "—Stacy Hubert."

"A pretty name for a pretty lady," he said mildly, turning to go. "See you later."

She had to resist the urge to laugh. *You mean a phony name for a crazy lady.*

Chapter Twenty-three

Gary McCullough looked around the general store, amazed at the assortment. If you were hungry, there were sandwiches of every variety; if you were cold, there were ski parkas and windbreakers; if you were bored, you could buy Monopoly or Scrabble. There were postage stamps in the tiny section devoted to stationery, and bolts of velvet and calico in the larger section devoted to sewing.

"Can I help you with something?" a man looking to be in his middle sixties asked politely.

"I hope so," Gary answered, pulling a picture of Elizabeth Ross from the leather folder he carried. "Does this woman look familiar to you?"

The man eyed him with sudden suspicion. "I couldn't say," he answered shortly, walking away.

Gary followed behind him. "I'm not asking out of morbid curiosity," he said, pulling ahead of the man. He extracted his badge from his jacket pocket and held it out. "Miss Ross is wanted for murder by the New York Police Department. You'd be doing me a big favor by looking a little more carefully."

Once again he extended the picture. This time the man took it and stared at it for a while. Then he shook his head. "Nope. I don't think I've ever laid eyes on her."

Gary began to walk away, then stopped. "Does any-one else work here besides you?"

"Sure," the man answered. "My daughter's here all week long." Once more, he moved off, eager to help two other people who had entered the store.

"Is she here now?" Gary asked.

"Yup." He turned away abruptly, addressing his next remarks to the other customers.

Gary tried to hold on to a vestige of patience. "Can I see her?" he called out loudly, interrupting whatever they were saying.

The store owner looked back at him and tipped his head toward the back of the store. "It's a free coun-try," he responded none too graciously.

Gary walked to the back of the store, seeing no one at all. What a mess, he thought, as he wandered through the crowded aisles of spices and cleaning sup-plies. The Boston police had located Elizabeth Ross's car in a garage, and various inquiries had led Gary to this tiny town in Maine. He needed to know ex-actly where she was. Or, he acknowledged to him-self, more likely *had been*. It was certain that the owner of this general store didn't care if he ever found a murder suspect. Gary only hoped the man's daughter had more information and was more forthcoming.

That is, he thought, looking around for the girl one more time, if he really had a daughter. After another couple of minutes of aimless wandering, he saw a teen-age girl emerge from what must have been a basement area. Chewing gum and moving listlessly, she reeked of dissatisfaction, from her heavily made-up eyes to her skintight jeans.

"Excuse me," Gary said, approaching her. "I'm from the New York City Police Department, and I'm looking for someone."

Ah, he thought, noting the instant excitement in the girl's eyes. At least the daughter actually *wanted* to talk to him. Thank goodness for small-town boredom, he thought, smiling at her in a friendly way. He held out the picture he'd shown to her father.

She smiled proudly as she took it in. "Oh, I know her. She was here a few days ago."

Gary felt his pulse quicken. "When, exactly?"

She shrugged her shoulders. "I don't know."

"Do you know where she was staying?" he asked, certain she was going to shrug her shoulders yet again.

"Sure," she answered, surprising him. "The Figueroa place. My boyfriend saw her walking out of there."

"How do you know it was this particular woman?" he asked.

She broke into an evil grin. " 'Cause he's a sadistic bastard and couldn't wait to tell me how much prettier than me she was." She gave a small cackle. "He paid for that, believe you me."

Gary had the urge to be a hundred miles away, but there was business to do. "Where is the Figueroa place?" he asked, willing himself to remain polite.

"Up the road," she answered, looking bored once again now that she could tell he was about to leave. "You can't miss it," she added. "It's the fancyass cabin about a mile up Mountain Road."

Gary thanked her and walked out of the store. Starting the engine, he envisioned Elizabeth Ross. She was beautiful and, unlike the surly teenager he'd just left, elegant and polite. Of course, he thought, frowning, she also most likely murdered her mother.

He drove up Mountain Road, checking the names on the mailboxes. Jack Ross's alibi had checked out, so Elizabeth was suspect number one. Thoughts of Elizabeth turned to thoughts of her sister. Now there was someone who really knew how to be surly. He laughed at the thought. Even when she was being as mean as a snake, Joanna Ross was worth every minute. He couldn't get over her, wished he could exonerate her damn sister and get on with the business of falling in love. Because that was just what was happening. There was no denying it. Joey was everything he'd

ever wanted in a woman. She had brains and beauty
and wit and—well, everything, he thought, smiling to
himself. And if her sister really had killed their
mother, he pondered. What then? Would Joey ever
even speak to him again?

Out of the corner of his eye, he saw the name Figueroa. He pulled into the driveway, happy to see a car
there. Maybe he'd get lucky and find someone home.
Maybe even Elizabeth herself.

But when he rang the bell, the person who came to
the door was much shorter and infinitely more stout
than the woman he was looking for.

He held out his badge as he spoke. "Hi. I'm Detective Gary McCullough from the NYPD. I'm looking
for Elizabeth Ross. I'd heard she might be here with
you."

The woman barely looked at the badge. "I have no
idea who Elizabeth Ross is. I'm just the maid. The
Figueroas are away and I'm here to clean."

Gary pushed forward a bit, hoping she would invite
him in, but the woman wasn't giving an inch. Nor was
she offering any further information.

"Are you sure this woman hasn't been here in the
past couple of weeks?" he asked. "Are there any signs
of anyone living here?"

She looked at him, unfazed by his probing. "For all
I know, she's on a space mission to Venus. Now, you'll
have to excuse me. I'm having my lunch. Of course,
if you'd like to search the house, feel free."

Without another word, she walked back inside.
Gary stood there for a while. Finally, he shook his
head and went back to his car. He sat at the wheel,
thinking through what his next move should be. He
doubted that Elizabeth was hiding in the house. The
maid hadn't seemed nervous at all. But neither was
she helpful. In fact, no one was being especially
helpful. Everyone he'd spoken to had raved about
Elizabeth. A perfect human being, seemed to be the
general opinion. Even coworkers who ordinarily could
be needled into a few jealous tidbits that might prove

useful had only splendid things to say about the sainted Elizabeth Ross. The boyfriend might as well have been a mute. The father was too drunk to say much of anything every time Gary spoke to him. And Joey, well, his darling Joey wasn't about to give up a thing.

Frowning, he took his cell phone out of his pocket and dialed the precinct in new York.

"Lieutenant Anderson," he said when the switchboard answered.

After a few minutes he heard his boss's voice.

"Martin Anderson."

"McCullough," Gary answered. "Listen, I'm getting close to nothing. I'm sure the girl was here, but she isn't here now. I guess it's time."

Gary felt almost ashamed of himself. His boss had wanted to place a wiretap on the telephones of the people dearest to Elizabeth Ross days ago, namely Jack Ross, Peter Grier, and—last but not least—Joanna Ross. Gary had argued with him. There were easier ways of finding Elizabeth Ross, he'd said. When the Boston police had notified him about locating the car, he'd been relieved. See, he'd said to his lieutenant, I knew we could do this on our own.

But that had been wishful thinking. This was a murder investigation, and Elizabeth Ross had disappeared of her own free will. As much as he hated the notion of intruding into Joey's life that way, it was time to be a cop.

And if Joey found out what he had just acceded to, he wondered, would she even speak to him again, let alone touch him? Well, he thought with a sigh, he would face that when he had to.

God, he thought with a shudder, he hoped he wouldn't have to face that more than he'd ever hoped for anything before.

Chapter Twenty-four

"There's not a lot here, but I did the best I could."

Joey gave Elizabeth the folded piece of paper. Just as Elizabeth had hoped, her sister had returned to their meeting spot at nine o'clock that night.

"Explanations of why I included each name are there too."

"Thanks, I really appreciate it." Elizabeth began to back away. "I have to get going now."

"Wait." Joey rummaged around in her briefcase and extracted a large manila envelope. "I spoke to my friend, Lisa, about you. She gave me a phone number. I think this might help."

"What is it?" Elizabeth asked, puzzled, as she reached for the envelope.

"It pays to have friends who are radical fugitives," Joey said with a grin. "They know how to do the darnedest things." She waved and turned away. "So long, big sis. Stay out of sight until you have the answers. When you emerge, you're going to owe me a big, fancy dinner."

Elizabeth opened the envelope. She extracted a small pile of documents and plastic cards. A driver's license, a Social Security card, a VISA card, and a passport with an old picture of her. God knows where Joey had come up with *that*.

All in the name of Stacy Hubert.

Elizabeth looked up, but Joey was already out of sight. So that was why she had asked what name Elizabeth was using.

She didn't know whether to be stunned or touched. It was so totally out of character for Joey to do anything for her. It couldn't have been easy to pull this together so quickly, and it certainly hadn't been free. Elizabeth felt almost humbled by an act of such generosity on her sister's part. If our positions had been reversed, would I have done the same for her, she asked herself.

She started to walk. Yes, I suppose I would have, she thought. But part of it would have been because I'm the big sister. It was my job to hold things together. I've always been on automatic pilot about keeping the family in one piece. Joey did this solely because she wanted to.

Elizabeth was shocked to find her eyes welling up with tears. She had never realized how happy it would make her to think that Joey actually gave a damn.

Her mind still on her sister, Elizabeth tucked the envelope under one arm and unfolded the yellow piece of paper Joey had handed her that contained names of those people who might have had some interest in harming Molly. She scanned it, anxious to learn whatever she could. That afternoon she had gone with a real estate agent to look at Molly's studio, which was now for rent. Pretending to be an artist from California, she had done her best to examine the space, but nothing struck her as odd or out of place. She prayed that following up on Joey's list would prove more productive.

Hector Rivera was first on the list. Elizabeth remembered him vaguely. He had been a doorman in her parents' building. According to Joey, Molly had informed the co-op board that he had been drunk while on duty six months before. She had had a nasty confrontation with him in the lobby the day he got fired.

His name was followed by Verna Nieman, a woman who also painted costumes for a living. Molly had beaten her out on several job bids. Joey listed the three productions on which this had occurred, explaining that Molly had mentioned it specifically to her because she was upset at how personally Verna seemed to be taking the losses. Elizabeth had never heard anything about it. She was pleased to see that Joey had provided her with the woman's address and telephone number. *I gave Dad some excuse to get him to look her up in Mom's phone book,* Joey's notes said.

Michael Weaver was third. He was some kind of artist who had the studio below Molly's. She had mentioned to Joey that he was around a lot, but in the past few months there was something about him that was disturbing her. She was uncomfortable whenever he appeared in her studio in a way she had never been before. *Don't ask me what that means,* Joey had written, *but it certainly fits the bill in terms of what you asked for. Mom and I never got into it further than that.*

Last, there was a description of a man in his forties, a homeless person who spent much of his time on the block where Molly and Jack lived. Joey could only describe him as having long, greasy gray hair and wearing a black overcoat. She noted that Molly had mentioned him occasionally because he was mentally ill and frequently vented his fury at her as she walked past him. Joey had spoken to Molly the afternoon he had roused himself to kick her as she went by. She had been frightened and extremely upset, both by the violence of the kick, delivered with all his might from his perch over a grating, and by the fury in his eyes. She told Joey she had a bruise on her calf that lasted for months afterward.

Elizabeth had never even heard about this incident. She shook her head. Boy, what she didn't know about her mother's everyday life was pretty much everything.

Glancing up, she was surprised to realize she was

nearing the NoHo Star, the place where she was to meet Kent Patterson. Her original plan had been to log on to a computer somewhere herself to check into Reda—and now these other four people. But her knowledge of computers extended little beyond her E-mail at the office and giving directions to the parale-gals and other research assistants. Getting names and addresses wasn't going to be enough. Only someone more conversant with computers than she was would know how to get access to the really useful informa-tion and get it quickly.

She pulled open the door to the restaurant and went in. It was noisy and crowded. She peered through her granny glasses, and ran her hand through her hair, noticing that she was actually getting used to its shorter length. I think I'll leave it this way, she thought. *Easier to take care of in prison,* a small voice inside her retorted.

"Stop it," she whispered to herself fiercely.

"Stop what?" A girl with a blond ponytail had ap-proached her, menus in hand, apparently the maître d'.

Elizabeth smiled. "Nothing at all. Just arguing with myself."

"I do it all the time," the girl said with a laugh. "Would you like a table?"

"Actually, I'm meeting someone." Elizabeth scanned the room. Kent was there, sitting at a table at the far end of the room, flipping through a magazine. "I see him, thanks."

She moved past the girl. As he reached for the bot-tle of beer on the table in front of him, he glanced up and saw her. He rose, smiling broadly, as he tossed the magazine, a copy of *Personal Computing,* aside.

"My mystery guest. Please join me, Miss Stacy, and tell me what I can do for you."

You can put your arms around me and kiss me. The words popped into her head so abruptly and with such force that for a moment she was afraid she had actu-ally said them out loud. She suppressed the laugh that threatened to escape.

"Let's just talk for a few minutes, okay? About nothing in particular."

"You got it. Would you like something to drink?"

"A glass of orange juice mixed with club soda, please."

He gave a low whistle. "I can't handle more than one or two of those myself. You're a drinker to be reckoned with."

She laughed. "Darn right."

He signaled to the waiter, ordering another beer for himself as well. Then he sat back, his eyes roving over her face, her hair, her shoulders. He was taking in every inch of her. She shifted in her chair, uncomfortable under his scrutiny.

"So . . . ?" he asked softly.

Slowly, she removed her granny glasses and folded them. "I just moved down here. I'm staying at a B-and-B until I find a place. So far, I don't know my way around too well, but I like it."

"Where did you move from?"

She decided to stick close to the facts. "Uptown, actually. Which is, as you know, a different city altogether. I never spent much time down here."

He looked at her curiously. "Why the sudden change of heart?"

She shrugged. "Life was getting stale."

He took a swig of Rolling Rock from the bottle the waiter set down before him. "That simple, eh?" he asked, clearly not believing her.

"Almost." She stuck the tip of her finger in her drink and swirled the ice cubes around.

"You have family in New York?"

"Some." She drank from her glass.

"Well, that tells me a whole lot of nothing about you," he said, folding his hands on the table like a schoolboy. "But far be it from me to ask."

"Let's hear about you," Elizabeth prodded. She observed how long and slender his fingers were, wishing she could reach over and touch them. Get a grip, she warned herself.

"I'm thirty-five, never been married, don't own any pets or have any bizarre personal habits. I floated through a series of meaningless jobs to support myself as a ski bum for a number of years. The computer thing just fell into my lap. I'm good at it, and I like it."

He paused to take a sip of his beer. Then he leaned forward and looked directly into her eyes.

"More to the point, I will be glad to help you find out anything you want to know about anybody. It's no big deal—the information is there for the taking. I assume you have a good reason for wanting to check someone out, but even if you don't, we can consider it sort of a date, hanging out together, snooping into the lives of your friends or, perhaps, your enemies. You don't have to bother explaining why."

"Really?" She took a deep breath. "You're making this very easy for me. I have four, no, five, people I need to get information about. Just see what's in their background that might be relevant to me. I promise you it's for a good cause."

"Your cause is my cause." He put some money on the table as he stood, then extended his hand to her. "Shall we log on, madame?"

"Where are we going?" she asked as she got up.

He tilted his head. "What you're asking for requires a little privacy, don't you think? We're going to my place. Two blocks from here."

"Of course." She nodded.

He laughed. "Before you get nervous about going to my apartment, let's try and remember who asked whom for what here, okay? We'll just get on the computer, as promised."

She smiled. "Of course."

I must seem like the biggest fool, she thought as she walked out ahead of him. Here I pick him up on the street, blatantly tell him I want to use him, and then get all scared about his offering to do what I want. What's with me?

But she knew the answer. If he hadn't been so attractive, she wouldn't have been nervous at all. I'm more scared of what *I* might do than what *he* might do, she realized. When I changed my hair, I must have changed my age, too—I feel like I'm about twelve.

They walked along, Kent making easy conversation, Elizabeth focusing on not making any mistakes that might give her away. His apartment turned out to be a large loft, most of its contents hidden by partitions walling off the personal part of the space. Near the front were several leather armchairs on casters and three enormous desks, each holding a computer and an assortment of papers and books in messy stacks that threatened to topple over at any second.

Kent shut the door behind them and sat down at the nearest desk.

"So who's contestant number one?" he asked, swiveling around to face her. "Oh, if you want a drink or something, you can help yourself. The kitchen's back there." He jerked a thumb in the general direction of the rest of the loft.

"I'm fine, thanks." She pulled up a chair next to him. "I want to find out about a woman named Reda Mathias. That's R-E-D-A. She's an attorney at Ross, Jennings, and Trent. In her forties, lives in Manhattan. I need to know what her story is. Does she have anything weird in her past? Or is she a totally upstanding citizen?"

Kent's fingers were already busy on the keyboard. "You don't happen to know her Social Security number right off the bat, do you?"

She shook her head.

"No problem." He was typing so quickly, she couldn't even see what he was doing. "The first thing is to access the National Crime Information Computer, NCIC. It's exclusive to law-enforcement groups, although private eyes can access it for a fee."

"You fit into one of those categories?" Elizabeth asked, surprised.

He grinned. "Hacker-slash-adventurer is more the description for me. We can go just about anywhere."

"Oh." She was hardly in a position to criticize.

"A date of birth would be a huge help." He turned to her expectantly.

Elizabeth started to say she didn't know, but hesitated. There had been a birthday party for Reda at the office. When was that? She searched her memory. It was snowing, she remembered that. And it was around Christmas.

"Got it," she cried. "December twenty-fourth. Everyone left for the holiday right after the party."

"The party?" Kent asked.

"Um, never mind. December twenty-fourth. If I remember correctly, she's about forty-six."

Kent did some quick figuring in his mind. "That would make her birthday 1952 or '53. Okay," he continued, still watching the screen. "NCIC has a subprogram called Triple I. That's the Interstate Identification Index. With a name and a date of birth we can see in what states that name and birth date has been arrested. And it'll give us the state's arrest I.D. number."

"The what?"

"SPBI. State Police Bureau of Investigation number." He kept typing. "You get assigned one when you get arrested. That'll also get us the Social Security number, so we can access other stuff. In Triple I, we get phonetic matches of the name, if the person ever used any aliases, and what they were. We'll go into the credit companies to get addresses, outstanding loans, marriages. We can find out pretty much anything you want to know. Lexis-Nexis will tell us a credit and personal history—houses she owns, spouses' birth dates, stuff like that."

"Great." Elizabeth was embarrassed to realize she had paid so little attention to how the law firm's staff got their background information. She made a mental note that she would immediately become conversant with what went on in Research at Ross, Jennings—if she ever went back. A big *if*.

"Here we go." He pointed to the name on the screen. "Reda Mathias."

Slowly they scrolled through the information Kent was pulling up, screen after screen of details about Reda's life. Elizabeth had been one of the people who interviewed her when she was being hired, and she had seen her résumé. Reda had neglected to mention several jobs she had held at law firms in and around New York. They turned out to be legitimate, respectable firms, mid-sized or bigger. Elizabeth was mystified. It didn't make sense for an attorney to leave jobs in the legal community off her résumé—unless there was something to hide. Reda had lived at several different addresses in Manhattan, New Jersey, and Westchester, an oddly high number in Elizabeth's opinion but hardly illegal.

"We're going into the New York City Division of Criminal and Civil Records," Kent told her, his fingers moving rapidly again over the keyboard. "We'll see if any actions have been brought against her."

He scowled, reading the lines scrolling up the screen. "Bingo!" He smiled and pointed. "A Marian Linden sued our Reda for emotional distress in 1993."

Elizabeth picked up the pile of pages Kent had printed out from previous screens they had searched. She flipped through, trying to find out where Reda had been working in 1993. There it was: Shaffer, Linden, and Meadows on Third Avenue, an address in midtown.

"Linden," she said aloud. "Linden is the name of the woman who sued Reda? Either one of the managing partners or the wife of one, probably."

Kent was already on to the next step. *"Harley Linden,"* he read from the computer screen, *"born 1943, one of the three founding partners of Shaffer, Linden, and Meadows, 1981."*

Elizabeth slid her chair closer to his, reading alongside him. "So, Marian is his wife. Or was. *Divorced from Marian Lebow Linden, December 1993.* Well, well, well."

"If you're game," Kent said, "you could always call up this Mrs. Linden lady and ask her what the deal was."

"Just what I was thinking," Elizabeth answered. She looked at her watch. "Although I guess waking her at one in the morning might not be the smartest move if I want her to open up to me."

Kent was quiet, and she could feel his eyes on her. Their chairs were close, angled so that their knees were touching. Elizabeth was suddenly aware of exactly how close they were, of the pressure of his leg against hers.

"Is one o'clock late enough to bring this portion of our date to an end?" he asked softly.

Her heart was beating so hard, she felt certain he could hear it. "You've been so nice to help me," she managed to get out.

"I didn't do it to be nice." He gently took one of her hands in his and interlocked their fingers. "I did it so you would *think* I was nice."

His face was coming closer to hers. She felt a thrilling surge of anticipation, knowing he was about to kiss her.

"And I do . . . think you're nice." She was whispering. "Very nice."

"That's good," he whispered back.

Her eyes closed as his lips met hers. They kissed, deeply, rising together from their chairs to stand pressed against one another, her arms going around his neck, his encircling her waist.

For an instant Elizabeth had the urge to run. I'm vulnerable because I'm lonely and alone, she thought. Peter's face flashed into her mind, almost making her pull away. But as Kent wrapped her in his arms, she knew she wasn't going to resist. She returned his kisses with hungry kisses of her own, as they moved over to a large couch several feet away and lay down on it, his hands stroking her back, her breasts, her face.

"Stacy," he murmured. "Stacy."

For a moment she stiffened. But then she pushed aside all her thoughts of her deception, of Peter, of how she herself didn't even know who she was anymore. As his lips trailed across her throat, she let out a long sigh and let herself get lost in her desire for this stranger.

Chapter Twenty-five

Joey looked out the window as she waited for a guard to bring Lisa Martin to her. How painful the sight of the beautiful expanse of trees and broad green lawn must be to the women locked up in the correctional facility, she thought. Valhalla itself was a typical small Westchester town, verdant and attractive, well-maintained houses dotting the appealing suburban landscape. The dreariness of the prison was a cold rebuke to its surroundings, a fact that must have made its inhabitants feel even more confined and hopeless.

"Hi," Lisa said with feigned brightness, as a uniformed guard led her to the seat across from Joey.

The guard left them alone, and Joey looked at her friend critically. Though Lisa was less pale than she had been the last time they'd met, in New York City, she still seemed only a shadow of the woman Joey had known.

"How's it going?" Joey asked, clasping her hand in greeting.

"Well . . . I got to see Hal and the kids for a while on Tuesday," Lisa answered. "Karen is confused and Josh is angry, but at least they know what's going on."

Joey nodded sympathetically. "I'm having dinner with them one night this week. I told them I'd take them someplace wonderful. What do they like?"

"Josh likes whatever Karen doesn't and vice versa. In short, good luck." After a brief smile, she seemed to sink back into herself. "I really do appreciate all your help. God knows, I've left them without much help of any kind."

"Hal seems to be coming through like a champ," Joey said enthusiastically. Although from Joey's brief conversation with him, Lisa's husband seemed about as lost as her teenage children.

"Poor Hal. For twenty years, he thinks he's married to a combination of Martha Stewart and Betty Crocker. Imagine his surprise . . ." The words seemed to die in her throat.

Joey looked on sympathetically, wishing she could magically free her friend from her heavy burden. Well, she thought, I may not have magic to offer, but sitting here chatting is not going to do anything at all.

"The sooner we get down to business, the sooner we get you out of here," she said authoritatively, removing a ballpoint pen, a sheaf of notes, and an empty pad from her enormous black leather pouch and placing them on the table in front of her.

Lisa looked back at her, her face almost devoid of expression. "Nothing's going to get me out of here, Joey." She heaved a sigh. "If it were up to me, *I* wouldn't even let *myself* out of here."

Joey narrowed her eyes. "Luckily, it isn't up to you." She picked up the pen and clicked it into working order. "I need to know more about the rest of the people with you at the time of the bank robbery." She lifted up the stack of notes in front of her. "I read through everything you wrote for me, but there are a lot of questions left."

Lisa shrugged her shoulders. "What difference does it make? I'm guilty no matter what."

"Just humor me," Joey answered. "First of all, Janie Saltzman was your roommate, right?"

"Uh-huh."

"She was the daughter of a dentist and his wife from Scarsdale?"

Lisa nodded yes. "We used to go up there for dinner once in a while." She breathed deeply. "They were really nice people. Conservative. They used to urge us to go to mixers at school. I remember one Sunday afternoon just before Christmas vacation, they picked us up and took us downtown to see *The Fantasticks.*" Her face grew dreamy. "After the play, we went to one of those coffeehouses in the Village, across the street from the theater, and drank cappuccino. God, they were nice. They were all excited about being in Greenwich Village, looking at all the hippies."

"You know, it's funny," Lisa continued, the set of her mouth turning grim, "they loved their daughter so much, but they had no idea who she was or what she was about to do."

"Was Janie the one who got you interested in the movement?" Joey asked.

Lisa looked thoughtful. "It's hard to remember. It was all so long ago." She turned her head to gaze out the window. After a few minutes, she looked back at Joey. "Well, I guess in a way she was. She started dating Bobby Sarkalian in the fall. I mean we were all doing antiwar stuff before that . . ." Her face grew rueful. "Everyone we knew was against the war, but Bobby and his friends were into more serious civil disobedience than the rest of us. Janie and I thought we were a big deal if we marched or took over the dean's office for a couple of days. Bobby and Tony and Paul had gone much further than that."

"What do you mean?"

"Well, the three of them were political science majors . . . no, maybe Tony was a history major. Anyway, they believed strongly in breaking the law to support the more important underlying human law."

"And what law was that?"

"Oh, the gross indecency of what we were doing in Vietnam, how many lies were carried on the news every night . . . made-up body counts and self-serving politicians." She smiled suddenly at Joey. "I forget

how young you are. You wouldn't remember. Trust
me, as ashamed as I am about what happened, I've
never been sorry about our stance on the war."

"Go back to the five other people."

"Well, Tony was from a political family. His grand-
father had been a union organizer in the twenties and
thirties. And Paul was kind of like me. He came from
a really religious Catholic family in Southbury, Con-
necticut, so his opposition was based on humanitarian
principles. Now, Bobby was different." Without realizing it, Lisa had begun to grin. "He would have been
a rabble-rouser in any generation. In the twenties, he
probably would have been a bootlegger, and in the old
West, he might have ridden alongside Jesse James."

Joey leaned forward. "It sounds as if you found
him attractive."

Lisa nodded thoughtfully. "Oh, I did. Everybody
did . . ." For a moment her face came to life. "But
Janie was the one he loved. She was the only person
who could even rein him in from time to time."

"Rein him in how?"

"Well, he'd wanted to break into the New York
draft board office and burn records. Janie had talked
him into sticking with acts that were somewhat less
criminal than that. At least, up until the time we got
to the bank in Peekskill."

"So what made all of you decide to go that far?"

"You know, I'm not really sure. By that time Freddie had come into the group."

"Whose friend was he?"

"I never really knew. One day there were five of
us, and it seemed like the next there were six."

Joey looked up from her notes. "Was he the one
who suggested sticking up the bank?"

Lisa shrugged her shoulders. "I don't know . . . I
don't think so." She rubbed a hand across her forehead. "You know, all this happened before the wom-
en's movement really took place. In those days, Janie
and I would be informed of decisions pretty much

after they were made. You'd walk into a room and suddenly there would be a game plan."

"So all of you lived in the dormitories?" Joey asked conversationally.

"Well, all of us except Freddie. He wasn't actually a student, I don't think."

Joey looked confused. "So what was he doing with all of you?"

Lisa shrugged once more. "There were thousands of guys like Freddie around the Columbia campus, people who preferred hanging out with students to actually growing up and going to work." She smiled.

"What's so funny?" Joey asked.

"Oh," Lisa said, "the notion of Freddie growing up or getting a job. The only thing he ever wanted to do was play cribbage."

"Cribbage?"

Lisa looked amused at her blank response. "What kind of childhood did you have, anyway? Cribbage is a card game where you keep score with pegs on a wooden board."

"So Freddie just lived to play cribbage?"

Lisa laughed out loud. "Freddie lived to *win* at cribbage. He used to make the rest of us play all night long, and he virtually never lost. Once, over Christmas break, I happened to win a few games in a row. Freddie threw his mug of coffee at the mirror above my dresser, he got so mad. God," she said, shaking her head, "did that guy hate to lose."

Joey rifled through the notes Lisa had given her, but she didn't seem to find what she was searching for. "So, how did Freddie live? I mean, if he didn't work and all he did was play cards . . ."

Lisa shook her head helplessly. "You're asking questions from almost three decades ago. I don't even remember who *I* was, let alone how anyone else got by."

Joey had only a few more questions. "Three of you were never caught," she said, straightening the loose notes into a neat stack. "You and Freddie and Tony.

Did you ever get in touch with either of them when you were underground?"

"Not exactly," Lisa responded. "I heard some things about Tony through the grapevine. A cousin of his helped me out for a few months in Pittsburgh. According to him, Tony ended up in Canada. Freddie, I don't know."

Joey stood up. "Would you still be able to get in touch with Tony's cousin?"

Lisa stood as well. "Maybe. His name was Raffia, same as Tony's, so if he hasn't moved . . ." Her voice trailed off as she saw a police guard come up behind Joey.

"Are you finished here?" the guard asked.

Joey hugged Lisa quickly and started to walk away. "I'll be back in a couple of days. Any messages for Hal and the kids?"

Lisa's face softened. "Love and love and more love."

Joey smiled.

Joey looked at her watch impatiently. She'd been stuck on the narrow highway for almost twenty minutes, because of a collision just a couple of miles south of Valhalla. Now the sudden appearance of a traffic light, smack in the middle of the speeding cars, caught her by surprise. She always forgot that there were three or four lights on the Saw Mill River Parkway. A good reason to take the Deegan next time, she thought, looking idly in her rearview mirror.

The man at the wheel of the red Ford behind her seemed familiar. She scrutinized his face as she waited for the light to change. Of course, she realized suddenly. He looked a lot like Charles Durning. She conjured up the image of the portly actor and once again observed the face of the stranger behind her. Yup, she thought. Charles Durning would definitely play that guy in the movie.

As the light went from red to green, she started up once more. There weren't that many cars on the road at three in the afternoon, and her mind began to wander. She had so much information to sift through. How could she get it all done while she was supposed to be readying a legal strategy? And how are you supposed to fit Gary McCullough into your life, an unexpected voice from within her head asked. Her foot grew heavier on the gas pedal. That was the last thing she had time to think about. She hadn't heard from him since the night they'd spent together, nor was she about to call him. It was crazy, impossible.

Damn, she thought, as another traffic light appeared, its yellow turning quickly to red. She frowned in annoyance and slowed to a stop. Miss one, you miss them all, she realized, taking her hands off the wheel and raising them above her head as best she could in the confines of the car. She couldn't really stretch in the few inches between the top of her head and the roof of the car. She pushed the button to open the sunroof. At least she could get some air.

She looked up, watching the glass as it receded, then twisted her head from side to side to stretch her neck. Funny, she thought as she glanced out the back window, there was the red car again, but this time, instead of being directly behind her, he was in the other lane. And he was hanging back twenty or thirty yards, although there were no cars in front of him.

Damn, she thought. He's a cop. He's following me. That was the only possible explanation. Thoroughly irritated now, she sped down the highway as the light turned green, then pulled off suddenly at an exit somewhere in Yonkers. Sure enough, the red car swerved off the highway as well. But this time, instead of pulling ahead, she slowed to a halt.

The red car slowed as well, waiting about twenty yards behind her. She sat there for a moment, undecided about how to proceed. Then, with a grunt of disgust, she opened the car door and got out. She walked toward the red car, stopped beside it, and stared in at the driver who'd been on her tail. The man hesitated, then drove off.

She could see him checking his rearview mirror as he pulled away. Hell, she thought, wishing she had the time to stay just where she was for the next few hours. She didn't. That was all there was to it. She got back in her car and drove to the corner. Sure enough, there was the red Ford, its motor idling. She pulled alongside the car and stopped. At first, the driver did nothing, not even catching her eye. But finally he rolled down his window.

"I'll be getting on the Henry Hudson, then taking the West Side Highway all the way to Fifty-sixth Street," she said conversationally. "I should be at my office by six or so."

The man smiled at her ironically, but that didn't stop him from falling in behind her as she maneuvered her way back to the highway.

It was many hours later when she managed to finish up for the day and leave for home. At least I won't be waking Tom up, she thought as she stopped at a small French bistro on Sullivan Street. Four days before, she'd thanked Tom profusely and moved out of his apartment into the small one-bedroom apartment that she'd sublet for the next few months. Situated near Houston Street, it was surrounded by restaurants of every possible ethnic stripe, but she'd eaten at Jean Claude every night since she moved in. Scouting out new places was the last thing she had time for. Besides, she told herself, taking a sip of the red wine she'd ordered and contemplating the simple menu, good French country food wasn't exactly ubiquitous in Montana.

She ordered the steak frites and pored over the notes she'd taken that afternoon. What could she really do for Lisa, she wondered as she read through the sections on all the people who'd been involved in the bank robbery. There was no denying Lisa's participation—that wasn't even in question. So the issue remained, what were the legal options here?

By the time she'd come up with the basics of a working plan for the next few days, her dinner was over. She'd barely tasted the morsels of rare beef or the perfectly cooked fries. All she was really thinking about was Lisa Martin. As she walked outside and turned toward the apartment, she thought of one new possibility, something that hadn't even occurred to her before. She strode along the crowded street, imagining what the difficulties might be.

She was paying little attention to where she was going, nor was she aware of anyone else around her, so she was shocked when Gary McCullough turned up beside her. She felt a small thrill of pleasure, quickly followed by a burst of anger as she remembered the man in the red Ford.

"Am I being followed all day every day, or do I get weekends off?" she asked, avoiding eye contact as they strolled along together.

"No rest for the wicked," he answered, taking her hand in his and interlacing their fingers.

She pulled away and began to walk at a faster pace. "At least the guy this afternoon kept his distance. You might want to master that technique."

He ruffled the curly brown hair at the nape of her neck. "That's just too hard. Sorry."

She wheeled around, her face betraying her rage. "I'm not kidding, Detective. You have obviously demonstrated who's in charge. Enough now."

Gary stopped, his eyes oddly guarded. "I didn't sleep with you to demonstrate . . . well, anything. I slept with you because I wanted to. Which, I assume, was the same reason you slept with me."

She backed away from him. "I slept with you because I thought you were human. Unfortunately, I was wrong." She turned to look in the window of a pottery store. "You're a policeman and I'm the woman you need to keep tabs on."

"The department is keeping tabs on you, not me," he said, coming to stand next to her. "I'm here because I want to be."

She glared at him. "Yeah, you're all about want, aren't you?"

He remained unfazed. "If that means I desire you, then the answer is yes."

"Well, I *desire* to know who killed my mother, and you cops don't seem terribly interested in that issue. Why don't you spend a little more time doing your job and a little less time harassing me."

Gary put his hand on her arm. "Wait a second here. How much of a cat-and-mouse game do you expect me to put up with?"

"I don't even know what you're talking about," she retorted, pulling her arm away.

He dropped his hands to his sides. "I'm talking about this bullshit with your sister. I know you know where she is, and you can't expect the entire New York City Police Department to ignore the fact that you're helping to harbor a criminal."

"I'm not expecting the NYPD to do anything at all—" Her voice broke. "Though, maybe . . ." she turned away and began to walk toward her apartment, "I expected something a little better from you."

She didn't look back as she quickened her pace. Damn you, damn you, damn you, she said silently, as she held back tears.

Nor did she cry as she fell into bed an hour later. She couldn't believe she'd allowed this man to invade her life, to make her feel this bad. She'd sworn to protect herself more carefully after Philip Gallent, she thought bitterly as she tried to fall asleep, and the first man who even bothers to try gets to decimate her. Raw pain ripped through her chest as she thought about their one night together. She was furious at herself for letting it happen, even more furious at Gary for *making* it happen. She turned over, then turned once more, punching the pillow one minute, changing the position of her legs the next.

Finally she gave up trying to sleep. She just lay there, flat on her back, staring up at the ceiling until a strange calm began to seep through her.

You're a liar, she thought, as the image of Gary filled her mind. You're not angry, she admitted in the silence of the room, you're lonely. She remained as she was, not moving, not even breathing, as an entirely new feeling overwhelmed her, an emptiness so vast that it threatened her very existence.

Gary stood outside her door, his finger resting on the buzzer. He couldn't bring himself to push it, nor could he get himself to walk away. He paced up and down the narrow corridor for a moment or so, praying that none of her neighbors would suddenly appear.

He willed himself to leave and made it almost as far as the elevator before doubling back. Damn, he thought. He had to see her one more time. Again he almost buzzed, but then changed his mind. If he rang, he knew she would refuse to let him in.

Damn her all to hell, he thought, knowing he was about to do something he shouldn't. I don't care, he decided, throwing caution to the winds. There were certain benefits to being a cop, after all.

Searching through his jacket pocket, he took out a small sharp instrument he'd once taken from a small-time thief he'd caught breaking into a liquor store on Lexington Avenue. Within seconds Joey's door was open. He looked around, accommodating his eyes to the darkness, then walked toward the door he figured had to lead to the bedroom.

God, he was going to scare her to death, he thought, wondering what he should say. But before he got a word out of his mouth, the lights blazed. Joey was sitting up straight on a queen-size bed, a gray comforter wound around her legs. With one hand she was holding on to the lamp, in the other was a pair of scissors, held in front of her for protection.

"You can't scare me," she said hoarsely, although the relief in her eyes was painfully clear.

He walked over to the bed, took the scissors out of her hand and put them down beside the lamp.

"I wish I could say the same," he whispered, lifting his hand to her hair and brushing one curly strand back from her forehead. "Frankly," his hand dropped to her cheek, lingering there before going down to her throat, "you scare me to death."

He bent toward her, his lips searching hers softly. Then he eased down beside her, putting his arms around her and holding her fast.

"Nope," she said, her voice quavery, her entire body shivering in his arms. "You don't scare me a bit."

Chapter Twenty-six

"Mrs. Marian Linden?"

The voice on the other end of the telephone was impatient. "Who is this?"

Elizabeth took a deep breath. At last. She had been trying to reach this woman for two days, but no one had answered the phone until now.

"My name is Stacy Hubert. I'm sorry to bother you, but I'm doing some background checking on a Reda Mathias. She's applying for a job with our firm. I understand you and she had a misunderstanding a few years back, and I wondered if you could elaborate on it for me."

There was a sharp laugh. "A *misunderstanding?* Yes, I guess you could say that. If stealing one's husband is something you would call a misunderstanding."

"I beg your pardon?" Elizabeth tried not to sound too eager for the details.

Marian Linden hesitated, then apparently decided to tell her story. "She was a lawyer at my husband's firm. To make a long, ugly story short, she had an affair with him, and he left me. He gave her a ton of money—*our* money, I might add—then she dumped him. Just like that, as soon as the divorce was final."

Her tone grew nasty. "You'd guess she did it for the money, but I tell you, I think part of it was the fun of splitting us up. She really got off on creating havoc in people's lives. And my husband never came back to me. I mean, we'd gotten legally divorced. He had moved into an apartment in the city, and I was still out here in Rye. Initially, I think he was pretty upset when she left him high and dry. That part was actually extremely satisfying to me. But that's ancient history. By now, he's been through any number of women."

Attempting to conceal her discomfort, Elizabeth tried to bring the conversation back to what she needed to know. "And for what reason did you sue Reda Mathias?"

"My horse's ass of a husband gave her a necklace of mine as a present. Can you imagine? It was worth a fair amount, but more important, it belonged to me, not him. He'd given it to me on our tenth anniversary. So I sued her for emotional distress. Years of living with a lawyer taught me you can always find a reason to sue somebody." She laughed sharply. "This is America, you know. He's free to dump me, she's free to dump him, and everyone's free to make everyone else miserable."

Elizabeth shuddered at the woman's bitterness. "Well, thank you, Mrs. Linden, I appreciate your candor."

There was the sound of a match being lit, and the inhalation of a cigarette. "You know, I'm not the only one with a story to tell about the divine Reda. I found out, too late, of course, that another woman lost her husband to this tramp three years before me. Same stunt. Worked for his firm, got him to leave his wife, then walked off into the sunset. It was in New Jersey somewhere, Wyckoff or something."

"You wouldn't know the name of the woman, or the law firm, would you?" Elizabeth held her breath for the answer.

"It's hard to remember now." There was a pause, the sound of the cigarette being inhaled once more. "Sanderson? No. Saunders. The wife's name was silly, like Sandy Saunders. I never met her. Only heard about it."

"Thank you again, Mrs. Linden." Elizabeth grabbed a pencil from the desk where she was sitting and wrote on the pad in front of her. Sandy Saunders. Wyckoff, New Jersey.

"I hope you won't be hiring that Mathias bitch. It would be a crime to let her keep going with this sick little game, don't you think, Miss—? What was your name? What firm did you say you were with?"

"We'll certainly look at her more closely," Elizabeth said hurriedly. "Thank you again."

She hung up and stared at the words on the pad. This was definitely a wrinkle she hadn't anticipated. Maybe Reda was interested in Jack because it was part of a bigger pattern of conning these men out of money. Nothing illegal about it, just leading them around by the nose until they coughed up whatever amount she deemed satisfactory and she could split. Of course, she'd been barking up the wrong tree with Jack Ross; she must not have had any idea how devoted he was to his wife. Would the frustration of failing, breaking her string of successes, make her so furious that she would go so far as to murder Molly?

Don't leap to conclusions, she told herself. Some further checking was in order here.

Kent emerged from behind one of the partitions, a towel wrapped around his waist. He had just gotten out of the shower and was in the process of combing his wet hair.

"Hey, look at you, all dressed already," he said, coming over and bending down to where she sat to give her a lingering kiss.

She stood up to nuzzle her face against his freshly shaved cheek. They had spent much of the night making love, but even after falling asleep just as the sky was growing light, she had awakened at seven without the aid of an alarm clock. She was anxious to get going. This would be an important day. Besides, she had wanted to try Marian Linden one more time before having to leave the loft. And she was glad she had.

"I spoke to the wronged wife in Rye," she told Kent, relishing the feeling of his hands sliding up and down her back. "Reda Mathias may have been up to something funny with at least a few of the partners at different law firms, making a few dollars in the process. At least, that's how it seems at first blush."

Kent pulled back slightly, looking amused. "Wow. She turned out to be a fun one. You do associate with some cool people, Stacy."

"Okay, okay. I know you're wondering what it's all about." She couldn't resist planting a kiss on his mouth before releasing him. "I want to grab some cereal before I hit the road."

He turned to watch her head for the refrigerator. "Come on, when are you going to tell me the story? Forty-eight hours is about my maximum for discretion and subtlety. Inquiring minds want to know!"

Elizabeth extracted a container of milk from the refrigerator, then pulled open the cabinet door to get the box of cornflakes. She sighed, knowing the inevitable was coming. It was ridiculous to think she could be carrying on a romance with Kent—or an affair, or whatever the hell this was—without telling him why she was investigating this random assortment of people. Besides, it wasn't fair to get him involved and keep him in the dark.

And after spending most of the past two days and nights with him, she felt reasonably secure that he wasn't going to rush to turn her in. He was more likely to get a charge out of it all, view it as a game. The same way he viewed using his computer to pry into the most intimate details of people's lives. She tried not to think about how uncomfortable it made her to know what was immediately accessible to the whole world through any computer. If so much was available about other people, it was available about her as well. I suppose I'm a relic, she thought, pouring cornflakes into a bowl, but it makes me mighty nervous.

She grabbed a spoon from the silverware drawer and took her cereal to the small kitchen table, gesturing for Kent to join her. He walked over to the counter and poured himself a glass of orange juice.

She took a bite of cereal, chewing slowly. When she spoke, she kept her head lowered, looking directly into her bowl.

"I'm suspected in a murder. Which I did not commit. They were about to arrest me, but I took off so I could try to find out who really did it before they put me away. The people we're checking on are the most likely suspects."

She lifted her gaze to his. He was facing her, leaning up against the sink, the hand holding the glass of orange juice frozen in midair.

His eyes opened wide. He set the glass down on the counter. *"Say what?"*

She gave a shrug as if it were no big deal, although her heart was pounding as she waited for his response. "That's my story. I'm hiding out. And that's why I needed your help. That's why I couldn't turn to any of the people I normally would have."

"And what kind of people might those be?" he asked, sitting down across from her at the table.

She hesitated. "I'm a lawyer. So they would be people at the law firm where I work. My father's firm, Ross, Jennings, and Trent."

Kent burst out laughing. "A *lawyer*. For Christ's sake, that would have been really low on my list of guesses. I suppose I don't need to point out that you've broken about a dozen laws just in the time you've been with me. I don't know what you were up to before that, so I can't add up the infractions properly—although disappearing on the police must count for something."

She looked at him directly, unaware of how tightly she was clutching her spoon. "Are you going to do anything about it?"

He was genuinely puzzled. "Like what?"

"Blow the whistle on me, as they say." Her voice was quiet.

He reached across the table to take her hand, his brow furrowing. "Are you crazy? Of course not. I'm offended you would even suggest that. Not to mention the fact that I'm the one who made it possible for you to break several of those laws. I would be liable as well."

She exhaled deeply with relief. "Thank you."

He grinned. "This makes it all the more fun, in fact. People usually go prying on-line for stupid or venal reasons. This is for something real. I love it." His tone was exaggerated. "I'm *honored* to assist in your noble endeavor."

She was a little disconcerted at how on-target she had been in guessing he would find it all to be a big game.

He leaned back in his chair, tilting it back on the two rear legs. "So everything else you told me is a lie. Where you're from, why you're downtown." Something suddenly dawned on him. "Your *name*? Is your name real?"

She shook her head. "My name is Elizabeth Ross. I grew up on Gramercy Park, although I've spent my adult life in my own place on the Upper West Side. Maybe you know who my father is, Jack Ross. He and my sister, Joey, are involved in defending this Lisa Martin, the sixties radical who just turned herself in. It's gotten a lot of press attention."

He turned both palms up. "I haven't seen the paper lately, so I'm not up to date on this one. Sorry." His eyes were amused again. "But this story gets better all the time."

Elizabeth felt a strong flash of annoyance at his string of flippant comebacks. "It's not a *story*. And I'm in trouble." She got up, reaching for her purse. "So I'm going off to meet that artist guy today and check him out. I'll see you later."

He jumped up to embrace her from behind. "Hey, I'm sorry. I didn't mean anything by it."

She told herself to keep calm. There was no point in blaming him for her problems. "It's okay. But I have to go." She broke away, trying to keep her tone light. "See you later."

He stayed where he was. "I have a job from about two to four. See you after that."

She glanced back and smiled, giving him a reassuring wave.

"By the way, who was it that you supposedly murdered?" he called after her.

She kept going as she answered. "My mother."

She heard him mutter, "Oh, Jesus" as she closed the door behind her.

There was a hollow feeling in her chest. This is not my life, she thought unhappily. But then again, I don't have a life anymore.

With relief, she left the building and stepped outside. She walked, replaying in her mind everything she knew about the man she was going to see.

She and Kent had easily ferreted out a somewhat scary piece of information. Michael Weaver, the thirty-nine-year-old sculptor whose studio was one flight below Molly's, had been arrested and then deposited in mental institutions on two occasions.

It turned out he was from an extremely wealthy family. He had grown up on Manhattan's Fifth Avenue in an enormous prewar building where his parents owned two apartments that they had converted into one. After attending college at the Rhode Island School of Design, he had moved around the country before returning to New York City, settling in a one-bedroom apartment on Tenth Street. He had gotten married in 1987, divorced two years later. The arrests had occurred in 1991 and 1994. He had spent a total of six months in the two mental hospitals.

It was a shame she didn't know more before she went to meet him, she thought. But she had simply run out of time. Much of the previous day had been spent tracking down Hector Rivera, the doorman on Joey's list whom Molly had gotten fired. He had moved to Los Angeles, where he had been employed at a hotel for two months. In fact, Kent had managed to discover that on the day the murder occurred, Rivera had taken a flight to Las Vegas for a three-day vacation with his wife, charged on his new credit card. It wasn't impossible that he had secretly flown on to New York to kill Molly, but it hardly seemed likely.

Ruling out Rivera had been useful, but it had diverted their attention from Michael Weaver. As soon as she discovered that Weaver had been institutionalized, Elizabeth knew she had to take a look at him as her potential killer. Without waiting to find out anything else, she had telephoned him.

She desperately tried to disguise her nervousness as she told him that she was an art student from his alma mater, RISD, and was considering dropping all her other courses to work exclusively as a sculptress. Claiming to have seen his work on exhibit—the place, date, and descriptive review of which Kent was able to provide her—Elizabeth regaled Weaver with how much she admired him. The tortured expressions of his bronze men and women, their bodies locked in struggle with one another, had captured her, she said. The flattery was effective. When she asked if she could spend a few days observing him at work, he agreed to it.

"I'm going to try to write an article about you for the school newspaper as well, or maybe the alumni magazine," she tossed in, figuring it would give her an excuse to take notes.

"Any publicity is a good thing in the art world," he had said. "It won't sell any of my work, but it may make a few people jealous who recognize my name from our school days."

Elizabeth was suddenly aware of the people on the avenue around her. For some reason she felt uncomfortable. She sprinted toward an empty taxi waiting at a red light several yards ahead of her. Casually shielding her face as she got into the taxi so the driver wouldn't see her clearly, she gave Weaver's address—

the address of Molly's old studio as well, she reflected sadly as she settled back into the seat.

Having reached her destination, Elizabeth paid the driver and got out, nervously ringing the buzzer to Weaver's studio. When she stepped out of the elevator on the fifth floor, she had to pause for a moment before knocking on the door. It was one thing to snoop on people via computer, another thing altogether to confront them in person. Taking a deep breath, she knocked. The door swung open.

Elizabeth hoped her expression didn't show how startled she was. She had expected an artsy type, maybe in dusty overalls, sporting either a long ponytail or some hip super-short haircut. A stereotype, she knew, but he was minimally successful, so she figured he would fit in some kind of artistic mold.

Michael Weaver had graying, shoulder-length hair that hung loosely around his face, straggly and greasy. He wore a black tank top, stained with food, and shorts that had once been white but were now yellowed and dirty. He was barefoot. The hand he extended to her was also dirty, the fingernails bitten down. His complexion was ghostly white, his skin glistening slightly from perspiration, although the room wasn't particularly hot. His eyes were bloodshot.

For a brief moment, Elizabeth was reminded of the way her father had looked the other morning when she saw him on the street, pale and nearly ill. She quickly pushed aside the uncomfortable thought.

She extended her hand. "Hello, Mr. Weaver. It's a pleasure to meet you."

"I thought you were a student at RISD," he said in a disappointed tone. "You're a lot older than I expected."

She resisted the urge to retort *And you're a lot more disgusting than I expected.* Instead, she forced a smile. "I spent a lot of years working at a job I hated before I went back to school to study art. That explains my advanced age."

"Oh." He gave a little shrug of resignation.

Her dislike of him was growing by leaps and bounds. Apparently he had been expecting a cute little coed whom he could impress right into bed. *Life is just so full of little disappointments, isn't it?* she wanted to snipe at him. Knock it off, Elizabeth, she told herself.

She took a deep breath. "May I come in?" she asked pleasantly.

"Sure," he said, stepping back to make room for her to enter.

She looked around. Oh, my God, she thought, Anthony Perkins in *Psycho.* Except the comparison wasn't actually humorous. The long windows should have flooded the room with light, but they were covered by some old, faded drapes, forcing the light to struggle through. There were art supplies and tools strewn everywhere, along with books, paintings, sketches, and the remains of a dozen meals. Pizza boxes, takeout containers, and waxed paper were shoved into corners and left on tabletops. A couch was practically hidden beneath clothing and unopened mail, its worn green-velvet covering stained and, in spots, completely bald.

There was no sign of any sculpting going on. No project started, waiting for him to return, nothing in any stage of progress that she could see.

He watched her take it all in, crossing his arms defiantly. "I'm thinking about what I want to do next," he said airily.

In the next second his face fell. "It's too hard, it's all just too hard," he moaned. "I can't take it anymore."

Elizabeth swallowed. Something was very wrong with this man. What kind of relationship could Molly have had with him? Of course, he might have been better in the past, but now he was on some kind of decline, working his way toward another trip to Bellevue. It would make sense, considering that a couple of years had elapsed between his two earlier hospitalizations. Maybe he got better for a while, then would fall apart again.

She wondered how much time she would have to observe him. Clearly, she wasn't going to be spending a few days here as she had planned; he was too crazy for her to sit around with him for hours every day. Better to jump right in, she decided.

"I noticed that there's a studio in this building for rent," she said. "I wonder if I should just stay in New York and start working."

His expression turned pained. "Molly's studio, yes." He shook his head, his eyes filling with tears. "My Molly, oh, God, my Molly."

Elizabeth stayed very still, trying not to disturb his train of thought. "You knew the woman who had it?" she asked gently.

"She was like a mother to me," he said, his arms thrust out in a nearly theatrical gesture. "I can't tell you what it's done to me."

"What what's done to you?" Elizabeth prodded softly.

He gave her a sharp look as if she were a fool not to know. "Some maniac killed my darling Molly. Shot her dead like an animal."

A shiver ran up Elizabeth's spine. "Why? Who would have done such a thing?" she asked, hoping she sounded innocently curious.

He closed his eyes, pained. "The world is full of the heartless."

The sudden buzzing of the doorbell nearly made Elizabeth jump. Michael crossed the room and yanked it open in annoyance.

"What?" he barked before seeing who it was.

The man on the other side looked about twenty-seven. He was wearing a black leather jacket and tight blue jeans. A diamond stud earring gleamed in his right earlobe. He was so good-looking, Elizabeth thought, he could easily be a model.

He immediately launched into a lecture to Michael. "I hate it when you stop answering your phone. Don't tell me you weren't screening my calls." He took a step inside and grabbed Michael by both shoulders.

"Look at yourself. I leave you alone for two weeks and you—" He broke off instantly as his eyes fell on Elizabeth.

"What's she doing here?" he asked Michael sharply.

"Nothing, some student," Michael answered offhandedly. "Eric, please . . ."

The young man glared at Elizabeth with overt hostility before turning back to Michael. "You're still trying, aren't you? I'd like to hear the line you fed her. When are you going to stop this?"

Michael drew himself up. "Could we please go inside to talk about this? I would appreciate some privacy."

Eric's face was grim as he took Michael by the arm and hustled him into another room, perhaps a bedroom or kitchen, Elizabeth guessed. He slammed the door shut. Quickly, she moved to stand beside it, hoping she could overhear what they were saying. It wasn't hard, because Eric immediately started yelling.

"Your family is never going to accept you, Michael. I don't know what it's going to take for you to get that. You are what you are. They are what they are. You're going to die still pretending, and they won't even give a damn that you've been robbed of your whole life. The smack won't make it go away, bringing girls up here won't make it go away. What, you think you're suddenly going to get a hard-on for some girl just because she's standing in front of you?"

Oh, my God, Elizabeth thought, taking a step back. This guy is being tortured by the fact that he's gay. Those rich parents of his probably wanted no part of that, and he couldn't deal with it. *She was like a mother to me,* he had said about Molly. One who probably cared about him and was accepting of him, unlike his real mother.

This poor man, she thought sympathetically. She couldn't imagine that Molly's murder was connected to the misery that must be his life.

Quietly, she made her way out of the apartment. She highly doubted Michael would care that she was gone when he finally emerged.

The field was definitely narrowing.

Chapter Twenty-seven

"Thank you, Mr. Raffia. I appreciate all your time."

Joey hung up the phone, the despair she'd been holding at bay suddenly threatening to explode inside her. Since her meeting with Lisa in Valhalla, she'd counted on the notion that Tony Raffia's cousin, Ray Raffia, would lead her to Tony—and Tony, in turn, would provide some mitigating factor to help keep Lisa from serving a prison sentence that would incarcerate her until she was well into her eighties.

Well, she thought grimly, how stupid that idea turned out to be. Not that Ray Raffia wasn't happy to help. In fact, Tony had actually called Ray when he saw an article about Lisa's arrest in the newspaper.

"He only wishes there were something he could do for her," Ray Raffia had told Joey earnestly. "That was such a terrible time in Tony's life, one he's atoned for in every way he can—short of turning himself in, that is. But he's changed completely. He's grown up. In fact, if you come out here to Pittsburgh, I'll show you pictures of all five of his kids."

It seemed that in the years since the robbery, Tony Raffia had emigrated to a city in Canada—the name of which his cousin, of course, refused to reveal—where he worked as a stockbroker, lived with his wife of twenty-some years, and happily coached the soccer team that several of his children played on. In short, with the exception of the fact that he lived under an alias and was still wanted for felony murder, Tony could be the winner of the local upstanding-citizen-of-the-year award. As for his youthful indiscretions, Ray informed her that Tony still felt guilty enough to send the bank guard's widow a thousand dollars anonymously each and every Christmas since the robbery.

Joey was surprised at the weight of her disappointment. She hadn't realized how much she had counted on the notion of Tony Raffia's leading her to some clue, some event, some unexplored territory that would help Lisa's legal case. Well, Ray's enthusiasm and support were boundless, but that plus a dollar fifty would get Joey on the subway. It certainly wasn't going to do anything for Lisa Martin.

Damn, she thought dejectedly, turning to look at the sun. It was only eight in the morning, but she felt as if the whole day had already gone to waste. Not that there weren't innumerable legal tasks to perform. Her father was proving to be no help at all, and there were hundreds of hours of work to do. If she worked twenty-four hours a day every day until the hearing, she still wouldn't get it all done. And, in addition to all that, she thought despairingly, her supply of Constance Truggle columns was getting low. Within the next couple of days, she had to take some time out to write another fifteen or twenty days' worth of them. Enough, at least, to get her through Lisa's preliminary hearing.

She couldn't spare the time to even think about that, she realized, forcing it out of her mind. What was important right now was Lisa Martin. And on that question, all the hours in the world might not be enough.

What she really needed was a big idea, a whole new direction. She sat back in the chair, pushing one of her shoes off her foot and flexing her toes absentmindedly. With distaste, she looked down at the black-leather high-heeled pump lying on its side under her chair. Some new direction, she thought bitterly. She seemed to have turned right back in her old direction. Here she was, tucked tightly into a conservative black suit, pantyhose, and a life she longed to be two thousand miles away from.

She listened to the quiet hum from the outer office as she looked out at the street. Everyone was busy doing what they presumably wanted to do. Well, she realized more fairly, what they probably *had* to do to keep their lives together. *I* was the one who finally found what I really wanted to do, and I thought I could do it for the rest of my life. I certainly was wrong about that.

I'm probably wrong about everything else in my life too, she mused. Like about Gary McCullough, the unbidden voice in her head said silently. Like believing that guy could really care about her.

After the last time she'd seen him, she'd actually believed he meant everything he said. Even the way he'd let himself into her apartment, crazy as it was, seemed romantic and impulsive. All his words, all his actions seemed galvanized that night, as if he were a man who wasn't in charge of his emotions, who simply couldn't keep himself away from her.

Which, she acknowledged to herself, was just about the only thing that made her own feelings in the matter at all palatable. She was falling in love with him, despite her best efforts, and it felt terrible. Because, in the light of day, it seemed so clear that his attention had more to do with keeping a closer eye on a murder suspect's sister than with anything about Joey herself. She wished she were wrong about that, but it seemed so obvious.

She had gotten a phone call from Cornelia only the day before, asking why the New York Police Department was so interested in Joanna Ross.

"The detective who called must have asked about a million questions about you and your sister," Cornelia had said. "How often she called you and how often she came out to Montana to see you, and who your friends in New York had been, and a whole bunch of stuff. And, my gosh, Joey, out here you barely mentioned her name!"

"Who exactly called you?" Joey had asked, dreading the answer.

"Oh," Cornelia had replied, "he was so nice and polite. I think he said his name was McCullough."

Joey had almost groaned. Yes, she wanted to say, his name is McCullough, though he answers to Gary when he's lying next to me in bed.

She was furious when she hung up the phone. How many times can I be this stupid, she asked herself, so mortified it felt like actual pain. Never again, she vowed, desperately trying to move her thoughts elsewhere. But she couldn't help the flush of desire that swept through her as memories of their night together crowded her mind. Viscerally, she recalled the path of his hands, the feel of his lips on her skin. It had been like magic, from the moment he frightened her half to death, appearing like that in the doorway, to the hours they'd lain together, intertwined, virtually always touching some part of each other, not falling asleep until daylight.

And yet, when she awakened, he was gone. And it had left her feeling as if she'd made it all up. Okay, she knew he had really been there. She could still experience the lingering scent of him on her pillowcase, still feel the urgency of his mouth, the warmth of his hands. But she knew full well *why* he had come, and that knowledge left her embarrassed and furious. He had been there to watch her, to monitor her every move so the NYPD could get to Elizabeth.

"That's not going to happen," she said out loud, hoping her secretary hadn't heard her.

Get to work, she urged herself, and right now. She might not be able to undo the other night, but she could do everything possible for Lisa Martin, and that didn't include mooning over Detective Gary McCullough.

She turned her chair and looked around her office,

trying to sort through the possibilities. She could look further into Tony Raffia, but her gut told her that what his cousin had said had been the absolute truth. He'd been a youthful radical who'd gone astray and was now a model citizen whose only continuing personal flaw was avoiding extradition to the United States.

But there was one other person who'd never been caught. She picked up the stack of notes Lisa had given her and began to look through them one more time. Page by page, she pored over what Lisa written, wondering if she had missed any information that would help. The names leapt out at her. Janie Saltzman. Bobby Sarkalian. Paul St. John. They had all been caught in the intervening years, and all three were still serving time.

Still, she thought, stopping at a line on one of the pieces of paper, there was Freddie Shore. He was the one person besides Lisa and Tony who had gotten away. Joey thought one more time about what Lisa had told her. Freddie had entered the group before their activities got someone killed. In fact, she realized, it had been pretty shortly before. Could there be anything in that?

She wondered where Freddie had gone after he'd left the crime scene. Lisa and Tony hadn't really seen each other, but they'd stayed in touch with the people underground who had helped them assume new identities. Freddie didn't seem to have taken that route. Lisa had spent a few months in at least twelve different cities before she settled in Montana, and she hadn't heard a word about him. Of course, Joey mused, Freddie hadn't been a student. Suddenly it seemed imperative that she locate Freddie.

She reviewed what Lisa had told her about him, but it was so little. He had hung around campus. He was competitive, and he loved cribbage. Well, she thought, that certainly wasn't much. She felt the curtain of depression once again threatening to descend. No, you don't, she told herself. If that's all you have, that's what you'll use. She drummed her fingers on her desk, then reached for the phone. The idea she had might prove ridiculous, but at least it was an idea.

Linda picked up the intercom on the first ring. Elizabeth's disappearance had left her sister's assistant free to work for Joey.

"Yes, Ms. Ross."

"Who in this city has a great photo library?" Joey asked.

Linda hesitated for a moment before responding. "Well," she said finally, "a girl I roomed with a couple of years ago has a job at *Sports Illustrated*. That's in the Time Life Building, and I'm pretty sure she mentioned that one of their magazines had an extensive library."

"See if she can get you in, okay? Right this second, if possible."

"What am I looking for?"

In place of an answer, Linda heard the phone slamming down, then looked up to see Joey standing in the doorway between their offices.

"Believe it or not, you're looking for cribbage tournaments. And we want pictures that go all the way back to the early seventies."

Linda reached for her handbag and stood up. "Are you thinking of taking it up as a hobby?"

Joey shook her head. "Yeah, right. That and my collection of pickup sticks should keep me busy." She reached into the pocket of her suit jacket and extracted a twenty-dollar bill. "Here's cab fare," she said, handing it to Linda. "Do you think people can change?" she asked abruptly.

"Well, sure," the girl answered, shrugging her shoulders. "At least, I hope they can."

Joey smiled grimly. "On the contrary, we're very much hoping they don't change much at all."

"So, what do you think?" Joey asked, the moment Lisa was shown into the visitors' room.

Joey tapped her pen nervously on the tabletop as

Lisa looked through the numerous photos Linda had brought back. Going to the photo library had been a great idea. It turned out that not only was there a national cribbage tournament held every year but the event was always preserved for posterity, winners and runners-up captured on camera holding their trophies, year in and year out. She only prayed that Freddie Shore still loved to compete.

Lisa examined photo after photo, starting with the oldest ones and concentrating on each face. "This is tough," she observed, holding one picture at a slight distance from her. "The faces are so small. And I haven't laid eyes on Freddie in so many years."

"Just keep looking," Joey urged. This was such a long shot, but it was about the only thing that held out any hope at all.

"Hey," Lisa suddenly exclaimed. She held up a black and white eight-by-ten. "This guy in front, the balding one. This could be Freddie Shore." She looked more closely. "You know, I swear this *is* Freddie."

Joey took the photo from her and scrutinized the man Lisa had identified. He didn't look any different from the men around him. Middle-aged, dark, slightly graying hair—or what was left of it. He looked very satisfied with himself as he smiled into the camera, the large trophy in his hands obviously giving him great pleasure. She read the caption across the bottom of the glossy print. The name of the man third from the left was listed as Robert Mallory.

"Okay, baby. More to come." She leaned across the table and gave Lisa a quick peck on the cheek. "Nancy Drew Ross is on the case. I'll let you know what comes next."

As she got up and walked to the door, she heard Lisa's plaintive voice from behind her.

"You really think this can make a difference?"

Joey turned and gave Lisa a bright smile. "I have no idea, but I'm going to do everything I can and you're gonna sit here praying or wishing or working black magic in your mind. And somehow, between us, we're going to get you out of here. I swear it."

She walked out of the visiting cell, knowing that a guard would close the heavy metal door behind her. God, I hope I'm telling the truth, she thought as she left the building.

"Do you want the burgers medium or rare?" the waitress asked, smiling at the two women in the booth.

"Rare," Joey answered, peeking over toward the bar in front to make sure no one was watching them.

Elizabeth sat across from her, her back to most of the other patrons. Fiddler's Green, a restaurant on Forty-eighth Street, was always busy at lunch and after five, but at three-thirty on a weekday, it was nearly empty. Joey had taken two subways and a taxi to make sure she wasn't being followed.

"Here are the pictures," she said, pushing an envelope across the wooden table. "Your mission, should you choose to accept it, is to check out Mr. Robert Mallory."

"Like I have unlimited time to go off checking out missing persons," Elizabeth answered, her annoyance plain.

Joey looked at her distastefully. Her sister's tight jeans and newly blond hair made her look like a denizen of the East Village, but her attitude certainly hadn't changed. "I hoped the fashion alteration might indicate a general loosening up," she said cynically. "Sorry I was so wrong."

"I'm not exactly out here doing nothing, you know."

Joey's lips tightened, but she didn't reply.

Elizabeth reached across and opened the envelope. She started examining the photos. "You know, generally when people ask for help, they try to be polite."

The waitress came over, two plates crowded with burgers and fries in her hands. Joey waited until she had put the plates in front of them and walked away from the table, then spoke in annoyance.

"Lisa Martin has lived over half her life hiding from the police. It's a concept you of all people should have sympathy for.

"Believe me," she went on, "I wouldn't dream of asking you if I weren't worried about the police following me. Which they're doing because of *you*, may I remind you. That's all I need—to lead them to this guy before I get a chance to find out what he can do for Lisa's case. I have no choice here."

Elizabeth's expression was the one she used to assume when Joey was about seven years old and would fling all the checkers onto the floor after losing.

"Okay," Joey amended, her tone chastened, *"please* can you find this guy and *please* can you find out what he's been up to for the past few decades?"

Elizabeth bit into her cheeseburger. She chewed it deliberately, then took a sip of her soda. "Well, since you asked so nicely . . ."

Joey was asleep when she heard the phone ring. She found that her heart was beating rapidly. At one-thirty in the morning, there were only two people it could be.

"Did I wake you?"

At the sound of Elizabeth's voice, Joey felt disappointment.

"So, what did you come up with?" she asked briskly.

"Robert Mallory counts among his family a perfectly manicured wife named Deborah and six horses, all of whom live in splendor on an estate the size of a county in Bedford, New York. His occupation is listed as 'Director of the Morris Corporation.' "

"Quite a long way to have come. Lucky Robert Mallory," Joey responded thoughtfully.

"And lucky me. I get to never think about him again," Elizabeth said, hanging up decisively.

Caught by surprise, Joey was still holding the telephone. As she reached to replace it in its cradle, she heard a small click. Thinking it might be her call waiting, she pressed the Flash button, but heard nothing.

Jesus, she thought, the son of a bitch is bugging my phone. She felt consumed by rage. Not just at Gary, but at herself. How many times would she try to fool herself into believing the man cared for her? If she needed more proof, here it was. Plain as day. To Gary McCullough, she was the means to an end. Oh, God, she thought, alarmed, had she of all people given her sister away?

She went over the conversation in her mind. Elizabeth hadn't identified herself, so Gary couldn't know anything for sure. And it had been short. There couldn't have been enough time for the police to trace her location. At least, she hoped not. Elizabeth, she begged silently as she put the phone down, please have called from a phone booth far from wherever you're staying.

That would be great, she thought, if doing me one favor caused Elizabeth to be arrested for murder. Then again, that was pretty much how her luck was running these days.

Contemplating that notion led her to another thought: just how did Robert Mallory get to be that lucky, she wondered, resting her head back on the pillow.

Chapter Twenty-eight

Joey rubbed her eyes tiredly as she paced around her office. She wasn't exactly sure of the hour, but the last time she'd even noticed the clock, it was after eleven, and that seemed like centuries ago. The phone was ringing, as it had several times before, but she made no move to answer it. She was sure she knew who it would be, and she had no intention of talking to him.

Damn you, Gary, she thought, willing the phone to stop, then wishing it would ring on forever. She walked over to the window, noticing as she looked out that most of the lights in the adjoining office buildings had already been turned out for the night. All the workers had gone home to their houses or their apartments, to their loving husband or perfect wife, to their two kids and their German shepherd.

Suddenly her own thoughts embarrassed her. There was her friend Lisa on the verge of being put away for murder, and she was focusing on her pathetic love life. So what if the man she was crazy about only cared about putting her sister under arrest. At least she could stay in her office or walk the streets or fly to Zanzibar if she chose to. If only Lisa had that option. If only Lisa had *any* option, she thought hopelessly, walking across to the couch and falling onto the cushions.

There was an answer here. There just had to be. Hauling herself up, she returned to her desk, sat down, and picked up the reams of paper she had been working on all day. The name Robert Mallory appeared on every page. She and a paralegal had assiduously surfed the Internet to find every word ever published about the man. Nothing had appeared in newspapers or professional journals until he was well into adulthood. But that was too little, too late. She still hadn't been able to conjure up anything about his current life that would help Lisa Martin.

One step at a time, she said to herself, not for the first time that day. Again she read through the various pieces of paper. There were any number of newspaper articles emanating from the many cribbage tournaments he had played in. And there was quite a lot of information about his corporation. But none of it helped. In fact, the company he headed up was an old one, with years of expertise in all aspects of the paper industry. It had a number of mills around the country, plus factories that handled corrugated materials and a large plant in Alabama that created bathroom tissue and paper towels.

Freddie Shore may not have gone to college, but he must be one smart guy, Joey thought with grudging admiration as she totaled the combined bottom lines of all his businesses. He must have worked his ass off to rise so high in that company. Especially a company like his, which had been in the hands of one family since its inception.

She turned her attention to the information she'd gathered about his family. His wife, Deborah Mallory, was on the board of the local Bedford Library, and also appeared in a number of newspaper articles covering local Westchester charities.

Then there were the children. Robert, Jr., was sixteen, and a handsome kid, judging by the picture of him carried by the Gannett newspaper chain when he won a prize at a swimming meet in White Plains. And his younger sister, Melissa, starring in the junior high school production of *Our Town,* looked like every other thirteen-year-old Lolita wannabe Joey remembered from her own teen years.

God, Joey thought, depressed at the realization. This guy had not only managed to stay scot-free, but was a real American success story. He's Horatio Alger, she thought bitterly. Everyone else ends up hiding out or spending decades in jail, while Robert Mallory or Freddie Shore or whatever his real name was gets to ride through the Bedford hills on his personal black stallion. She picked up the next piece of paper, scanning it with disgust. It was three columns from the society page of the Bedford paper. *The afternoon was made especially worthwhile,* it read, *by the radiance of the hostess, Deborah Mallory.*

"Sickening!" Joey exclaimed out loud. Her voice sounded alarmingly loud in the silence of the empty offices. She felt foolish, like a little girl caught being inappropriate in company. Then she began to laugh.

"There's no one here to listen and I can say anything I want," she practically screamed at the top of her lungs. "Screw you, Robert Mallory, and the same to the lovely Mrs. Mallory. . . ."

She knew she sounded slightly hysterical, but she was enjoying herself. It wasn't as if anyone were there to observe her craziness. In fact, she thought, it felt great to be nuts. Then she caught herself. If she kept this up, she really was going to go crazy. She was clearly too tired to get anything done, and if she didn't go home and get some sleep, she wasn't going to be any good the next day either.

Wearily, she collected the papers on her desk and pushed them carelessly into her pouch. Maybe she'd get a second wind before she fell asleep. Shutting off the lights and closing the door behind her, she walked out of the office.

Luckily, a cab rolled by almost as soon as she got out of the building. She gave the driver her address and leaned back against the seat. Closing her eyes, she almost fell asleep, the weight of all the useless information she'd collected exhausting her. Then a thought popped into her head. She'd actually read some of the Horatio Alger novels when she was a kid. They'd studied them when she was in seventh or eighth grade. And she remembered something about them. Their heroes, the embodiment of the self-made man, youngsters who worked their way to the top, were, in fact, not so self-made. Invariably, in the course of the story, they married the boss's daughter.

Curious suddenly, she rummaged through her briefcase, leafing through until she came to the articles about Deborah Mallory. She read several before she came to a sentence that stopped her in her tracks.

Deborah Langdon Mallory graduated from Sarah Lawrence College magna cum laude in 1968, according to the blurb in her alumni magazine.

"Deborah *Langdon* Mallory." Joey rolled the name around in her mouth, as the driver looked at her with some alarm through the rear-view mirror.

Joey felt the excitement rising in her chest. The name of the bank guard Freddie Shore had shot, for whose felony murder three people were already in jail, was Henry Langdon.

The taxi pulled to a stop and Joey was surprised to see she was in front of her building. She pulled a twenty-dollar bill out of her wallet and handed it to the driver.

"It's yours," she said gleefully as he tried to hand her more than ten dollars in change.

She rushed inside, hardly able to breathe. At last there was something to explore, something real. This couldn't be an accident. The shooting had never made sense. After all, the robbery was over, the money was safely in the hands of the four people who'd already left the scene. Why should Freddie have shot Henry Langdon in the first place? Finally, there was a hint of what the reason might have been, and one that had nothing at all to do with Lisa Martin.

Joey rushed upstairs, threw her door open and went to the stove to make a pot of coffee. As she waited for the water to boil, she took the pages from her leather bag and lay them out on the kitchen table. She searched through them until she found what she was looking for, the corporate profile that had accompanied a stock offering more than thirty years before.

On page five, Joey found the anecdotal history of the Morris Corporation. She looked down the list of company officers, stopping when she came to the single largest shareholder from the mid-nineteen-forties through the early seventies, a woman by the name of Emily Westman. Eagerly, Joey switched to another stack of papers, extracting the copy of another of the annual reports the company had issued a few years later.

She went carefully from page to page, noting family names, trying to draw links among them. Then, on the inside back cover, she struck gold. Inscribed in beautiful full color detail was the Westman family tree. The corporation had done her work for her.

What she saw made her smile widely. Emily Langdon Westman had been married to William Westman, who died during World War II. He had had a sister who died at the age of eleven. Emily's only immediate family was her brother, Harry Langdon. He died in the early nineteen-fifties.

But I'll bet my life that he had a son, she thought, shaking her head, and that the son lived on. She had no doubt that Henry Langdon's real name had been Harry Langdon, Jr. That was something she could check on tomorrow. She heard the water boiling, and got up to fill the coffee filter with freshly ground beans. Now why would Henry Langdon, presumably heir to a fortune in stock, have been working as a cop, let alone as a moonlighting bank guard, she wondered as she poured water through the filter.

The answer to that wasn't something she was likely to find out from company records and public newspaper articles, she knew. That could wait to be answered later. But she could feel in her bones that she had finally found the answer for Lisa. Not that there was any doubt of her client's complicity in the robbery. But felony murder, now that was another story.

Her thoughts were interrupted by the ringing of the doorbell. She froze at the sound, simply staring at the pot of water in her hand until it started to spill over the sides of the glass pot she had been pouring it into.

"Joey, I know you're in there."

Gary's voice was soft, but it carried perfectly. She felt almost as though he were already standing next to her, running his hands down her face, kissing her. . . .

She had to make him go away, had to keep him at a safe distance where she wouldn't lose sight of who he really was, what he really wanted from her.

"You know I could let myself in," his voice went on, even softer now, "but I want you to want me there."

"You want me to tell you where my sister is, that's what you want!" she cried, putting the pot of water down and going to stand near the door.

Gary stayed silent for a while, then spoke plaintively. "Please just open the door and let me have my say. If you tell me to leave, I'll leave. No questions asked, I promise."

She stood there, wracked by indecision, then took the chain, which had been hanging loosely, and drew it across to lock it. Only then did she open the door, allowing five or six inches of open space between them.

He didn't attempt to touch her, didn't even put his hand out. He just stared at her, his expression utterly serious.

"I don't know what it is you're afraid of," he started quietly, "but that's what this is—it's fear. It's not the truth, it's not your sanity speaking, it's terror."

She couldn't believe how sincere he sounded, how almost wounded. But, she thought, of course that's how he would sound. Con artists don't seem like con artists. That's why they're so very good at their craft.

"Gary, I don't know where Elizabeth is. She doesn't report in to me, we aren't close and never were"— she knew she should stop there, but she couldn't—

"and no matter what you think, she never could have killed my mother."

Gary's mouth tightened, and she found herself going on.

"Ask anyone—of the two of us, she's the one with all the virtue. She's never been so much as rude, let alone hurt anybody—"

Gary interrupted her. "I know you love your sister, but that isn't why I'm here."

Joey couldn't help but laugh. "*Love* my sister?" she replied mockingly. "I don't even *like* my sister. In thirty-odd years, we've never said a civil word to each other."

"I don't really care."

Joey's eyes suddenly blazed with rage. "Well, you certainly do care. You care enough to put a wiretap on my telephone!"

There was silence on the other side of the door, which only made Joey more infuriated. She knew she should stop talking, but there was no way in hell she was going to.

"You care enough to make love to me. You care enough to hound me, to break into my apartment, to stand here at—" her eyes searched the room for the nearest clock—"three o'clock in the morning," she finished.

Gary slapped the door frame with his open hand, amazement in his eyes. "You really think that's what I care about? Do you really imagine that I go out of my way to seduce the relatives of every suspect I investigate?"

"How do I know what you do?" she answered wildly, her mind reeling from his nearness.

"My God, Joey," he exclaimed, taking his hand from the door and putting it through the empty space between them to touch her cheek. "Don't you know when someone loves you? Can you really be that blind?"

She could only stand there, frozen. The man she saw in front of her seemed like the answer to a prayer.

But she didn't trust the power of prayer. She never had. How on earth could she start now?

Gary watched her for a few seconds, then turned and began to walk away. His words trailed behind him as he approached the elevator.

"I can't force you to see what's right in front of you. I can't and I won't. You'll have to do that for yourself."

She held her breath as the doors opened and he got inside. She stood there, helpless, as he lifted his hand and pressed a button. The doors closed and the noise of the car going down to the lobby sounded as loud as a gunshot. But she remained where she was, looking out into the empty corridor, unable to move.

Chapter Twenty-nine

The intercom buzzer startled Joey, who was deep in thought, glancing through the papers in a folder on her desk.

"Ms. Ross," announced her secretary's voice, "there's a Dennis Foley here to see you. He doesn't have an appointment, but he says he was a friend of your mother's."

"Who?" Joey replied in surprise. What would a friend of her mother's, whom she had never heard of, be doing popping up in her office in the middle of the day? "Never mind. Please send him in."

The door opened almost immediately. Joey looked up to see a nice-looking middle-aged man standing in the doorway. She rose.

Hello, Mr.—?" She started to walk toward him.

He came forward, his hand outstretched. "Dennis Foley. I worked with your mother."

They shook hands. Joey ushered him forward and they sat down in two armchairs in the corner of her office.

"I'm sorry, I don't believe we've ever met," Joey said.

"No," he smiled, "no, we haven't. Your mother and I worked together on the production of *West Side Story*. I was in the building at a meeting with my own lawyer on the fifth floor, and I saw your firm's name on the directory as I was leaving. I recognized it, of course, not so much because Molly had mentioned it but because it's been in the news quite a bit. I stopped by on the off chance that I could meet you. Molly often talked about you and your sister."

He stopped, grimacing. "I'm sorry, that was indelicate of me. I've read about your sister's situation."

Joey shrugged. "As has everybody else in the world. It's all right."

He looked bemused. "And normally it would have been Elizabeth I would have met by dropping in. You're not usually here. You live in—was it Michigan?"

"Montana."

He nodded. "Right. Sorry."

"Why was it you wanted to meet me, Mr. Foley?"

"Dennis, please." He smiled. "I guess I wanted to see Molly's daughter." His expression grew serious. "And I would really like to know if anybody has any idea who killed her."

Joey regarded him for a moment, the kind gaze of his eyes, the obvious caring behind the question. "Do you mind if I ask what your relationship was with my mother?"

"We were simply friends on the set of a job. But I liked her. Very much. To be perfectly honest, I would have liked to have been more than a casual friend. But she was married and loyal, and she wasn't going to entertain any such notion."

Joey's eyes were wide. It took her a moment to find her voice. "I'll be damned . . ."

"Please." Dennis held up his hand. "I didn't come here to cause trouble for you or anybody else in your family. Nothing went on between us. But I was deeply upset about her death, and something just drew me in here to see you."

"Who would have guessed?" Joey muttered under her breath, shaking her head.

"She was truly talented, you know," Dennis went on reflectively. "I admired her work very much."

"Thank you," Joey replied. "I thought the same."

"In fact, I'm a producer, and I had been planning to hire her for my next show. She was going to do some sketches for me. It's for a play set in Ireland, so we were discussing how the costumes could suggest the countryside." He looked pained. "Of course, I've hired someone else, but I wish we'd been able to work together."

"Did she do the sketches for you?" Joey asked.

He shrugged. "I have no idea. I never saw her again after our one job together."

Joey tilted her head. "Would you still want them if I could find them?"

"Now?" He was surprised. "Well, I don't know if we could use them. I mean, I'd want her to get credit, and that probably wouldn't sit well with my new painter. In fact, she would no doubt go through the roof at the suggestion. On the other hand, I'd love to have them, if only for sentimental reasons. Do you think you could find them?"

"I don't know. But I'll give it a try. Can you give me a number where I can call you?"

He reached for his wallet and extracted a business card. "Your mother was a very considerate person, always willing to go out of her way to help. I see she passed the trait on."

Joey bowed her head with theatrical modesty. "Thank you."

He laughed. "No, I mean it. Molly was really somebody special. At least, I always thought so."

He stood up. "I won't take up any more of your time. I'm glad I got to meet you. Thanks for indulging a sentimentalist."

Joey got up and shook his hand. "A pleasure to meet you. And fascinating. I'm sorry to say I never thought much about my mother's professional relationships."

"I have to admit," he said as they walked toward

the door, "that we didn't have to have that extensive a professional relationship, given our respective jobs. I sought her out more than was necessary. We liked one another's company. There was just something about her . . ."

Joey smiled. "I liked her, too," she said.

"I hope I didn't upset you," Dennis said, one hand on the doorknob. "I didn't really think it through before I just showed up. That wasn't very nice."

Joey waved off his concern. "Not at all. And I promise to see what I can do about digging up those sketches, if there were any."

"Good-bye, Joey. And thanks."

"Good-bye." The door closed behind him. Joey stared at it. "Goodbye, White-Knight-on-a-Horse-Who-Wasn't-Meant-to-Be," she said quietly.

She strode back to her desk. "What were you up to, Mom?" she asked aloud. "Were you in love with him?"

Sighing, she sat down in her chair. "That's one question I'll probably never get answered."

Her encounter with Dennis Foley made her think about her relationship with Gary. Was he telling the truth about himself? Was he *her* white knight? It was all so confusing.

Back in her apartment that evening, she was surprised to see how glad she felt when she picked up her ringing telephone and heard Elizabeth's voice on the other end. But, at the same time, she panicked, remembering the wiretap.

"You're just the one I've got to tell this story to," Joey began, "but I can't talk right now, Natalie."

There was a momentary pause.

"Oh," Elizabeth said slowly. "I see."

Joey was relieved. Obviously her sister understood.

"But let's get together soon," Elizabeth said with great deliberation. "We could meet at Tang's."

Elizabeth hung up. Joey jumped up and threw on sweatpants and a shirt, grabbing a jacket on the way out the door. She raced downstairs toward the Chinese restaurant on the corner, catching her breath as she waited for the pay phone a few steps from the entrance to ring. It seemed to take an eternity until it did.

Joey grabbed it on the first ring. "Finally," she said into the receiver.

"Sorry," Elizabeth answered.

"Listen, you're not going to believe this. A man came to see me today, Dennis Foley. He worked with Mom, and from what he said—and what I saw on his face—he was in love with her."

There was stunned silence on the other end.

"Did you hear me?" Joey asked.

"Was Mom having an affair?" Elizabeth suddenly found her voice.

"He said they weren't. But not for his lack of trying."

"God," Elizabeth breathed.

"Exactly," Joey said. "There wasn't a hint of any such thing."

Elizabeth seemed to hesitate. "Joey, I've got to tell you something. I've been afraid to. Or I just didn't want to. I don't know—it doesn't matter. But it's time." She took a deep breath. "Mom was leaving Dad when she died."

"What?" Joey couldn't comprehend what her sister was saying.

"She was going to get a divorce. Move out. The whole thing."

"Are you serious?" It was Joey's turn to be surprised. "How do you know?"

"She told me." Elizabeth's tone was rueful. "In fact, it was the last conversation I ever had with her. I told her she couldn't, that it was cruel and a terrible mistake."

"Jesus, Elizabeth," Joey said with disgust, "that sounds like you."

Elizabeth bristled. "Thanks, I appreciate the sympathy. It's not as if the fact that our last interaction was an argument hasn't tortured me every day since she died."

"Sorry. I guess that's pretty upsetting for you," Joey said.

"Well, now you know."

"Boy, what the hell was going on with Mom and Dad? He was drinking, while she was finding love and getting a new lease on life. There's a reversal I would never have expected to see."

"I don't know," Elizabeth said. "It's a lot to sort out."

"This Dennis said Mom was doing sketches for him, for a new play he's producing. He wanted to hire her to paint the costumes."

"Oh."

"I told him I'd try to find the sketches. You know, give them to him as a sort of keepsake."

Elizabeth didn't say anything for a minute. "Joey, let me go to the apartment and look around for them. Maybe there'll be something there that'll be helpful. I can go in the middle of the day when Dad's at the office."

Joey considered the proposal. "Okay, I guess. I don't know what you're hoping to find, but be my guest. The sketches will be something about Ireland, greens representing the countryside, something like that."

"Fine. I'll go tomorrow, midday."

"Good luck."

Elizabeth sighed. "Boy, do I need some of that."

With a click, she was gone.

Slowly, Joey hung up the phone on her end. Would her father ever really have permitted his wife to leave him?

Chapter Thirty

As Elizabeth reached the corner, she knelt down, pretending to adjust the laces of her boots. From that position she was able to peer around the corner and see the doorman. He was standing in front of her parents' apartment building, rocking back and forth on his heels, his hands clasped in front of him. She recognized him, an older man named Jimmy who had worked there for more than a decade. He would doubtless recognize her as well, despite her new look.

She would have to find the right opportunity to slip past him. The entrance was about fifteen feet from where she was kneeling, so she would need a moment to make the dash inside.

She didn't have to wait long. A man emerged from the building and said a few words to Jimmy, who stepped into the street to hail a taxi. Both men had their backs to her. Elizabeth stood up and sprinted into the building, then, without looking back, yanked open the door to the stairwell and raced upstairs. She didn't hear anyone behind her or any voices calling out to her as she took the steps two at a time.

She slowed as she got to the higher floors. At last she saw the number eleven painted on the wall as she rounded a landing. She pulled open the door and hastened down the deserted hall to her parents' apartment, reaching into her jeans pocket for her keys.

Her hand was shaking as she tried to get the key into the lock. She glanced around to see if anyone was coming. She fumbled a few times before it finally went in and she was able to unlock the door and get inside, slamming it shut and flipping on the light as fast as she could. She leaned against it, her heart racing, and waited until her breathing slowed.

The light inside was dim despite the bright sunshine outside, and she realized that the curtains must have been drawn in the rooms surrounding the foyer.

"Hello?" she called out tentatively.

There was no answer. Good. She hadn't expected anyone to be here, but it would hardly be pleasant to be taken by surprise.

She walked down the hall, glancing quickly into the rooms, not certain where to start. It was an eerie sensation, knowing she wasn't supposed to be in the apartment, and, at the same time, finding her childhood home oddly unfamiliar. She felt as if she hadn't set foot in it for months, even years. The apartment itself seemed to have aged. It wasn't dirty, she thought, but it somehow looked run-down, shabby. Amazing how quickly it had happened. Without her mother's supervision, it was no doubt getting only minimum upkeep and cleaning. Her father wouldn't have a clue what it took to keep a home from slipping into shoddiness. She started up the stairs, deciding to go into her parents' bedroom first. Her hand slid lightly along the banister, the feel and shape of the wood so familiar to her.

Theoretically she was here to look for those sketches Molly had done for Dennis Foley. But she was hoping to find more—exactly what, she would have been unable to say. Still, she had to come up with something.

Kent had ascertained that the homeless man on Joey's list, a Christopher Lily, had been in the hospital the day of Molly's murder; he had gotten into a fight on the street and wound up in St. Vincent's with two broken ribs and a fractured nose. They learned that Molly was far from the first person he had attacked; several had filed complaints that provoked his arrest. Sooner or later, though, he always ended up back at that spot on the same block. Elizabeth had no idea what the circumstances of this particular fight were. She only knew that he could no longer be considered a suspect in Molly's death.

Then there was Reda Mathias. She had, in fact, played out the same scenario of breaking up marriages with the managing partners of three law firms. Once Kent had the idea, it was a simple matter for him to put it all together. He tracked down the places she had worked and the managing partners who had gotten divorced during that time frame. He was able to see who had withdrawn large amounts of money from their bank accounts, perhaps to settle their divorces or perhaps to keep their girlfriend Reda happy. Elizabeth was astounded by both his ingenuity and the ease with which he put the puzzle pieces together once he got rolling.

It looked as if Jack Ross had indeed been Reda's next intended victim. He fit the bill perfectly. God only knows, Elizabeth thought, what Reda's thing was with lawyers. Her own father, they discovered, was a bartender, and Elizabeth hadn't looked any further than that for a connection. But she obviously had a grudge against lawyers or philanderers or some combination of the two. The answers were for a psychiatrist to discern, not her, she decided.

As creepy as she found it to realize that her suspicions had been right, that Reda had indeed been circling around Jack like a spider around a fly, the critical information didn't support her as Molly's killer. Reda had been in court on the day of the murder and then at dinner with a group of lawyers that night. It had been a simple matter to confirm that. Her time was accounted for. Of course, the second Elizabeth had the chance, she would get Reda out of her father's firm. She was bad news, but she probably wasn't guilty of killing anyone.

Verna Nieman, the woman who had competed with Molly in their field of costume painting, was more problematic. Elizabeth had visited her in the guise of writing a freelance magazine article on theatrical costumes, telling her she hoped to sell it to a publication after it was completed. The woman had been pleasant and helpful, although she seemed somewhat high-strung. That might have accounted for how badly she had responded to losing those jobs to Molly. She was clearly a nervous person, and it was easy to imagine her flying off the handle. Her killing someone was a more difficult scenario to conjure up, although Elizabeth knew better than to judge a suspect by appearance. Some of the most angelic-looking defendants she had come across in court had committed the most depraved crimes.

In the course of the supposed interview, they had gone over various things Verna had done in the past few weeks. Elizabeth asked her to describe a sample day—she picked a date, seemingly at random, that was the day Molly was killed. The woman seemed to think the request odd, but she pulled out her datebook and complied. She claimed to have been in her studio painting for several hours that day, something Elizabeth was hard-pressed to confirm. Maybe she was and maybe she wasn't. Elizabeth left there knowing little more than when she had come.

All of this was leading nowhere. She could only pray that while she was here in the apartment she would see something that could be of help, any little thing her mother might have left around that would speak to Elizabeth in a way it might not have spoken to the police.

She entered her parents' bedroom, a pang in her chest as she smelled the fragrance of her mother's perfume still hovering faintly in the air. At the dresser, she pulled open the drawers one by one and went through their contents, careful not to disturb anything.

It was painful to see her mother's sweaters and stockings there, still seeming to be part of someone's life. Her father had done nothing about getting rid of Molly's things, she noted. Not a single item had been removed from the dresser top or the drawers, as far as she could tell.

She headed for her mother's closet and searched through the dresses, checking the pockets, hoping to find a note or a list or anything that might be of some use. Nothing. She opened her mother's pocketbooks, neatly lined up on a shelf, but found only her makeup, wallet, and checkbook in the one she used most often; the others contained stray hairpins, receipts, pens, and the like. She poked through hats and shoes, scarves and gloves. She knelt down and looked under the bed, unsurprised to see only dust. If there had been anything of interest in this room, the police had already taken it.

Dejected, she went downstairs, deciding she would come back up later to check out the rooms that had been hers and Joey's as a last resort. First she wanted to go through her mother's other personal place in the house, the so-called sewing room. The last place she had seen her mother alive, she reminded herself, before she had screamed at Molly and stormed out.

Heavy with her own guilt, she looked through the bookshelves, pulling down titles at random and flipping through them, wondering if something would miraculously fall out from between the pages to answer all her questions. It would take hours to go through every volume, and she doubted that it would be productive anyway. It was unlikely that Molly would have stashed sketches in a book. She was hoping for a note that said, "So-and-So killed me," buried in a copy of Shakespeare or Updike, she thought cynically.

She turned to the desk in the corner. The drawers revealed job bids, receipts for art supplies, letters of thanks and recommendations from clients, photographs of her mother with this or that performer or producer or director at openings of plays and operas for which she had painted the costumes. There was a file marked "House," nearly three inches thick, containing bills and receipts for furnishings and work done in the apartment going back to 1975.

In a slim, unmarked folder, she came upon two pieces of construction paper, both with childish crayon scrawlings, one marked "Elizabeth, age 6," the other "Joey, age 4." Molly had kept one example each of their childhood artwork. Elizabeth's appeared to be a picture of a house, dwarfed by the large, leafy tree beside it. Joey's was a drawing of a horse and rider, the horse purple with stars on it, the rider a barely recognizable human form with big red lips and long yellow corkscrews of hair.

Elizabeth was touched to think that her mother had kept the art. It gave her a moment's pause as she stood there, staring at the drawings, the once-vibrant colors now faded.

She put the drawings back in their place. In the last drawer she opened, she saw the bulging files of sketches, labeled by production name and date, with the thickest ones in back marked "Ideas" and "Research." Flipping through the tabs, she was assaulted by memories of the shows on which her mother had worked, the hours she had put into the costumes, the trips to theaters, telephone conferences, her feverish sketching in the early stages of a job on whatever scrap of paper was handy.

But it was in the file marked "Ideas" that the power of her mother's imagination was apparent. Mesmerized, Elizabeth leafed through the drawings, taking in the array of skirts and hats, dresses and gloves, all decorated in astonishing flights of fancy. Many of these designs could probably never be used; they weren't necessarily practical, or even possible, to wear onstage, let alone execute at any reasonable cost. But they showed Molly's artistry. *I never realized she was so talented,* Elizabeth thought, abashed. Good, yes. Competent, yes. But from what she saw before her, it was clear to Elizabeth that Molly hadn't yet achieved all she was capable of. If she could have made these drawings, she could have done incredible work, given the right opportunities.

With a sigh, Elizabeth put the folder back and quickly glanced through the remaining ones. Capes, tutus, tulle fairy costumes, and the like flashed by. But there was nothing that matched the description of sketches for Dennis Foley.

She shut the drawer before reaching for the large black-lacquer box that Molly always kept on the desk. Elizabeth and Joey used to love playing with what they called "the magic box." It was a hand-painted jewelry box, streaked with delicate gold and orange designs. Their mother had once shown them the trick to opening up its secret compartment. Molly used it to hold paper clips and Scotch tape. The secret compartment, a long, flat drawer beneath, was always empty. Elizabeth could remember how she and Joey would hide their own little treasures inside it, coming back days or weeks later to squeal with delight at seeing them still there.

She lifted the box and felt underneath for the familiar spot. Finding it, she pressed, releasing the latch. The drawer sprang open. But this time it wasn't empty.

Elizabeth extracted the folded papers that were inside. She put the box down so she could open them gently. Scanning what was before her, she saw page after page of her mother's handwriting, hurried and sloppier than her usual proper script.

My Darling Daughters,

Will you ever get this letter? Will I ever have the courage to tell you the story I'm about to write down? I hope so. I think so. But for now, I need to see the words myself.

Only then will you girls have a mother who can make her life her own.

I was seventeen when it happened, the event that was to alter my very existence. My parents and I were living

*in the big house in Riverdale. I was a senior in high
school. Studious. Popular even. It was a Monday. I
had had all my morning classes and was at lunch in
the cafeteria when my stomach started to hurt. Finally,
the pain got so bad that I went to the school nurse. She
wanted to call my mother, but Mom had gone to visit
her sister in Chicago. She wasn't due home until later
that night. No one would be home at two in the afternoon, so the nurse let me go.*

*I walked to the house, stopped to say hello to Mrs.
Henderson, who lived next door. Everything was normal until I reached the front door. I was turning my
key in the lock when I heard the voices. I was about
to turn around and yell for Mrs. Henderson when I
realized one of them belonged to my father. I would
have called out to him, but I heard a woman screaming.*

*I walked inside and listened. The sounds were com-
ing from the living room. The woman was still yelling,
and she sounded terrified. Then there was a thump, and
then my father's voice raised in fury.*

"Shut up, you bitch!"

*I couldn't believe what I was hearing. I remember
my bookbag slipping to the floor. I heard the woman
screaming for him to stop. I realized the voice belonged
to his secretary, Pia.*

*I'll never forget the rest of it. My father's words. "I
told you. I told you fifty times to get rid of it." And
the words were punctuated with the sounds of blows.
With each blow came Pia's groans of pain.*

*"You think you can blackmail me into leaving my
wife? For some bastard baby, no less. As if I give a
good God damn!"*

*My heart was pounding so hard it finally made me
move. I raced down the hall, but I stopped when I saw
what was going on. My father had her locked in his
grip, and he was striking her over and over. Pia had
one arm covering her stomach, obviously trying to protect it, while she struggled to push him away. But he
was so much stronger and heavier. Her efforts were
useless.*

From where I stood, I could see the blood running from Pia's nose. Her eyes were already swollen shut.

She was crying, begging my father to stop. "You'll kill the baby! You'll kill me!"

My father just kept hitting her. "Who would care if I did?" That was all he would say.

I can't describe how horrified I was, standing there, watching him. He punched Pia so hard her head snapped all the way back.

I couldn't bear what was happening. I screamed as loud as I could, "Daddy! Stop it!"

I tore across the room and grabbed at him, trying to make him stop, but he shook me off so hard I crashed backward onto the floor. I sat there for a few seconds trying to catch my breath, but then I saw him punch her again, even harder this time, driving his fist right into her stomach.

I don't remember actually deciding to pick up the brass clock. It was as if it had been decided for me somehow. It was on the mantelpiece. I used to love the chimes when I was a little girl, used to wait for them to ring when the big hand reached the hour. But now it was just something to stop him with. I held it high over my head and brought it down hard. I couldn't think what else to do. There was so much blood. So much blood.

I'm not sure when I found out that he was dead. That I had killed him. Or when I knew that Pia had died too. All of it had been for nothing.

And I'll never exactly recall the moment I realized your father was there. Jack Ross. The young man who raked the leaves and did odd jobs around the house to put himself through law school. He'd been there all along, outside the window. Watching my father and Pia. Watching me.

I never told anyone what had happened. Not the police, not even my mother. Jack was so insistent on that point. "Don't say anything. *I've spoken to a lawyer friend of mine, and uttering even a word about what happened could end up in an indictment of murder." He drilled it into me before the police arrived. I never*

understood where he found the time to make the call.
I never even knew how the police got there or what he
told them. All I knew for sure was that they were gone.
And the blood was on my hands.

Elizabeth paused in her reading, struggling to envision
her mother as a young girl, confronted with this violent
argument between her father and the woman Molly
claimed here was his mistress. She tried to imagine
Molly grasping that her father was out of control. That
she was the only one who could stop him. *Seventeen*
years old. And she had virtually been forced to kill him.

After all this, what else could I do but marry Jack
Ross, the one who had taken care of me? It's almost too
painful for me to consider how my life might have gone
if I had only faced up to everything. But I was in a daze.
As for Jack, he saw his opportunity to have me and he
seized it. He didn't care that I didn't love him. What I
wanted was utterly unimportant. He needed to own me,
and that was that.

But now I want to take away the power of his threat
to tell my secret. I believe I have repaid Jack Ross in
full by being the possession he desired for thirty-six
years. I've kept my end of the bargain.

Molly went on for another page, quickly summarizing
the painful years of her agoraphobia, her recovery, and
the unbearable sadness of having abdicated responsibility for her life to a man she didn't love.

He is still threatening to reveal me as a monstrous
killer. He cannot bear the idea that I could leave him,
Molly wrote in conclusion. *But I'm done with it. Let*
him do his damnedest.

Elizabeth set the papers down on the desk. She
stared ahead, unseeing, for several minutes, thinking
about what she had just read. Then she buried her
face in her hands and wept.

Chapter Thirty-one

Elizabeth inserted a quarter and dialed the number for Kent's beeper, reading it from a slip of paper in her hand. She punched in the number of the pay phone, then hung up to wait for him to call back. It wouldn't take long—Kent always had his cellular phone with him. Even so, she was glad there was no one else standing at the bank of telephones in the Plaza Hotel lobby with her.

In less than a minute, the phone rang. She picked it up immediately.

"Hi," she said softly. "It's me."

"What? I can't hear you," Kent yelled into the telephone, his voice rising above the noise surrounding him on his end.

"It's me," she said as loudly as she dared. "How's the ball game?"

"Good. It's tied, three-three, top of the sixth." He sounded distracted. "What's up?"

"Sorry to interrupt. I need a favor. After the game, could you go to Joey's office? I don't dare call there. Tell her I need to see her. Tonight. Seven o'clock."

"What time did you say?" he asked as the crowd cheered loudly in the background.

"Seven. Tell her to meet me where the seals are in the Central Park Zoo."

"Seals, zoo, seven o'clock. Got it."

"I'll go back to the apartment. Call me there if you run into any problems. Remember, it's Park and Fiftieth."

"Yup." There was a sudden roar on Kent's end. "Jeez, I don't believe that!" he yelled about whatever had just transpired on the field.

"Thanks, Kent. It's important."

"Don't worry, hon. See you later."

"When I get back from seeing my sister."

"Right. Bye."

He disconnected the call.

Elizabeth hung up and hastened out of the quiet lobby, eager to be back on the street, walking among the indifferent crowds of Fifth Avenue. She looked at her watch. It was almost three-thirty. She regretted having to bother Kent during the ball game. He had had tickets to the Yankees game for a couple of months, and he was going with a friend he hadn't seen in a long time. But she knew his friend had to leave right after the game, and he would be driving straight back into Manhattan, so it wasn't as if she was asking him to cut anything short.

She was afraid to call Joey, knowing she would run the risk of the secretary recognizing her voice or, even worse, the possibility of a bug or tracing device on Joey's line. She had no way of knowing how far the police had gone in trying to track her through her sister. But Kent could just zip in and out of Joey's office with the message and be done with it. They had already discussed his taking Joey a message should the need arise.

The need had arisen now, that was for sure. Elizabeth had spent hours wandering lower Manhattan that morning before ending up in midtown, trying to make sense of her mother's notes. Her mind was going in circles, around and around her misconceived sense of her parents' marriage and the way it actually had been.

She headed downtown. She would go back to Kent's

apartment in case he called there because he was unable to contact Joey or she couldn't make the meeting. But seven o'clock was her best shot at finding Joey available; her sister wouldn't have to leave work during the day, and she could probably squeeze it in before any evening plans she might have.

Elizabeth fervently hoped Joey would come. She had to tell her what she had learned. Maybe Joey could shed some light on things. Maybe Joey even knew more about their parents than Elizabeth thought she did. Joey was the one who supported Molly, and maybe her favoritism was based on an actual reason she had never shared with Elizabeth. Was it possible her sister could have known some of what those notes contained? Elizabeth doubted it, but she had to find out, and she had to fill Joey in if she didn't know.

The confusion about her parents had kept her thoughts cloudy all day. She couldn't seem to wrap her mind around the misconceptions she had held for so many years. It was almost too much to take in. Her beloved father wasn't the devoted, heartsick victim of love, as she had always viewed him. He had taken advantage of a tragic incident and manipulated a young girl who was alone and terrified, incapable of thinking clearly. Not to mention encouraging her to believe that she would have gone to jail for what she did, which was in no way a foregone conclusion.

Molly had been a scared, unhappy girl, trapped with a terrible secret. The years of staying inside were a symptom of her terror and self-hatred. Her notes were filled with agony. Of being unable to raise her babies. Of being so depressed and weakened that she couldn't do the one thing that might have given her happiness. And, according to what Molly had written, her husband had done nothing to encourage her to get better. Having his little princess locked up inside was fine with him. He had all the money and contacts anyone needed to get help for someone suffering from her condition, but he hadn't made a move to do anything about it.

I can't imagine it, Elizabeth thought in anguish. And then, of course, I grew up to give her nothing but grief night and day, always looking down on her, barely deigning to speak to her. After that, I was the big benevolent lawyer, polite and accommodating but still utterly superior.

Elizabeth turned onto Sixth Avenue, her shame so intense she actually bowed her head with the weight of it. There were clearly all sorts of things between her parents that she had no idea about, yet she had somehow come to believe she understood everything there was to understand. How could I have been so stupid, she asked herself. The hubris.

She couldn't begin to imagine what it had been like for Molly to live with the memory of smashing her own father's skull in and having him bleed to death at her feet. It was so difficult to put that image together with the woman who had been her mother. All the years of her being so distracted, so *not there,* suddenly made sense. I'd want to be distracted too, Elizabeth said to herself, if I had to see two corpses in front of me every time I shut my eyes. Dear God.

She was exhausted from the hours she had spent going over it. She walked without thinking anymore, not wanting to feel anything else. On Houston Street, she stopped at a deli and bought a sandwich to take home, then continued on until she reached Kent's apartment.

She ate her sandwich, then spent the remaining time she had going over the notes she had made about her mother's death. Verna Nieman was still an open question, but Elizabeth had an instinct that she was going in the wrong direction with Verna.

She was growing more agitated. She was anxious to talk to her sister. After what seemed like an eternity, six-thirty approached, and Kent still hadn't called to tell her of any problem. Gratefully, she grabbed her purse and headed out. What a relief it would be to discuss this all with Joey, she thought as she got into a taxi to go uptown.

It was a balmy evening, and the zoo was full of people enjoying the pleasant summer weather. Elizabeth made her way to the seal tank and looked around. No sign of Joey, but it was only five to seven. Elizabeth propped her elbows on the side of the tank and leaned over, gazing at the shiny seals, some swimming in the green water, some resting on the rocks. Were they seals or sea lions? She could never remember the difference.

At seven-fifteen, she stretched and began pacing around the tank. By seven-thirty, she was frowning, unhappy at how conspicuous she was, standing in one area for so long. She moved away, strolling around but staying close enough to keep the seal tank in view. The sun was beginning to set. Well, she thought, a million things could have kept Joey. Still, her sister hadn't taken Elizabeth's situation lightly, and she would know better than to let her stand here, exposed.

At eight-thirty, Elizabeth decided she didn't dare stay any longer. She hastened out of the park and back into a taxi. Sighing, she wondered what the hell she should do next. She *had* to get to Joey.

When she let herself in at Kent's apartment, he was sitting at the table, eating pizza from an open box beside him.

"Hi. I didn't know how long you'd be, so I ordered in," he said cheerfully as she approached.

She dropped her purse on the table.

"Joey never showed up," she said. "I can't understand it."

The look on Kent's face immediately explained why.

"Oh, Christ, I'm sorry," he said, wincing. "The game went into extra innings, and I completely forgot. We didn't get out of there until about seven ourselves."

Elizabeth stared at him. "You never gave her the message?"

"I couldn't," he said defensively. "I was stuck at Yankee Stadium."

"You were stuck," she repeated. "You were prevented from leaving?"

"No," he said in annoyance, "you know what I mean." His tone grew placating. "It was three-three, and the damn thing went thirteen innings. The Yankees won."

Elizabeth stood where she was, just looking at him in disbelief.

"I said I was sorry," he went on, "and I'll make it up to you, I promise. I'll go see her first thing tomorrow."

Elizabeth was about to speak, but thought better of it. If he didn't understand what was wrong about leaving her stranded, a goddamn fugitive from the police, so he wouldn't have to miss the end of a ball game, then she doubted she could explain it. Sure, Kent figured he could go tomorrow. It was all a big joke to him. What was one day more or less? But tomorrow, Joey would have a full day of work scheduled. And, tomorrow, Elizabeth would be another day further into this mess. Kent didn't seem to feel any sense of urgency about her situation. All along, she had had the uneasy feeling that he was having far too much fun with it. It struck her suddenly that she never would have had a problem like this with Peter. Peter understood things.

She turned away. "It's not necessary for you to go tomorrow. That's too late."

"No, no, I'll do it," he protested. "I don't mind."

Her eyes met his, but she remained unsmiling. "No, Kent, don't bother," she said with finality.

He shrugged. "Suit yourself."

She headed back to the area near the bed, where her few belongings were stashed in a dresser drawer. Kent had been an enormous help to her with his computer, and she would always be grateful to him for that. But what she thought she'd seen in him simply wasn't there. She had been making an enormous mistake because of her own loneliness and need.

It was time to go back to the bed-and-breakfast on Horatio Street. Time to stop pretending that she wasn't utterly alone out here.

Chapter Thirty-two

Joey touched Lisa's elbow as the deputy entered the vast blue-carpeted courtroom. She felt Lisa stiffen in fear as the man began banging his hand heavily on the dark, wood-paneled wall.

"All rise," he said loudly. "The Honorable Judge Willard Schneider presiding, the case of the United States versus Alice Lynn Carter."

As Lisa came to her feet, her hands were trembling. Joey watched with concern as the fingers of her friend's right hand grasped the side of her beige skirt, as a baby might hang on to a blanket. Reassuringly, Joey looked back toward the right gallery, leading Lisa's eyes toward the first three rows, where her husband and their two children were joined by Lisa's parents and her brothers and sisters, plus assorted nieces and nephews of whose existence she hadn't even known before the last couple of weeks. Also on hand was Cornelia Wrightson, who'd flown in from Montana the day before. Lisa, Cornelia, and Joey had had some time together in Valhalla, a joyous reunion despite the circumstances.

Joey knew how important it was to keep Lisa's hopes alive. Otherwise, the depression that had seemed to consume her when she first turned herself in threatened to become a permanent condition, regardless of the outcome of today's hearing. Joey herself had called Lisa's brothers and sisters, begging them to come today. For some of them, that had been hard. After all, their sister had disappeared for nearly three decades. As far as they knew, she had no interest in them, no sympathy for what their direst fears had been all this time.

But most of them had come anyway. I guess Robert Frost must have known what he was talking about, she mused, whatever that line was about home being the place where they have to take you in. Suddenly she wondered who in her family would come to her aid if she needed help. Mom, she realized sadly. She would have been here in a minute. Clearly her father would be no good. In the old days, he wouldn't have cared enough. Now, he could barely get through the day.

Of course, there was Elizabeth. Sure, she thought automatically, like my sister would lift a finger. Then she caught herself. Elizabeth had been the one who had in fact helped her on this case. Not that she could count on anything. But maybe it had been a start.

Then she caught sight of her friend Tom Abrahams, who was seated in the back row of the courtroom. He was on vacation all week while the school where he taught was closed for asbestos clearing. That's fine, she thought. Perhaps Tom was family enough.

Enough self-obsession, she chided herself. I've got a client to take care of. And that client had been terrified when Joey and Cornelia had left the correctional facility the night before.

Joey gave Lisa a warm, reassuring smile. "Of course, I can't promise anything," she said fervently, "but with every fiber of my being I'm going to do my best to get us back to Montana for breakfast as soon as humanly possible."

Lisa smiled back, and today, with all her family around, the smile seemed genuinely hopeful. Having those she loved most at her side in support seemed to make her as close to happy as she could get. Straightening her shoulders almost imperceptibly, Lisa stood tall as Judge Schneider took his seat at the bench.

Of course she's nervous, Joey thought sympathetically. This hearing, which preceded an actual trial, would test the strength of their case. Joey had pieced together information she found startling, information that might exonerate Lisa from the most serious of the charges against her. If the charge of felony murder could be dropped, the amount of jail time the U.S. attorney might ask for at the trial would be relatively minimal.

But there was no guarantee that the case would go that way. It was all up to Judge Schneider. At this stage, there was no jury, no one other than the stern-looking middle-aged man in the dark robe, who would decide Lisa's fate.

Everyone in the courtroom sat back down as the judge sorted through a stack of papers in front of him, then exchanged a few words with his law clerk, who was seated at a table just to his right. Finally, he looked out to the gallery, first to Lisa and Joey, seated at the defense table, then across the room to Frank Warner, the short, bald, aggressively mustached U.S. attorney whose job it was to put Lisa Martin away for as long as possible.

"So, what do we have here?" Judge Schneider asked with deceptive geniality.

Frank Warner rose, his hand poised on a stack of notes. "As you know, Your Honor, the case against the defendant involves—"

"Before we start, Your Honor . . ."

The sound of Joey's voice startled the federal prosecutor. Judge Schneider also looked at her curiously. It was most unusual for the defense attorney to interrupt at this stage of the hearing.

"What is it, Ms. Ross?" The judge's tone had grown measurably less genial.

Joey stood and faced Judge Schneider squarely. "Thank you for the indulgence, Your Honor." Her voice was smooth and steady, but inside she could feel the tension building in her stomach. Everything rested on the next few minutes.

"Alice Lynn Carter is here today to face the charges resulting from a robbery and murder almost thirty years ago. There were certain facts that had been understood at the time Ms. Carter turned herself in to federal authorities." Joey turned to include the U.S. attorney in her gaze. "Now other facts have come to light that I believe will change the nature and the substance of the indictment."

Judge Schneider's annoyance was visible in the tightening of his mouth. "Whatever those facts are should have been shared with the U.S. attorney's office long before today."

"Of course, Your Honor," Joey said respectfully. "Unfortunately, those facts weren't known until now. It was only this morning that the final piece of evidence came into my possession."

"This seems precipitous, Your Honor." Frank Warner glared at Joey.

"My apologies to the U.S. attorney," Joey said politely. "I promise you I'm not wasting the court's time. In fact," she put a protective arm on her client's shoulder, "I believe that what I have to tell the court will save everybody a great deal of trouble, and"—she looked back up at the judge—"form the basis for an entirely new prosecution for first-degree murder."

There was a sudden hush in the gallery.

"Okay, Ms. Ross," Judge Schneider said, "let's hear what you have to say."

Frank Warner sat back down in his chair grudgingly, still leaning forward as if he might rise again in an instant.

"Gentlemen," Joey walked around to stand midway between the judge and the prosecutor. Out of the corner of her eye she saw an artist begin a pencil sketch, which she assumed would include all three of them when it was used on some broadcast later on. "The crime for which Lisa Martin—pardon me if I use the name the defendant has gone by for the past twenty-nine years. She has lived under that name, has raised two children under that name, has been my friend under that name, for a very long time." Joey turned back to her client for a moment, smiling at her encouragingly.

Then she focused her attention on the case. "At the time Lisa Martin disappeared, the murder of Henry Langdon, the bank guard who was also a member of the Peekskill police force, was thought to have been part and parcel of the bank robbery, which would form the basis of a felony murder charge. And there has never been any question of Lisa Martin's participation in that robbery. She has openly admitted to having taken part in what at the time was considered by her and her friends to be a political act in a highly charged climate, one that divided the country, indeed the whole world."

She noticed the opposing attorney growing impatient. The last thing she needed was to be interrupted by Frank Warner, so she hurried on. "It has now come to my attention that the murder of Henry Langdon"— her eyes narrowed—"and it *was* a murder, let me assure you—came not as a consequence of the bank robbery but as a separate and malevolent action performed by its only participant, a man who then called himself Freddie Shore."

Warner rose to his feet quickly. "Mr. Shore has been under indictment all these years. We know his part in the crime."

"No," Joey answered, "you don't."

Warner shook his head. "Your Honor, it is not the defense attorney's job to tell me what I know."

The judge cut him off before he could say any more. "Let us allow Ms. Ross to have her say." He turned to Joey sternly. "I assume you're getting to your point."

Joey breathed deeply. "Thank you, Your Honor. The man then known as Freddie Shore wasn't part of the group referred to as the Peekskill Six for the political reasons shared by its other five members. Freddie Shore, now known as Robert Mallory, distorted the idealism of five naive young students to gain a personal fortune."

The courtroom erupted in noise, members of the press who were in the back of the gallery pushed forward in their seats to hear more clearly, relatives of Lisa's exclaimed to each other in surprise.

Joey pressed on. "We always knew that four of the young people, Lisa Martin included, had left the scene of the robbery several minutes before Freddie Shore shot Henry Langdon." She paused and walked back to the defense table, took a sip of water, then turned once more toward the judge. "And Freddie Shore, also known as Robert Mallory, was indisputedly the man who pointed the gun at the victim. Why he should have fired on the bank guard long after the the robbery had taken place has always been a mystery, to the police investigating the incident and to my client and her friends. But, as was confirmed only this morning, there was a very good reason. That reason was approximately fifty thousand shares of the Morris Corporation."

Lisa heard several people in the gallery gasp in surprise. "These were shares owned by Emily Westman, which would have been inherited upon her death by her nephew Henry Langdon, had he lived. Instead, they went to his cousin, Deborah Langdon, now Mrs. Robert Mallory."

Frank Warner stood up, his face flushed. "Are you saying that a twenty-year-old war resister went to such ridiculous lengths to get his hands on the *future* inheritance of a woman he hadn't even yet married? How could he know she would inherit those shares? How could he be so sure they would marry?"

"Because," Joey said patiently, "of the proof I received at eight-fifteen this morning." She reached back to the table and retrieved several pieces of fax paper.

Frank Warner joined her as she approached the bench. The paper she put in front of Judge Schneider had a facsimile of the Maryland state seal at the top. The official-looking document, dated May 15, 1967, certified that Deborah Langdon and Robert Mallory had been joined in matrimony—well before the murder.

The judge examined the document, then looked up at Joey. "This is not uninteresting, but how does the court know that Mr. Mallory had any reason to suspect that the death of Henry Langdon would lead to his wife's inheritance?"

Joey took a deep breath. "Because I also have confirmed evidence of Mr. Mallory's proven knowledge of the terms of Emily Westman's will, wherein the shares go to Deborah Langdon in case of Henry Langdon's death."

"And you're claiming that Robert Mallory actually went to these lengths to cover up a premeditated murder? And that this Mallory is the same man as Freddie Shore?"

Joey nodded solemnly. For the next thirty minutes, she went through her findings in detail, pulling out reams of material, including numerous interviews with Emily Westman's household staff and legal staff regarding conversations they had had with Robert Mallory. She showed them documents ranging from Emily Westman's last will and testament to two marriage licenses issued to Robert Mallory and Deborah Langdon, one preceding the death of Emily Westman, the other a year after.

When Joey had gone through most of the evidence she had collected, she walked back to the table where Lisa sat, tears streaming down her face. Joey stood behind Lisa's chair and placed both hands on her client's shoulders.

"While he was calling himself Freddie Shore, idealistic war resister, Robert Mallory was already laying the groundwork for a murder that had nothing whatever to do with anything but his own pocket." She squeezed Lisa's shoulder softly. "I assure the court that all of this is as much of a surprise to Lisa Martin as it is to everyone here. For almost three decades, she has been feeling incredible guilt about a crime she had absolutely no part of. What was made to look like an accident of radical politics was, in fact, one man's extraordinary dance of violence and greed."

Frank Warner looked almost shell-shocked as Judge Schneider called for a lunch break.

"I'll see you back here at two-thirty," he barked to both attorneys as he strode out of the courtroom.

"What will happen now?" Lisa asked, her brow furrowed in worry.

Joey sighed as she sat down in her chair. "That's up to the judge. Either he'll bind it over until tomorrow or he'll make some kind of ruling."

One of the federal marshals came over to them to collect Lisa. Joey hugged her for a long moment before releasing her.

"Look for a four-leaf clover while you're eating your tuna on rye," she urged Lisa whimsically.

As the guards led her toward the side door, Lisa's face brightened. "Who needs a four-leaf clover when they have you on their side!"

Joey watched them escort her out, then began stacking the papers that lay in front of her. She had done all she could. Now it was up to the judge.

"Joey, you were magnificent."

Cornelia was beside her suddenly, along with Lisa's oldest brother, Carl, and her mother, Ruth Carter. Joey responded warmly at first, but then she pulled away.

"It's not over yet," she said cautiously. "You never know what a judge is going to do."

Lisa's mother spoke up firmly. "I'm her mother. I *know.*"

Suddenly Joey felt helpless. So many people would be affected by this. Not just Lisa. Not just Hal and the kids. So many lives would be changed forever. She prayed she had done enough.

Lisa's husband came to stand beside her. "Let me buy you lunch."

Joey looked up at Hal Martin, struck suddenly by his bravery. How many men could have their lives explode this way and still be as consistent and thoughtful as Lisa's husband continued to be? Here he was, two thousand miles away from home, working hard to maintain Lisa's spirits. Would any man do the same for her, she wondered, the image of Gary McCullough inserting itself in her head. The thought made her want to cry, but now was no time to give in to that feeling. If Hal could be hopeful at a moment like this, she owed it to him and to the kids to do likewise.

"I'm starved," she said, smiling up at him as she lied.

At precisely two-thirty, Judge Schneider walked to his seat at the high bench. Joey and Lisa stood together, their hands clasped for luck.

"Based on the record before me, the court hereby dismisses the felony murder charge against Lisa Martin. The robbery charge will stand."

With those few words, he stood up and strode out of the courtroom.

"All rise," instructed the courtroom deputy, although by the time the words were out the judge was practically gone from the room.

Lisa and Joey looked at each other. For a moment, they were too overwhelmed to move. Only when Lisa's family surrounded them did the two react. Lisa threw her arms around Joey's neck, holding on for dear life.

"You're amazing," she breathed, "absolutely amazing."

Cornelia Wrightson came up behind them, hugging both of them as tears flowed down her face. "You certainly are," she echoed Lisa's words.

Lisa removed herself finally, searching the crowd for her husband. Finding Hal, she flew into his arms, then turned and brought her children into the crush of their embrace.

Lisa's brother put his hand out to congratulate Joey. "What happens now?" he asked.

Joey looked thoughtful. "With a simple robbery charge, Lisa will probably get jail time of a year or two. Possibly even less, given what's come out about Freddie Shore's role in getting all of them into the robbery to begin with." She smiled at him. "We'll have to wait and see, but the worst is over."

"Jeez," he said, pumping her hand energetically. "You are one smart woman."

Tom came over to them and put his arm around Joey. Clearly he had overheard their conversation. "We always knew she had a brain," he said, ruffling Joey's hair. "Now, let's see if she has some courage and a heart."

Joey scowled at him. She didn't even feel up to asking him what he meant, although she was pretty sure it had nothing to do with the case she'd just tried. She couldn't remember when she'd felt so exhausted. Or so claustrophobic. The stately federal courthouse in White Plains was almost elegant, but right now it felt suffocating.

"Excellent job, Counselor," Tom said, giving her a quick kiss on the cheek.

"How'd you like to do me a favor?"

He smiled. "For Perry Mason—anything."

"I could really use some air. How about we explore the beauties of Westchester County? I have my running stuff in my trunk."

They began to walk toward the exit.

Tom looked down at his outfit. "You think that because I'm wearing blue jeans and loafers, you'll be able to keep up with me," he said playfully. "But I've got sneakers in the car. You don't stand a chance."

Within fifteen minutes they were jogging together alongside the Bronx River Parkway, a stretch of trees and grass too beautiful to be wasted on the cars that sped by all day long.

Joey breathed a sigh of relief. The day had taken everything out of her. "Thanks," she said, shooting Tom an appreciative smile. "I needed a friend."

He looked back at her, his eyebrow raised cynically.

"What?" she asked, slowing down.

Tom shrugged his shoulders. "I don't know, pal. Maybe a friend is what you need. Or maybe that's what you'd like to *think* you need."

She ran in silence. She had a feeling that she knew where he was going with this, and she wasn't going to make it easy for him to get there.

"Lose your voice, Counselor?"

"What exactly is it you want me to say?" she finally replied sarcastically. "That all I really need is a good—"

"Don't demean yourself, Joey," Tom interrupted. He caught her upper arm with his hand and slowed them both down, stopping completely at the base of a large tree. "What you need, damn it, is to admit you're in love with the man who loves you."

Joey found herself breathing heavily, whether from the jogging or from what Tom was saying she wasn't quite sure. She wished fervently that she'd never told Tom about Gary McCullough. He didn't understand. There was no way he could.

"Tom," she said quietly, "I really appreciate your trying to help. And I know that for whatever reason, you actually do think someone could love me. Honest," she looked up at him plaintively, "if there were a prayer in hell that the man you're referring to even *thought* about me for a single minute, I might try to do something about it. But . . ."

"What the hell is the matter with you?" he exclaimed in frustration. Then he reached for her hand. "What is this?" he asked, holding it up in the air.

"It's my hand," she answered, jerking it away petulantly.

"And what are those?" he continued, pointing at her feet.

"Nikes. Size seven and a half." She met his eyes blandly. "So what?"

"Well, at least you can see *some* of the things that are right in front of you." He didn't even bother to sound angry. He just kept looking at her sympathetically.

"I don't need this from you," she snapped defensively.

"Yes," he answered patiently, "you do. You have a man who adores you, who would literally break down doors for you, and all you can do is run away like a four-year-old child." He strode away from her, stopping at the next tree to stretch out his calf muscle. "You'd rather tell yourself a story that even a mental midget would throw out of court, let alone a Harvard-educated attorney." He finished stretching one leg and extended the other. "Like some fancy Manhattan detective would claim he loved you in order to spy on you."

Joey could barely control the sadness that was welling up inside her. If only he were right, if only he understood how impossible it all was. "Tom, you're my friend, you actually believe it could happen. But nobody ever cared the way Gary claims to, so why should it be so different now? How could it be?"

Tom finished his stretches and walked back to her. He put his arms around her, swaying rhythmically as if she were a helpless infant. "It could have been different, Joey, if you had let it. All those years, all that hostility . . . honey, it was *always* up to you."

Joey allowed her head to rest against his shoulder. She didn't know if what he was saying was true or not, but something inside her forced her to listen, to really hear the words instead of automatically throwing them away as she'd done so many times in the past. "Do you really believe this crap?" she asked finally, a sob in her voice.

Instead of answering directly, Tom kept right on cradling her. But now he started crooning in the sing-song voice she herself had used to taunt her sister thousands of times throughout their childhood.

"Gary luh-uhves Joey . . . Gary luh-uhves Joey."

Instead of lashing out at him, Joey found herself grinning like an idiot.

*   *   *

Joey approached the restaurant slowly. What if he didn't eat here anymore? What if he had been here and had left already? *What if he were here and she really had to say what was on her mind?* Now, there was a truly terrifying notion.

She willed herself to go through the door, to keep going until she was far enough inside to see to the back. Oh, God, there he is, she thought. Gary was all alone, his head buried in a hardcover book.

Fearfully, she backed up a few steps, praying he wouldn't see her there. But his eyes met hers almost immediately. Coolly, he seemed to assess her. He neither rose nor indicated that he wanted her to come over. He simply sat there, forcing her to make her own choice.

Her feet moved without her consciously telling them to. She found herself standing near him, staring at him, uncertain about what to say, not even sure of what she really wanted.

He didn't push her. In fact, with slow deliberation, he took a bite of what looked like a slice of lamb, chewing it thoughtfully while watching her in silence.

"Did you mean it?" she asked finally, sounding like an incoherent fool to her own ears.

But he didn't laugh at her. Nor did he pretend not to understand. "I mean everything I say. That's the thing about me. I tell the absolute truth. All the time. Whether you want to hear it or not."

Tentatively, she sat down on the chair opposite his. "That's just what my sister used to say about me when we were children. That I told the truth all too often. That I could learn to be polite instead of shattering everyone with frankness."

"Shatter me with the truth, Joey," he said, putting down his fork. "Let's hear it." He was looking into her eyes now, his expression unreadable.

She found she couldn't look at him any longer. She wished a tornado would blow in and take her away, that she would wake up suddenly and this would turn out to be a dream. But the words came anyway.

"I love you." Unwanted tears were stinging her eyes. "And if you really are only interested in finding my sister, I love you anyway." She looked at him, her glance a question.

She was shocked to see the unguarded happiness on his face.

"It's about time, honey," he said softly, putting his hand out to draw her face toward his. His kiss went on for what seemed like hours.

Finally he pulled away. "So, what would you like to eat?" he asked with a grin, as he enfolded her hands in a grip that felt as if it would never end.

Chapter Thirty-three

Elizabeth looked carefully around the room. The second floor of Miss Ellie's, the cozy restaurant on West Seventy-ninth Street, was nearly empty, as it usually was in the middle of the afternoon. Getting the message to Joey about meeting her here had been dangerous, but the secretary who answered her sister's office phone sounded utterly unfamiliar to Elizabeth. Even so, she had lowered her voice considerably.

Well, she thought, there's nothing I can do about it now. She looked at her watch. Joey would be here any minute, She took the pages her mother had written out of her bag and spread them out on the table in front of her, covering them with her hands when the pretty young waitress walked over to take her order.

"I'll just start with a Coke, thank you," Elizabeth said, glancing past her with relief at the sight of her sister emerging from the staircase in the smoking area beyond.

Joey threw her handbag and briefcase onto the chair next to Elizabeth and sat on the one opposite.

"So, sister dear, what is it that's brought us to the beautiful Upper West Side?"

Elizabeth looked at her curiously. "You're in a jaunty mood, aren't you?"

Joey broke into a broad smile that Elizabeth could barely remember ever having witnessed before.

"I have quite a lot to feel jaunty about, thank you. For one thing, I'm about to stop being a lawyer. Again."

"I read about the Lisa Martin decision," Elizabeth said warmly. "Congratulations."

Joey nodded. "It almost made the law look good." She smiled yet again. "But not good enough."

"Does this mean you'll be going back to Montana?"

An even more unusual look came over her sister's face. "Well, maybe not. That is, I may write my columns from New York for a while." She seemed to be debating something in her head, but instead of explaining whatever it was she was thinking about, she changed the subject. "So why am I here?"

Elizabeth pushed her mother's handwritten pages across the table. Joey turned them around so they faced in the right direction and started reading. It only took her five minutes or so to get through them.

"My God," she said raspily. Her earlier good humor had evaporated completely. "Where did you find these?"

"In the magic box," Elizabeth responded, knowing that she didn't have to explain what she meant to her sister.

Joey sat still, clearly turning the information in the notes over in her mind. Elizabeth could almost read her thoughts. The sympathy for their mother. The anger at their father, never exactly a stretch for her sister. Then she saw the light in Joey's eye. She knew exactly what her sister was about to say. Somehow, it seemed easier to voice the thought herself.

"It had to have been Daddy, right?"

Joey looked at her. "I never thought I'd hear you say that."

Elizabeth's mouth tightened. "It was obvious to anyone who knew she was leaving him. I just refused to see it."

Joey expelled a long breath. "You know, he claimed to be with a client that day."

"Somehow, I think that claim might just turn out to be unsubstantiated, don't you?"

The quiet acceptance of their father's possible guilt was the last thing Joey ever would have expected to witness.

"I think we have to check out what he told the police," Elizabeth continued, her voice quietly business-like.

Joey looked at her admiringly. "Well, I can find out exactly what he said he was doing pretty easily. Then we can figure out how to check into the truth of it."

She got up and left the table for several minutes. When she got back, she had written a name and a place on a piece of paper.

"That's the name of the client Dad said he was with the day Mom was killed."

Elizabeth looked down. "Eli Kasarsky." She thought for a moment. "He's the one Daddy defended for mail fraud about two years ago. Got him off without a minute's time, despite ten million pounds of evidence against him."

"How did he do that?" Joey asked, impressed despite herself.

"It turned out that most of the evidence was collected by the police slightly before the time the search warrant was issued. Everything was thrown out of court—and I mean everything." She shook her head. "They would have had him in jail for ten years, minimum, if we hadn't noticed the time discrepancy."

Joey gave her sister a long look. *"We?"*

Elizabeth didn't flinch at the implication. "I found the discrepancy. Daddy told the client about it."

Joey sighed. It was an old story, one that didn't bear dwelling on.

Elizabeth picked up the piece of paper. "It says here that Mr. Kasarsky resides on Amsterdam Avenue. I suggest a visit."

Joey couldn't believe how matter-of-fact her sister

sounded. They were about to try to unravel their father's alibi for the murder of their mother, and here Elizabeth sat, as cool as a cucumber. She had to hand it to her.

"I'm with you," she said simply, gathering up her belongings and following Elizabeth out the door and down the steps.

They emerged onto Seventy-ninth Street just as the sun was setting over the Hudson River.

"Pretty, huh?" Joey observed, before she turned right, toward Amsterdam.

Elizabeth looked west, then joined her sister. "I guess something about today had to be pretty," she said, her voice quavering slightly in the breeze.

It took fifteen minutes for the sisters to walk up Amsterdam, finding the address Joey had gotten at Ninety-ninth Street. The building Eli Kasarsky lived in was run-down on the outside, but when they announced themselves through the speaker and went upstairs, they found a pleasant, if slightly shabby, one-bedroom apartment, its living room long and narrow, a galley kitchen beyond that undoubtedly led to the bedroom.

"How lovely to see you, Elizabeth," Kasarsky said as he ushered them in. "You've changed your hair."

Either Eli Kasarsky hadn't known anything about Elizabeth's disappearance or he was doing a good job of pretending.

"This is my sister, Joanna," she said. "I don't think you ever got to meet her."

"Well," he said, "both of you sit down. Let me get you a soda, or maybe a glass of wine."

Elizabeth caught his hand as she sat on the sofa he had indicated, forcing him to sit down beside her. "This isn't a casual visit, Eli. But I'm sure you know that."

Elizabeth could see that Kasarsky wasn't about to acknowledge anything, but she pressed on.

"The day my mother was killed, you had a long lunch with my father, right?"

"Of course, dear. That's exactly what I told the police when they asked." He looked relaxed, leaning back against the sofa and smiling affably as he answered.

Joey sat across from the two of them, choosing a straight-backed chair and bringing it close to where he sat.

"Mr. Kasarsky," she said sternly, "perjury is a very serious offense. In fact, in the state of New York, protecting a murderer makes you culpable as well."

Kasarsky laughed uneasily. "You girls use such big words. 'Culpable,' my goodness."

"How about 'guilty of being an accessory to murder'?" Joey shot back. "Is that clear enough?"

"You have no way of proving that I was not with your father that day," he answered, the smile gone from his face. "The police were satisfied. They even talked to our waiter."

Elizabeth drew closer to him on the couch. "Why do I think that if we question the rest of the staff, and the other people who were eating there, we can prove that you two weren't there at the time you and my father claimed?" She held his eyes with her own. "For that matter, if we check carefully among all your friends and neighbors and acquaintances, I bet we can find out exactly where you were at that time."

"Why should I tell you something different from what I told the police? It can only get me into trouble, and that's the last thing I need," he said, his growing upset plain.

Elizabeth spoke once again. "Eli, I learned quite a lot about you at the time of your trial. I remember *all* of it."

Kasarsky bolted off the couch. "I can't be tried again for that crime. Double jeopardy. I know all about that."

Elizabeth watched him pace nervously back and forth.

"What I know about you has nothing to do with double jeopardy."

"But you were my lawyer, for God's sake. You can't tell them I'm guilty of anything," he said plaintively.

Elizabeth's gaze at him didn't waver. "There are all kinds of ways for information to get out."

Kasarsky looked miserable as he turned his back on both sisters. His shoulders slumped—in fact, his whole posture looked like that of a beaten man.

"What is it you want me to tell you? Your father was very good to me. I was happy to be good to him in return."

Joey looked up. "Meaning you weren't with him that day?"

Kasarsky nodded unhappily. "I backed him up because he asked me to. I owed him."

"And how much did he pay the waiter to lie?" Elizabeth asked quietly.

Joey looked at her sister. There was no triumph on her face, nor was there any particular sadness. Rather, she bore the resolute expression of a boxer going to the center of the ring for the very last round.

Chapter Thirty-four

It was a little over a mile from Eli Kasarsky's apartment to Peter's restaurant on Seventy-fifth Street. While Joey headed back to Ross, Jennings, Elizabeth herself had something she had to do. As she walked along, she knew she should be preparing some kind of speech, but no words came to her. Between the enormity of what she had just learned about her father and the frightening prospect of what she might encounter, she found herself unable to plan anything.

It made her happy to see the words "Hey There" on the canopy of the restaurant. She watched a couple disembark from a taxi to enter, the man reaching to open the door for the woman he was with. It was so comfortingly familiar.

Maybe I shouldn't feel so comfortable about it, she thought unhappily. Maybe from now on, I'll be just another person passing by on the street, just another customer if I sit down to dinner there. Which would never happen. If what she dreaded came to pass, she knew she would never be able to bear seeing the restaurant again.

Breathing deeply, she came to stand in front of one of the windows. It was crowded inside. She took a step closer and looked in.

There he was. Peter was off to the side, talking to

a man in a green shirt whose back was to Elizabeth. He was laughing. She felt a stabbing in her stomach, a combination of fear, desire, and joy. The wonderful sight of his grin, his easy stance, the way his hair fell against his forehead, were all like a warm bath enveloping her.

Please don't let me have ruined it, she begged silently.

Peter glanced in her direction, and they made eye contact through the window. Elizabeth smiled. Peter gave her a quick smile in return, then went back to his conversation.

No, no, Elizabeth thought, it wasn't possible. Please, don't let him be so indifferent that he could spare her only a glance. It had to be that he hadn't recognized her. She yanked off her sunglasses and stepped closer to the window.

Peter's gaze was attracted by the movement, and he looked at her again. This time, he didn't look away. He stared, puzzlement on his face for a few seconds, then an expression of shock. She smiled at him, a wide grin this time. Without taking his eyes off her, he put a hand on the arm of the man he was talking to, said something, then moved away. Elizabeth watched him quickly making his way through the crowd of people at the bar. Then the door opened and he was standing in front of her, close enough to touch.

He grabbed her by the shoulders. "Is it you, is it really you?" he asked urgently.

She nodded.

"Thank goodness you're all right." He closed his eyes with relief. Then, as if remembering something, he opened them and released her, the look on his face turning distant and impersonal.

"Well, I'm glad it worked out," he said, his tone cool. "Which it did, I trust."

Her smile faded. She made her tone match his. "I wouldn't put it quite that way, but thank you."

He was looking her up and down, taking in the

difference in her appearance. "So, is this the new you?"

"Actually, yes." Elizabeth hoped he couldn't see how crushed she was by his cold reception. "I sort of am a new me."

She couldn't read the expression in his eyes.

"You just dropped by to say hello?"

"Actually, I—" She stopped. The old Elizabeth would have continued on like this for a few minutes, keeping up the facade. Then she would have gone on her way, refusing to show how upset she was. But that girl wasn't who she was anymore.

"Peter, please," she said, her voice full of the emotion she had been holding back, "I know you must be angry at me. I wouldn't blame you. But in the time I've been gone, I realized how much I need you."

"You need me?" he repeated flatly. "For what? A date for a party, maybe? Need to borrow my car?"

She felt as though she had been slapped. But she refused to let herself back down. "Peter, for God's sake, I'm trying to say that I love you. I've loved you all along."

"You're ready to come back and resume things the way they were, eh?" He folded his arms across his chest. "Gee, thanks but no thanks."

She knew she sounded frantic, but she didn't care. "Not like that at all. I know I kept you at a distance. But please try to understand. I'm just starting to understand it myself. I was my father's protector all these years. I couldn't let myself be distracted by having my own life, my own real love, because that would have taken me away from my mission in life. I know it sounds insane. But that's the truth of it. When you strip away everything on the surface, that's the sad truth of it. I couldn't permit myself to have anything or anyone that implied disloyalty to him." She was exhausted, as if all the air had suddenly been let out of her. "It would have been wrong under any circumstances," she finished sadly, "but it was particularly pathetic given what I now know about him."

Peter's mouth tightened. "So now everything's supposed to be okay between us. Your disappearing, not letting me know where or for how long, not trusting me enough to tell me even that."

"I didn't want to put you in jeopardy, to make you lie."

He turned to go back inside the restaurant. "Goodbye, Elizabeth."

She watched, stunned, as he disappeared through the door, into the crowd of diners.

Her worst fears had been realized. She couldn't make it up to him. She had run away, because cavalierly discarding him at the time was what was most convenient. She hadn't explained anything or even promised that she would come back.

Tightly clutching her sunglasses and the strap of her purse, her head bowed, she rushed away from the restaurant, hurrying along the street in a blind panic. I destroyed the one thing I had been smart enough to hold on to for all those years, she thought miserably. As deluded as I was, somewhere in my heart I must have known better than to let Peter out of my life. Yet now I've finally managed to drive him away once and for all.

She was afraid she might burst into tears right in the middle of the street. Playing the good girl had become automatic to her, but it was a role that left little room for being a real person. With Peter, she had sometimes forgotten to be the perfect Elizabeth, and he had loved her anyway. He was the only real thing in her life. Except he wasn't going to be in her life anymore.

She turned the corner, not even knowing where she was going, just desperate to get away. Then, suddenly, she stopped.

She couldn't let it end this way. Of course he was mad. He was entitled to be mad. She could hardly expect him to fall into her arms, grateful just to have her back. She had been wrong to think it would be that easy. If she was serious about getting him back, she would have to do whatever it took.

She turned around and went back in the direction from which she'd come. As she approached the restaurant she was surprised to see Peter standing in front. He must have come back out after she'd left. His back was to her, so he didn't notice as she came up behind him.

"You're right, you know."

He turned around at the sound of her voice.

"You're absolutely right," she went on hurriedly. "I don't deserve another chance. But I don't care. I want one anyway."

His expression remained guarded and he continued his silence.

"Being without you is the worst thing in the world," she cried. "Please forgive me. You have to forgive me. I won't let you *not* forgive me."

Finally he spoke. "What do you want from me?"

"I want everything. I want marriage. I want children. I want a home. And I want all of it with you."

He walked over to her and looked into her eyes. "Are you sure?" he asked, his voice husky.

She kissed him in reply. "One hundred percent."

His arms went around her. "Are you free to come home now?"

She grimaced. "I will be soon. There's one thing I have to do first." She pulled away. "I'll see you in a few hours. Then I'll be with you forever."

Chapter Thirty-five

Elizabeth braced herself as she stepped into the hallway, dreading what she was about to do. But she was anxious to get it over with. At last, all the secrets would be exposed.

As she reached her parents' apartment, she decided against using her key to open the door. Joey had said she would be sure to get their father home by seven o'clock. Elizabeth didn't want to frighten him by suddenly materializing in the doorway. She rang the bell.

She could hear Joey's heels clicking on the floor as she came to answer the door. When she pulled it open, her expression was tense.

"Are you ready?" she asked Elizabeth.

Elizabeth nodded. Clearly, her sister had been anticipating this with dread as well. Before either of them could say anything else, they heard their father coming into the foyer. Elizabeth saw him, dressed in a blue suit, sorting through a stack of mail as he walked.

"Who is it?" he asked, his eyes on the letters in his hands. "Why didn't the doorman—"

Looking up, he caught sight of Elizabeth. He appeared puzzled, and then his face registered confusion and fright. Of course, she thought, the outfit and hair were completely throwing him.

She took a step inside, setting her shoulder bag down on the floor beside her.

"Hi, Dad," she said gently. "It's me, Elizabeth."

It was as if her very words triggered the draining of all the color from his face. He turned so pale, she was concerned he might actually faint. He dropped the pile of mail on a nearby table and momentarily leaned on the edge for support.

"Dear God," he whispered. *"Elizabeth."*

She nodded. "It's true."

He hurried over and embraced her. "I didn't know what had happened to you . . . I was so worried . . ."

"I'm okay, Dad, really I am." She glanced over at Joey, who was watching grimly. Now was the time. "We need to talk to you."

Jack released her and took a step back, as if fearful of whatever was to come.

"Darling," he said with forced joviality, "come in. I'm so happy to see you safe and sound. We'll have some champagne to celebrate your return."

"Come on," said Joey, taking his arm, "let's go inside. We don't want any champagne."

There was a spark of panic in his eyes. "No, no."

Elizabeth looked at him sadly. "Dad, please . . ."

He stopped, his expression hardening. "Well, then, fine," he answered in an almost childishly defiant tone, turning to go into the living room. "Say what you want to say." He dropped down onto an armchair.

Joey stood in front of him. "It's not what we *want* to be saying."

There was a long silence, none of them willing to take the step that would change things forever. At last, Elizabeth moved forward.

"It was you, wasn't it, Dad?" she asked softly.

He looked up at her, motionless. She thought he was going to express shock or indignation. But he closed his eyes and said nothing. His shoulders sagged perceptibly, as if all the fight had left him. When he opened his eyes again, she saw that they were filled with tears.

His voice was barely audible. "I've been waiting for this. I knew it would come."

Joey came closer. "Dad," she said hoarsely, as if unable to comprehend, "you actually killed Mom?"

He ran his hand through his hair. "God knows I didn't want to. You know how much I loved her."

Elizabeth exploded. "You *shot* her! You killed your own wife. That's not anybody's idea of love."

He looked at her in anguish. "She was going to leave me. She didn't love me anymore."

Elizabeth looked at him coldly. "She *never* loved you. But that didn't seem to bother you before."

Stunned, Jack jumped up and clutched her arm. "Why do you say that? Of course she loved me. We were married for thirty-six years."

"No, Dad," Elizabeth said, "you"— she cast about in her mind for the right word—*"appropriated* her when she was at her most vulnerable. You took advantage of a young girl who had been caught up in a terrible, tragic circumstance."

Jack looked as if he had seen a ghost. *"You know?"*

Joey spoke up. "We both know. Mom wrote down the whole story." Her voice rose. "We wish you had seen fit to tell us. We could have handled it. Instead, there was just a lot of lying, everybody pretending all the time."

"But I loved her more than anything in this world," Jack said piteously. "I couldn't have lived if she left me, I really couldn't."

"So you stopped her by killing her," Joey said in disbelief.

Jack's shoulders sagged. "I went out and got drunk that night she told me she was leaving. I slept at a hotel. When I came back to confront her the next morning, I didn't plan for anything so terrible to happen. But, I don't know . . ." He covered his face with his hands. "It must have been after you were here, Elizabeth, when you and your mother argued. I was so angry and so hurt. And then I saw the gun, that gun I gave you when they threatened you after the

Enders conviction. It was right there, in the drawer of the night table. I didn't even know your mother had it."

"I had told you I didn't want a gun," Elizabeth said quietly. "I gave it to her to get rid of it. I didn't want it in my house."

Jack looked at his daughters as if trying to make them understand. "I lost control. I couldn't let her divorce me. When she came out of that closet, so casual, as if she was packing for a vacation instead of ending my life—I shot her. Then I left. I came back later and pretended to discover the body." He shuddered visibly. "That sight will stay with me forever." He was quiet for a moment, then continued. "No one saw me here the first time. Certainly, the police asked the doormen about that morning, and nobody knew I was here until I came back the second time. So I was able to line up an alibi."

"I wasn't so lucky," Elizabeth said sharply.

Jack's voice grew anguished. "That was the worst part, seeing the police go after you. It broke my heart."

"Dad, for God's sake!" Elizabeth cried out.

He looked at her. "Sweetheart, don't you understand? You've always been so understanding, so good to me."

Elizabeth started to pace. "That was the problem. I was a fool, believing you had been deceived by Mom, feeling sorry for you. But you deceived everyone. Then you took a gun and shot her." Her eyes blazed. *"For what? Why did she need to die?"*

Jack grabbed his head with both hands. *"I don't know, I don't know!* It's been a misery, thinking about it night and day, going over it. Seeing her face, the blood. Knowing my daughter was out there running away from the police."

He choked back a sob. "All my life, my greatest fear was that I would lose what I loved. I had already lost so much. I couldn't bear it. Then I destroyed everything."

Joey put a hand on his arm. "Take it easy, Dad."
She eased him back into the chair.

Elizabeth stared at her in surprise. "Now you feel
sorry for him?" she snapped. "You've hated him all
these years."

Joey shot her a dark look. "Elizabeth, please. Yelling isn't going to help."

"But he betrayed Mom. And he betrayed *us*," she
burst out.

"It's not about us," Joey responded sadly, "not
really."

Elizabeth turned away, struggling to regain her com-
posure. "You always did see him for what he was,"
she murmured, the reality of what she was acknowledging hitting her for the first time.

Joey knelt before Jack and remained there, not saying anything. At last she spoke to him, the force of
her words startling both her father and her sister.

"I hate you. You killed my mother because you're
a spineless son of a bitch." She got to her feet, her
tone changing more to one of disgust. "But I almost
feel sorry for you."

Jack winced at the contempt in his younger daughter's voice.

"Well, *I* don't feel sorry for you," Elizabeth was indig-
nant. "You used Mom and you used me," she shouted.
"You're a selfish bastard. And you thought you were
going to get away with murder, didn't you?"

Jack looked from one daughter to the other, his
pain evident in his eyes. Then, heavily, he stood up.

"It was just a matter of time before it came out,
don't you see? The second I pulled that trigger, my
life was over. It was just a question of what day,
what hour."

"Not if they locked me up first," Elizabeth added
angrily.

Jack nodded. "I deserve that, of course."

He turned and walked over to the desk where the
telephone was. Picking up the receiver, he glanced
over his shoulder at them.

"Do you know what I dial for the police who are handling this? I'm ready to talk to them now."

Joey hesitated. "You want Gary McCullough. Call him directly." She recited his telephone number.

Jack didn't question how or why she knew the number by heart, but dialed, his hand shaking slightly. His daughters stood there, listening, immobilized, as Gary apparently picked up the telephone on the other end, and their father informed him that he was the person who had murdered Molly Ross. Then he was silent, listening to Gary's instructions.

"Fine," he said. "Yes, I do. Good-bye."

He hung up. "I'm going to get a few things together. The detective is on his way."

Elizabeth's voice was almost a wail. "Oh, God, Dad, why did you have to kill her?"

Jack looked at her in sorrow. "I'm sorry, princess," he whispered, using his special childhood nickname for her, one she had all but forgotten about.

Tears filled her eyes. "You were my hero. My idol."

"And you made me proud every day of my life," he said tenderly. "I'm so sorry I let you down."

She turned away, crying in earnest.

"Do you need help, Dad?" Joey asked.

He shook his head, speaking distractedly. "No, there's not much I can take. As we know, they don't let you bring a lot when you're arrested. I'll change out of my suit, get my reading glasses, that sort of thing, I guess . . ."

He trailed off as he left the room. They could hear him making his way upstairs, his footsteps heavy.

Elizabeth wiped at her eyes. "I still can't believe this is happening."

Joey sighed. "Unfortunately, I'm not as shocked as you are. It's not that I would have dreamed he could have done such a thing. But I wasn't the one who worshiped him."

She paused. "Still, I meant it when I said I feel sorry for him. I actually do. To be that desperate when someone wants to leave you, to believe there's no choice but to kill her . . ."

"You're lucky you can feel sorry for him," Elizabeth replied. "I only feel furious. And deceived. Everything I grew up believing was a lie."

Joey came over and put her arms around her sister. "We were little kids, and they were two people carrying on a charade. No wonder we got it all mixed up."

Elizabeth leaned her head against her sister's shoulder and closed her eyes, suddenly worn out. The strain of being in hiding, the underlying terror of being arrested, and her guilt at her unfairness to her mother had all been weighing on her more heavily than she had been able to admit, even to herself.

She smiled weakly. "Hey, I guess it's time to start from scratch—what the hell."

Joey laughed. "A lot of people would love to be able to start again."

Nodding, Elizabeth moved away and sat down on the sofa. It was true, in a way, that she would be starting all over. Which meant she had a chance to do things better this time.

"You know," she began slowly, "I missed out on a lifetime with Mom, years when we could have had something together. And I've missed out with you in the same way." She gazed at her sister. "I don't want that to continue. We could change things between us. Don't you think?"

"You mean you're expecting us to get along?" Joey asked wryly.

"Okay, okay, it's never been our strong suit," Elizabeth said. "I thought you were irresponsible, and I was wrong about that, too. You've really come through for me, not to mention your friend, Lisa. Obviously, you're nothing like the picture I painted of you. I'm sorry for that, deeply sorry."

Joey looked thoughtful. "Then I guess I have to admit my part in it as well. Because, of course, even though I would have denied it under torture, I was always insanely jealous of you. I mean, who wouldn't be—you were the perfect girl, the gorgeous, smart one with all the attention and accomplishments? I could never compete with that. And then there was always Dad coming between us. You and he—you just never saw reason when it came to him."

Elizabeth shook her head. "That's me, martyr and protectress. And village idiot."

"Don't be so hard on yourself." Joey smiled again. "Let me do that for you."

Elizabeth found herself smiling. She looked at her sister, feeling almost as if she were seeing her for the first time. She walked over to Joey and put her arms around her.

Joey returned the hug.

They turned at the sound of their father reentering the room. He had changed into gray trousers and a white tennis shirt. His hair was freshly combed.

He stopped short at the unfamiliar sight of his daughters embracing.

"Well," he said quietly, "wouldn't it be a miracle if something good came out of all this?"

Elizabeth came over and took his arm. "Are you ready, Dad? Is there anything we need to do for you?"

He turned to her, pain etched on his face. "The only thing I would ever want . . . If you could ever forgive me . . ."

They all looked at one another, but no one said anything. Then the silence was broken by the sound of the doorbell.

"That'll be Gary," Joey said softly.

"That detective, you mean? Yes, I suppose so," Jack said.

He straightened up and cleared his throat. "All right. I'm ready."

Joey nodded and went to answer the door.

Epilogue

Ten Months Later

"You can throw your coats here." Elizabeth dropped her blazer onto the bench by the front door and moved in the direction of the kitchen. "I'll get some cheese and stuff. Peter, would you pour the wine?"

Peter pulled off his leather jacket, nodding. He looked over at their guests. "Red or white, guys?"

"Red, if it's easy," Joey said. "How about you?"

"For me, too," Gary replied.

Peter followed Elizabeth into the kitchen to get the bottle of wine. "What time is your flight?" he called out over his shoulder.

"Eight in the morning," Joey called back. "Needless to say, we're not packed yet."

"Not that we have to take much, right, dear?" Gary asked archly. "It's just for a couple of weeks. Isn't that so?"

Joey smiled angelically. "Naturally. But you know you're going to love Montana just as much as I say you will. You'll never want to come back to New York. You might as well just take everything now."

Elizabeth emerged from the kitchen carrying a tray laden with several types of cheese, crackers, and fruit. "Joey can be very persuasive, Gary. If she says you two are resettling in Montana, something tells me that's what's going to happen."

Gary sighed. "That's what I'm afraid of."

Joey laughed. "I promise you won't have to do anything against your will." She grew more serious. "But I did give Lisa my word that we'd be there for her coming-home party on the twelfth."

Peter joined them, holding a bottle of red wine in one hand and four wineglasses, grasped upside down by their stems, in the other. "Can't you keep an apartment here so you can go back and forth?"

"We're exploring all the possibilities," Joey said. "but we can't decide on anything until Gary sees Montana for himself."

Elizabeth settled back on the couch. The couch had originally been hers, but she had brought a lot of her furniture over to Peter's apartment when they'd gotten married six months before. It had made the transition easier. She could certainly understand Gary's trepidation about leaving the city, recalling how difficult it was for her to give up her own apartment and move only blocks away. But it had been fine, in the end. Now the apartment was a blend of both their things. And, by extension, she reflected, both their personalities. Whatever Gary and Joey decided to do, it would be fine in the end.

These past months with Peter had been nearly perfect, their sweetness marred only by the sad contrast between her new life and her father's new life.

When Jack was initially sent to prison, Elizabeth had stayed away in anger and bitterness. But, over time, she had come to view her father as more pitiful than anything else. He passed his days reading in his cell, claiming he finally had the time to study and reflect on the law the way he wanted to. By now, he was thin and pale, his shoulders sagging with the weight of his own self-loathing. The shine was gone from his hair, the sparkle from his eyes. He was almost docile when they visited him, rarely complaining, grateful for their company. He was merely passing the time until . . . Elizabeth didn't wish to pursue that train of thought. Should he even live until the first possible date when he could be paroled, he would be a very old man upon his release.

The only time he seemed to come back to life was when he discussed the law firm with Elizabeth. It was she who had taken over from him as managing partner of Ross, Jennings. At first she had been reluctant, thinking she would go out on her own. But she soon realized that things didn't have to remain the same. Little by little, she began making changes, refusing to take on certain cases she found repugnant, aware now of how her father had justified doing work he knew in his heart was morally reprehensible. She trimmed the staff and attempted to create a more intimate atmosphere. Her father had always encouraged competition among the lawyers to get them to do their best work. She chose to encourage the team attitude. The firm was not quite where she wanted to see it, but she was pleased with the direction it was taking.

Still, there were so many times in the course of the day that she was reminded of her father. His presence was everywhere—in every room, in the halls, in every meeting. A great sadness would often descend upon her. Joey felt it too, and they had been glad to have one another to turn to, as unfamiliar as that was at first.

Today was actually the first time they had visited their father together, along with Peter and Gary. Gary had been wildly uncomfortable with the situation, Elizabeth saw, but he knew he had to come along. Joey wanted him there with her when she told Jack that she and Gary would be married in the fall. Jack had been smart enough not to pretend that things were normal between Gary and himself. He said a quiet congratulations at the news and let it go at that.

"Oh, by the way,"—Joey's voice interrupted Elizabeth's reverie—"I'm having some papers messengered to your office tomorrow. Just leftovers from Lisa's case and a few stray items."

"Thanks." Elizabeth picked up a handful of grapes and spoke thoughtfully. "It'll be quiet without you in New York." She grinned. "An easier place to live in, but quiet."

"Don't start with me," Joey retorted. "You know, I have the power to pick any matron-of-honor dress I want for you."

"Wait a minute," Gary said to her. "What happened to the small dinner at a cozy restaurant? I thought we were having something like three and a half people at this wedding."

"We are," Joey answered, "but you still need a matron of honor for the ceremony, and I can still dress her any way I like. Prerogative of the bride."

"You wouldn't!" Elizabeth said in horror.

Joey closed her eyes, imagining. "I'm thinking hoop skirt, and I'm thinking fuschia. Maybe a nice big taffeta bow on top of your head."

Peter laughed. "A sight I'd give anything to see."

"Don't hold your breath," Elizabeth said with a smile. "Members of the bridal party can also develop the flu at the last second, you know."

Gary drained his wineglass. "I hate to break up the planning session, but we'd better get going. Okay?"

"Right." Joey went over to the bench to retrieve her jacket. "I'll call you when I get home to Montana." She hesitated. "It's been so long, it doesn't sound right to say that anymore."

"I couldn't agree more," Gary said encouragingly. "New York—now that sounds like home, doesn't it?"

Elizabeth got up and went to give Joey a hug. "Don't disappear, okay?"

Joey kissed her on the cheek and embraced her tightly. "Never again."

Elizabeth pulled back and looked into her sister's eyes. Her voice was barely above a whisper. "Thank you for everything. Thank you for coming back, even if it wasn't initially for me. Thank you for all you did. Thank you for letting us be sisters again."

She was shocked to see Joey's eyes fill with tears.

"Gee," Elizabeth said, "I didn't mean to make you cry. I didn't even know I *could.*"

Joey wiped hastily at her eyes. "Well, you can. Happy now?"

Elizabeth smiled. "Yes."

Joey smiled back. "Okay, good. Now let me get out of here."

She reached for the doorknob, then stopped and turned to face Elizabeth.

"I love you," she said quietly.

Elizabeth gazed at her for a moment. "I love you, too."

Joey stepped outside without looking back. Gary gave Elizabeth a quick hug and shook Peter's hand.

"See you soon," he said.

"So long." Peter waved. "Good trip."

Gary nodded, closing the door behind him. Elizabeth went to Peter and put her arms around his waist. He gently put a hand on her cheek.

"You okay?"

"Sure." She smiled up at him. "It's just that . . . well, it's just that I never really had a sister before."